KEEP ME I

Monica Murphy is a *New York* ~~~~~~~~~~~~~~~~~~~~~~~~ nal bestselling author. Her book~~~~~~~~~~ translated in almost a dozen languages and have sold millions of copies worldwide. Both a traditionally published and independently published author, she writes young adult and new adult romance, as well as contemporary romance.

ALSO BY MONICA MURPHY

Lancaster Prep: Next Generation

All My Kisses for You

Keep Me In Your Heart

New Young Adult Series

The Liar's Club

Kings of Campus

End Game

Lancaster Prep

Things I Wanted To Say

A Million Kisses in Your Lifetime

Birthday Kisses

Promises We Meant to Keep

I'll Always Be With You

You Said I Was Your Favorite

New Year's Day

Lonely For You Only (a Lancaster spinoff novel)

The Players

Playing Hard to Get

Playing by The Rules

Playing to Win

Wedded Bliss (Lancaster)

The Reluctant Bride

The Ruthless Groom

The Reckless Union

The Arranged Marriage boxset

Billionaire Bachelors Club (reissues)

Crave & Torn

Savor & Intoxicated

College Years

The Freshman

The Sophomore

The Junior

The Senior

Dating Series

Save The Date

Fake Date

Holidate

Friends Series

Just Friends

More Than Friends

Forever

The Never Duet

Never Tear Us Apart

Never Let You Go

The Rules Series

Fair Game

In The Dark

Slow Play

Safe Bet

The Fowler Sisters Series

Owning Violet

Stealing Rose

Taming Lily

Reverie Series

His Reverie

Her Destiny

KEEP ME IN YOUR HEART

MONICA MURPHY

PENGUIN BOOKS

PENGUIN BOOKS

UK | USA | Canada | Ireland | Australia
India | New Zealand | South Africa

Penguin Books, Penguin Random House UK,
One Embassy Gardens, 8 Viaduct Gardens, London sw11 7bw

penguin.co.uk
global.penguinrandomhouse.com

First published in the United States of America by Monica Murphy 2024
First published in Great Britain by Penguin Books 2024

001

Copyright © Monica Murphy, 2024

Edited by Rebecca, Fairest Reviews Editing Services
Proofread by Sarah, All Encompassing Books
Typeset by Jouve (UK), Milton Keynes
Printed and bound in Great Britain by Clays Ltd, Elcograf S.p.A.

The authorized representative in the EEA is Penguin Random House Ireland,
Morrison Chambers, 32 Nassau Street, Dublin D02 YH68

A CIP catalogue record for this book is available from the British Library

ISBN: 978-1-405-96537-8

www.greenpenguin.co.uk

Penguin Random House is committed to a
sustainable future for our business, our readers
and our planet. This book is made from Forest
Stewardship Council® certified paper.

To the girls out there who are deemed "too much". No, you're not. You're just right.

PLAYLIST

"Guilty as Sin?" - Taylor Swift
"Butterfly Wings" - FELIVAND
"It's Me & You" - Tokyo Tea Room
"like we're an indie movie" - MKSTN, Tiger La Flor
"Art Deco" - Lana Del Rey
"imgonnagetyouback" - Taylor Swift
"Risk" - Gracie Abrams
"BODYGUARD" - Beyonce
"I Look in People's Windows" - Taylor Swift

Find the rest of the **KEEP ME IN YOUR HEART** playlist
here: https://spoti.fi/3W62nU4

Or scan the QR code below:

ONE

ROWAN

NOVEMBER

I'M APPROXIMATELY one third into my senior year and so far, it's for shit.

Shifting carefully so I don't hurt myself, I wince with the subtle movement anyway, fighting the anger and frustration that bubbles within me. Getting injured on the football field is a risk we all take when playing a sport. But getting injured during our last regular season game, thanks to a massive linebacker who sacked my ass and somehow in the fray fractured my goddamned ankle?

I was over with. End of the season for me, just like that.

Done.

That was weeks ago. It's mid-November, and I'm bored out of my skull. Cursing the awkward boot that keeps my still-healing ankle in place. I didn't need surgery, which the doctor reassured me was a good thing. But at the time, I couldn't focus on anything good. Playoffs had ended extra early for me, and I'm still bitter about it.

I'm bitter about a lot of things. I just try not to let on to anyone that I feel this way.

"Uh oh. Here she comes." Callahan Bennett—my best friend – slaps me in the chest a couple of times with the back of his hand, not even looking at me. His attention is fixed on the girl who's approaching the front of the building where we're standing. The way she moves is effortless as she comes closer, reminding me of a model striding down a runway wearing the latest designer clothes.

Which she is, of course. Her family is almost as rich as mine and everything she owns reflects it. The amount of money she must spend on her wardrobe would blow most people's minds, and don't even get me started on where she might store all of her clothes. She has a private room but still. I know the closet space in the dorm suites is for shit. Suites reserved for Lancasters are the only exception.

Why I care about any of this, why I even bother thinking about it—about *her*—I'm not sure.

I take her in as subtly as possible, not wanting her to know I'm checking her out, even though the only reason I'm standing out here in the freezing cold is because I want to witness her daily appearance. This girl knows how to modify her uniform like no one else, and she pushes the dress code limits every single day. She makes outrageous fashion choices, yet always manages to somehow pull it off.

Arabella Hartley Thomas.

She's stunningly beautiful and I'm certain she knows it, but she never comes across as arrogant. Her features are delicate—the high cheekbones and the button nose. The sweet curve of her chin and the elegant length of her neck. Those flashing dark eyes and full, pouty lips. I've had dreams about that mouth where I wake up sweaty and aching. Not that I'd ever admit it.

Hell no.

All that beauty is offset by the quirky glasses she wears. I swear to God, she's got a new pair on every day. Different colors, different sizes. I never know what to expect from her.

She surrounds herself with plenty of friends. The girls gravitate toward her because she's the type of person who makes other people feel good. When she talks to you, she focuses her full attention on you, and she actually listens. Always nodding along and offering her support with a murmured response here and there. Every tiny little detail about a person, she makes it her mission to remember. To know and even bring it back up later, so you feel like she actually cares. I hate it.

I don't want someone to remember my faults or the dumb stuff I said two years ago. And I sure as shit don't need someone like Arabella reminding me of those things either, even though she does. Always with a big smile on her face. As if she finds me amusing.

I found her annoying when I first met her. She talks nonstop. Like, she never shuts up. And while she has a beautiful, lilting voice with the faintest hint of a British accent—there's a link to royalty somewhere in her bloodline according to campus gossip —I brace myself every time she speaks to me. Like it's going to hurt, though it never actually does.

Arabella Hartley Thomas wouldn't harm a fly, let alone me.

My shoulders grow tense just watching her approach, my gaze sweeping over her. Always assessing, taking note of what she's wearing. There's the school uniform—mostly. The skirt, the white button-down shirt, the form-fitting vest that always, *always* emphasizes the perfect shape of her tits. But as usual, she's added a bit of her own flair to the outfit. Instead of the standard blue jacket, she's wearing a cropped black furry coat that's unzipped and offers us a stellar view of her chest. And covering her legs?

Black tights that have threads of silver glitter running through them, making them sparkle.

"Cal," she greets as she draws closer, shifting past me to pull my best friend into the quickest embrace that I immediately envy. Her sweet perfume seems to wrap all around me, tickling my nose. For the briefest moment, I'm tempted to press my face into her neck and see if her scent lingers there the most. "Looking strong and handsome this morning."

Callahan fucking blushes because he turns into a bumbling idiot every time Arabella says a single word to him, and she loves to lay on the praise. You'd think he'd have grown used to it by now, but he hasn't. And he doesn't even like her like that.

Arabella turns her dark gaze upon me, and my entire body stiffens. Those big brown eyes sparkle with barely contained amusement, and her thick eyelashes flutter as she blinks, making me think of that one Disney character. What was that little deer's name?

Oh yeah. Bambi.

"Rowan." She seems to enjoy calling me by my full name. Very rarely do I hear her call me Row, when that's what pretty much everyone calls me, including my parents. "Looking grumpy as per usual."

The right side of my upper lip lifts in the faintest sneer and I blatantly check her out, my gaze lingering on her legs. "Nice tights, Bells."

I call her Bells, only because I think she hates it. And she completely ignores my compliment.

"How's the ankle?" She gently kicks at the boot I'm currently wearing on my right foot, her Gucci loafer barely touching it, but I still put on a show, wincing like the kick hurt me. Even though we both know I'm made of stronger stuff than that.

"Aches like a bitch," I bite out, which isn't necessarily a lie. I do too much and don't rest enough. My doctor—and my mother—would kick my ass if they saw my definition of rest.

"That's too bad," Arabella croons, taking a step closer to me. God, she smells incredible. It's infuriating. "Maybe you need someone to take care of you. Like your own personal nurse."

"Are you volunteering?" I cock a brow, waiting with anticipation for her response.

This is what we do sometimes, Bells and me. Flirt. Banter. Give each other endless shit. My sister told me a long time ago after I complained about this girl and how she wouldn't stop talking to me that I should try to beat her at her own game.

Keep up the conversation, Willow said. *Give as good as you get. Eventually she'll grow tired of you, especially if you never make a move.*

That's exactly what I've done ever since that first day of school when Arabella sat next to me in chemistry and I was forced to be her lab partner for the entire year, which was pure torture. The problem?

We've kept talking. It's like we can't stop. We talk, we flirt and we give each other endless grief, and damn it, I would never admit this out loud, but our conversations are freaking...

Enjoyable.

I look forward to our early morning encounters. Our classroom interactions. And when she joins our table during lunch, she sits right next to me, pressing her thigh into mine like she wants me to touch her, even though we never talk about that. The chemistry. It's there. It's always there and it drives me out of my mind because she is the last person that I should ever be interested in. She's too needy, too kind, a little odd sometimes and what makes it worse?

My mother would probably love her.

But no. Arabella and me? We can't be anything. I try to ignore her during those lunchtime moments, but it's impossible. Especially when she's right next to me. When I ponder what she might do if I settled my hand on her slender thigh before I slipped my fingers beneath her skirt. She'd probably slap me the moment I brushed my fingers across her soft skin. Or maybe she'd tremble when I touched her, her thighs slowly parting, giving me better access. Would she slap my face if I touched the front of her panties?

Probably. And I'd deserve it too.

I never touch her though. Not like that. It's like I can't. I worry that the moment I break free from all of these self-imposed restrictions and actually rest my hand on her leg, forget it. I'm afraid I'll never let go. I'll want to touch her more and more until my fingers are actually slipping beneath her panties and encountering nothing but wet heat. Hearing her moan my name would do something to me, I just know it, and I can't risk it. I can't.

I'm too young for that shit. I don't need a steady someone in my life. Not yet.

What makes everything worse is that Arabella doesn't seem interested in anyone else. She's never dated anyone and, trust me, people have asked. Upperclassmen when we were younger were constantly trying to get her to hook up with them, and she'd always say no. Bitter, they spread rumors about her being into girls, which caused a few of them to ask Arabella out as well, but she was always kind in her refusal. Always smiling and shaking her head almost shyly, like she couldn't believe she was rejecting them either.

When she does that, she reminds me of...me. I'm not interested in anyone at this damn school, save for Arabella, and deep down, I tell myself that's impossible. There was one girl—she was older than me and led me on and left me for another guy. I've never admitted this to anyone, but she broke my heart. That's why I don't give it so freely. Fuck that. I'm too young to let another girl destroy me.

And I'm definitely not attracted to Arabella. Nope. Not like that. She's a challenge and I enjoy arguing with her. Flirting with her. She has a nice body and she smells good and those big brown eyes seem to eat me up most of the time when I catch her watching me, but we're not interested in each other beyond giving each other endless grief or the occasional flirtatious remark.

Commitment isn't her thing either. She has shitty parents who don't care about her. She's told me that in casual conversation, like it's no big deal. They've taught her love is a lie and you can't count on anyone. You can only count on yourself.

That's pretty much a direct quote straight from her pretty mouth.

"Oh come on," Arabella says, pulling me from my thoughts. "I can barely take care of myself, Rowan. How do you expect me to take care of you?" Her smile is saucy—that is a stupid word but I have no other way to describe it—and she flips a wavy lock of dark brown hair over her shoulder, giving me a better view of her tits.

My gaze drops because I have zero control and she actually laughs.

"Eyes up here, Lancaster."

I jerk my gaze to hers, and I swear to God, now I'm the one blushing, which is bullshit. Cal is laughing. The smile on Arabella's face is enough to make the heat on my cheeks increase, and if I could run out of here, I would, but I can't.

The goddamn boot on my foot slows me down like nothing else, and I hobble around campus like an idiot. I hate it.

"Maybe I'll come by your room tonight," she says, her casual offer sparking a flicker of hope inside me, which is stupid. "Check in on you and make sure you're doing okay."

Cal actually chortles like an old man, slapping me in the chest again with the back of his hand. "Bro, you've just found yourself your own personal nurse."

"Shut the fuck up," I say through gritted teeth, fighting the wave of jealousy that wants to take over when I see the way Arabella looks at Callahan. "She doesn't want to be my nurse."

"How do you know?" She turns her gaze upon me, blinking. The absolute picture of innocence. "Maybe I will show up tonight just because you don't think I will."

"You wouldn't," Callahan tells her, his tone like a dare.

"I so would." Her expression turns...sad? "Though let's be real with each other. I could never take good enough care of you, Rowan, and you would end up disappointed in me. You know how I am. I don't think I'm up to the job."

With that, she walks away, leaving behind a few sparkles of stray silver glitter from her tights lingering in the air, accompanied by her delicious, sweet scent that makes me think of vanilla and spice.

Cal actually sags against the wall, gently banging the back of his head against it once. Twice. "I don't know why, but I always feel like a complete idiot in her presence."

"No shit," I mutter.

He sends me a look. I can feel his gaze on me. "And you don't?"

"Never," I say without hesitation.

"Right. Because the two of you are hot for each other, yet neither of you can admit it." He turns to face me, but I won't do the same. I can barely face myself. "She embarrassed you."

"She did not."

"Cut the shit, Row. You blushed."

I turn it around on him. "She always makes you blush."

"At least I can admit it."

I finally swivel my head in his direction. "Then go ahead and admit you want to fuck her."

He appears vaguely taken aback. "I don't want to...*fuck* her. I mean, she's beautiful, I can't deny it."

My hands curl into fists at his compliment, as if I have no control over them. Why am I jealous? Why do I feel this incessant need to tell every motherfucker who even glances in her direction to back off, even my best friend?

"But she's so far out of my league." Cal shakes his head, whistling low. "Like, she's almost too much, you know?"

"Sure," I say with a nod, my attention elsewhere. In constant search of Bells, who I spot standing at the top step right in front of the double doors of the building, talking to a group of girls who are chatting nonstop.

As if she can feel me watching her, Arabella glances over her shoulder, her gaze finding mine in an instant, that faint smile curving her lush lips just for me. I don't bother smiling back, but I don't glare at her either and I hope she takes that as a good sign.

She dismisses me with a turn of her head, returning her attention to her friends, her laughter ringing in the air. I know the sound of Arabella's real laugh, and that isn't it.

I continue watching her, not caring if she catches me again, Cal's words running through my head. How he thinks she's almost too much.

Sometimes, when I'm being real with myself, usually late at night when I can't sleep, I wonder if I could ever get enough of her.

Probably not.

TWO

ARABELLA

GOD, it's difficult being halfway in love with a grumpy Lancaster who constantly snarls and snaps at you and somehow thinks that's flirting. He's like a pissed-off, injured dragon who seethes with anger and broods like he wanders the moors of Scotland in search of his long-lost love in the middle of the night, frustrated because he can't find her when, damn it, she is standing directly in front of him. I can't help that he's an idiot who doesn't realize what we could be...

Shaking my head, I push the far too dramatic thoughts from it and enter the building upon the first sound of the warning bell that indicates we have five minutes left until class. I could feel him watching me the entire time I spoke to those girls—they were all younger than me and I have no idea what their names are but that's beside the point—and I was desperate to turn around and fling myself at him. Beg him to touch me just once. That's all I ask.

Just one time.

But if that actually happened, I know he'd turn me into an addict, and I don't feel like making a fool of myself over an angry, sexy boy who would most likely rock my world the first time he touched my lips with his. Instead, I try to keep a healthy distance between us because I'm not reckless.

At least, I'm not reckless with my heart. Everything else? Most definitely. And besides, I don't do a good job trying to keep away from him. I'm a moth and he's the flame, and I'm drawn to him despite knowing that the closer I get, I'll get burned.

The moment I enter my statistics class, our teacher shakes her head, her disappointment in me obvious.

"Arabella." That's all Mrs. Guthrie says as I make my way across the classroom and settle into the desk that's closest to hers. My usual desk because I love math and I love Mrs. Guthrie and plus, I'm a bit of a suck-up.

As per school rules, she wields a certain amount of control over me and I know it.

"What?" I blink at her as I shrug out of my coat—it's quite toasty but that's thanks to the thick faux fur it's made of—and drop it carelessly across the back of my chair.

"You're violating dress code." She pauses for emphasis. "Again."

I violate dress code pretty much every single day of the school year but no one does much about it. Being my senior year, I really push the boundaries now. Today's outfit is nothing compared to some of the things I've worn in the not-so-distant past. Or the things I have planned for the near future.

I need to get my thrills somehow.

"Are you going to write me up?" I stick out my lower lip in a worrisome pout. If I was a talented actress, I could make my lip quiver, but I'm not made for the theater, unfortunately. And while I do take the advanced theater class because I so very much wish I was brilliant on the stage, my talents usually lie in costume or set design.

"As your first period teacher, I'm obligated to write you up." There's that power I referred to earlier.

"Oh no." I rest my hand against my chest, playing dumb.

A sigh leaves Mrs. Guthrie and she shakes her head. "At least you're mostly covered up."

She's probably remembering that one time at the beginning of the school year when I wore a Missoni blue and white knit bikini top underneath my white button-down. And how I knotted the button-down at my midriff, exposing my stomach completely while not bothering to wear the uniform jacket because my God, it was hot that day. I felt like a goddess the moment I saw Rowan's reaction. He appeared to swallow his tongue, his green eyes never straying from my bare stomach, and I swear his heated gaze was so intense, it felt like he was actually touching me.

I wish.

All the boys loved the outfit, and all the girls were desperate to copy me by wearing the same thing, though that idea was squashed immediately.

I got written up for that one and was even put into detention for three days. I had to be, Guthrie implied, her tone beyond exasperated. I frustrate her beyond measure every single day, and I always think that's how my mother feels about me too.

I just bring out the worst in people, I suppose. Maybe because I take things too far? It's like I can't help myself.

"That's a good sign, right? That I'm covered up?" My voice is hopeful, as are my thoughts. I really don't want to go to the headmaster's office this morning. She's a delightful old woman who seems amused by all of us with her grandmotherly ways. A big improvement on the last headmaster we had who turned out to be a total creep.

"I'm going to let this one go," Mrs. Guthrie tells me as more students pour into the classroom, bringing their loud and distracting chatter with them. "Just—please watch yourself, Arabella."

Curling my hands together, I clasp them on top of my desk, ever the dutiful student. "Of course. Thank you, Mrs. Guthrie."

Someone approaches her with a question before she can respond to me, her attention turned elsewhere, and I nearly sag with relief. I don't know why I choose to push the envelope or do such outrageous things—say, provoking things. I have provoking thoughts too, though all of them are centered on a certain six-foot-two dreamboat with dark hair and beautiful green eyes and the smartest mouth around.

Truth be told, I secretly love it when he's mean to me. All snappy and growly like an injured animal, which he truly is currently with that boot on his foot. My poor baby got his ankle broken by some horrible brute out on the football field, and my God, the scream that ripped from my throat when he first went down...

Let's just say I'm glad everyone else was yelling in the stands too. My reaction had been completely embarrassing but thankfully, no one noticed.

It's only when the bell is about to ring that Rowan Lancaster slips into the classroom, flashing the teacher an apologetic but charming smile as he settles into the desk that is in the same row as mine, but on the complete opposite side of the room. I don't even bother looking in his direction because there's no point. He won't acknowledge me. He never does in statistics, and that's because he has to keep his focus on the subject at all times.

My boy has a few flaws and one of them is math.

We're in every single class together this year, and if that isn't some sort of sign, I don't know what is. And I'm a big believer in signs, while Row is most definitely not. He told me that before, one night when we were at a party in someone's dorm room. His dorm room, as a matter of fact, which is more like a full-fledged suite. He was a little drunk and freely speaking to me like I wasn't his mortal enemy, and it had been a glorious moment.

A moment like that has never happened between us again, much to my regret. Rowan's lips are tighter than Fort Knox when it comes to personal stuff. Deep, dark, secret-type stuff. Not that I think he's full of secrets but come on.

He has a few. We all do.

My favorite person to chat with at parties besides Rowan is his bestie. I just adore Callahan Bennett with my whole heart because he's funny and sweet and easy to talk to. I like embarrassing him when I flirt with him because I know it infuriates Rowan. He hates it when I pay attention to his best friend and ignore him. I'm sure they've had conversations about me.

Or maybe that's my ego. Maybe they never talk about me at all.

Anyway, when Cal drinks? His lips become looser and looser, and the next thing I know, he's spilling all sorts of tea. Interesting little tidbits are shared without much explanation and afterward I'm left lying in bed deep into the night, trying to put it all together, which I can never fully do. Is Cal trying to send me secret messages? Is he trying to tell me without blatantly saying it that Rowan is interested in me? Or is that just wishful thinking on my part?

I'm not even sure if Callahan is aware of his big, drunken mouth.

Now, I pay attention in statistics because I'm not left much choice. And I keep paying attention throughout the morning, only able to let my guard down and have a little fun once I enter the beautiful old theater where our class is held right before lunch. Everyone is sitting on the stage, the spotlights shining upon them so brightly it's hard to make out their features. The moment they spot me striding down the aisle toward them, they burst into applause.

I put some extra strut into my step because at least here I'm appreciated for my unique twists on our standard and so very boring uniform.

"Love the tights," someone shouts, and I kick out a leg, loving how the lights make them appear extra sparkly.

"Rather boring choice for today though, don't you think?"

I glance over my shoulder at the sound of his deep voice. The one person who never seems impressed with me.

Pausing, I wait for Rowan to catch up, unable to contain the smile that curves my lips at seeing him limp his way toward me. He hates the boot, and I don't blame him. "You find my accessory choices *boring*?"

I feign annoyance because my God, the boy loves to give me endless shit and it's exhausting.

"I've seen you do better," he drawls, his gaze flitting over me, heat sparking on my skin everywhere his eyes seem to touch. "Why am I in this class again?"

He asks me this question at least once a week. He despises being here, which I find amusing because it's advanced theater, meaning he took beginning theater already. But he has a soft spot for our teacher Mr. Thorson, and I swear, that's the only person I've ever seen Rowan have a soft spot for.

But we all feel that way. Thorson is an easy person to adore.

"Because you want to spend as much time with me as possible," I tell Rowan, increasing my pace so I can walk ahead of him. Maybe he likes to check out my butt, I don't know.

He chuckles and the sound reaches deep inside me, settling in that dark spot between my legs. The one that throbs to life every time he comes near me. "In your dreams, Bells."

If he only knew that's exactly where he resides almost every single night.

The bell rings and I settle into the first row that faces the stage, joining a few stragglers who chose not to go up there with the rest of them. Rowan sits at the end of the row, his foot stuck out awkwardly, that clanky boot he's wearing at an odd angle that doesn't look comfortable. He's immediately on his phone, his head bent, his dark hair falling across his forehead, and I lean forward, watching him.

Not worried at all if anyone notices.

It's getting worse, my obvious staring. Is it because I don't care anymore? When I was younger, when my crush on Rowan Lancaster first started, I was shy. Secretive. I didn't want anyone to know, especially him. But as the crush grew into this overwhelming, all-consuming thing and as the years have passed, I've come to realize I sort of don't care anymore who knows how I feel about Rowan.

Especially...Rowan.

He doesn't take me seriously, and that's where I run into road blocks. Is it that he doesn't view me as a sexual being? That can't be it—I see the way he always looks at my boobs. Is he not attracted to me? I notice the way he watches me sometimes. Almost hungrily if I'm being truthful.

Or maybe I'm delusional. I can't tell.

I absently reach for the necklace I keep tucked under my shirt, tugging on the delicate gold chain, my thumb drifting across my empty heart-shaped locket. I wear it every single day and never take it off, not even to shower. I designed it myself when I was thirteen and thought I wanted to be a jewelry designer, and it's the only piece I've ever had brought to life from a sketch. My mother took the sketch to her personal jeweler—yes, she has her own jeweler and yes, it's ridiculous, I totally agree—but I appreciated that she did so. It's one of those rare gestures she makes when she pretends that she cares about me.

I'm waiting for the moment when I can put a special someone's photo inside, along with my own. But the one I'm most interested in is in complete denial, so I doubt his photo will end up in my locket. It will most likely remain empty forever.

And isn't that just the saddest thing?

THREE

ROWAN

"IT'S ALMOST THANKSGIVING BREAK," Callahan announces once we've settled at our usual table. It's finally lunch and I'm relieved. The day has dragged on and it's good to know I only have two classes left before school is finished for the day. And considering seventh period is a study hall at the library, I might even skip it. Though I do like using that time to finish up any homework I might have.

Today? I'm in a fuck-it mood.

"Thank God," I mutter, readjusting my leg, though it's no use. I can't get comfortable with the damn boot—still. Will I ever be comfortable again?

"Got any plans over the holiday?" Cal asks the table, his gaze landing on me.

The rest of our friends are too busy shoving food in their mouths to answer, including me. I'm starving. Flirting with Bells in advanced theater always seems to work up my appetite.

Figures she'd be in every single class I have. How does that even happen? Did she make a special request at the beginning of the year? Knowing how she is, I wouldn't put it past her.

"We're going to Mexico," Cal continues when no one answers him. He's smiling, looking pleased with his vacation plans, and I can't blame him. "The whole family will be there, even Rhett. His team has a bye week. Fucker got lucky."

"My sister is going?" I ask.

Willow is with Callahan's older brother, Rhett. Their relationship is pretty serious, and if they get married, that means we'll be brothers and I can't lie, I like that idea. Cal and I are close. He's the best friend I've ever had, and I wish we would've met earlier in life, but I guess I should be grateful he's in my life at all.

"Yep. Your sister will definitely be there," Cal confirms.

Can't believe Mom and Dad are cool with Willow spending the holiday with her boyfriend's family, but there are so many damn Lancasters running around during the holiday, I'm guessing one won't be missed too badly.

"You should come with us," he says.

I frown. "You leave in like, what? Two weeks?" When Cal nods, I continue, "Not that I can't get a flight, but I'll still have this."

I wave a hand at the boot. Cal frowns.

So do I.

"And that'll suck," I finish.

"Yeah." Cal exhales loudly. "I bet getting sand in there would irritate the shit out of you."

"I wouldn't even be able to go to the beach. I'd be poolside the entire time and this thing is a pain in my ass." The resentment I have over my injury and subsequent healing process is strong, and while I know I should be glad what happened to me wasn't something worse, I'm still not over it.

When you're a Lancaster, you feel untouchable. That's something I've always noticed but have never discussed. The generational wealth in our family makes things easy. If I didn't want to, I'd never have to lift a finger or work for the rest of my life, but that's not my plan. I can't stand the thought of sitting idle and doing nothing. How freaking boring.

That's half the reason I started playing football. It felt like something different—a challenge that I was eager to accept. My parents didn't like the idea from the start, not even my father. He was worried I would get hurt, and look. His worries came true.

"We'll have to go somewhere tropical for spring break then," Cal says.

"For sure," I agree with a nod, relaxing some when Cal turns his attention to another one of the guys at the table.

I toyed with the idea of leaving after the first semester and finishing my senior year early, but what would I do? I don't have a clue. Not that much is happening on campus anyway, and I already have all the credits necessary to graduate. Yeah yeah, I know I'd be missing out on all of those senior moments that will happen during the rest of the school year, but is it really that big of a deal?

I don't know.

I'm restless. That's my problem. And frustrated with the fractured ankle and the boot and not being able to play football any longer. I had visions of our team winning the state championship, and when that didn't happen, I sort of gave up on this place. There aren't many people I would miss if I left. Definitely Callahan, and I know that fucker would miss me too...

My gaze snags on the one other person who I think I would miss once I left campus.

Arabella. Bells.

She's standing in line at the salad bar, loading her bowl with a wide variety of veggies while chatting with her friends. She doesn't even notice me, which gives me ample time to stare at her without worry of getting caught.

Felt like something shifted a little between us during theater. It was the way she blatantly said that I wanted to spend as much time with her as possible in that class. How I responded with *"In your dreams"* and she didn't deny it. In fact, her cheeks turned the faintest shade of pink, which never really happens because usually she's the one who goes around making people blush.

Does she dream about me?

Would she ever admit it if she did?

Probably not. She plays it coy. Acts like half the time she's not into me, as if it's all for show. Yet again I wonder if she's actually interested in Callahan and I turn my attention to him, staring.

Hard.

He catches on quick.

"What's your problem?"

"Tell me the truth." I do my best to smooth out my features and put out a neutral vibe. Like nothing is bothering me. Life is fucking *good*. "You into Arabella or nah?"

Cal looks at me as if I'm crazy. "Definitely nah. I already told you this. *Multiple* times. When are you ever going to believe me?"

I lean back in my chair, watching him carefully. "Just wanting to confirm."

His expression switches to perplexed in an instant. "Why do you care so much anyway? If I was into her, would it bother you?"

"I don't know." I snap my lips shut, startled by my response. That is about as close to the truth as I'm willing to get. Why? I'm not sure.

That's a lie. Admitting my feelings to someone—even to myself —is opening my heart wide open, only for someone to crush it.

Would Arabella do that? Crush my heart if I gave it to her? That's some sappy shit, but a warranted question. After all, she is a little reckless.

"You don't know if you care? Or you don't know if it would bother you that I liked her?"

"My answer was to both of those questions." I go quiet, realizing I sound like a jackass.

"Uh huh." His gaze narrows and I look away, not wanting to be scrutinized. I don't need Cal trying to figure me out right now, when I can't even figure myself out.

"I just wanted to make sure you're not playing her," I tack on, grimacing the moment the words leave me.

Talk about an excuse.

He actually laughs, the asshole. "*Me* playing her? That's more your game, my friend."

I frown. "What the hell are you talking about?"

"You've been playing her for years. She's had a thing for you since we were freshmen."

He's right. I know he is.

"I think the two of you are totally into each other, but neither of you will ever make a move. Not sure why." Cal shrugs and resumes eating his lunch.

I stare at my tray, my appetite gone. The truth hurts—that's how that clichéd saying goes, and it's one hundred percent accurate. There's a small part of me that can admit that I'm...curious about Arabella. To see if the banter and the spark and the goddamned chemistry we seem to share would carry over into... what?

A relationship?

I don't think that's what I want. Not right now. I know my parents' relationship is solid, and they first started seeing each other in high school during their senior year, which is unfathomable to me. How did they know they would be right together? How many people had they been with before?

That's a question I've never asked because I didn't want to know the answer. My parents seem to fit, like two pieces of a puzzle. As if they were made for each other. Dad is still into Mom. He looks at her as if she's his entire world, and lately, I wonder about that. How do I look at any girl? Particularly Arabella?

Maybe I need to talk to her and clear the air once and for all. I'm positive the two of us could never actually work. She's too all over the place and I'm too tightly contained. She's a free spirit and I'm more reserved. She wants all of the attention all the time, whether it's good or bad, while I'd rather lurk in the shadows.

Damn it, the way I'm mentally describing myself, I sound like a freaking vampire.

"Hello, boys."

We all glance up to find Arabella standing at the head of the table, on the complete opposite side of where I'm currently sitting. Two of her friends linger behind her, all three of them each clutching their tray with a heaping salad bowl on it.

The table offers a murmured hello with the exception of me. Sometimes I act like a dick just because I can.

This is one of those times.

"Mind if we join you?" Bells asks this every time she wants to sit at our table, and every time, we let her. It's almost like a little ritual she enjoys participating in.

"Please." Cal kicks out the chair closest to him. "Sit."

They all settle in, taking the last available chairs, and my friends watch them covertly, almost as if they're spying on them. Which makes sense considering...

Arabella's friends are almost as beautiful and fashionable as she is.

Hadley Michaels is an ice queen and Simone Vincent never stops smiling. The fact that they're friends has always confused me because they're complete opposites. But I don't think about their friendship much. Only when it comes to Arabella, who spends most of her time with them.

Hadley sits next to Callahan, immediately turning her back on him to speak to Simone, who sits on the other side of her. Cal sends me a helpless look, amusement in his gaze, and I just shake my head.

Hadley can be a total bitch, but she owns it, so I don't hold it against her. It's just part of her personality.

Arabella sits in the empty space directly across from me. I watch as she grabs her fork and points it straight at me, her eyes glittering with an unfamiliar emotion.

"I'm mad at you." She stabs her fork in my direction with each word spoken, as if she's making a point.

"What did I do now?" I purposely try to sound bored, stretching out my legs so my feet nudge closer to where hers rest directly under her chair. Trying to get under her skin in any way possible by invading her space. She invades mine on the daily, so it seems appropriate.

Bells glances over at Simone, who takes that as her cue to lean over the table, her gaze meeting mine. "I have it on good authority that you're meeting up with Lydia Fraser after school."

I make a scoffing noise. "Who told you that?"

"I can't name my sources." Simone's voice is prim, her lips thinning. Giving me the impression that she's making good on her statement and won't talk.

Jesus. This is how rumors are spread.

"I'm not meeting up with Lydia after school," I declare to the girls. The guys aren't paying us any attention, save for Cal who has no choice, considering he's sitting in the middle of all of us. "I don't know who told you that or why."

"So it's not true?"

I glance over at Arabella, surprised to hear the relief in her voice. "No, it's not. Who said that?"

"She did." Bells nods toward Simone. "And Lydia told her."

"Arabella!" Simone scolds, her eyes practically bugging out of her head. "I told you not to say a word."

"I can't lie to him." Arabella shrugs, her gaze meeting mine, all the sincerity shining in her dark eyes. I'm tempted to reach over and whip off her glasses. Have I ever seen her without them before? I don't remember. "He needs to know who's spreading rumors about him."

Lydia. She's beautiful. A pain in the ass and mean as a snake. We rarely talk—I prefer steering clear of her, which means I'm baffled why my name is coming from her lips anyway. It's fucking wild.

But this wouldn't be the first time someone was talking about me and making up stories. When you're a Lancaster, this sort of thing is fairly common.

"You have a problem with me meeting someone after class?" I ask Arabella, my voice low.

She slowly shakes her head, her dark brown gaze never straying from mine. "Not at all."

FOUR

ARABELLA

I AM LYING through my teeth. I would be furious if he was seeing someone, especially if that certain someone was Lydia Fraser. She's the worst. Unkind. Downright cruel. Believes she's better than everyone else. Rude to everybody she encounters, even teachers. Condescending. I could go on and on.

I can't stand her, obvi.

Worse? She's gorgeous. Absolutely stunning. Tall and willowy with long blonde hair and crystal blue eyes and a perfect little rosebud mouth. She looks straight out of a fairy tale if I'm being truthful. Too bad that sweet princess mouth spews some of the vilest things ever. It's so unfair that someone so terrible is also incredibly beautiful.

But I can't admit any of that to Rowan. He might take great pleasure in knowing I was jealous of a girl he would give even an ounce of attention to. When Simone told me earlier about Lydia and his "supposed" meetup with her, it took everything I had within me to offer my restrained response. Deep inside, I was spiraling.

"Really, Bells?"

I blink Rowan back into focus, admiring for about the millionth time his handsome face and those pretty green eyes that are fringed with thick, dark lashes. The strong eyebrows and perfect blade of a nose. His high cheekbones and sharp jaw and that mouth, *God*, his mouth. His lips are perfection, and I want to know once, just one single time, what it would be like to feel those decadent lips on mine.

"Really." My voice is flat, my expression as neutral as possible. "You know how I feel about you, Rowan."

His gaze lingers on mine as he murmurs, "Right. And I feel the exact same way about you."

His words mean nothing, but my heart hammers extra fast just the same. We are in a strange position that is of my own creation. The constant back and forth conversation laced with sarcasm and innuendo. The pretending I don't like him when sometimes I feel like I might die for him if he asked me to. Like leap off a tall building, run an extra sharp blade across the inside of my wrist kind of devotion.

Sick and twisted but I'm only being truthful with myself.

"You two are ridiculous."

This stellar observation is made by Callahan, who appears disgusted by our entire conversation.

"What crawled up your ass?" Rowan asks loud enough for the entire table to hear. A few of his friends laugh. Simone and Hadley both grimace with obvious disgust.

"I'm tired of the way you guys constantly flirt."

"Flirt?" I rest my hand against my chest, my eyes wide as I watch Callahan. "You call our conversations flirting?"

Callahan switches his attention to Rowan, his gaze...knowing? Hmm.

"You two can deny it all you want, but it's pretty fucking obvious that you're into each other. I wish you'd just hook up with her and get it over with." Cal leaps to his feet so quickly, his chair falls backward with a clatter, effectively silencing the entire dining hall.

"Hey. Watch what you're saying," Rowan snaps, his narrowed gaze on Cal. I can practically feel the anger emanating from him and I frown, wondering at that.

Why is he mad? Does he not like being called out by his best friend? And why is he mad at Cal anyway? He's usually the most easygoing person at this table, save for this outburst.

Callahan glares at Rowan, slowly shaking his head. "I've never seen two people in such denial before in my life. Get your head out of your ass, Row. There's a perfectly good girl sitting across from you who's probably dying for you to ask her out. Put us all out of our misery and just do it."

My heart trips over itself. I can't believe Callahan called out his best friend like that. And over me? What is this life?

"What? Now you're trying to tell me what to do?" Row leans back in his chair, his expression icy cold. "Stay out of my personal business, Cal."

"You're fucking ridiculous." Cal sends me a look full of apologies before he returns his attention to Rowan. "Why are you being so stubborn?"

"Guys." I snap my fingers and they glance over at me at the same time. I rear back a little, overwhelmed to have their focus. It's rather intense, I can't lie. "Are you seriously fighting over... me, right now?"

Rowan's assessing gaze settles upon me and I go still, my breath lodging in my throat. "Absolutely not."

My mouth drops open. Why that little liar.

"This is ridiculous." Cal turns and stalks out of the building, the double doors clanging behind him making me jump in my seat.

Eventually conversations start back up in the dining hall, including ones at our table. Save for me and Rowan.

We're not saying a word, especially to each other.

I keep my gaze focused on my salad, turning the various vegetables over and over again with my fork. My appetite has evaporated. My mind is a whirl with questions, none of them I can ask out loud. So Callahan and Rowan have talked about me. I suppose I shouldn't be surprised, but I am. I had no idea I was a topic of conversation for Rowan. Most of the time he acts like I annoy him. Like I'm a gnat buzzing around his head and he takes great pleasure in swatting at me.

But he never actually slays me dead, so maybe there's something there, like Callahan said. Or perhaps I'm delusional, as usual.

"If you're trying to save my feelings by denying you're going out with Lydia, you don't have to be careful around me," I finally say, hating every single word that leaves my mouth.

Rowan makes an irritated sound like a growl deep in his throat and God, I hate myself for thinking this, but wow that sound was sexy. "This is stupid."

I sit up straighter, my voice coming louder. "What's stupid?"

"What's happening here." He waves a hand between us. "We've been doing this for years, Bells."

"I know."

"And we've gotten nowhere."

"Was this?" I'm the one waving a hand between us now. "Supposed to actually go somewhere?"

He frowns.

I do too.

"Tell me something—have you ever had a boyfriend?" His question is casual. His expression is not. He appears to be bracing himself for my answer.

"Don't you think you'd know if I had a boyfriend?"

"I don't know what you do during your private time." He shrugs. "It's none of my business."

I want to make it all of his business, but if I were to say that to him now, would he laugh? Or would he consider it?

For the first time since sophomore year, I have a feeling that he would consider it. Consider *me*.

My heart is in my throat. There's a buzzing in my head and ears that makes it hard to hear, and I lick my lips, trying to come up with the right words to say something. Anything.

"Rowan Lancaster, there you are!"

We both swivel our heads to see the dreaded Princess Lydia herself approaching us, stunningly gorgeous as usual. Being in her presence immediately makes me feel frumpy and awkward and I clamp my lips shut, forgetting my true confession plans.

"Hey, Lydia." He reluctantly—was it reluctantly?—drags his gaze from mine to acknowledge her.

While I sit in silence, jealousy bubbles inside me. It's something I deal with all the time, it seems. Jealousy. Envy. People have things I want. Things I crave that I don't get. Ever. Like love from their parents, their family. A boyfriend who is obsessed with them. And I hate admitting even to myself that I'm a jealous person, but I am.

I so am.

Putting on a brave face, I glance over at my friends, who both watch me with sympathy practically dripping off them.

Ugh, I hate that.

Looking away, I keep my attention focused on Lydia and Rowan.

"I was hoping we could get together after school sometime," Lydia says, twirling a lock of perfect blonde hair around her finger as she studies him with hunger in her eyes. "We have that American Government project to work on, and we're supposed to partner up with someone."

I send a quick look toward Rowan, but he's not paying attention to me. He's too enraptured with Lydia and her stupid, beautiful face.

I'm in their class. I have that project to work on too, and I don't have a partner yet. I don't think any of us do. I figured our teacher would assign us partners, which is how she normally operates. As a matter of fact, Mrs. Wallace only just mentioned this project at the very end of second period. And look at Lydia, rushing in to try and pin down Rowan as her partner.

So smart. I wish I would've come up with that.

"Right." Rowan nods, his gaze sliding toward me. "I already have a partner though."

Lydia's rosebud lips part in surprise. "Who?"

"Bells." He inclines his head in my direction.

I gape at him. So does Lydia, who slowly turns her narrowed gaze upon me. "You're partnering with Arabella?"

"I am," he says firmly.

"You are?" I clear my throat when I realize I sound like I'm questioning him. "I mean, yes. You are. We are partners. In American Government. For our new project."

I sound like an idiotic robot.

"Oh. I see." Lydia's voice is hollow, and she returns all her attention to Rowan. "Are you sure you want to work with...her?"

"Hey," I murmur, vaguely irritated. What's that supposed to mean exactly? "I didn't ask him. He asked me."

"I did," Rowan confirms. "And I definitely want to work on this project with Arabella."

I like it when he says my full name, which isn't often. I do adore the nickname he has for me too. If I'm being truthful, I love it when he acknowledges me in any way possible, which makes me sound pathetic and sad, but I don't care. It's not like anyone can hear my thoughts.

"If you say so." Lydia sniffs. "Have fun."

The moment she's gone, I'm leaning across the table, my voice lowering to a whisper. "What exactly was that?"

"That was me getting out of working with Lydia," he responds without hesitation.

Hmm. Why wouldn't he want to work with her? Does he find her beauty too distracting? I think her face would even distract me. "Maybe I don't want to be your partner."

"Come on, Bells. Give me a break."

"You make it sound like it'll be a privilege for me to work with you." My tone is haughty because if he's implying that, ugh. I know Rowan has a tremendous ego and for good reason. Look at him. He rules this school, and everyone adores him. I swear the entire campus was depressed after he broke his ankle out on the football field. No one likes to see their prince injured, including me.

He doesn't say a word to my statement. Just watches me with that gorgeous face of his, his eyebrows lifting, his expression challenging.

"It'll be an easy project," he finally says.

"For you, only because I'll do everything," I retort. I have no idea if that's true. Rowan isn't dumb. He's actually quite smart and I'm just being mean, insinuating that he won't put in the effort.

"I won't let you do it all," he says, leaning across the table as well, though he grimaces when he does it. That boot always gets in his way, and I immediately feel bad for him. "I can hold up my half of the project. I'm not a slacker."

I know he's not. I had no business accusing him of being one.

"What's this project about anyway?" I ask, because I haven't a clue.

"I don't know, but I'm sure we'll figure it out." His slow smile is lethal, sending an arrow straight to my heart and making it ache. "Together."

FIVE

ROWAN

"HOW'S THE ANKLE?"

I smile at my parents, pretending everything is cool. Nothing is bothering me. It's after dinner and Dad FaceTimed me like he usually does a couple of times a week, but during this call, Mom is with him. I have to put on a brave face or else Mom will get overly concerned and demand I ease up. And right now, well basically all the time, I don't want to hear it. "It's fine. Hurts a little."

"Oh no. Are you doing too much?" Mom asks, her brows drawn together, looking as concerned as ever.

"Not at all," I lie, shaking my head. I mean, I'm not out trying to run a marathon. And I'm definitely not on the field tossing a football. At least I'm keeping the boot on. I've been tempted more than I'd ever admit to her to take it off. "But I do have to walk around campus every day, which is...tiring."

Mom turns to Dad. "Maybe he shouldn't be walking everywhere. The campus is huge."

"What do you suggest? We make him use a wheelchair?" Dad sounds amused.

But Mom is dead serious. "Yes. That's a great idea."

"No way," I interject. "I'm not using a wheelchair, Mom. I'm fine."

"Row, you have to be careful. Your ankle needs time to heal properly, and you can't be on it all day."

"I'm not on it all day," I reassure her, sending a *help me out here* look at my father. "Trust me. I'm going to be okay. It's healing properly."

"He's right," Dad says, his voice firm. "I'm sure his ankle is doing well, and he'll be able to get rid of the boot soon."

"But not too soon," Mom says, like she can't help herself. Her big green eyes lock on me. "Take your time, sweetheart."

"Right. Sure," I say, desperate to change the subject. "So what else is going on?"

"You and Beau are coming home soon." Mom's face visibly brightens. "I can't wait to see you both."

My younger brother is a freshman, along with a bunch of our cousins. Supposedly, there are more Lancasters on campus right now than there ever have been in the history of Lancaster Prep, and most of that is thanks to all the Lancasters that are Beau's age. Not all of them have Lancaster as their last name, but the family blood is flowing through their veins and we're running rampant around here.

Can't wait to leave and get away from the majority of them, not that my cousins bother me. They don't really. My little brother can be a pain in my ass sometimes but for the most part, he's okay. Helps that he worships the ground I walk on and I can get him to do whatever I want. Maybe I should take advantage of that in my currently hobbled state.

"I'm ready to come home too," I say, though I don't one hundred percent mean it. It'll be nice to get away from campus and I won't mind being back in my room. But Mom will want to pamper me, which is code for smothering me with attention, and she'll be so stressed out over the state of my ankle that I'll get annoyed.

I know I will.

And then there's the fact I won't see Bells for a solid ten days. That's a long time. I'll miss arguing with her. It's the only thing that cheers me up.

"But we won't have Willow with us," Mom continues, her tone a little bleak. "I'll miss her so much."

"Cal told me they're going to Mexico."

"She'll have a wonderful time," Dad says, slipping his arm around Mom's shoulders and giving them a squeeze. "It's good for her to spend more time with Rhett's family."

"So true." Mom sighs, all of her romantic imaginings showing on her face. "I assume Rhett will ask her to marry him soon."

I make a face, panic making my insides clench up. They're only twenty. Two years older than me, and they already want to get married? Get the fuck out of here.

"And you're cool with that?" I ask Dad because come the fuck on.

His baby girl getting married at such a young age? How can Dad approve of that? Shouldn't she be out living her life and figuring out what she wants? I'm sure she'd say she only wants Rhett, but that seems like such a big decision at such a young age. And it's not like I enjoy it when people call us out for being too young for whatever, including myself, but marriage?

I'm not ready for it. Can't imagine Willow and Rhett are either.

"Why wouldn't I be cool with it? We got married pretty young." He glances over at Mom, who just smiles at him, her adoration for him shining in her gaze.

While I sit in my dorm suite all alone, just the way I prefer it, rolling my eyes. Engaged at twenty. That is freaking incomprehensible.

"It's not so bad, being married to your father," Mom says, making Dad nudge her in her side. "Hey!"

"Come on now. You guys can flirt later," I mutter. "Need anything else from me?"

"We were just checking on you," Mom says, her voice soft, her eyes glowing as they meet mine through the screen. "I worry about you, Rowan."

Guilt swamps me but I shove it aside. "I'm okay. I promise."

"Take care of yourself," she murmurs. "We miss you."

"Miss you, Son," Dad adds. "Can't wait to see you in a couple of weeks."

"Yeah, yeah." I'm about ready to end the call when they both tell me they love me, and I say it back because of course I do. I do love my parents. They're great. Supportive and encouraging and they treat all of us with respect, which a lot of my friends don't get that kind of treatment from their parents, save for Callahan, who's lucky like me, I guess. It just sucks that my parents won't let me wallow in my misery for too long. They always force me to snap out of it. This is why a part of me dreads going home.

Mom won't let me hole myself away in my room like I'll want to. She'll expect me to interact with the family and participate in whatever activities she might have scheduled. Because knowing her, she'll have activities. She lives for that kind of shit. Bringing the aunts and uncles and cousins together, making sure we're all spending what she calls "quality time" together as a family.

Yeah, that's not my thing. Most of the time, I just want to be alone. I've been surrounded by family my entire life. My sister and my brother and all my cousins. While everyone has a cousin or cousins that are the same age and they can hang out with them—save for August but he hates everybody—I'm the one standout. The cousin with no one who's closer in age to me.

When we were younger, I tried to tag along with Willow and Iris, but after a while, I didn't want to be with the girls. And the cousins who are all the same age as Beau—there are a ton of them—drove me nuts. The age difference is still noticeable. They're pretty damn immature if I'm being real.

I'm my own island and most of the time, I like it that way.

Particularly now.

After my call with my parents, I remove the boot and take a quick and agonizing shower, grumpy as fuck because I'm sick of dealing with my still-healing ankle. I'm in a state of constant pain, but I kicked the meds a while ago, not about to get hooked on them. The ankle is an incessant reminder of what happened to me out on that field. The boot is a symbol of my dreams shattered and my senior year ruined.

I hate it.

I'd give anything to change that night, and when I go over the moment in my brain, I wonder if it would've happened if I'd jagged left instead of right. Maybe that lineman would've sacked me, but I wouldn't have broken my ankle. The injury wouldn't have been as bad. Could I have avoided getting injured at all?

I'll never know. I can't change what happened that night. What's done is done. I just have to deal with it.

It fucking sucks, but I don't have a choice.

THE NEXT MORNING, I decide to change up my routine. I walk a different path from my suite to the dining hall, and once I get there, I purposely stay inside longer than usual, holding court with my friends who also remain at the table with me far longer than normal. I eat a breakfast burrito instead of an egg and sausage sandwich. I drink a vanilla latte instead of a mocha. By the time the warning bell is ringing, I'm only then hustling out of the dining hall the best I can, slower than usual thanks to the fucking boot, limping my way across campus as I head toward first period.

"Hey, Lancaster, need a ride?"

I glance over my shoulder to see Artie Daniels, our newish groundskeeper sitting behind the steering wheel of his golf cart, a grin on his weathered face. He's a good guy, Artie. Prefers to keep to himself and doesn't talk much, though I have caught him talking to the plants and flowers in his garden and all over the grounds.

Normal me would refuse the offer because I don't need any help from anyone, but again, I'm trying to make a change. "Sure."

I climb into the passenger seat and grip the side bar hanging from the golf cart roof, grateful I do when he takes off at a rapid speed, causing my body to sway toward the right. We pass the last-minute stragglers who are hurrying to beat the first period final bell, including a very familiar figure breaking into a light jog just in front of us, her dark hair swinging from the ponytail that sits atop her head.

She's not wearing sparkly tights today. Nope, Bells is barelegged in the middle of November, her skirt hiked up so high I swear I see the curve of an ass cheek as she runs, the hem of her skirt flapping.

Huh. Arabella is late and she is never, ever late.

"Bells!" I cup my hands around my mouth and yell her name, causing her to slow down as she glances over her shoulder. "Let's pick her up," I tell Artie, who comes to a screeching stop.

She leaps out of the golf cart's way, obviously out of breath, her gaze shifting from the cart to mine. "There you are," she breathes, puffing.

I sit up straighter, frowning. "You were looking for me?"

"You weren't in your usual spot." She glances toward the building where our first period class is, her delicate brows drawing together in concern.

"Get in." I jerk my thumb behind me.

"The back seat is full," Artie says, voice full of regret. "She won't fit."

"Don't worry about me. I can walk." She starts doing exactly that, and I wave a hand at Artie, who lets the golf cart roll forward.

"Get in," I command as Artie drives the golf cart, keeping pace with her brisk stride. I envy her ability to walk on two legs. "Now."

"You can't tell me what to do." She says it with a blissful smile, her dark eyes sparkling behind her heavy-framed glasses, and I huff out an irritated breath. Normally she'd agree with whatever I say, but for whatever reason, she chooses this morning to be difficult.

"Sit on my lap, Bells. Artie is going to get us to class on time. Come on."

She stops walking, her gaze going to the spot on my thigh that I'm currently patting. Where I want her butt perched because I guess I feel like torturing myself.

"I won't hurt you?" she whispers, her worry obvious.

"Not a chance," I say with more confidence than I feel.

And I'm not referring to my ankle either. She might have the power to hurt me in a multitude of ways.

Most of them I don't even want to consider.

SIX

ARABELLA

I STARE at temptation personified patting his thigh as an invitation to...sit on his lap? Is he for real right now? The very morning that I choose to wear the shortest uniform skirt I own and a skimpy pair of undies beneath it? My bare butt cheeks are going to settle on his leg and um...

That's a lot to consider.

The groundskeeper checks the clunky watch on his wrist. "You have less than two minutes until the final bell rings."

"Arabella. Come on." The commanding tone of Rowan's voice has me spurring into action and next thing I know, I'm on his lap.

Perched on his leg.

His thigh.

One large hand owned by *the* Rowan Lancaster suddenly rests on my waist, keeping me in place, while the other reaches up and grabs hold of the black bar above us, caging me in. "Hold on to me."

He doesn't have to ask me twice.

I grip his shoulder, my hand sliding upward as if I have no control over it, closer to his neck. He's warm and solid and he smells so freaking good. Like a fresh pine tree in the middle of a forest. Like crisp mountain air and sin, if sin had a smell.

It would be Rowan Lancaster.

The golf cart jerks into motion and I fall against him, making him grunt. I immediately start to pull away but his hand tightens on my waist, pinning me to him.

"I'm fine," he mutters, his annoyance obvious because I'm sure he knows I was going to ask him if he was okay. If I hurt him.

This boy hates when people show concern for him, and it's the oddest thing.

The brisk November air blows against us as we hurtle toward the math and science building, and I shiver in Rowan's arms, my butt settled right on his firm thigh. I can feel his gaze sweeping over me, tingles erupting everywhere his eyes touch, and when he tilts his head back to look into my eyes, his dark brows are drawn together as if he's confused.

"What the *fuck* are you wearing?" he whispers, his voice harsh.

"My uniform?" I say it as a question, which is how I often speak to him. He makes me feel like my answers might be wrong every time he awaits a response.

"Your skirt. It's fucking indecent." His hot gaze seems to burn a hole through my exposed legs as he stares at them. "One wrong move and we'll see everything."

My outfit choices are dictated by him, and he doesn't even know it. I wanted to capture his attention in the most extraordinary way today, and only moments ago, my disappointment in not finding him at his usual morning spot had nearly overwhelmed me. Seeing him on the golf cart immediately lifted my spirits, but now...

Now I'm worried he thinks I'm too much. Too obvious. Too brash and cheap and unattractive.

These are all of my old insecurities roaring back to life. There are other, more personal reasons as to why I dress the way I do. Act the way I do. All my life, I've never received the attention from my parents I so desperately craved. I'm an only child with a workaholic dad and a mom who travels with him everywhere he goes. They're too wrapped up in their own lives to worry about me. I've spent the majority of my life away at boarding school. Family holidays don't exist. My father is in finance, and according to him, the finance world never rests, not even on Christmas or New Year's or even Thanksgiving, which is coming up soon.

I'll be spending the holiday like I usually do—on campus here at Lancaster Prep, eating dry turkey with the other unfortunate souls who don't have anywhere to go during the holiday season. It is truly the most depressing thing ever.

"Maybe I want someone to see everything," I finally murmur, just as the golf cart comes to a screeching halt directly in front of the steps that lead to the building where our first period class is.

Rowan ignores my comment, nudging my hip with the firm press of his fingers, indicating he wants me to get off his lap. I jump off him, gripping my backpack so it doesn't slide out of place as I run up the stairs and I can hear him behind me. Note the groan that escapes him as he follows me.

"Jesus, Bells. I can see your ass."

I scurry into the warm building, my heart racing, my cheeks heating. "It can't be that bad, is it?"

"You're delusional," he says as he keeps pace with me as best as he can, remaining close. "You need a bodyguard to block everyone's view."

I am mortified. I must look atrocious. "I should go back to my room and change."

He reaches for the classroom door before I can, holding it open for me right as the final bell rings. "Too late for that."

I go inside, Rowan practically on top of me, and I flop into my seat, wincing when my bare skin meets the cold, hard plastic of my chair. This is just...

A giant mistake. I got his attention in the worst way, and he seems downright disgusted with me. Maybe he thinks my butt is too skinny because lord knows, it's not too big. My figure has always been a little more on the boyish side, and I only just got decent boobs last summer after they remained as flat as can be since I was twelve. Most of the boys I know have reminded me of that fact too, save for Rowan.

He's never commented much on my appearance at all. That might be part of the reason I try to wear something completely outrageous every day. I want him to comment, to notice, to see me. To appreciate the view, the fashion, the time I take each morning to catch his attention in the hopes that he'll notice and fall madly in love with me.

Instead, I gross him out with my skinny butt cheeks on display. I'm a disgusting human being. Maybe I should start drinking protein shakes. Or I should work out more. I should definitely cover up...

"Arabella." The exhaustion in Mrs. Guthrie's voice is obvious. I know she's tired of my antics. I completely understand why. "You're breaking dress code."

I don't even argue with her. "May I be excused to go change?"

She seems startled by my lack of protest. "Of course, you can. But hurry back. I'm starting on a new section and you'll want to be here for it."

I grab my backpack and rise to my feet, immediately turning so my back is to the wall and no one can see my butt. I send Rowan an apologetic smile and edge out of the classroom, walking funny so, again, no one can see something they shouldn't. I only breathe a sigh of relief when I'm in the empty hallway.

I hear the clanging slam of a door only seconds later, just as I'm about to go outside, and I pause at the double doors, glancing over my shoulder to find Rowan hobbling toward me.

He's so adorable with that irritated look on his face, his dark hair hanging over his forehead in the most appealing way. He's getting better at maneuvering with the ankle boot, and I wait for him, pinning my back against the door so he can't see my backside.

"Did I offend you?" he asks the moment he's standing directly in front of me. Close enough to touch.

Now that I've actually touched him, even sat on his lap, I want to do it again. Immediately.

"Offend me how?" I blink at him.

"By telling you your skirt is too short." He got rid of his winter coat and he rests his hands on his hips, shoving back his uniform blazer with the movement. "I, uh. I didn't mean to hurt your feelings."

Did he just stumble over his words? That is so un-Rowan-like of him.

"If you don't want to go back to your dorm room, you can have this." My jaw drops as he takes off his blazer and holds it toward me. "This should cover you up."

It takes me a few seconds to find my words. "But then you'll be out of dress code."

"They won't punish me for not wearing this. Here." He thrusts the coat closer to me. "Put it on."

I'm in my uniform vest, which is what the girls wear if they're not feeling the jacket, which is me almost all the time. The vest is easier to work with when I'm tweaking my outfit. And dumb me shrugged out of my heavier coat and left it in the classroom when I could've wrapped it around my waist and hid my skirt.

"I don't want you to get too cold," I start but he shakes his head once, cutting me off with just that movement.

"Stop being ridiculous and wear the damn thing, Bells." He literally pushes it against my chest, and I have no choice but to take it from him and slip it on.

The blazer completely overwhelms me in all ways possible. It's far too large and hangs practically to my knees, which was his intent. And the sleeves are too long. I'm shoving them up my arms, but they fall back down, covering my hands completely. Then there's the fact that it smells like him, his scent clinging to the fabric.

"That's better," he says, satisfaction lacing his voice. "Come on. Let's get back to class."

I follow after him in a daze, my steps slow, my thoughts racing. He ran after me. He sort of apologized. He offered me his blazer and forced me to take it and now I'm wearing it. I think he felt bad for cursing at me and telling me my skirt was too short and oh my God.

Right now, I feel like the luckiest girl alive.

SEVEN

ARABELLA

"INTERESTING OUTFIT CHOICE TODAY, ARABELLA."

This comment comes from my friend Hadley at lunch. She scanned me up and down the moment we saw each other in the hallway but didn't say a word until now.

I decide to take her words as a compliment. Better than being defensive. "Thank you."

"Where did you get the oversized blazer?" Her question seems innocent but I spy the gleam in her icy blue eyes. She has suspicions, I'm sure.

"Well..." I glance around to see if anyone is paying us any attention, but no one is. We're sitting at our own table today, all of us deciding not to sit with the boys. We only do that a couple times a week because we're all under the assumption that if we keep pushing ourselves on them, they won't want to spend time with us anymore.

God, why does life always feel like a game? Sometimes I'm tired of playing.

"The rumor going around is that Row gave you his blazer during first period because your skirt was too short and you were being written up for breaking dress code," Simone interjects, leaning into our conversation, a knowing smile curling her lips.

"That's exactly what happened," I admit, not bothering trying to hide it.

Hadley's brows shoot up in obvious surprise. "You're telling us that Rowan gave you his blazer."

I nod.

"To cover up your short skirt," she continues.

I scoot away from the table so she can see said short skirt. "I was a little too daring this morning."

She examines most of my thighs on display. "Not even wearing tights, huh?"

I shake my head.

"Aren't you freezing?" Simone asks.

"No. Not really." It helps that I'm wearing a piece of clothing that belongs to Rowan and that his scent is still wrapped all around me. I could live a long time dressed like this, wearing his clothes. I now want to steal whatever I can from him and keep it forever. A T-shirt, a sweatshirt. A girl's prized possession is the hoodie that belongs to the boy she's dating, and I'd wear Rowan's like a badge of honor all around campus. I'd probably never wash it either.

That's so gross, but I'm just being honest.

"Row giving you his blazer is so very...nice of him." Hadley makes a little face after using the word nice to describe Rowan because no one says that. No one calls him nice.

"Isn't it?" I agree, cheerfully digging into my salad. The vegetables are fresh and delicious, and I munch away, lost in my thoughts of kind Rowan and the way he touched me while I sat on his lap until Hadley has to ruin everything with her next question.

"What's he up to anyway?"

I swallow hard, setting my fork on the edge of my salad bowl. "What do you mean?"

"What's his motive? Why is he being nice to you? He's never nice," Hadley says. "To anyone."

"He's an asshole," Simone adds.

I'm offended on his behalf but I can't act that way in front of them. I mean, they do know I have a crush on him and that it's been growing for years. I can't deny it. They are my closest friends and they know how I feel.

"He's not that bad—"

Simone cuts me off before I can finish my sentence.

"He's awful. An absolute menace. Girls won't date him because they're terrified of him and boys are his friend because they're too scared that he'll ruin them if they're not. He's barely tolerated you for years. Why is he suddenly acting nice and wants to help you?"

"I don't trust him," Hadley adds. "You need to be careful."

I absorb their words, turning them over and over in my brain while they continue eating as if their world hasn't been rocked.

Not that mine was rocked, per se. How they described Rowan is correct. He's extremely closed off, casually cruel to almost everyone around him and he doesn't date. Ever.

"Maybe he has a...secret girlfriend?" Hadley winces when I jerk my gaze to hers. "She could go to a different school, or maybe she's older? That could be why he's so grouchy all the time. He's pissed off at the world and wishes he was with his one true love. That would make anyone frustrated."

"That is a valid point." Simone points her fork in Hadley's direction, her gaze sliding to mine. "Have you ever considered that?"

Impossible, is what I want to tell them. I would know if he had a girlfriend. There would be clues. Signs. And if he had a girlfriend, then why does he tolerate me hanging around him all the time? I see the way he looks at me sometimes.

Or maybe he feels sorry for me, which is—God, that's awful to even contemplate.

"He didn't used to be this way," Hadley continues. "The first two years of high school, he wasn't as grumpy. Definitely a lot more friendly and flirty. What changed him?"

"The fact that his secret girlfriend doesn't go here," Simone says before she starts giggling.

I send her a stern look and she immediately stops laughing.

"We're speculating when we have zero facts to back up what we're thinking. Besides, I find it hard to believe that I wouldn't know if he had a secret girlfriend. There's no reason for us to spread any rumors." I sound prim, but I can't help it.

"We're not spreading rumors, Bella. We're just talking about him amongst ourselves," Hadley says, and I know she's right. I'm just defensive about him. Protective. And I sort of hate it when anyone calls me Bella, but I never correct them, so I let it go. "I was kidding about the secret girlfriend part. If she existed, we'd know. But here's what's weird—lately it feels like the only person he can tolerate is...you. Oh, and Callahan, of course."

"He doesn't tolerate me," I start, but Hadley shakes her head. My voice weakens. "He doesn't."

"He most definitely does. You two have this weird relationship going on and none of us can figure it out. We've been trying to understand what's going on between you two for a while, but we don't get it," Hadley says, Simone nodding her agreement.

"You've been trying to figure us out?" I'm baffled by this. I didn't even realize Rowan and I were a topic of conversation for anyone. My mind is a little blown, I cannot lie.

"Of course. And we've both come to the conclusion that he's either sexually frustrated because he's into guys or because he's into *you*," Simone says.

I gape at my friends, my thoughts scattering to the wind. "He is not into me."

They both watch me with matching skeptical expressions, neither of them saying a word.

"He's not," I stress. "I annoy him. I'm like a little bug buzzing around his head and he's desperate to swat at it. Swat at me."

"You really believe that?" Simone asks, her voice full of doubt.

"Yes. With my whole entire heart."

Hadley changes the subject, asking if a certain couple from the junior class is still together or not and I keep rolling with the conversation, not missing a beat. Simone does the same, all discussion of Rowan completely forgotten, though he does linger in the back of my mind.

It's impossible to think he could be interested in me. No one is. No one ever has been—not really. I sometimes even wonder if my friends actually like me, or if they merely tolerate me like Rowan. Teachers care because they have to and same with the staff at school. And my parents? I don't matter to them.

This is my daily reminder that truly, I matter to no one.

THE LAST CLASS of the day is my favorite. Psychology. Ms. Skov has been at Lancaster Prep forever, and I remember Rowan saying in class once that she taught his parents when they were seniors. Meaning the woman is positively ancient. I don't hold that against her though. More like I view her as a wealth of knowledge on human behavior and why we do the things we do. Though I never like to examine myself too closely, I adore observing other people and trying to figure out what makes them tick.

We have less than ten minutes left on the clock before Skov makes a declaration, causing all of us to sit up straighter and pay attention.

"We have a group assignment," she announces, her gaze scanning the room. "I'm going to partner each of you up with someone and you'll all have to do both an analysis on yourselves and one on your partner."

"So we'll be in groups of two?" someone asks from the back of the classroom.

"Yes, indeed. And don't bother asking—like I said, I'll be in charge of picking your partners," Skov says.

A variety of people groan their frustration while I visibly squirm in my seat. It doesn't bother me to work on group projects. I don't mind when a teacher assigns us our partners either. I just hate it when it's someone I don't particularly like or respect. That makes things *extremely* difficult.

"Here's a worksheet for all of you to complete." She starts to pass them out, going row by row. "And I'm going to announce your partners right now so tomorrow you can start working together."

I clutch my hands together, mentally noting how cold they are. Nervous anticipation races through me, and God, I really hope I don't get paired up with a terrible someone. I'd much prefer to be partnered with Rowan, but that's just wishful thinking.

Once she's passed out the sheets and we're able to look over the questions, Mrs. Skov heads toward her desk, where she picks up another piece of paper and starts rattling off names.

My eyes cross as I stare at the form that she gave us while listening to her name off students in the classroom. I breathe a sigh of relief when she pairs a boy who gives me the creeps off with another girl. She keeps going, making the wait agonizing, and when she finally calls my name, I almost sag with relief.

"Arabella Hartley Thomas." Ms. Skov pauses, her gaze finding mine. "And Rowan Lancaster."

If I could jump for joy and do a little dance at this miraculous pairing, I so would, but I'm not interested in making a fool of myself. Instead, I sink deeper into Rowan's uniform blazer, the collar rising up and around my face, his scent flooding my nostrils and making me breathe in deep.

Thank you, Ms. Skov, for giving me the partner I was hoping for.

"This project isn't easy," she says once she's done reading off everyone's names. "You're going to have to take a cold hard look at your partner, as well as yourself. If you understand who you're dealing with—both the people around you and yourself—you'll have such an advantage when handling people when you're out in the real world. Whether in the workforce, with family members, and even with friends."

I know how to handle people. I am a confident almost eighteen-year-old who knows exactly what she's doing.

At least, that's the lie I keep telling myself.

The bell rings and everyone makes a mad dash for the door, a mass exodus flooding into the hallway. With the exception of a few stragglers still gathering their things before they leave, including myself. And Rowan.

He's only slow because of his injury, I tell myself as I shove the last of my things in my backpack and zip it up. It has nothing to do with me.

I sling my backpack over my shoulder and make my way toward him, stepping to the side as I walk past, offering him a weak smile when he glances in my direction.

"I thought I'd return your blazer to you," I tell him, dropping my backpack onto the desk closest to me before I start to shrug out of it.

"Keep it," he says, making me pause. "You still have to walk across campus in that skirt."

I slowly pull the blazer back into place, unsure if he's being extra mean or just normal. God, I really can't tell. "Thank you."

"We're partnered up." He's stating the obvious.

"I know." I shrug. "Is that a problem?"

"Is it for you?" he throws at me.

"I asked first."

He runs a hand through his hair, messing it up. Somehow, he still looks perfect. Perfectly gorgeous. "No."

My smile is back and bigger than ever. "Good."

"Don't get any funny ideas though."

"Like what?" The smile is gone, replaced by a frown.

"Don't get all silly and...you know. Fall in love with me."

Fall in love with him? Is he serious? "Don't worry. That's not going to happen."

His frown deepens. "It's not?"

"Not at all." I shake my head. "I won't fall in love with you because I don't think I'm capable of it."

"Capable of what?"

"Love." I shrug. "I've never been shown it in my entire life, so how would I be able to reciprocate it?"

I'm all about a crush—and I've had a mad crush on Rowan for years. But love? That's big and scary and I have no idea what it actually feels like.

He blinks at me, as if my confession shocked him. Maybe it did. "What about your family?"

"I don't really have any."

"Brothers and sisters?"

I shake my head.

"What about your parents?"

"They're too wrapped up in their own lives to ever worry about me." I might have mentioned that to him before, but did he forget?

His expression switches to straight disgust. "What are you talking about? You're their kid."

"I know, right? But that's just how they are. Sometimes I wonder why they even had me." I grab my backpack and sling it over my shoulder. "I'll see you tomorrow?"

He just stares at me, his gaze roving over my face, and it looks like he wants to say something but changes his mind at the last second. "Yeah. See you."

"I'll bring your blazer back to you." I start to exit the classroom, pausing in the open doorway to glance over my shoulder at him.

To find Rowan staring at me, his brows drawn together, adorable confusion written all over his handsome face.

Hmm. I think I threw him for a loop.

EIGHT

ROWAN

I CALL my cousin after dinner, bracing myself for a blast of icy indifference, and he doesn't disappoint.

"Why are you calling me at eight o'clock on a weeknight?" This is August's usual greeting, always so warm and open.

Ha.

"What, are you an old man who's in bed early on weeknights?" I'm giving him shit because it's one of the only ways to disarm him. My father describes August as a, and I quote, tough nut to crack.

I'll say. The guy never cracks. Ever.

"No. You just never call me out of the blue like this unless you want something." He pauses for only a moment. "What do you want?"

"I need you to do some research for me if you have the time." I settle into my desk chair and crack open my laptop, logging in and going straight to Google, opening the search page I conducted earlier.

"On who?"

August has become my go-to person for digging up information. He's really good at it, with hacker tendencies he claims he picked up from his aunt Sylvie. I wouldn't doubt if what he's told me is true. She's pretty sly, and I heard back when she went to Lancaster Prep, she could actually hack into the computer system and change grades and shit.

Talk about lucky.

"Winston and Marietta Hartley Thomas." My gaze locks on the photo of the couple I'm talking about. They're attractive for old people, I'll give them that. From what I could glean off the internet, he's a big-time finance guy and she doesn't do shit but spend his money and hang on his arm at various social events.

After what Bells told me earlier, I hate them on sight.

I hear the clacking of keys as August types and I wait patiently for what he might discover while I scroll through the boring articles I did find. Whatever search engine and access August has, he discovers way more information on someone than I ever could. This is why it's good to keep him in your back pocket. His scary stealth searching skills are unmatched.

"Why do you give a shit about these two?" he asks me at one point.

"I go to school with their daughter."

"Hot for her?"

"No," I lie.

"Uh huh." There are a few taps and clicks on the other end. "Check your email. I want to Zoom with you."

I go into my inbox and open the Zoom link he sent me. Within seconds I'm facing August, who's sitting on his couch, the glow of his laptop the only light in the room. He's scowling, which is a normal look for him, and I realize I've basically modeled myself after him over the last couple of years.

"I'm going to share my screen with you." A couple of clicks and there's his screen, showing a large photo of Winston and Marietta standing together at some party where he's in a tux and she's clad in a black sequin gown, both of them wearing phony smiles and lifting their glasses in a toast. "These two hang out with some of Manhattan's most elite."

"How much are they worth?"

"Approximately..." He's tapping away again before he goes quiet for a moment. "Twenty-five mill, give or take."

Compared to Lancasters, that doesn't feel like much.

"Where do they currently live?" That I couldn't figure out, which was frustrating. If they live in New York and were purposely ignoring Arabella, I might come for them.

Correction. I know I'll come for them. Hurting their daughter is the equivalent of kicking a puppy in the gut. When I think about these people, all I can see is red.

"Hong Kong."

"Hong Kong?" I repeat.

"Financial capital of the world. They come back to New York often though."

"How often?"

"Umm...they were here last week. Brief stay for the both of them."

"And they didn't even try to see her," I mutter.

"Who?"

"Their daughter."

"The one you want to fuck."

"I don't want to fuck her," I practically growl, which only makes August laugh.

"Uh huh. Sure. Why else would you be pissed at her shitty parents?"

He's right. Not that I view Arabella as a casual fuck. Honestly? I don't view any girl like that. But I do look at her like she's some-one...different.

Like she matters.

As if she's special.

What the hell? I don't think anyone is special. But I am protective over her. Abnormally so. Seeing her walk around campus and in class all day wearing my jacket? Felt like a claiming. As if I were telling people *hey, she's mine.*

She belongs to me.

But that's impossible. No one belongs to anyone, and she would agree. I have a lot of nerve, getting all territorial over her when I don't feel for her like that.

Feel for her like what? My brain asks me.

I can't even begin to explain it.

"She's a nice girl and I feel bad that her parents are never there for her." This is all true—it's just not all of my truth.

"That is some bullshit," August mutters as he still types. "But you can't change her parents. What's done is done."

"I know that," I say irritably. "I'm just—curious. Who are these people? Why are they such shit parents? How much of a life has she had with them?"

"Are you referring to Arabella Margaret Hartley Thomas?" The amusement in August's voice is obvious.

"Yes," I bite out.

"Age seventeen. Birthday is November 29th—coming right up. Born in London, England, to her British father and American mother. Supposedly he's a distant cousin of Princess Diana."

A somewhat confirmation of the royalty rumors that swirl around her. "That's her."

"She lived all over the world when she was younger. England. The US. Japan. Her father bounces around from one firm to another." August is quiet as he takes in information. "She's been in boarding schools since she was in the fifth grade."

"Fifth grade?" We went to day schools where we got to come home and be with our parents every night, and only went to boarding school beginning our freshman year in high school because it's a Lancaster tradition. "That's young."

"Eleven and on her own. She went to a few different schools in the early years but remained steady once she showed up at LP her freshman year. Graduating with you this May." August taps a few more keys. "I'm sending you links so you can read up on the Hartley Thomas family."

"Thank you." I grip my phone tightly, feeling the vibration of my text notifications. "I appreciate you taking care of this so quickly."

"That's what family is for. Need anything else?"

"No—"

"See you at Thanksgiving." August ends the call before I can say another word.

Typical.

I go into my text messages and hit the first link to find it's an article about Arabella's father and his enormous success in the finance industry. There are brief mentions of his wife. An even briefer, singular mention of their daughter, but that's it.

The next article is from a magazine featuring their home in the English countryside. It's about eight years old, which would make Arabella around nine or ten and she's in a few of the photos. One in particular, she's wearing a short white dress constructed almost entirely of rows and rows of ruffles. Ruffled skirt and bodice and sleeves. Her hair is pulled back in a matching white headband and her little face is solemn as she stares into the camera. She's not wearing glasses but she's squinting, and I wonder if she could see.

I wonder if she was happy. She doesn't look like she was.

My heart actually fucking pangs in sympathy and that never happens. I can't even pinpoint the exact moment when I switched over from my even-keeled self to a grumpy motherfucker—

That's a lie. I can pinpoint it. It was a girl's fault. A girl who doesn't even attend Lancaster Prep any longer, who was a year older and toyed with me only because I was a Lancaster. She acted like she cared, while behind my back, she was fucking some other guy. I was so gone for her that when I found out about her betrayal, I told myself never again. I'm too young and we're too fickle at this point in our lives. I'd rather wait it out and find a woman when I'm in college, if I even go. Maybe I'll meet a woman who's part of the same social circles. Who understands this life I lead, because not many do.

Bells would. She lives it too. Though no one really has money like my family does...

I find another photo of Arabella from the home interior article. She's sitting atop her massive bed, the pink velvet comforter so thick I swear I can see the texture of it in the photo. Her room is straight out of a fairy tale, and I wonder if she loved it. If she ever got to spend time there when she was a child, considering she was always shipped away to boarding school.

Probably not.

NINE

ARABELLA

AFTER A GOOD NIGHT'S sleep and a minor attitude adjustment, I feel better this morning. Not so caught up in my own insecurities and worries about a certain boy. On the plus side? I had a few things work in my favor despite yesterday being such a disaster, and I'm currently clutching one of those things as I stride across campus in search of Rowan.

Today he's where he should be. I still don't know what happened yesterday when he wasn't in front of the building waiting for me as usual, but I see him now, hanging out with his friends like normal. They're all laughing and chatting away while he stands in the middle of them, his expression serious, his gaze searching. Searching for me?

Of course not.

Adjusting my hold on his uniform jacket and giving myself a mental pep talk that I can do this, I march straight toward him, passing his friends by as I approach Rowan, stopping directly in front of him.

"Here's your jacket." I keep my voice quiet and measured, not wanting to act too excited, which is my usual mode when I'm near Rowan. I offer the jacket to him. "Thank you for letting me wear it yesterday."

He doesn't even look at the article of clothing that belongs to him. Instead, he keeps his gaze on mine, catching me in his spell. I could stare into his beautiful green eyes forever and never get tired of it. "You didn't have to give it right back."

Why does he argue every single point with me? He should just take the damn jacket and say thank you.

"I wanted to. I was afraid I might forget." I try to shove it at him but he still won't take it, which is the slightest bit frustrating. "Plus, it's just cluttering up my room."

That is the biggest lie. Yes, I'm clean and everything in my room has its place. I don't like messy things. It comes from a lifetime of living at a boarding school or with my mother, who is the fussiest person I know.

Cleanliness is next to godliness, is what she would always say. Which is funny, considering my parents aren't what I would call religious people.

"I'm clutter, huh?" He sounds...amused?

Odd.

"You're not clutter. Your jacket is." I practically press it against his broad chest. I can feel the warmth from his body seep into my hands, and I would give everything to have the opportunity to run my hands all over him. I know once I started, I would never be able to stop. "Thank you again. It was very—sweet of you to loan it to me."

I hear Callahan chuckle at my use of the word sweet, which no one would ever say in regards to Rowan. It's why I chose the word in the first place.

"You're welcome." He finally takes the jacket, staring down at it clutched between his hands before he returns his attention to me. "Not sure what I'm supposed to do with it right now though."

"Take it back to your room?" I raise my brows.

"It's pretty far and my—my ankle is bothering me," he admits.

I'm shocked at his confession. He's not one to say when he's in pain. "Do you want me to take it back for you?"

"You don't have to—"

"I would like to. I'm the one who brought it with me, after all." I take the jacket from him before he can protest. "I'll run it back now. What's your door code?"

All of the dorm rooms have a keypad code to gain entry.

"Won't you be late for class?"

I check my phone. "I still have twelve minutes. I can do it."

"I'll text you my code."

I frown. "You don't have my number."

"Ah, but I do." Within seconds my phone vibrates, and I check to see I have a text from an unfamiliar number.

I send him a look, baffled as to how he has it. "How did you get my number?"

"I have my ways," he drawls, his smile slow. Be still my rapidly beating heart. "You better run if you're going to drop that jacket off in time."

Without another word, I take off, dashing across campus toward the building where all the Lancaster family suites are. I've never been over here before and my curiosity is increasing with every second that passes. I'm going to be in Rowan Lancaster's room.

Alone.

In under two minutes I find myself in his dorm suite and I pause in the doorway, taking it all in. The room is huge. All of the Lancaster family is housed in a different building when they attend here, and their rooms are twice as big as ours. I have my own private room as well and mine is the size of a closet compared to this.

I'm jealous. There's so much room where I could store all of my clothes, and I have a lot. Too much, some might say, but I adore fashion so I tell myself it is my one indulgence. And I don't have many.

Checking my phone for the time, I decide to do a quick perusal of Rowan's room, though I would never go through his things. I'm not that bold, and I wouldn't want someone going through my stuff so there is that. I'm a big believer in always treating people how you want to be treated.

I wander around his room, stopping at the foot of his bed, noting how he didn't make it. The comforter is thick and black, the sheets a dark gray, and I'm tempted to lie in the very spot where he does every night...

But that's creepy. I'm not an obsessed stalker.

With minor apprehension I check his connected bathroom to find that it's clean, which is a relief. I scan the top of his dresser and find there are no personal items. Not even a picture frame of his family, his besties, a girl, nothing. He left his laptop open on his desk and without a thought I tap the space bar, making the screen light up. There's a login page but it glitches, switching over to show his open tabs on his browser.

Blinking, I lean in to examine the page he must've last looked at. It's an article from an architectural and interior design magazine and I recognize the house immediately.

It used to belong to my parents. And the photo that appears is of me, sitting on my princess bed in the princess bedroom I never really got to enjoy because I was never home.

My heart pangs looking at that photo of myself. How sad I look in my eyes, even though I'm smiling. The smile isn't very big though and I'm not showing any teeth.

God, I look miserable. I was such a solemn child. There was no real joy in my life then. When I got a little older and went to therapy during middle school, I realized I had to make my own joy. Clothes make me happy. My friends. Even my crush on Rowan.

Checking the time, I toss the jacket on his bed and zoom out of there, hurrying back to the math and science building and praying I beat the final bell. My mind is full of questions, none of them I can ask because then I'd have to admit I was snooping on his computer and I had no idea his browser would show up. They never do.

It's like fate wanted me to see that he's checking up on me. But why? Why does he care? Why do I matter? I never felt like I did to him before. The flirting and the banter are fun but it never seemed like it meant anything to him, though it always meant a little something to me.

Fine, not a little something. It is a big something. And now my new discovery feels like something even bigger.

Rowan Lancaster wants to know more about me. He somehow found that old article about my parents and checked it out. Did he read it? Could he tell how pretentious and money-hungry my parents are? How callous and cold? Probably not. The article I'm sure shone them in a good light. Everyone believes the Hartley Thomas's are a wonderful couple who move about society and never have a bad thing said about them. I wonder what would happen if their business associates and social circle found out what neglectful parents they are?

I make it into our statistics class with two minutes to spare, though I'm out of breath. Thank God I wore regular loafers today. Well, they are Miu Miu loafers and cost a fortune, but still. They're comfortable and surprisingly easy to run in.

"You made it," Rowan says when he spots me from his desk.

I pause in front of where he sits, reluctant to go to my desk. Trying to savor this moment of Rowan speaking to me first without tossing a little insult in my direction. "I did. With a couple minutes to spare."

His expression turns serious. "Thank you for taking that back for me. I don't normally have a problem getting around campus, but you know."

He points at the cumbersome boot he's wearing.

"I understand. And you're welcome." I offer him a tentative smile, practically bursting with the need to tell him I saw what was on his laptop.

But I can't.

"You didn't go through my things, did you, Bells?"

"Absolutely not." I shake my head repeatedly, hoping I don't appear suspicious.

Rowan contemplates me for a moment, his assessing gaze moving over my face before it drops, checking out my outfit. "You're fairly subtle today."

Instead of the usual white button down, I'm wearing a hot pink one under my navy vest. I personally love the look of dark blue and pink together, but of course, I'm breaking dress code. Though in the least offensive way possible.

"You call this color subtle?" I tap at the collar of my shirt.

"It's subtle compared to you having your ass hang out of your skirt yesterday." He grins. Literally grins.

I have to grip the edge of his desk so I don't pass out.

The bell rings, jolting me into moving over to my desk, and I can feel the weariness of Mrs. Guthrie as she takes in my outfit while I shrug out of my coat.

"Hot pink, Arabella? Seriously?"

"Seriously," I say with a nod, not about to regret my life choices. "You don't like it?"

A long-suffering sigh escapes her. "I'm going to pretend I don't see it."

"Perfect." I rest my clutched hands on top of my desk, trying my best to act like the dutiful student all while my mind is busy trying to comprehend the fact that Rowan grinned at me just now. How faint the sight of that beautiful smile made me feel.

How warm and fuzzy I got when I realized he was doing research on me. I have nothing to hide. I really don't have any secrets, save for the one I wouldn't mind him finding out.

The fact that I'm completely infatuated with him.

I'VE JUST LEFT theater class and am headed toward the dining hall when I hear someone call my name.

"Arabella, there you are! I've been looking everywhere for you!"

I lift my head to find Lydia making her way toward me, a beautiful smile lighting up her fairy-tale princess face. I pause, waiting by the water fountain for her, my smile strained and my nerves frazzled.

I don't like talking to her. Something about her sets me on edge. Maybe it's all the perfectionism that bothers me. There has to be a flaw hidden in there somewhere.

"Hi, Lydia," I greet her when she's standing directly in front of me.

I'm starving and dying to eat lunch, but she's holding me up. Of course.

"I was wondering if I could talk to you for just a moment?" She tilts her head to the side, all of that beautiful blonde hair cascading past her shoulder.

"I need to go meet my friends." That is the weakest excuse ever and she sees right through me.

"It won't take long." Her smile brightens. "I was hoping to make a deal with you."

"A deal?" I'm frowning. What do I have that she could possibly want?

"Yes." She nods. "I was hoping you would relinquish your partner in American Government and let me work with Rowan instead."

"Oh." My voice is hollow. I forgot all about that. It dawns on me that I'm project partners with Rowan in two classes, which is kind of wild. And wonderful.

"Yes, *oh*. You lucky bitch. God, he's hot." She nudges my side like we're good friends and she's trying to be funny, but I'm guessing she really does think I'm a bitch for snagging him from her. "You don't have a thing for Rowan, do you?"

I thought everyone knew I had a thing for Rowan, but maybe Lydia doesn't realize it. Not like we've talked much over the years. She's definitely not someone I would consider a friend, though I don't view her as an enemy either.

Maybe I should start looking at her like that though...

"We're...friends." That sounds lame but I don't know how else to describe what Rowan and I share. Truthfully?

We don't share much at all.

"Really?" Her voice is full of doubt. "That's funny. I never see the two of you together."

"You just saw us in the dining hall at lunch a couple of days ago," I remind her, my voice frosty. "Together."

Lydia blinks at me, that smile still on her face. "Just friends then, hmm? So you won't mind giving up your *friend* for the project?"

She makes air quotes with her fingers when she says the word friend.

"Actually, I would mind." My smile is just as phony as hers. "Rowan and I work well together."

"Hmm."

That's all Lydia says. Hmm. There's so much doubt and annoyance in that one sound. It kind of spurs me on.

"And we enjoy each other's company," I tack on, sounding like a grandma.

"Every time I see Row with anyone, he doesn't seem to be enjoying their company," Lydia says.

She's observant because her assessment is one hundred percent correct.

"Well, he enjoys mine." I lift my chin, hoping I look confident. As if I know what I'm talking about. "Sorry I couldn't be more help, Lydia."

Her smile fades, her gaze shifting to my right, and that's when I feel it. A presence looming behind me, the scent of him lingering in the air. I lock my knees so I don't do something stupid like faint, secretly praying he didn't overhear our conversation or the things I said about him.

"You just don't know when to let up, do you?" Rowan asks Lydia and my stomach sinks into my toes.

He most definitely overheard our conversation.

Lydia's overly cheery expression is back, her eyes magically sparkling. How does she do that anyway? "What are you talking about?"

"I told you I was working with Arabella and here you are, trying to get her to what—switch out with you?" He sounds shocked, but he really shouldn't be. He's a hot commodity on this campus. I'm surprised this sort of thing doesn't happen more often.

"That is not what I was trying to—"

"Cut the shit, Lydia."

His tone is dark. Almost menacing. And I can feel the look on his face. A glower. A scowl. Whatever you want to call it, I know it's scary and I wouldn't want it aimed at me.

Lydia takes a step back, all signs of her sunny disposition gone in an instant. "You can't talk to me like that."

"Who says?" He shrugs, taking a step closer to me, and I almost wilt when I feel his hand lightly rest on my shoulder. "Leave Arabella alone. She's my partner in American Government. I'm not interested in working with you."

Lydia works her jaw, her gaze shifting to mine. I see the irritation there. She's not happy being denied what she wants. Worse? She doesn't like that who she wants is choosing someone else. "Looks like I made a mistake. Because truly? I don't want to work with you any longer either."

She flounces off before we can say anything and the moment she's gone, Rowan drops his hand, which makes me immediately miss his touch.

"She needs to back the fuck off," he mutters.

"I think Lydia has a crush on you." I turn to face him, surprised by how close he's standing in front of me. My chest brushes his and I swear I can feel goosebumps dotting my entire body from the brief contact.

"I'm not interested."

"Apparently, you're not interested in anyone." I think of my conversation with my friends yesterday. How they suspect he might be into...me.

Please.

Please?

Oh, I need to stop.

"That's not true." He sounds vaguely defensive.

"Really?" I arch a brow, ready for a challenge. "You haven't gone out with a girl for the entirety of our high school lives."

"Maybe I keep my dating life private."

I can't help but laugh. "Nothing is private here, Rowan. Especially who anyone is dating."

"Maybe I don't date girls." His smile is wicked and he leans in, his mouth practically at my ear. "Maybe I only fuck them."

I suck in a sharp breath at hearing the curse word whispered so intimately. He pulls away slowly, that naughty smile still on his face, and I can't help myself. I slap him on the chest, my fingers tingling where they make contact.

"You're rude," I chastise, though my voice is weak.

My problem is I'd love it if he whispered in my ear again. If he said something completely filthy in reference to what he wanted to do to me. With me. Whatever. I would eat that *up*.

He chuckles, the rich, warm sound doing something to my insides, and I realize there is no fighting going on between us. Just flirting.

"You like it."

Oh God, can he read my mind? Maybe my body language is too obvious. He probably thinks I'm easy when I'm not. Not even close. My sexual experience is very limited. I mean, I've had sex, but it was terrible and it probably doesn't count.

Well, it does count. Unfortunately.

"How many girls have you been with, then?" I ask him.

"Been with how?"

Is he being purposely dense?

"Been with as in had *sex* with." I smile serenely at him, this close to laughing at the shock I see on his face. I don't think he expected me to ask that particular question. "Tell me, Rowan. How many?"

TEN
ROWAN

DID she really just ask me that? Not like I'm going to answer her.

"Have you had sex with anyone?" I throw back at her, confident in what her answer will be. Either a non-answer or she'll admit she's a virgin because she has to be one. I've never seen her with anyone on this campus or heard even a whisper about her love life. And that's because it's non-existent. I'm sure of it.

"Yes." She nods, not even hesitating with her response. "Though it was a long time ago, and it wasn't that good."

Arabella makes a little face, scrunching up her nose.

"Wait a second..." Surprise washes over me as I contemplate what she just said. "You've had sex, but it was a long time ago? It's not like we're old, Bells."

"I know that."

"So how long ago are you talking?"

"The summer after our freshman year."

"Freshman year?" What the shit? I was still playing video games every night with my friends and jerking off to free porn videos on the internet while Arabella was actually getting laid?

"Yes." She nods, her expression serious. "One of my biggest regrets."

"Who did you have sex with?" I can't help but ask.

"Bentley Saffron Jones."

"What the fuck? Who the hell is that?"

"You don't know Bentley Saffron Jones?" Her brows shoot up and I'm so damn grateful it's lunchtime so we can keep having this odd conversation.

"To be totally honest, that name sounds completely made up."

"Believe me, it's not. He's a real person and I gave him my virginity when I was oh...fifteen?" She grimaces. "That's terribly young, isn't it."

"Terribly," I echo, in absolute shock. "Where exactly did this happen anyway?"

"Why are you being so nosy?" She's smiling. I'm sure she can tell that I'm curious and I want all the details but damn. I am being nosy. And she's right, it's none of my business, what happened between her and this Saffron Jones dude.

"Because it sounds like a made-up story," I tell her. Hopefully she accepts that as a decent answer.

"I'm not a liar, Rowan. But if you really want to know, let me explain. Bentley and my parents are dear old friends. A couple of summers ago, we went over to Bentley's parents' house in the Hamptons and stayed with them for a few weeks. I was thrilled.

It felt like the first summer since I could remember that my parents actually wanted to spend time with me." Her smile is full of sadness, and I get the sense that they ended up disappointing her that particular summer. I'd guess they disappoint her on a constant basis.

God, her parents sound like they're the fucking worst.

"Bentley and I have known each other since we were in diapers. We've always been close, but we sort of hate each other too? It's hard to explain, but that part doesn't matter. One night we were sitting outside enjoying the salty air, getting drunk on his mom's good pinot grigio and the topic turns to sex because of course it does. We're teenagers, we're horny."

I'm frowning because I don't want to hear about her being horny with some asshole I don't know.

"Bentley admits to me that he's a virgin. I confessed that I was one too, and feeling bold thanks to all of that wine, I suggested we get rid of the burden together so...we did." She shrugs, like it's no big deal.

"You're telling me you had sex with this dude that night?"

"Oh no. We prepared for it. We got drunk again of course before we did it, and snuck out to the pool house after everyone else went to bed. We had sex on a broken lounge chair, and I'm pretty sure we broke it even more." She wrinkles her nose, and it's the most adorable thing, despite the words coming out of her mouth. "It was terrible."

An irrational and completely unexpected wave of jealousy sweeps over me at the thought of Arabella having sex with another guy. Even someone with the most ridiculous name I've ever heard, like Bentley Saffron Jones. I think she might be playing me.

"What was so terrible about it?" I ask her, wanting more details even though I know they're only going to make me angrier.

"You really want to know?" She peers up at me, caution alighting her eyes as she brushes her fingers against her pursed lips. "I probably shouldn't have told you that story."

I can see the regret written all over her face.

"Don't worry, Bells. Your secret is safe with me."

"It's not really a secret. I would tell anyone who wanted to know who I lost my virginity to. I mean, sex is just...sex, right? There was no emotion involved and I wasn't in love with him. Not even close."

This girl blows my mind. I got the sense that she was a total romantic who believed in falling hopelessly in love, and instead she's talking about casual sex and how she gave up her virginity to a family friend when she was only fifteen. I can't even wrap my head around this revelation.

"We should go to lunch," she suggests when I still haven't said anything.

"Okay."

I walk with her toward the dining hall, tuning out her incessant chatter while I try to absorb the fact that she's had sex and I want to know what this guy looks like. I want to know how much he might mean to her. Girls don't just casually hand over their virginity like it's an old sweater they want to get rid of. The ones I know treat their virgin status like a prize, and only the guy they're madly in love with gets to win it.

That's how I've always viewed it at least. But maybe I'm wrong. Maybe Arabella is as casual as anyone else, and I'm the one with a stick up my ass.

Just before we enter the dining hall she touches my arm, stopping me. "You don't think less of me after what I just told you?"

"Think less of you?" I don't know what to think, if I'm being honest. I hate the swirl of emotions inside me that make my chest hurt. It has nothing to do with her not being a virgin, but the fact that she had sex with another guy instead of...who?

Me?

I'm being ridiculous.

"Yes. I don't want you thinking I'm a...whore or whatever." She sinks her teeth into her lower lip and fuck, that's cute. Why is everything she's doing right now so fucking adorable? "I've only ever had sex with Bentley. There's been no one else."

The relief I feel at that admission is way too strong.

"Though we did have sex five times," she adds.

"Five times?" *Five??*

She nods. "We were trying to...figure everything out."

"And did you?"

"Not really." Her soft sigh is tinged with sadness. "He wasn't very good at it. Not a great kisser either."

"Bells."

"Yes, Rowan?"

"I don't like hearing about you kissing another guy. I really don't like hearing about you having sex with this guy either." I bite the words out, my chest aching with the confession.

"You don't?" Her surprise is obvious.

I shake my head.

"Why?" She seems truly confused. "Does it bother you?"

"Yes," I bite out.

"I don't understand." She drops her hand from my arm, and I immediately miss her touching me which is fucked up. This entire situation is fucked up. I shouldn't have told her that. I should've dealt with my feelings on my own versus admitting that her confessions bother me. "Why does it matter who I've had sex with?"

Here is my chance to be real with her and admit that I sometimes think about having sex with her. Not that her past experience has any sway on how I feel about her currently, it's just...

I don't know. I can't explain it.

"Look, there's this stigma wrapped around the sexual act and it's just...it's silly. It's human nature to have sex. We're all built to procreate. Boys can have sex with all kinds of girls and no one judges them but I have sex with Bentley, and now you're thinking I'm some sort of slut who sleeps with any guy she meets."

There is pain in her voice, and I wonder if she called herself a slut so she'd beat me to the punch?

"That's not true. You don't know how I feel. And I definitely don't think you're a—slut." It's not even a word I use as a part of my everyday vocabulary.

The relief on her face is evident. "Okay good. You still seem mad though."

"I'm not mad." I grab hold of her arm, yanking her close to me. Our bodies collide and mine reacts, just like that. Just like usual. Her sweet floral scent swirls around us, and her curvy softness seems to melt into me. Like we're two pieces of a puzzle locking together.

Which is absolute bullshit. I know it is. We're not like that, Bells and me. I need to be a realist.

"Then tell me how you really feel, Rowan," she murmurs, her voice lulling me into submission. "Why does it bother you that I've had sex?"

The truth hangs on the tip of my tongue and I part my lips, ready to confess my sins, when Callahan approaches us with a giant smile on his face.

"Rowan! Arabella! There you guys are." He slaps me on the back before yanking Arabella in for the briefest hug. "We were missing you guys at the table so they sent me looking for you."

Irritation floods me at my best friend's appearance. "We were having an important discussion," I tell him, my voice serious.

"About what?" Cal asks.

"My wild sex life," Bells says, making Cal laugh. She laughs along with him, her gaze cutting to mine, and all I can do is scowl.

I'm fighting my emotions that threaten to bubble up and unleash all over...Cal and Bells and whoever else is in my path. Damn, her admission is just so unexpected.

She's had sex. Some asshole has touched her naked body and... fuck, did he make her come? Did she give him a blowjob? Did he go down on her? Finger her? Kiss her so deeply that she cried out because it felt so good?

Five times gives them ample opportunity to do all kinds of stuff.

I cup the side of my head with my right hand, threading my fingers in my hair and tugging on the strands until it hurts. I cannot fucking stand the images that are now appearing in my brain.

Arabella and Callahan are still talking—about what, I don't know, and I can't take it anymore.

"I've gotta go," I say, completely interrupting their conversation, just before I leave them where they stand.

And I never look back.

ELEVEN

ARABELLA

I WATCH ROWAN WALK AWAY, regret making my stomach twist. There is no way I can eat lunch now. And I was so looking forward to it too. I was absolutely starving until I started to run my mouth and ruin everything.

"What's his problem?" Cal mutters.

"I have no idea," I lie, knowing exactly what triggered him.

Me and my stories. If only I could chase after him and tell him what happened between Bentley and me meant nothing because it's true. We were young and dumb and ready to shed our virginity, so why not do it together?

Bentley was terrible, but that wasn't his fault. He had no idea what he was doing, and I didn't either. It didn't help, coming from a home that doesn't show much love. My parents weren't affectionate toward me, and they weren't that affectionate with each other either. What did I know about romantic love back then?

I don't know much about it now either, but I crave it, even though it scares me. Am I capable of that type of love? I'm not sure, but I want it so badly and I want it with the very boy who is stalking off at a slow pace thanks to his boot.

Suddenly not caring what Callahan or anyone else might think, I take off toward Rowan, calling his name when I draw closer. He comes to a stop and turns, that handsome scowl on his face easing when he sees it's me.

It's the way his scowl fades when he watches me that gives me hope. That makes me feel like chasing after him might be worth it. I stop directly in front of him, my heart in my throat, my breaths coming faster, and he just watches me, his brows drawn together, his gaze locked on mine.

"You never did tell me," I start, purposely being vague.

"Tell you what?"

"Who you've had sex with." My smile is blissful. Without a care in the world. "You can tell me. I can take it like a big girl. Is it a girl who goes here?"

Rowan averts his head, the sudden gust of cold wind making his hair blow across his forehead. "No."

"An old family friend like what I did?" At least you can trust those people. It might've been kind of terrible, but Bentley was sweet and he tried so hard. He was so awkward and even came all over my leg twice out of the five times. I'm still not quite sure how that happened.

"No. Not an old family friend." His gaze returns to mine, and he appears so conflicted. Like he wants to tell me but doesn't know how.

"You don't have to say." My smile falters a little but I keep it pasted on my face. "You've always been a private person."

"So have you."

My laughter is loud and I don't even bother trying to contain it. "No, not really. I have a big mouth and I'll tell people whatever they want to know."

"Have you ever been in love?" he asks out of nowhere.

I blink at him, slowly shaking my head. "No. I'm not even sure if I know how to love someone." The closest I've ever been to love are the feelings I have for Rowan, but most of the time they feel like a silly crush and nothing else. "Sometimes I think I'm broken."

"Broken?"

"My parents aren't the best, but you already know this." The words come out in a hoarse rasp and I clear my throat, telling myself now is not the time to get emotional. "I have no family that I'm close with. I have friends, but I've never had a real boyfriend or fallen hopelessly in love. I don't think I know how."

"Bells." I jerk my gaze up to his, surprised at the gentle emotion I can hear in his tone. "You're not broken. You've just...never been given a chance."

"Well, maybe someday, right? Guess I'll have to get out of here first. Once I graduate, the first thing I'm going to do is travel across Europe."

"Alone?"

I nod. "It'll be wonderful."

"Sounds unsafe." He's scowling again. "There are a lot of assholes out there who'd want to take advantage of you."

"Stop trying to scare me, Rowan. I'm not afraid of traveling alone. It'll give me the freedom I've been seeking for what feels like forever."

"I'm not trying to scare you. Just speaking truths. But you mean it, don't you?" He doesn't give me a chance to answer him. "You want to travel alone and you're not scared to do it either."

"Not really." Actually, I'm terrified but I can't say that now. I'm trying to impress Rowan. "Life is meant to be lived, right?"

"Right." He nods slowly. "Are you seeing your family for Thanksgiving?"

"No. They're in Hong Kong. They can't come see me because my father is working and Mother worries about me traveling over there for such a short vacation and dealing with the time difference and all that. It's not worth it. Besides, they don't even celebrate Thanksgiving in Hong Kong." I believe and agree with everything my mother says because I have to. Otherwise, I'll just feel pitiful and unwanted, and I've dealt with both of those emotions enough to last me a lifetime.

"What will you do for the week we're off then? Stay here?" He sounds incredulous but that's because he comes from a large family who all love and support each other. I envy him that and wish I had something similar.

But I don't.

"Yes, that's exactly what I'll do, but it's not so bad." My voice is purposefully cheerful and I'm smiling, otherwise known as putting on my fake act that I'm so good at. The one where nothing bothers me and I'm accepting of my circumstances. "I always catch up on my homework. And reading. And they serve a Thanksgiving dinner for everyone who's staying here with turkey and pumpkin pie."

I can see the sympathy in his eyes and I don't want him feeling sorry for me. "Sounds—nice."

"It really is." Unable to help myself, I reach out and pat his chest. I would keep on touching him forever if he'd let me. "Maybe someday I'll get it out of you."

"Get what out of me?" He's frowning again.

"Who you lost your virginity to. But it's fine. You can go on and keep your secrets. I don't like to pry."

I'm dying to pry but I won't. Rowan keeps things to himself. Who he's had sex with is none of my business.

He doesn't say a word. Just watches me with those gorgeous green eyes, and I'm left with no choice but to walk away from him, dragging my feet the entire way back to the dining hall.

But when I glance over my shoulder to see if he's still watching me, I discover that he is.

And I can't help but smile.

"Are you sure you can't buy me a first-class ticket and I can hop on the plane to Hong Kong?" I FaceTimed my mother at seven o'clock at night my time because it's early morning there and I knew she'd be up. And for once she didn't ignore my call. She picked up after the second ring.

"Darling, Thanksgiving is next week." A heavy sigh escapes her. "I would love, *love* to see you but it's too last minute. Besides, we have plans."

My stomach lurches. "You have plans?"

"I didn't want to tell you." The stress on her face is beyond obvious. Mother is always sneaking around and doing things she shouldn't. Like making plans during Thanksgiving week when she knows her only daughter is left at boarding school alone. "We're going on vacation with the Feldmans for a few days. Your daddy works with Jim and they've become friends. Ginny is wonderful. That's his wife. You would just adore them! They have a private jet."

"That's nice," I say, my voice hollow and downright echoey in my head. I should've known they made other plans. That they would forget all about me. Disappointment settles over me like a wet blanket and I wish I could shrug it off. "I'm sure you'll have a great time."

"You aren't upset?" Mother mock pouts, her lips already glossed and shiny despite it being seven in the morning there. "I know you don't like spending the holiday alone, but it just can't be avoided, Arabella. We'll try to see you for Christmas. I do have a surprise gift planned for you. I can only hope that it'll all come together..."

She won't see me. I used to believe her when she said stuff like that but not anymore. I won't be with my parents for Christmas or New Year's or any other holiday because they don't care.

They. Don't. Care.

Facing hard truths is never easy. My chest is tight and my throat is clogged. I try to swallow past the feeling but it doesn't budge.

Only seems to swell and grow and I'm surprised I can even speak.

"It's my birthday next week, too," I say, my voice soft. "Or did you forget?"

"How could I forget my only child's birthday? Of course, I remember! I can't believe you're going to be seventeen."

"I'll be eighteen," I remind her.

"Ah, right. Eighteen! A grown-up. You can do whatever you want." She pauses. "Within reason."

She laughs.

I don't. I'm too mad to pretend any longer.

"Do you have any birthday plans?" she asks when I remain quiet for too long.

"I'll be here."

"None of your friends will want to take you out and celebrate?"

"No, of course not. They'll all be with their families over the holiday." My eyes start to sting and I blink rapidly, fighting off the tears that threaten. "I need to go. I'll talk to you later."

"Bye, darling! Take care! Happy—"

I end the call before she can get those last words out, flopping backward on my bed so I can stare at the ceiling.

It was a dumb idea, calling my mother. All it did was remind me that I'm an afterthought in their world and I don't matter. Again, I wonder why they even had me in the first place. Was I not what they wanted? Am I a giant disappointment? It hurts when you realize that your parents don't really care about you. And it doesn't get any easier either. I thought it might...

But it doesn't.

I was twelve when it really hit me that they viewed me as more of a burden than anything else. Middle school is the worst. Talk about feeling unlovable and wretchedly ugly. I had frizzy hair and braces on my very crooked teeth. Spots on my face and knobby knees. I was taller than all the boys in my class but that changed eventually.

When you're twelve though? It matters. I towered over them. I wore glasses. I was flat-chested, and the boys made fun of me because of my glasses. My height. My frizzy hair. That's where I first met Hadley. She took me under her wing and was a very good friend. She still is.

Hadley offered for me to accompany her with her family to the Bahamas for Thanksgiving week but I declined. Her dad stares too hard when he sees me in a swimsuit and he makes me uncomfortable. Simone is taking her boyfriend with her home for the first time to meet the family, and I can't infringe on that. It's too important of a moment.

I close my eyes, trying to stop the tears from rolling, but it's no use. They slide down the side of my face and I sniff, thinking of that article Rowan found about my parents. Those phony photos and how sad I looked in them. Anyone with half a brain could see it.

I wonder if he did.

TWELVE
ROWAN

MY MOM WON'T STOP CALLING me. I've avoided her FaceTime calls over the last couple of days because I didn't want to deal with her over-the-top concern, but I finally answered on Wednesday night.

"There you are!" She beams at me and I take her in, noting how beautiful she is even though she's my mom. I remember being young and telling her I wanted to marry her someday. I think I was four. She just laughed and said she was already married to my dad and I burst into tears.

She loves that story. I used to hate it but now I get it. My four-year-old self was completely enraptured by my mother and I see why. She's the best—when she's not nagging me.

"Sorry, I've been busy. School." I lean back against my headboard, bracing myself for the endless questions she's about to ask me.

"Well, I've got good news." Her mysterious smile has me curious. "I've made an appointment with your doctor on Monday and if all looks well, you'll be able to rid yourself of the boot."

"Seriously?" I sit up, excited for once in my life. Feels like I've been wearing this stupid thing for years. "That's great."

"As long as you're healing properly, you should be good. I hope you've been taking it easy."

Here we go.

"I definitely have."

"Good. I miss you and your brother so much. I'm so glad you'll be home soon! Did you arrange for a car to pick you up yet?"

"I need to do that."

"Or I could talk to Pat for—"

"No, I've got it," I say, cutting her off. "I need to do shit on my own, remember?"

She's frowning. I'm sure she doesn't love that I just cursed at her. She rarely says those types of words. Neither does my sister. "I know you're busy. I just want to help."

"I've got it. You want us coming home Friday after school?"

"Absolutely. Why spend the weekend there? Get your vacation started as soon as possible."

"Right." I think of Bells stuck here by herself for a solid ten days and how fucking miserable that must be. Without her family or friends. Catching up on her reading and homework. Eating shitty turkey with the other students who are stuck on campus during the holiday.

That must suck.

"Row, you look sad. Is everything okay?"

"What? Yeah, everything's fine." I shake my head but she just peers at me through the screen and I know she's going to keep asking. "I'm thinking about a friend."

"Is something going on with your friend?" She sounds concerned when she doesn't need to be.

"Everything's fine, there's just this—girl who goes here that I know. Her parents live in Hong Kong and she's stuck on campus for every holiday."

"She doesn't get to go home to see them?"

I shake my head.

"And they don't come here to see her?"

"Nope."

Mom rests her hand against her chest, horrified. "That's terrible! The poor girl. She must be so lonely. Can you imagine spending the holidays by yourself?"

I can't, and that's why I can't get Arabella out of my head. The thought of her being holed up here pretty much by herself for ten days makes me feel...bad.

And no one makes me feel bad. Not really. I just live my life and I'm grateful for what I have—to a point, because let's be real. My life has always been like this. I'm not necessarily grateful for it either. I expect things to be a certain way. Meaning I'm privileged as fuck.

Knowing that Arabella has wealthy parents and supposedly this great life, yet spends most of her time all alone, breaks my fucking steel-infused heart.

"How close are you to this girl?" Mom asks when I haven't said anything.

"I mean..." I let my voice drift, pondering how I should answer her. Truly? We're not that close. Though lately we've been talking more. Sharing more. Getting closer. "We're friends."

"Good friends?"

I shrug. "Sort of?"

"Do you like her, Rowan?" Mom's brows lift. This is the last thing I want to talk to her about.

"Not like that." Lies, all lies. "I don't know."

Her lips curve into the faintest smile, and I don't want to give her any kind of hope. I haven't dated a girl in years. According to my parents, I've never dated anyone period. They don't know about the one girl who broke my heart and taught me that relationships are for suckers because I didn't tell them about her. It was such a brief moment of time it makes me wonder...

Why do I let that experience keep me in such a chokehold? I can't even think her name in my brain, let alone say it out loud, and I'm letting what she did wreck me for life?

Stupid.

"You should invite this girl home with you," Mom suggests.

"I couldn't" is my automatic reply.

"Why not? The poor girl spends the week of Thanksgiving alone. That's dreadful! What kind of parents does she have anyway?"

"Shitty ones," I mutter, making Mom laugh, which makes me smile too.

"You are correct in that assessment. But really, Row, invite her here. You don't have to entertain her the entire time. There will be plenty of people around both at our house and at Whit and Summer's. It'll be a busy time for us. She'll have something to do every day if she wants."

"And what if she doesn't want to?" I hate the thought of asking Bells to come with me and she turns me down. I don't like rejection. Who does?

Guess I need to put my feelings aside for once in my life and think about hers.

"Then that's on her. At least you asked," She pauses. "It's the right thing to do, Row."

I groan. Mom knows just how to make me feel like a dick. "I know."

"So do the right thing and ask her. The worst she'll say is no."

I get the feeling Bells won't say no. She's been crushing on me hardcore for what feels like years, and lately...the feeling is reciprocated. Though I have no idea what to do with that. With her. My feelings aren't easy to process and most of the time I want to banish them and forget they exist. I just want to live and not worry or think about anything. Or anyone.

Lately, I've been focused more on my future. Get this fucking boot off my ankle. Get through the rest of senior year. Graduate. Move on. Become an adult and live my real life.

But what the hell does that even mean? Aren't I living my real life right now?

See? It's all confusing.

"I'll ask her," I say reluctantly, and Mom actually claps her hands together like an overexcited little kid. "But don't get any weird ideas."

"What in the world are you talking about, weird ideas? I would never." She's laughing, and I already know she's got plenty of weird ideas running through her mind.

And every single one of them has to do with me and Bells.

It's the next day at school and I'm waiting for Arabella in my usual spot, surrounded by my friends. Nothing unusual or out of sorts. I didn't try to change my routine save for that one time and it threw everything off.

Best to stay in my lane and do my normal thing.

Except, the moment I see her making her approach, I break away from my friends and start heading toward her. It's extra cold this morning, the sky dark and gray. A storm is headed our way and they predict freezing rain this afternoon and the possibility of snow overnight.

Winter is unofficially upon us.

As Arabella gets closer, I take in the fine details of her outfit. She's got on her normal uniform. Not much looks out of place, save for the clunky moonboots she's wearing on her feet. They're white and puffy and remind me of my own boot, but much more stylish. Even a little ridiculous.

Somehow, she can pull them off.

"Bells, I'm disappointed," I announce to her.

Her shoulders sag a little and I note the dark circles under her eyes. She looks tired. "What did I do now?"

"Just the shoes, huh? That's the only change to your outfit?" I focus my gaze on her feet and she kicks the right one up, like she's showing off for me.

"I'm tired, Rowan. This was as good as I could manage." Even her voice sounds weary and I'm hit with an unfamiliar emotion.

Fuck, I think that's...concern I'm feeling?

I take a step closer and curve my fingers around her elbow. She has on her uniform and a thick coat, and still when I touch her there's a buzz that jolts through me the moment we connect. It's so wild.

Unexplainable.

"Are you okay?" I ask her, my voice low.

She tilts her head back, her dark eyes wide and unblinking. "I'm fine."

There is no emotion in her voice. Meaning she is clearly not fine.

"Maybe I should ask if you're okay," she says, taking a step back, allowing me no choice but to let my hand drop from her arm. "Why did you run over here to meet me anyway?"

"I didn't run—" I clamp my lips shut, not in the mood to argue with her this morning. "I wanted to talk to you. Alone."

Arabella winces. "You're freaking me out, Rowan. What's going on?"

"I have a question to ask you."

"Okayyyyy." She drags the word out, clearly off-center. Is it wrong that I enjoy rattling her?

Probably.

"I wanted to know if...you'd like to come with me."

"Come with you where?" she asks.

"To my house. For Thanksgiving break."

She goes silent, blinking at me once. Twice. Her lips part and close together until finally she manages to speak.

"Really?" Her voice is hopeful, as is her expression and I can't help but shrug. Trying to play it off like the asshole I am.

"If you want." I flick my hair out of my eyes with a jerk of my head, hating that I witness her face crumpling. For a moment, I think she's going to cry, but her expression transforms and just like that...

She's mad.

"I'm not your charity case, Rowan."

And with that shitty statement, she turns on her heel and strides away.

Fuck.

I chase after her, pissed at myself for making her feel bad and extra pissed at the boot that slows me down. I call her name once. Twice. And still, she won't turn around. She's walking with no rhyme or reason, meaning I can't figure out where she's going, and when I finally yell out, "Bells! Give me a break here!" She slows down. Comes to a stop.

And waits for me.

When we're finally face to face again, I realize she's shaking. Her eyes are wide and full of unfamiliar emotion and that's when it hits me.

She's not just mad—she's *furious*.

"What's wrong?" I start to reach toward her again and she jerks away from my touch, taking a leaping step back.

"I don't need your sympathy, Rowan. I already feel bad enough."

Say what? "I'm not trying to make you feel bad, Bells. I just—I want you to come home with me."

"And what? Are you going to introduce me as your girlfriend?"

"Of course I'm not. Because you aren't my girlfriend."

Arabella rolls her eyes, a strangled sound escaping her before she stomps off again. I'm too tired and pissed off to chase after her so I watch her go, not surprised at all when she comes to a stop, turns around and marches back toward me.

"You don't even like me," she practically screeches, poking my chest with her index finger. "I annoy you most of the time and now you're asking me to come home with you? Make that make sense."

Damn it, she's right. It makes zero sense. But none of the feelings I have toward Bells make any sense to me. I can't figure them out. I can't figure her out.

"We have an—understanding. Right?" I send her a look.

She just scowls at me in return, her arms wrapped around her middle like she needs to ward me off of her. "I have no idea what you're talking about."

I decide to take a different approach. "I consider you a friend, Bells. We spend a lot of time together, don't you think? We're in every single class together this year. We hang out at lunch. Before school starts."

She doesn't say anything. Just watches me with that moody expression on her face.

"We share mutual friends. Cal loves you."

"I love Cal," she murmurs.

The normal jealousy I experience in regards to these two and their friendship rears its ugly head and I mentally tamp it down. "I invite Cal to my family's house when we're on break."

"But that's different."

"How?"

"You're a boy. So is Callahan. And I'm a girl."

"Meaning we can't be friends?" Why the hell am I trying so hard with her?

"Is that what I really am to you, Rowan? Your *friend*? Because I always figured I was that annoying girl who constantly fluttered around you and drove you crazy."

Her description isn't too far off, but I've started to realize there's something about her that I'm attracted to. And when she's not around, I...

I miss her.

And I don't miss a lot of people. I'm pretty self-sufficient and can handle my shit on my own, despite what my mother believes. Yet I don't like the idea of not seeing Arabella for ten whole days.

"You don't drive me crazy." The skeptical look she sends me almost makes me laugh. "Much."

"Exactly." She drops her arms to her sides. "I don't know how to feel about this invite, Rowan. It's hard for me to believe you want me to come to your house and spend the next week with you. I'm sure I would get on your nerves. And I don't know your family—I might get on their nerves too. Won't they think it's weird, you bringing home a girl that's not your girlfriend?"

"I don't care what they think," I say vehemently. "All I know is that I can't stand the thought of you being here on campus all by yourself through the holidays."

Her eyes go wide at my outburst and I clear my throat, trying to gain some control over my sudden turbulent emotions.

"Come home with me, Bells."

She says nothing, though I can tell from the look on her face that she's probably going to say no.

Damn it, I don't want her to say no.

"Please?" I tack on the extra word. A word I rarely use because it's always felt like begging. There's an appropriate time and place to say please and in this moment, I need to. I'm losing her.

Arabella's expression softens. Even her shoulders go slack, and I see her answer reflect in her gaze before she actually says it.

"Okay," she murmurs.

Right as the warning bell rings.

THIRTEEN

ARABELLA

I STOMP into statistics class in my moonboots, feeling silly. The boots are a little awkward to walk in because truly, they are ridiculous. I'm not quite sure what I was thinking when I slipped them on earlier, but I'm feeling no regrets.

Despite the boots, it's like I'm walking on soft, fluffy clouds because of what just happened between Rowan and me.

Am I really going to his family's house for the entire week? Like, seriously?

Pretty sure I am. Unless he changes his mind.

I hope he doesn't change his mind.

Rowan enters the class right behind me and heads for his desk, while I go to mine. I can feel Mrs. Guthrie's gaze land on me, quietly assessing, and when she finally speaks, there's surprise in her voice.

"Extremely understated today, Arabella. And you're in your full uniform."

I kick a foot out toward her, letting her admire my boot. They're bright white with pale gray lettering on them and they're puffy and huge, nearly reaching my knees. I blame my lack of decent REM sleep last night for wearing them. I was definitely not in the right frame of mind this morning when I made this choice.

"I sort of hate them," I admit to Mrs. Guthrie, making her laugh.

"They're not so bad."

"They're ridiculous."

"Well, they're not worthy of being written up so you're safe today." Her smile is warm. "I have to admit, Arabella, I do look forward to seeing what you're wearing every morning when you walk into class."

"I'm glad I can entertain you," I say solemnly, meaning every word. At least someone appreciates the work I put into my silly outfits beyond just me.

Someone approaches Mrs. Guthrie's desk and asks her a question, and I lean forward in my desk, spying on Rowan. He's got his long legs stretched out in front of him, slouching in his seat as he taps away on his phone. His brows are drawn together and his teeth are sunk into his bottom lip, like he's concentrating extra hard, and oh my God, I've never seen him look better.

I have issues. Rowan Lancaster issues.

My phone buzzes and I check it to see it's a text from an unknown number.

You're staring.

I lift my head to find Rowan smiling at me, still clutching his phone.

I immediately add his name as a contact and fire off a text to him.

Me: **So are you.**

Rowan: **I let my mom know you're coming home with me.**

I want to melt into the floor at the idea that he's telling his mom about me. What is this life?

Me: **I'm sure she's confused by this turn of events.**

Rowan: **Not at all. She's glad you're coming.**

Me: **You're just saying that.**

Rowan: **No way. My mom is a total sweetheart. Unlike me.**

Me: **You're a sweetheart.**

Rowan: **According to who?**

Me: **According to me.**

My heart leaps to my throat the second I fire off that last text. I probably shouldn't have sent it but I'm feeling reckless. And what he's done is very sweet, inviting me to his home out of the kindness of his heart. I can't figure out what his ulterior motive could be so I'm assuming he doesn't have one. Is that dumb on my part? Perhaps.

I'm just going to live in my delusion and believe he actually wants me there because he likes me.

We have a test in statistics so the moment I'm finished, I leave class because Mrs. Guthrie doesn't care. I make my way to the bathroom, stopping short when I find Lydia inside with her mean friends, all of them surrounding her as they stare at her phone screen. The moment they catch me in the room with them, they all go silent, still wearing sly smirks on their beautiful faces as they watch me.

"Arabella! We were just talking about you," Lydia greets warmly.

Her voice drips with kindness and my defenses rise. I don't trust this snake as far as I can throw her. "All bad I assume."

Lydia is slightly taken aback by my reply. Good. I want to keep her on her toes. "Not all bad."

"Uh huh." My sarcasm is thick.

"We just found a photo of you," adds one of her friends. I don't know her name. She's in the grade below us, and I realize all of the girls surrounding Lydia are younger. Meaning Lydia doesn't have many friends who are seniors because she's so awful.

"From a long time ago," another one says.

I rest my hands on my hips, contemplating all of them. "Are you guys for real right now? You're all hiding out in the bathroom laughing over old photos of me? I'm sure I look just as awkward as you all did back in the day."

They are silent, shocked by me essentially calling them out. Seriously, I'm so tired of this sort of thing. We're almost out of high school and will be considered adults. I turn eighteen in a matter of days. This type of behavior is beyond immature.

"I think I'll use another bathroom," I announce before I turn and leave, letting the door shut behind me.

Unfortunately, I hear it slam shut again within seconds of me escaping and Lydia's unmistakable screechy voice calling my name.

I don't slow my steps. I pick up my pace instead but the girl is determined and next thing I know she's in front of me, making me stop. I'm not that fast anyway thanks to the stupid boots I'm wearing.

"You're really completely unbothered by me, aren't you?" I don't think her mean little brain can fathom this.

"I am utterly unbothered by you." That's not the whole truth. She bothers me some but I can't let her know it. "You really need a hobby or something. This mean girl business isn't a good look for you."

Lydia arches a brow. "You think you're better than me?"

"I never said that." I shake my head. It's obvious she wants a fight.

"Then what exactly are you saying, hmm? You may flaunt all of your designer clothes when you add them to our uniform. We all know your parents are rich, you don't need to show off." Her gaze drops, and she sneers at my boots. "We all know the truth anyway—that you're just a lonely little rich girl who's been abandoned by her parents. Is that why you're always looking for attention?"

I keep my expression as impassive as possible because wow, her words sting. She's not far off of her assessment of me, and I hate that.

I also kind of hate her.

"And the way you follow after Row everywhere he goes is pathetic. Do you really think he's interested in you? If he was, he would've done something about it a long time ago. Truthfully, I sense he enjoys having his little fangirl trailing after him," she continues, her lips curving into a gleeful smile.

Her words are like tiny knives, carving into my sensitive heart, and I remain still. I can't falter. I can't let her see how much her words hurt, and how accurate she is when she describes me. If her goal is to bring up all those insecurities I try to keep at bay, then she's successful.

"We're friends," I say, my voice stiff. I'm terrified it'll start shaking, and then she'll know she has an effect on me. I refuse to let that show.

"Please." Lydia makes a dismissive noise. "He merely tolerates you."

"Lydia, leave her the fuck alone."

We both turn at the familiar male voice to find Rowan standing there, glaring at Lydia. The relief I feel at seeing him is brief though because I'm also a little annoyed.

I wanted to fight this battle on my own. I don't need him running to my rescue.

"Rowan! How are you?" Lydia's entire face brightens. Even her body language shifts as she thrusts her chest out. Like she wants him to check her out.

I roll my eyes, not caring if she sees. And she calls me pathetic?

"Stop with the bullshit," he continues, stalking his way toward us. He's not even looking at me, and if he did, he'd see I'm irritated by his interrupting our conversation. Again, I can handle this. Handle her.

It's obvious he thinks I can't.

"I'm not doing anything. Am I, Arabella?" Lydia's narrowed gaze lands on me.

"We were talking," I say, my voice cool. He still won't look at me. All of his anger is focused on Lydia, and I can practically feel him vibrate with the emotion, he's standing so close to me. "Privately."

That word gets his attention. He glances over at me and I see the questioning in his gaze. I wish I could telepath to him that I've got this, but I don't think he'd get it even if I could.

"What are your plans for Thanksgiving?" Lydia asks him, completely ignoring me. "My family and I are going to Lake Tahoe."

"I'm going home and spending it with family." Rowan slips his arm around my shoulders, tugging me firmly into his side. "And with Arabella."

Lydia's jaw about hits the floor at his response and I almost want to laugh. Almost. "You're lying."

"Why would I lie about that?" His voice is calm, his fingers gripping my shoulder, and I let myself enjoy the moment. The way his warmth seeps into me. How solid and muscular he is. He's tall, the top of my head doesn't even reach his shoulder, and he makes me feel small and protected.

Which I also can't help but find annoying because I was trying to stand on my own two feet here in my little argument with Lydia.

Lydia's gaze shifts to me and there's something different glowing in her eyes. Respect? No. I doubt that. More like curiosity. She's struggling with the idea that Rowan isn't interested in her and she probably can't believe I'm her competition, which is the furthest thing from the truth.

"You two have fun then," she murmurs before she leaves, heading straight into the bathroom she was just in. Her friends never came out so I'm sure she's giving them all the tea on my going home with Rowan.

Great.

The moment we're alone in the hallway I slip out from under his arm and give him a light smack on the chest. I keep doing that. Maybe it's my signature move. "You shouldn't have told her that."

"Told her what?"

"That I'm going home with you for Thanksgiving."

"Got her to leave you alone, didn't it?" His voice is a challenge and I decide to challenge him right back.

"I am perfectly capable of handling Lydia on my own." Ooh I sound snotty but I can't help myself. I am not a defenseless princess who can't take care of herself. I've been on my own pretty much my entire life. I need no one to fight my battles for me.

"I'm sure you are." He backs down somewhat. I can sense he's a bit confused. "Just wanted to help."

"I don't know if you running to my defense helped at all. Now that she knows what we're doing, she's going to tell all of her friends. She loves spreading gossip," I say.

"What friends?" He scoffs. "No one likes her."

"She has friends with her in there." I point at the bathroom. "That's where I ran into them a few minutes ago."

I am not going to tell him how awful they were to me. That encounter doesn't count anyway. I stood up to them and it felt good. It was Lydia's cruel words from only moments ago that got to me.

"Are you sure they're her friends? Because, seriously, no one likes Lydia. She's the worst." He shoves his hands into his pockets. "How'd you do on the test?"

"I probably failed it." I did great. I knew every answer.

"I might've too." He shrugs. "It's fine though. I always feel like we can make it up in class. Guthrie is pretty good about giving us extra credit."

"She is," I agree as I pull out my phone and check the time. "We still have fifteen minutes until our next class."

"I know." He smiles, and oh I hate when he does that. He could say anything in this moment and I'd readily agree with him. He could suggest we go murder Lydia with our bare hands, and I'd say yes without hesitation.

We start walking, our steps slow, and he keeps his head bent, though I can see the faint curl of his lips as he studies my boots. As if he might be smiling. "You wear those to make yourself feel like me?"

"What do you mean?"

"You're moving slower and I'm sure it's thanks to the boots. I know what that's like."

"Oh. Yes." I'm nodding, going along with his suggestion. "That's exactly why I wore them. I wanted to shuffle around campus like Rowan Lancaster."

He's full-blown smiling now, aiming it right at me, and I glance around quickly, making sure I'm not going to walk into a wall. "I have a doctor's appointment early next week. If all's well with my ankle, they'll let me take off the boot."

"That's great news!" I know he's been miserable wearing it.

"Yeah. Trying not to get my hopes up though. What if it's not healed?"

"It'll be healed," I say with authority. "I'm positive you won't be wearing it by Thanksgiving."

"I hope so." He aims that smile of his right at me.

I smile back, absently reaching for my locket, rubbing my thumb across the top of it. We're not actually flirting. Nor are we arguing, bantering, whatever you want to call it. We're having a real conversation and it feels like maybe we could be friends. Maybe we already are.

But could we be more?

Earlier this morning I would've said no. Now I'm starting to wonder...

Maybe we could.

FOURTEEN

ROWAN

THE FRIDAY BEFORE THANKSGIVING BREAK, we only have school until one. Class times are cut in half and those of us who are still in class—a lot of people have already left—are completely checked out and not paying attention. The teachers realize this and don't make us do much on this last day. Makes me wish we would've left first thing in the morning for home but my little brother didn't want to.

Once school is over, I head to my room. We're all meeting the driver who's taking us home out in the front parking lot at one thirty. I texted Pat and asked him to come to my room and help me carry out my luggage, and he's already there, waiting for me. I only have one suitcase and a duffel bag, but it's a bitch with the boot and Pat never minds helping us out.

We stop off so he can grab Beau's suitcase too, and my brother and I follow Pat to the parking lot, Beau talking a mile a minute.

"I'm so freaking mad. I don't want to leave. Mom and Dad are making me come home. I tried telling them I had other plans but they wouldn't hear it," Beau says, sounding pissed.

"What other plans did you have? Staying here?"

"No, of course not. Cecilia Bancroft invited me to her parents' house in Cape Cod. A lot of people from my class are going. They're doing a tour of where the Mayflower first landed and everything." His bitter disappointment at not being able to go rings in every word he says.

"You want to go on a tour of where the Mayflower landed?" That sounds fucking lame but I'm not going to say that out loud.

"That's not the point. I wanted to hang out with CeCe." Beau sends me a quick look. "She's hot."

"Uh huh."

"Mom was like, no way. Dad just went along with her because he always does." Beau kicks at a rock, sending it skittering across the walkway. "They treat me like a baby."

"You're only fifteen," I point out, and he shakes his head furiously.

"You were out fucking around and doing whatever you wanted when you were fifteen," he says. "But Mom always thinks of me as her baby."

"You are her baby."

"Yeah, and I hate it." He sounds miserable. "What's your problem anyway? Are you sad because Cal's not coming home with you? I know I'm going to miss him. He makes you less grumpy."

"Ha ha, real funny, motherfucker." I reach for Beau, scrubbing the top of his head, and he ducks away from my hand, scowling at me.

Realization hits. My brother is going to be even more pissed when he finds out who I'm bringing home instead of Callahan.

"See? Already giving me shit and we haven't even left campus yet." Beau glares at me.

"I'm always giving you shit."

"I know, and it sucks," Beau grumbles, a sulky expression on his face. It's weird how much he looks like Mom. If he grew his hair out long, he'd look exactly like her. And he's right. Mom does treat him like a baby. She's extremely overprotective of him, and Dad is always telling her to relax, which only makes her mad.

Dad should know better than to tell any woman—especially his wife—to relax.

As we approach the giant black SUV, I realize Arabella is already there waiting beside it, three giant suitcases surrounding her.

Three.

Artie the groundskeeper is just behind the car, sitting in his golf cart. The moment he spots us, he salutes Arabella before taking off. "Have a good time on your break, Miss!"

"Who the hell is that?" Beau asks, sounding downright hostile.

"Relax." I slap him in the chest, annoyed. "That's Arabella. She's a friend."

"Your friend? Is that what you're calling them now?"

"She's a friend," I repeat firmly. "We're not dating."

"Do you date anyone?"

Not really.

"And Mom is cool with this?" When I shrug, Beau looks ready to punch something. Or someone. "Such bullshit! She's a hypocrite."

"I'm eighteen," I remind him. "And like I said, nothing is happening between Bells and me."

"Right. You just have a nickname for her, and she's bringing three suitcases because you two are *friendly*." Beau shakes his head. "Looks more like she's moving in."

"She's into fashion."

"And you're into her?"

"Beau..."

"What? Does it make you mad I'm asking you that?"

My fucking brother knows how to get under my skin. He's so annoying.

"This will be interesting," Beau mutters, raising his voice when we draw closer to where Arabella stands. "You going to introduce me to your girlfriend, Row?"

I growl but no one notices.

"Oh, I'm not his girlfriend. But hi, hi! You're Beau. We've passed by each other on campus but I don't think we've ever spoken." Arabella rushes toward my brother, enveloping him in a big hug.

Beau just takes it, seemingly surprised by her enthusiastic greeting, and eventually he wraps his arms around her, patting her back awkwardly.

Another growl escapes me. I can't help it. I don't like seeing another guy touch her, even if it's my little brother, which is stupid. Since when did I turn into such a territorial asshole over my so-called friend?

Arabella pulls out of Beau's embrace and makes her way toward me, shading her eyes with her hand. It's unusually sunny after the last couple of stormy days that were nothing but rain, though the air is crisp and cold. She's bundled up in a thick brown coat that makes her look like a teddy bear.

"Hello, Rowan."

"Three suitcases, Bells?"

She shrugs. "I wanted to be prepared."

"I don't know if we'll be able to fit it all in the car."

Her eyes go wide behind her glasses. "I didn't even think of that. Should I take one of the suitcases back to my room?"

"I'm joking."

"Oh." She drops her hand, glancing over her shoulder to study the three suitcases before returning her attention to me. "I completely overpacked."

"You did." I glance down at my single carry-on sized suitcase. "But don't base your overpacking on this. I have stuff at home."

"True." Her smile is kind of sad. "I'm used to bringing large suitcases everywhere I go. I never feel like I have a permanent home."

Fuck, that is heartbreaking.

"Come on, you two," Beau groans. "Tell me the truth. You're fucking on the low."

I snarl. Bells actually gasps, resting her hand against her chest.

"Beaumont Lancaster, you did *not* just say that," Arabella chastises before I can manage to form words.

"How do you know my full name?" He sounds freaked out.

"I did my research." She lifts her chin, fiery yet dignified. "You shouldn't speak so...bluntly."

"Aw, come on. You two act like you're together."

"We absolutely do not," Arabella tells my brother without hesitation, which makes me chuckle. "I drive Rowan crazy most of the time."

"Doesn't take much. His tolerance level is low for pretty much everyone," Beau notes.

Arabella glances over at me. "You're right, Beau. He's actually the worst."

"No shit, huh? He's also mean to me," Beau adds, eating up the fact that Arabella is paying attention to him—and acting like she's on his side. "I could tell you stories."

"You better not tell her any stories," I say, thrusting my index finger at him.

"Rowan, be nice to your brother." Arabella grins, just before she gives a high five to Beau.

Great. Now they're ganging up on me.

We pile into the car after Beau helps Pat add the luggage to the back. I would do it but I'm taking advantage of my injury and besides, it's about damn time Beau steps up. We may have servants but our parents haven't raised us to be completely helpless.

We all slide into the middle seat, Arabella in between us, her body snug against mine.

"Buckle up," Pat says once he's in the driver's seat and starts the engine.

Arabella pulls the seat belt across her front, looking for the latch to lock it into place. "I can't find it."

I help her, my fingers brushing her hip as I take the seat belt from her. I slide the belt into place, my knuckles up against the side of her ass and I linger there, making it seem like I need to even though I don't.

I'm just trying to touch her. See if she has any sort of visceral reaction. And she doesn't disappoint. I hear the soft intake of breath. The way it catches. How she shifts ever so slightly to get a little closer to my hand.

Or maybe that's all in my imagination. I can't tell.

"You guys comfortable back there?" Pat asks before he takes off. "Can't use the back seat thanks to all the luggage."

"That's my fault. Sorry," Arabella murmurs.

Pat just chuckles. "No worries. But if one of you wants to sit in the passenger seat, it's open."

"I'm fine." Beau bunches up his navy Lancaster Prep sweatshirt he was wearing only moments ago and pins it against the door with his head as a makeshift pillow. "I'm gonna sleep."

"I'm okay," I say, glancing over at Arabella. "How about you?"

"This is fine." She nods, smiling. "It's perfect."

I stare at her full lips. Take in her whole face. Today's glasses have bright red frames, and her big brown eyes are sparkling with pure hope.

I'm suddenly aware that everything between Bells and me might change this week. And that could be a good thing or it could end up being...

Really bad.

FIFTEEN
ARABELLA

I COULD BARELY CONTAIN my excitement during the entire ride to Rowan's parents' house, but I did my best. Calm and collected on the outside.

Screaming, crying, throwing up on the inside.

The ride was longer than expected. Traffic was terrible, the roads crowded and full of bad drivers. I could hear Pat cursing under his breath, tapping his fingers impatiently against the steering wheel. Considering how long we were in the car, some of us got restless—like me. Constantly shifting my legs. Bumping into Rowan again and again.

On purpose I might add. I'm not dumb.

There wasn't much talking going on, but it wasn't awkward. There was almost something comforting about the soft snores that emanated from Beau, who slept with his mouth open almost the entire time. Which Rowan thoroughly enjoyed and documented by taking multiple photos.

"I'll use them against him later," he murmured to me after he took a bunch, and I immediately felt bad. I thought it was mean of Rowan to catch his brother in such a vulnerable state, but then I remembered I don't have any brothers and sisters and I have no idea what that's like.

So I remained quiet, which I kept up for the majority of the ride, savoring the feeling of Rowan's big strong body pressed so close to mine. He spread his legs wider to accommodate the boot on his right foot, causing his thigh to be aligned right next to mine and oh my God, I had a complete moment. My imagination went wild, considering all of the many things that could happen this week.

Only for all of those happy thoughts to come crashing down because good ol' self-doubt crept back in, making me reconsider everything. What if he gets sick of me? It could happen. I always feel like I must wear people out. I have my friends but we don't do every single thing together. We never really have. Maybe that's because in my younger years I never stayed long enough at any particular school to forge long-lasting friendships.

Wow. Just the idea of that makes me sad, but maybe that's my problem. I can't hold a lasting friendship because I was never given the opportunity.

Ugh. I should probably go back into therapy. I probably need it.

By the time we arrive at the house, I'm warm and sleepy from the long car ride, and my body is cramped up. I'm not even paying attention to the house until we're all climbing out of the SUV. Poor Beau practically falls out, thanks to his brother giving him a not-so-polite shove, and when I lift my head to take in the house before me, I'm awestruck.

I have seen plenty of beautiful homes in my lifetime. I have lived—briefly—in a variety of gorgeous, expensive houses and apartments. My mother is an interior design snob and everything has to be perfect. Translation: immaculate.

Untouchable.

We've always lived in a museum-state, and for a kid who loved to run around and touch everything, I was stifled by our past houses. Muted. I might've wanted to come home when I was away at school but I was desperate to go back after only a few days at my parents' house.

Because that's what it was—my parents' house. Not mine. I never felt like I belonged there. Truth be told, I never feel like I belong anywhere.

But this house? The Lancaster house? The exterior is beautiful. Two stories with a massive porch and sweeping driveway in front of it. There are rose bushes everywhere, and while they're mostly devoid of any flowers, I can see the occasional dried up one here and there, all of them a deep red color. There are giant pots all over the porch filled with fall-colored flowers. Yellows and oranges and a dark burgundy. A scattering of pumpkins in a variety of colors are nestled among the pots and there are two giant wreaths hanging on each double door.

I swallow past the lump in my throat as I take it in, blinking when one of the double doors swings open and a beautiful woman appears. A smile forms on her face when she spots us and she runs across the porch, practically skipping down the steps before she tackle hugs Beau first.

"My babies, you made it!" She kisses Beau's cheek, and he grimaces, leaning his head away from her. She wipes at his face, removing the faint lipstick print she left on his skin. "Stop. You know you love it."

"Not really, Mom," Beau grumbles as he disentangles himself from his mother's embrace. I can see the hurt on her face from his actions but she masks it well, turning her shining attention onto Rowan next.

"Look at you." She marches right up to him and cups his face, her arms stretched out because he's so tall. "You look more and more like your father every time I see you."

Lord help me, then Daddy Lancaster must be the handsomest dad on the planet.

"Mom." Rowan rolls his eyes but I can tell he loves it. Loves the attention from his mom. His entire demeanor visibly softens, and when he pulls her in for a hug, they cling to each other for a moment longer than necessary.

My heart swells witnessing the moment.

"Where's Dad?" Beau asks as he marches up the steps, heading straight for the front door.

"He'll be home soon," their mom calls just as she lets go of Rowan and turns her attention on me.

I go stock-still, my nerves eating me up inside because all I want is for this woman to like me. Approve of me.

Accept me.

She watches me carefully, not hiding her curiosity, and I blatantly stare back at her, taken in by her beauty. She doesn't look like a mom—I should say, she doesn't make me think of my mother. This woman's expression is totally open and her smile is genuine. She's absolutely beautiful and equally mesmerizing, if

I'm being truthful, and when she pulls me into her arms, fiercely hugging me, clinging to me much like she did to Rowan who's her actual child?

I melt into her, clinging right back, struggling to fight the tears that sting the corners of my eyes.

"Look at you!" She pulls away from me, holding on to my upper arms as she continues to study me. I almost start squirming but I do my best to keep myself contained. "It is *so* nice to meet you, Arabella Hartley Thomas. Rowan never brings anyone home except for Callahan and he doesn't count."

"Hey," Rowan protests, but his mother ignores him.

"Row says the two of you are friends," she says.

"Um, yes. We are." I don't look at him. It's like I can't. I'm afraid I'll give myself away if I do.

"He told me how you were going to spend the entire week on campus by yourself, and I absolutely hated the thought." Her smile somehow turns brighter, if that's possible. "I'm so glad he was able to convince you to come here and spend the week with us. I hope we don't bore you."

They could never bore me. I can already tell.

"Thank you so much for inviting me, Mrs. Lancaster. I really appreciate it." My voice is shaky, full of emotion. She still makes me nervous, but not in a bad way. More like in a, I really want this person to like me, kind of way.

"Please don't call me that. My name is Wren." She hugs me again like she can't help herself before pulling away from me, sliding her arm across my shoulders as she steers us around to face Rowan. "You two are adorable."

A small part of me—okay, a big part—wants to die of embarrassment at her declaration.

Rowan shakes his head. "Don't get any funny ideas."

"Who me?" Wren Lancaster's face is one of pure innocence. "I would never."

"Yeah, right." Rowan's gaze shifts to mine. "Don't believe her."

"What funny ideas are you talking about?" I'm genuinely confused. I don't speak Lancaster as well as everyone else at this place.

"She thinks the two of us are a secret couple."

I blink at him, shocked that he's not holding back his thoughts.

"That's preposterous." I don't believe I've ever used that word before in my life, but it feels appropriate for the situation.

"I totally agree," Rowan says, filling me with disappointment.

Oh well. I suppose I asked for that.

"You two." Wren shakes her head. "Come on. Let's give you the tour."

I let his mother take my hand and lead me up the steps toward the entrance.

"See you in about thirty minutes," Rowan calls, not moving from his spot in the driveway.

I glance over my shoulder, staring at him. Thirty minutes? Is he serious?

"He's exaggerating," his mother reassures me as we enter the house. My head immediately tilts back, taking in the soaring two-story—wait, make that three-story—foyer. There's a massive, glittering chandelier hanging above us, and I swear I could stare at it forever, it's so beautiful. "I promise it won't take long. Plus it'll be fun, just us girls."

She smiles at me, and I can't help it. I smile back, eager to get to know this woman. Rowan's mom. I feel like I'm in a fever dream.

And I never want to wake up.

———

By the time I'm left alone in the bedroom that will be mine for the next ten nights, I collapse on the bed and stare up at the ceiling, secretly thrilled to find another, smaller but just as beautiful, chandelier above me. I let the happy sigh I've been holding in escape and spread my arms and legs out wide, my body sinking into the comfortable mattress.

The tour was a little over twenty minutes but worth it. The entire house is opulent. It screams old money with all the antiques scattered about and ancestral portraits on the wall. Not to mention all of the art strewn about that Rowan's mother has collected over the years. Some of it is modern yet fits with the house's aesthetic completely; and when I say I'm in awe of her decorating style, I mean it. Wren explained that they've owned the house for only the last ten years or so, and that they fully moved out of the city and into this home full-time soon after they purchased it.

"We loved living in the city," Wren told me as she led me up the stairs of the west wing to where my bedroom is. "But we also loved spending time out here with my husband's cousins, who live down the road. They come over often so I'm sure you'll meet them before Thanksgiving. They usually host the event, but this year I asked to, which means you might miss out on going to their place. Their house has been in the family for generations."

Generations? I hope I get a chance to see it.

There's a knock on my bedroom door and I leap from the bed, rushing to go answer it. And when I crack open the door, I'm not disappointed whatsoever to find who's waiting for me.

It's Rowan.

"Dinner is at seven," he tells me. "My mom wanted me to tell you."

He could've texted me that. I suppose I shouldn't get my hopes up, but I do.

"And she expects us to dress up." He makes a face. "Sort of."

"Exactly how should we dress?"

"Semi-formal."

"Rowan." I sigh, leaning against the door. "That could mean anything. A prom dress. A gown. A nice skirt and sweater. I need more information."

"I don't know. I'm just a guy. I'll show up in khakis and a button-down shirt and I'll be good." He sounds the slightest bit annoyed by me, and there is something comforting about the fact that he's not treating me any differently just because I'm a guest in his house.

"You are no help." I smile at him.

He scowls in return, making me laugh.

"At least you're consistent," I tell him.

Rowan changes the subject. "You like your room?"

I nod. "It's beautiful."

"I'm right down the hall." He glances to his right. "So if you uh, need anything, let me know."

My heart beats a little faster at his words. Right down the hall. Does this mean I could sneak into his room in the middle of the night and have my wicked way with him? How thrilling.

Though I suppose I'm putting the cart before the horse, or however that saying goes. Just because I want us to be a secret couple, and his mother is hopeful that we're a secret couple, doesn't mean that Rowan wants the same thing. I can't bear the thought of him feeling sorry for me though. That is just...the worst. The absolute worst feeling in the whole entire world.

"I need to go talk to my dad," he says as he takes a few steps back. "See you at dinner?"

I nod. "I'll be there in my ball gown and tiara promptly at seven."

He grimaces and I can't help it. I start to laugh again.

This is going to be an interesting week.

SIXTEEN

ROWAN

"BRINGING a girl home for the holiday feels like a big step," Dad says as casually as can be while we're sitting together in his study.

I almost choke on the smooth-aged whiskey he poured me not even two minutes before he made that statement. I could pretend my choking is because of the liquor and not what he said so I lean into that, bringing my fist up to my mouth as I cough into it.

Dad just sits there in the overstuffed chair opposite mine, a faint smile on his face. Mom is right. I look a lot like him. Definitely more than Beau and Willow. My sister is the absolute spitting image of our mother, save for her blue eyes that are just like Dad's.

"She's just a friend," I croak once I sort of find my voice. Damn, that whiskey really did burn going down my throat. "I didn't want her to spend the week alone on campus."

Dad frowns. "Where are her parents?"

"Hong Kong. Her dad is some big financial guru. She doesn't see them much." The words are bitter on my tongue. I don't even know her parents, and Bells hasn't said anything bad about them but...

I hate them.

"Does she have any brothers or sisters?"

I shake my head, taking another smaller sip of the whiskey. I love that Dad brought me into his study and gave me alcohol. Not that I want to party with my dad or anything, but I feel very much on his level right now. Almost like we're equals—which we're not—but it's nice that he's treating me like an adult.

"Her parents sound like assholes," Dad mutters into his glass before he drinks from it.

I chuckle. "My thoughts exactly."

"I know what that's like." He polishes off the rest of his drink, rattling the ice in his glass. "And it's awful."

I remain quiet. My grandparents aren't the best, but according to Dad, they've softened since they've gotten older. When Dad was my age, his father put all sorts of pressure on him and had all of these expectations that Dad never believed he could meet.

My parents don't do that to us. They're open and accepting of all of us, and they rarely try to tell us what to do because they believe we know what we're doing already—to an extent. Mom is always worried about our safety. Dad harps on us about respect and treating others how we want to be treated.

All the normal parent stuff. Plus, they trust us.

Until you give us a reason not to, we trust all of you.

We've heard that more than once and it always makes me want to keep earning their trust. I'm not about to fuck up a good thing.

"What are your plans this week?" Dad asks after he's poured himself another whiskey.

"We don't have any. We're just going to hang out." I shrug.

"Here?" Dad's brows lift.

"What else are we going to do?"

"Row." He sits up, leaning forward in his chair. "Are you interested in this girl beyond friendship?"

I remain quiet, staring into my whiskey glass. It feels like I've been in denial when it comes to Arabella for weeks. Months. Years. "I'm not sure."

"What kind of answer is that?"

"A truthful one." I lift my gaze to his. "How did you feel about Mom when you were my age?"

He falls back into his chair as if I startled him with my question. A myriad of emotions seems to cross his face, one after the other until he finally says, "I thought I hated her."

Him saying that is exactly my point, and I know he would never admit that sort of thing to Willow, who is a giant romantic and has been entranced with our parents' love story since she was in diapers. "I thought I hated Arabella at first too."

"Your mother says she's beautiful. Stylish. And that she wears glasses."

"She is beautiful and stylish and wears a different pair of glasses almost every day." That I notice makes me look like I care and...I do. I care about Arabella. And sometimes my caring feels more than friendly.

Shit, it's definitely more than friendly. I stare at her mouth way too often, wondering what it would be like to kiss her. I enjoyed every second of that car ride with her soft, curvy body nestled against mine. She's warm and smells fucking amazing, and her hair is soft. Her skin is smooth and perfect, save for the tiny scar I noticed on the right side of her nose, and her right ear has three piercings in it. There's a tiny mole on the underside of her jaw, and she has a long, elegant neck. All of these things I noticed on the drive where I blatantly stared at her while she stared off into space like she was in a daze or something. We barely spoke.

We didn't need to speak. Words weren't necessary. All I wanted to do was take her in and I did.

"You've never had a girlfriend," Dad says, his voice pulling me out of my thoughts. "Though when I was your age, I wasn't big on having a girlfriend either. Commitment to any one person scared me."

I feel that more than he knows. "What made you change your mind?"

"Your mother."

"But why?" I drain the rest of my whiskey and it goes down smoothly. Dad grabs the decanter from the table in between us and pours me another one as if he knows I need it. "What happened to make you realize that she could be the one for you?"

I was told forever ago that once a Lancaster meets their person, they are loyal until death. That it is instantaneous and our minds won't be changed. Some of the Lancasters just take a little longer than others to figure it out. I hear my uncle Grant was one of those. Uncle Finn too. My aunt Charlotte was forced to marry Uncle Perry and they're probably the most in love couple I've ever seen.

There's a lot of pressure put upon you when you're told that story as a child. When you know you're a Lancaster and you're going to fall fast and hard for that one person who belongs only to you. I wonder if that's why I keep my distance from most girls, because I'm secretly terrified to find that one person, only for them to break my fucking heart.

"I got to know her. I hated her because she was beautiful and she wasn't mine. She acted like she wasn't aware of me, but I found out that's because I scared her." Dad's smile is small. Almost menacing. "I was an asshole in high school."

"You can be an asshole sometimes now," I tell him, making him chuckle.

"True. But yeah. I scared her. And at first, I liked that. Her fear made me feel powerful." He grimaces. "That's really fucked up to admit."

I'm shocked he'd confess that. "It kind of is."

What's worse? I can relate. I know Arabella doesn't fear me, but I get a thrill out of treating her like shit. Knowing she'll just come back for more, though she dishes out just as good as she gets.

"Then I started to fall for your mother. I fell hopelessly in love with her to the point of being completely obsessed with her. All I ever wanted was to see her happy. I still do." His gaze turns distant, as if he's lost in his thoughts. Memories. "She's the most important person to me beyond the three of you."

Growing up they were such a unified front. We never witnessed a fight. Maybe a minor argument but those ended up being nothing. He'd make her laugh so she couldn't stay mad at him for long and the next thing we knew, they'd be making out again.

My parents are very affectionate with each other. Lots of hugging and kissing and touching and hand-holding. I witness that sort of thing now with Rhett and Willow. Those two can't keep their hands off each other, and I love to give them shit for it.

"It'll happen to you someday," Dad says, his tone almost cryptic. "It might happen sooner than you think."

"Doubtful" is my automatic reply.

Dad just shakes his head, chuckling. "Just wait, Son. Just wait."

By DINNERTIME I'm buzzed after consuming two and a half glasses of aged whiskey. My dad is as calm as ever, sweeping Mom into his arms and delivering a kiss to her lips the moment he spots her in the dining room. I stumble in after him, taking in the table in front of me that's decorated with fresh flower arrangements lining the center and the family's finest china with our crest delicately etched into the center of each plate and bowl.

"Someone brought out the big guns," is my first vocal observation, which has Mom scowling at me as if I insulted her.

"I wanted everything to look nice for our guests," Mom says, vaguely defensive.

"Don't you mean guest?" I notice Mom even put place cards by each plate and that I'm right next to Arabella because of course I am.

"Your aunt and uncle are joining us."

"Which ones?"

"Grant and Alyssa. The kids are having a movie night and friends over so they needed somewhere to escape for a few hours," Mom explains.

"They're trusting everyone on their own for the night?" That doesn't sound like Uncle Grant at all. He's a complete control freak.

"He's got cameras all over the house, and I'm sure he'll be monitoring them all night." Dad chuckles.

Beau enters the dining room seconds later, not as sullen as he was when we first arrived home. He lets Mom hug him this time and doesn't try to pull away. I think he's still mad at them for not letting him go to that girl's house for the weekend or however long he was invited, but I think he's gotten over it. He doesn't ever hold a grudge for long.

"You both look nice," Mom says as she watches the two of us. "You clean up well."

"Anything to get out of the uniform," Beau says.

"I'm so sorry I'm late." Arabella practically runs into the room, coming to a skidding stop right next to Beau. "I got lost."

She's breathless. Beautiful in a simple black long-sleeved dress that hits her at about mid-thigh, with black tights covering her long legs. Her hair is up, piled on top of her head in a messy but somehow elegant bun, showing off that beautiful neck that I was tempted to kiss earlier in the car.

I blink, shoving the wild thoughts out of my mind as I watch my mother introduce Arabella to my father. He smiles at her and pulls her into a hug, complimenting her glasses, which are bright pink frames tonight. What looks like giant pink diamond studs dot each ear, and her lips are a glossy pink too.

She stretches those lips into a friendly smile that she turns onto me, her hopeful gaze meeting mine, and I have a sudden epiphany.

When it comes to this girl, I'm completely fucked.

SEVENTEEN

ARABELLA

DINNER at the Lancaster residence is quite...entertaining.

Whenever I was at my parents' house, which was never often and never for long, we rarely had dinner together. My father was always working late, or my mother would be out with her friends at some sort of party or gathering. Charity gala or bullshit ball. Most of the time I ate meals in the kitchen with the servants, who'd always watch me with pity filling their eyes.

Those rare times when we ate dinner as a family, my mother and father would mostly ignore me. They'd talk about their day and what happened, never really asking me any questions until near the end of the meal, when they'd realize that I was there and it was only polite to have me join in the conversation. I was an afterthought, always.

At the Lancasters', the conversation is lively. Constant. And they include me in it, so I don't feel like an outsider. Any private reference or inside family joke is explained by someone so I'm not left out and I love it.

Love it.

Rowan's Uncle Grant is grumpier than he is, and I can see where he comes by it naturally. The man scowls at everyone at the table, save for his wife. He looks at her as if the sun rises and sets on her head, and that is the sweetest thing I've ever seen. My romantic heart can barely take it. His parents are just as in love with each other, always sharing secret glances and fond smiles. I watch both couples unabashedly, enraptured with the way they speak to each other and include all of us. The adults at the table ask me plenty of questions, some I have no problem answering, while a few others make me a little uncomfortable. Such as the fact that Grant realizes he knows my parents.

"We've definitely crossed paths over the years," he tells me. "My brother sold them their penthouse in Manhattan years ago," he explains to me.

I hate the penthouse in Manhattan. It's sleek and modern and cold as ice. "I have fond memories there," I lie to him with a fake smile.

Grant bursts out laughing at my lie and shakes his head. "That apartment is very..."

"Cold?" I supply for him.

"Yes. That." His gaze is full of sympathy, and I hope he doesn't feel sorry for me. That is the last thing I want.

The food is amazing. Fine restaurant quality with a multitude of courses that grow more impressive every time the next dish is brought out. Dessert is a pumpkin cheesecake with caramel sauce drizzled over the top that has me moaning in delight every time I take a bite.

The look on Rowan's face each time I moan is worth me making an extra big deal about dessert. He seems pained by my reaction and I love it. Sitting next to him is part of the bonus, though it's also torture. Whatever cologne he's wearing I don't recognize because he doesn't use it when we're at school, and I want to take a giant bite out of him. But that would make me a cannibal and that's literally disgusting so I restrain myself.

Barely.

When dinner is over and we're leaving the dining room, Rowan touches my arm, causing me to stop and turn to face him.

"Sorry if they made you feel uncomfortable."

I'm frowning. "Who? Your family? They're wonderful."

"Even my uncle?"

"Especially your uncle." I smile at him. "He reminds me of you."

Rowan shoves his hands in his pockets and I blatantly stare at him for a moment. The light blue shirt he's wearing has a few buttons undone at the neck, giving me the perfect view of the strong column of his throat. The bob of his Adam's apple when he swallows. I take a deep breath, inhaling his scent as subtly as possible when he speaks.

"My dad says I need to entertain you this week."

"Entertain me?" My voice is hollow, my imagination running wild. "Like how? Will you sneak into my room and kiss me for hours every night and it'll be our dirty little secret?"

The moment the words leave me I'm pressing my trembling fingers against my lips, shocked. Embarrassed. He hasn't said anything, and I feel like a fool for blurting my most secretive inner thoughts out loud. "I didn't mean to say that."

"But you did." He is grinning.

Might I add he's grinning widely and looking terribly pleased with himself.

"But I did," I whisper, shaking my head as I drop my fingers from my mouth. "Seriously. I don't know why I said it. That's not what I want."

His brows shoot up.

"I don't! I swear." I mark an X across my heart with my index finger.

"That's not a very friend-like thing to say, Bells," he drawls.

I glance around, realizing we're the only ones left in the dining room. I don't know where Beau went but I'm glad he's not nearby to overhear this conversation.

"Which part? Me saying I don't want that or suggesting you sneak into my room and kiss me?"

"Both." He's smirking. Acting extra flirtatious this evening. I have no excuse for what I said but I think I'll blame the house and everyone in it. It's cozy here and makes me feel far more comfortable than I should.

"I beg to differ. I think you sneaking into my room so we can make out in my bed is an extremely friendly thing to say." I laugh at myself because I am truly being ridiculous. "You know I'm joking, right?"

He doesn't move or make a sound. Just continues to watch me with his hands in his pockets, looming in front of me. Big and broad and slightly intimidating, I must admit. I might even start quaking in my black suede ankle boots a little bit.

"Is this how you ended up having sex with Bentley Saffron Jones?" he asks.

My frown deepens. "What do you mean?"

"Did you suggest sneaking around with him and making out and next thing you know, he's balls deep inside you?"

I rest my hand against my chest at his words. *Balls deep?* Lord, I don't even think Bentley was two inches deep before he orgasmed. The boy could barely stick it in without coming too fast. "We didn't really kiss."

"You didn't?"

"I mean, we did but here's where I confess that he was incredibly bad at it." I shake my head. "But I don't want to talk about Bentley."

"I don't either."

"Then why did you bring him up?" He always brings him up.

"Because I can't stop thinking about what you told me—that you had sex with that guy," he admits, his gaze dark as it lingers on mine. "And how fucking jealous it makes me feel."

I am full-on gaping. Jaw unhinged and swinging like an old-timey puppet on a string. Did he really say that? I remember that he kept sipping from a highball glass of amber-colored liquid throughout dinner. He must be drunk. And his parents are okay with this? Oh my God, why am I thinking of his parents at a time like this?

"Jealous?" I squeak. I sound like a mouse. "You can't be serious, Rowan."

"I am very serious, Arabella," he says without an ounce of hesitation. "I am baffled by the fact that you had sex with a guy named Bentley."

"Don't forget the Saffron part," I remind him, my voice weak. "That makes it even more baffling."

"True," he agrees. "I feel like every time I talk to you, I peel back another mysterious layer."

"Mysterious? Please. I am not mysterious." I laugh.

Rowan doesn't, of course. He rarely does if I'm being truthful, and I think that's a little sad. "You are to me."

I stare at him, all of my laughter disappearing. "You are to me too."

He glances around the giant dining room, spotting the servants starting to clear the table at the same time I do. Withdrawing his right hand from his pocket, he gently grabs hold of the crook of my elbow and steers me out of the room, guiding me toward the massive staircase that leads to the west wing.

Where our bedrooms are.

His parents must be idiots to put our rooms so close together. They should've put me in the east wing or a guest house on the property under lock and key because oh, the look on Rowan's face right now as he turns to study me once more is...feral. And he's studying me with that feral expression like I'm a tasty treat he's hoping to enjoy later.

My mind is spinning. How is this already happening? Maybe I should blame the alcohol that I think he consumed. Because he is acting like a completely different person than the Rowan I know on campus.

"Did you mean it?" he asks.

"Did I mean what?"

He drops his hand from my arm and I immediately miss his touch.

"That you hope I sneak into your room so I can kiss you for hours."

My throat goes dry and my ability to speak completely leaves me. All I can do is nod my answer.

"And you really didn't kiss that Saffron dude?"

"Only a couple of times," I whisper, glancing around like someone might be lurking in the dark and overhearing my confession. "It was so bad, Rowan. The entire experience was terrible."

"But you kept going back for more."

"We were fifteen and stupid." I throw my hands up in the air. "I was hoping it would get better. It didn't."

I can hear people talking and I realize it's Rowan's parents. They're drawing closer. And Rowan realizes it too. He takes a step closer to me, bending down and dipping his head so his mouth is close to my ear. "Leave your door unlocked."

That's all he says before he walks away to speak to his mom and dad, leaving me standing at the base of the stairwell alone, my entire body trembling.

For him.

EIGHTEEN

ARABELLA

I TAKE A QUICK SHOWER. I lather my entire body with my favorite lotion and put on a thin white T-shirt with no bra and a pair of pale pink pajama bottoms dotted with white hearts. No panties.

I am a slut. But only for Rowan Lancaster because I wouldn't do this for anyone else. Not a single person. Only him.

Lying in bed, I'm quaking in anticipation of his arrival. I can't even scroll mindlessly on my phone like I usually do because being on my phone makes me realize that time is ticking by oh so slowly and he still hasn't arrived, and God, it's painful. Deliciously so.

What got into him to say such a thing to me?

Leave your door unlocked.

I swear my panties were immediately soaked when he whispered that in my ear. The timbre of his voice. The heavy suggestion behind those seemingly innocent words.

The boy makes me want to melt into a puddle. I don't recall Bentley Saffron Jones ever making me feel like that.

I'm shocked that Rowan would even agree to my flippant suggestion. I've said that sort of thing to him before. Plenty of times, and he never takes me seriously because I don't take myself seriously either. It's fun to goad him. To witness his always irritable reaction. Until tonight. There was nothing irritable about his reaction whatsoever beyond his references to Bentley.

A part of me wishes I would've never made that confession, but another part of me is glad because I think it helped Rowan see me as a sexual human being. Someone to be desired instead of just annoyed with.

Oh, my thoughts are...not the best sometimes. I know I am the sort who wants attention constantly, whether it's good or bad. I blame that on my neglectful parents obviously. And praise be to the therapist I went to when I was fifteen and struggling, who helped me have that realization. I told her everything about Bentley, and she said I was just searching for love since I couldn't find it with my parents.

A painful realization but it's true. I still want someone to love me. This is probably why I'm enjoying myself so much in this house and I haven't even been here for twelve hours. The entire place just overflows with love and affection. I adore it. I want more of it.

I want to feel like I belong here in this massive house that feels like a cozy little home.

As I lie there waiting in my bed for a certain someone to show up, clutching the silken duvet cover in my hands so tightly I'm sure it's permanently wrinkled, I eventually start to drift off. It's hard to focus, considering how long the day has been and how late the hour currently is. The bed is soft and fluffy, and my head sinks into the pile of pillows that are like clouds. The room is blessedly dark, and I can hear the wind blow outside, gently rattling the windows.

It's peaceful.

And then I realize I'm being woken up by the sound of someone entering my bedroom. I can hear footsteps shuffle across the floor but no slight drag of the boot.

Hmm.

But I can smell him. I can sense him standing beside the bed, watching me sleep, and I pretend to be exactly that, my eyes gently closed, not moving a muscle. He walks around to the other side of the bed and I feel the tug of the covers being pulled down. The dip of the mattress when he crawls onto the bed. The smooth sound of the sheets and duvet being pulled over his body, indicating that he's in bed with me. Right next to me.

What is this life?

Rowan Lancaster is in my bed. And he's not doing a damn thing about it. Just lying there and...what? Spying on me? Do I need to light a firecracker under his butt or what?

Deciding to let him know that I am fully awake, I flop over onto the other side so I'm facing him and crack open my eyes to find that yes, he is watching me. His expression is soft this late at night. Almost vulnerable. And he's looking at me as if he can't believe we're sharing a bed, which I can totally relate to.

"You're not like other boys," I murmur to him, keeping my voice low so I don't break the spell.

"What do you mean?" He appears confused.

"I'm assuming any other boy who would have the balls to sneak into my room would pounce on me immediately," I tell him.

"Do lots of boys sneak into your room?"

"Not a single one ever has."

"Is that what you want? For me to pounce on you?"

I am so grateful that he didn't bring up Bentley. "Is that what you want to do?"

He ignores my question. "I didn't think you would be asleep when I snuck in here."

"I waited for you—I tried to stay awake." I hesitate and decide to ask the question that's at the forefront of my mind. "What took you so long anyway?"

"I was working up the nerve to actually do this."

What?

Rowan had to work up the nerve to sneak into my room?

"Are you serious?" He's always so confident about everything.

He nods. "You...throw me off."

"How?" I am baffled. I never thought I had any sort of effect on him beyond utter annoyance.

"I never know what you're going to say or do. I never know what you're going to wear. You're a constant surprise."

"Is that a bad thing?" I whisper, scared that it might be.

"Not at all." He stretches his hand out toward me, his fingers grazing my cheek, making my eyes close. I wish he would keep touching me forever. "Can you see me?"

"What do you mean? Yes, I can see you." He presses his thumb against my chin, making my lips part.

"You're not wearing your glasses." His gaze roves over my face. "You look...different without them."

"Different bad? Or different good?"

"Different good." His smile is faint, his voice dropping an octave when he murmurs, "Tell me to leave, Bells." His hand drops away from my face and he sounds like he's in absolute agony.

I rise up on one elbow so I can really look at him. The covers fall away from my top half with the movement and even in the dim light I can see his gaze go straight to my chest.

Typical. The boy is fascinated with my boobs. I glance down to see that my white shirt is extremely thin and my nipples are hard, and oh wow, he is *staring*.

"I'm not going to tell you to leave," I say when I return my gaze to his, my voice firm. Maybe even a little too loud. Though right now I could not care less if someone heard me. Us. "I would be a fool to say that."

"You're a fool to let me stay." He sounds serious. Is the boy blind? I'd let him do whatever he wanted to me, I'm that desperate for his attention.

"I'm a bigger fool if I encourage you to leave," I whisper, shocked I would lay myself on the line like this. For him.

His fingers are on my neck, tracing my necklace, coming to a stop at the heart pendant. The one I never take off. "Is this a locket?" Before I can answer he's already got it open. "There aren't any pictures inside."

"I know."

His gaze lifts to mine. "Why not?"

"I'm waiting for the right person to come along," I admit.

His mouth kicks up on one side in the faintest smirk. "Are his initials BSJ?"

I realize that Bentley has some terrible initials. BS could equal bullshit. BJ—blowjob. Poor Bentley. "Absolutely not. You need to stop bringing him up, Rowan. I'm starting to believe you're obsessed with him."

"That is the furthest thing from the truth." He carefully snaps my locket closed, his hand dropping away from my neck and God, why won't this boy just touch me? Kiss me already? That's what I want the most. I wasn't lying when I suggested we make out for hours. That sounds like a dream come true. I want his hands all over me and his mouth fused with mine to the point that our jaws will be aching when it's over. I want to wake up the next morning and still feel the imprint of his mouth on mine. I want to sit across from him at breakfast and share secret smiles with him because we know what we've done.

And no one else would have a clue.

Instead, he's just lying there staring at me like he can't believe we're in the same bed, and I catch his gaze dropping again to the front of my chest. Most likely my nipples. I'm half tempted to grab his hand and place it right on my breast. Force him to feel me up but he might think I'm too forward.

Despite my meager sexual experience, I have no idea what we're doing. No clue as to how we should navigate these unchartered waters. And when I start spouting clichés in my thoughts, that's when I know I'm overthinking everything.

"Rowan." I startle him by saying his name and I wonder if he's in as much of a trance as I've found myself over the last few hours. He is making me impatient and I don't like it. "What are you doing?"

"Staring at you," he admits truthfully. "You're pretty, Bells."

My impatience evaporates at his compliment. "You really think so?"

"I know so." His hand settles on my hip and he gently drags me closer to him. My heart starts to pound in my ears, tingles erupting all over my body when I feel the dig of his fingers into my skin. Our legs collide and I slip one between both of his, desperate to get closer when I realize something.

"Where's your boot?"

"I'm not wearing it."

"Why not?"

"I don't sleep in it," he points out. "Talk about uncomfortable."

"Oh." I'm careful when I drag my toes along his ankle and calf, making sure I'm not touching the one that's broken. "True."

He starts to reach for me, hesitating for only a moment, and I withdraw my leg from between his. My frustration and impatience must be showing because he says, "I don't want to fuck this up."

"Fuck what up?"

"This. Us. You. Me." He slides his hand from my hip to the small of my back, jerking me into him, making me gasp. I like a forceful Rowan. "We should keep this a secret."

"Yes," I breathe, knowing full well if he asked me to murder someone at this very moment my response would be the same.

"Just between us? I don't want to get my parents' hopes up." Somehow, he rearranges our bodies and he's on top of me. On. Top. Of.

Me.

I spread my legs and he settles in, bracing his hands on either side of my head, caging me in. I'm completely surrounded by him and I lie there breathless, heart hammering a million miles a minute, waiting.

"Please don't bring your parents up during a moment like this," I tell him, dead serious.

He dips his head, his mouth hovering above mine. I can feel his breath, minty fresh like he might've just brushed his teeth, and I wonder what brand of toothpaste he uses. Once I find out, I'm buying it immediately. "Probably best if we don't talk at all, right?"

"Right," I whisper just as his lips brush mine.

It's a tease of a kiss. Barely there yet completely earth-shattering. I have been thinking about this moment for years. Anticipating it for what feels like forever. His mouth touches mine again and I inhale softly but otherwise do nothing else. Just let him kiss me in the gentlest way. It's agonizing.

It's wonderful.

"How many guys have you kissed, Bells?" He asks this question while his lips are still on mine.

"How many girls have you kissed, Rowan?"

"Not many," he returns, leaving me shook.

"Exactly how many then?" My number is low. I figured because he's Rowan Lancaster, he would've already kissed an infinite number of girls.

"I'd rather not say."

"You don't kiss and tell?"

He kisses me like he wants me to stop talking. Forceful and quick. "I don't kiss anyone much at all."

Wait a second.

Wait.

A.

Second.

I'm almost afraid to ask but I have to know. I must. It's imperative. And might change everything. Not in a bad way but in a *this is so interesting* type of way.

"Rowan. Are you trying to tell me you haven't really kissed... anyone?"

NINETEEN
ROWAN

I CAN'T BELIEVE I have this gorgeous girl pinned beneath me in her bed. Her soft, lush curves fit perfectly under me and I have this vision of me sinking into her body…

The idea leaves me hard and frustrated because fuck. I haven't been in a situation like this before. Arabella is more experienced than I am, and this shit is embarrassing to admit.

"Well?" she asks when I haven't answered her. She's so damn impatient most of the time.

I lift away from her so I can stare into her eyes. Memorize every single part of her beautiful face. If I'm being real with myself, I sort of miss the glasses, but her face is open and her skin is bare without a lick of makeup on and she's the most gorgeous girl I've ever seen.

Maybe it's the alcohol I consumed earlier. Maybe it's the fact that I jerked off in the shower to thoughts of her, trying to alleviate the pressure before I snuck into her bedroom. But it's like I'm seeing her, *really* seeing her for the first time.

"I've kissed other girls. It's not like you're my first." I scoff because come on. I'm eighteen. I've kissed girls.

Just not a lot of them. None of the girls I've been with before were what I considered worthy. I fell for one hard and she fucked me over so badly I've been in protection mode ever since.

"How many beds have you snuck into?" she asks in that soft, infinitely appealing voice with the faint accent that makes her sound vaguely snobbish.

But she's not a snob. She's open and sweet. Sometimes too open, and she wants me to be the same way with her, which is difficult for me. I keep my feelings bottled up. I don't blurt the first thing that comes to my mind, and she always acts like that.

"Not many."

"I find that hard to believe," she starts, her voice loud, and I automatically cover her mouth with my hand to silence her. She blinks up at me, her breath coating my palm, and I can't deny that she looks hot like this.

Sexy in her white T-shirt that's so thin I can see the outline of her nipples. Those cute pale pink pajama pants she's wearing with the little white hearts that are extra soft. I can see myself slowly pulling those pants off and exposing her completely and fuck, I think my dick just got even harder.

"It's true," I tell her. "I've kissed girls. The first one, we were in the seventh grade."

I drop my hand from her mouth just in time for her to say, "She doesn't count."

"We were playing seven minutes in heaven."

"And did you kiss her the entire seven minutes?"

"Well...no." It was at a birthday party and we were locked in a darkened closet. I only got up the nerve to kiss her at all when the other kids started doing a countdown to the end of our seven minutes.

The girl went on to brag to anyone who would listen that it was the best seven minutes of her life. That I was the perfect kisser and she was madly in love with me. It dawned on me then that I didn't have to do a damn thing to prove myself. People were infatuated with the idea of me more than my actual self. Rowan Lancaster the name has all of these connotations and expectations put upon it but Rowan, the actual, real person?

No one knows the real me, save for my closest family and a couple of friends, and even then, I feel like I put on a front sometimes. Who the fuck am I anyway?

"We are wasting time," she whispers, bringing me back to the present. To the fact that I'm still lying on top of her and she's not telling me to leave because of what I just confessed. "Kiss me, Rowan."

I don't hesitate, dipping my head and brushing her mouth with mine. I go on pure instinct, kissing her over and over, our lips parting with every pass, lingering. She shifts beneath me, her arms coming around me, her hands settling on my back, and without thought, I press my torso against hers, my kisses becoming fiercer.

"Go softer," she murmurs against my lips, her hands slowly sliding up my back. "We have all night to do this. We don't need to rush."

I soften my approach, kissing her like we have all night, which we do. Paying attention to every little sound she makes, how her breaths quicken when our lips part wider. I swipe my tongue against her lower lip, and she moans. The sound shoots a bolt of lightning down my spine, settling in my balls.

Fuck.

Without hesitation I do it again, her tongue darting out to meet mine this time and that's it. The kiss turns deeper as I search her mouth, sliding my tongue against hers and we don't stop. It's like we can't stop. We're too hungry for each other but all we do is kiss. Kiss and kiss and...

Kiss.

I don't know how long we keep this up but eventually I have to pull away from her intoxicating lips because I need to breathe. She seems to need to catch her breath too and I nuzzle her neck with my face while she lies there and pants.

"You smell really fucking good," I practically growl against her neck.

She's smiling. I can feel it, though I don't see it. "Thank you."

"Should we stop?"

Arabella doesn't even hesitate with her answer. "Absolutely not. Though I do have a question."

"What is it?" I lift away from her neck so I can stare into her eyes. They're dark and hazy and her lips are damp and swollen, and I'm tempted to kiss her before she can ask.

"Are we moving too fast?"

"It's just kissing, Bells." I kiss the right corner of her mouth. Then the left. "Nothing serious."

"Nothing serious," she echoes. "Right."

"I don't know how to manage a relationship," I continue, deciding to be completely honest with her. "What's the point in starting one?"

"So you're just looking for...noncommittal kissing."

That sounds perfect.

"Accompanied by equally noncommittal sex." She pauses, her hands falling away from my back. "Am I right?"

"Well." I stare into her eyes, noting the flicker of irritation I see in them. "Yeah?"

"Oh, Rowan." She lifts her hips like she's trying to buck me off her, and I go willingly, sliding off and onto my side, still facing her. "You need to leave."

"What the—why?" This girl and her mixed messages leave me fucking confused.

"I should've never told you about Bentley. Now you've just reduced me to your nightly plaything. Ugh." She climbs out of bed, pushing her hair out of her face with both hands, clutching the back of her head. My gaze drops to her chest because I can't help myself. That see-through T-shirt just does something to me and I cannot stop staring at her perfect tits. The hard nipples poking against the thin fabric. She catches me staring for what feels like the millionth time and then does the absolute craziest thing I think I've ever seen Arabella do.

She whips her T-shirt off in one smooth movement, standing in front of me bare-chested and those perfect tits on display.

"Is this what you want to see? Is this what you've reduced me to?" She reaches for the waistband of her pajama pants and shoves them down, revealing she is completely naked beneath them. Meaning she is standing in front of me without a stitch of clothing on. And I can't stop myself from drinking her in.

She's beautiful because of course she is, and I immediately feel like an asshole because damn, she's pissed.

"No, of course not," I start, but she's shaking her head, thrusting her arm toward the door.

"You need to go."

"Arabella…"

"Don't try to convince me you see me as something more. You never have. Like, ever. I'm just that girl who follows you around like a lost puppy dog. The one you felt sorry for and invited to your family's house for Thanksgiving break. This big, beautiful house with your beautiful family who all actually cares about each other and talks to each other. Do you even know how lucky you are? Probably not. You're too secure in the fact that this is just your normal life. Not all of us have it as good as you do, Rowan."

She reaches for the blanket draped across the foot of the bed and wraps it around her body while I just stand there, shocked by her outburst. Shocked even more by the pain in her voice. Arabella is right. I've never considered what's going on with her personal life until recently, but that's only because we've started talking more. And she's the one who wanted me to sneak into her room. I do exactly what she wants, and now I'm the bad guy?

This girl makes no sense.

"I'll leave you alone," I bite out, a mixture of misery and anger coursing through me. "I didn't mean to make you feel like that."

I stalk my way out of the bedroom, pausing in the doorway when I hear her murmur, "It's fine. I'm really good at making myself feel like that too."

I WAKE up the next morning grumpy as shit because I slept terrible. All I could think about was Arabella getting so pissed at me that she stripped off all of her clothes, accusing me of reducing her to nothing more than a body for me to get off on. In.

Whatever.

The more I thought about her outburst, the shittier I felt, and now I'm in the dining room picking at my breakfast since I have no appetite, my brother right next to me and just as quiet as I am. I'm waiting for Arabella to make an appearance so I can apologize to her but it's already past ten o'clock and she's still not downstairs.

Did she leave in the middle of the night? Is she already back at Lancaster Prep? I wouldn't doubt it. Talk about making me feel like absolute garbage. Like I drove her right out of this place in less than twenty-four hours because I couldn't keep my hands to myself, even though she claimed she wanted it. Wanted me.

Jesus. I cannot win.

"You boys grumpy this morning or what?"

Beau and I both glance up at the same time to find our father watching us, his hands on his hips, clad in golf gear—dark green pants and a crisp white polo shirt, a white visor on his head. I'm sure he's off to the country club. It's his new favorite pastime, playing golf with Whit.

"Grumpy," I say at the same time that Beau says, "Or what."

Dad laughs. We don't.

"I'm going back to bed." Beau leaps to his feet and leaves the dining room in a huff.

"What's his problem?" Dad asks me once he's gone.

"I don't know." I shrug.

"And what's your problem?"

"Women," I mutter, making Dad chuckle. "Seriously. I don't get them."

Dad settles into the chair at the head of the table. "Want to tell me what's going on?"

"Not particularly," I answer, making him chuckle.

I can't share with him what happened last night. First of all, it's none of his business and second of all, there's no way I'm going to admit that I was in her room and she stripped off all her clothes in a fit of anger. Just thinking about it reminds me of how completely out of character the moment was.

But was it actually out of character? Arabella is so damn impulsive sometimes. She just—does things and thinks about them later. While I'm over here agonizing over every little point.

"I thought you two were getting along pretty great last night," Dad says, interrupting my thoughts.

"Yeah, I guess. It's like we're sending each other...mixed signals," is what I tell him instead.

"That happens." He nods. "Do you like her?"

Why is it so fucking hard for me to admit that I like a girl? That I might care about a girl and want to be with her? And didn't he already ask me this yesterday? Why do they keep questioning me about her? Mom is just as bad.

All I can do is shrug my answer, which makes Dad frown. "Come on, Son. If you can't even admit that you li—"

"I like her," I say, cutting him off. "But please don't mention it to Mom yet. She'll make it this big deal and I don't want to feel under pressure."

I can tell it takes a lot for him to suppress the smile he wants to let loose. "Well, then. Does she like you?"

"I'm fairly certain she's been into me for years."

Dad lets the grin fly. "Confident much?"

"I've been into her too," I admit, hanging my head so I can take a deep breath. "I just—it's hard for me to realize that. Admit it."

"You've got a lot of walls. I know what that's like. I did too when I was your age, though for different reasons." Dad leans forward, propping his arms on the table. "If you want to get closer to her —and she seems like a sweet girl—you're going to have to let her break down those walls. You'll need to be your real self with her."

"I don't feel like I'm my real self with anyone," I say, sounding miserable. Feeling it too.

"What do you mean?"

"Everyone has all of these expectations of me, but no one knows who I really am. At one point, I thought it was football that made me who I was. That's different, you know? Lancasters have never really been big into sports." Dad remains quiet, and I keep talking. "But then that all went to hell when I broke my stupid ankle."

"What do you want to do, then?"

"I don't know." I keep my gaze fixed on the table in front of me. "I'm still trying to figure that out."

"If you tell her that, she might understand. She's probably trying to figure herself out too," Dad says, his voice soft. "Your mom and I were kind of a mess when we first got together. We helped each other out."

"Really?" I don't ask much about their early years. That's more Willow's thing, and most of the time, I don't care. I'm not into the romantic stuff, or so I thought. But now? I'm curious.

"Oh yeah. Your mom's relationship with her parents wasn't the best and she was a prissy little snob." Dad bursts out laughing while I sit there in shock. I don't think I've ever heard him describe her quite like that. "And I was a punk asshole with a giant chip on his shoulder who hated everyone, including your mother."

Damn, it almost feels like he could be describing me.

"I didn't think I liked her but honestly? I was just fighting my feelings. And once I was hooked, once I realized just how special she was..." Dad shakes his head. "I knew I could never let her go. And I was going to do whatever it took to make her happy."

"Yeah." I nod, letting that sink in. "I don't know if I feel the same way about Arabella that you did about Mom."

"You'll figure it out." He says this with such confidence. I wish I felt the same way he did, but I'm confused. Conflicted.

We both whip our heads in the direction of the foyer, which is filled with the sound of women's laughter and nonstop chatter. I watch in disbelief as my mother enters the dining room with Arabella trailing after her. The two of them looking and acting like they're old friends. The joy on Arabella's face, the big smile stretching her mouth wide is a complete contradiction to the Arabella I saw last night.

I absently rub at my chest, right across my aching heart. I wish she smiled at me like that. Laughed with me like that. I need to earn this girl's trust back and redeem myself.

Hopefully, I haven't missed my opportunity.

TWENTY

ARABELLA

I COME to a stop in the open doorway of the dining room, my gaze automatically going to Rowan like I can't help myself. He looks utterly miserable and completely traumatized, and I hope I did that to him. I'm still not over what happened last night, though I know deep in my soul that I overreacted. Whipping my clothes off like that in front of him—what in the world possessed me?

He did. That's who. And my own insecurities. I've been reduced to nothing for so long by the people who supposedly care about me the most, and I'm sick of it.

Over it.

Done.

Perhaps Rowan ended up in the crossfire of my emotions, but he'll survive. This beautiful life he lives with his wonderful family will take care of him whether I'm in his world or not. We're just two young teenagers who don't know what the hell they're doing, right? That's what I feel like. A confused, hormonal mess who pitched a naked fit.

He probably thinks I'm too much. Too irrational, too impulsive. And if that's the case? He was never the one for me. If he can't handle me, maybe now is the time to realize and bail before he ends up breaking my heart...

Hmm, too late. I think he always had that power. I'm sure he doesn't realize it though. He's rather clueless.

"What are you two up to?" Crew Lancaster rises to his feet and heads straight for his wife, kissing her like he hasn't seen her in weeks. "Your face is cold."

"We were outside. Power walking." Wren smiles at me. "I found Arabella about to leave the house for a run and offered to join her."

"You don't run, Birdy." He slings his arm around his wife's shoulders and pulls her into him, pressing a kiss to her forehead. "You never really have."

"I convinced her to walk instead." Wren smiles up at him, and my heart is a crushed little pulp of dying flesh at seeing them so adorable together. I want that. I desperately, undeniably want it and I don't know how to get it.

My gaze flicks to Rowan, who's watching me with sympathy filling his pretty green eyes. Defeated, I look away from him and offer a weak smile to his father. "Yes, we walked. Though it was cold out there, I agree."

"Freezing," Wren adds.

"You weren't trying to escape the house before everyone woke up?" Rowan asks me.

I glare at him. His dad scowls. And his mother automatically chastises him.

"Rowan, please. Don't be rude to your guest." She glances over at me with a smile. "Your Arabella is an absolute darling. We had a great conversation while we were walking. Plus, she told me a secret."

Crap. I was hoping she would keep that secret.

"What kind of secret?" Rowan asks, curiosity filling his deep voice. Curiosity tinged with a healthy dose of fear because he's probably terrified that I spilled my guts over what happened between us last night.

As if. I'm not that stupid.

"You'll never believe it." Wren steps away from her husband, clutching her hands together in front of her. "But she's going to be celebrating a birthday while she's here!"

"Oh." That's all he says, and I want to roll my eyes but restrain myself. It's not like we've ever been close enough that he's paid attention to my birthday before, but he could at least sound somewhat enthusiastic.

"Yes, Arabella is turning eighteen on Friday. The day after Thanksgiving. We should have a party. I already have plans to order her a cake and we'll have a special dinner catered—"

"You don't need to do that," I say, feeling bad that I cut her off. When she frowns at me, I go on. "Seriously. My birthday is not that big of a deal. Besides, you barely know me."

"Aw, Arabella. It's not every day that someone turns eighteen." Her voice is soft and her eyes are glowing, and I realize this is what it might be like if I had a mother who cared and wanted to do something for me like celebrate my eighteenth birthday. "It's a special moment that should be celebrated."

"I don't need a party."

"At the very least you should have birthday cake. With candles to blow out. And a nice dinner." She drops her hands at her sides. "I would love to host that for you."

"It's okay. Really. I don't need anything big—"

"It wouldn't be big. Just a few family members invited over."

"Mom, stop. She doesn't want you to make a big deal about her birthday," Row says, his voice firm.

Everyone goes silent. So quiet, I hear a clock ticking somewhere in the house, and God, the lack of sound is stifling. I feel awful. Worse that Rowan snapped at his mother in my defense. She was only being kind.

"You're right. Of course." Wren's smile is small. I don't think she liked that Rowan said that. "I understand. Let me know if you want anything special to eat on Friday," she says to me before her husband escorts her out of the dining room, leaving us alone, much like we were only last night, when everything shifted and changed between us.

Now it's shifted and changed again and we're in a shit place where we're both to blame for it.

"Your mom was just being nice," I tell him. "She got excited when I told her it was my birthday."

"Do you want a party though? You didn't act like you did."

I shrug. "I'm not used to that sort of thing anymore. My parents haven't thrown me a birthday party in years." And back when they did, it was only for their business associates and so they could get a write-off. It never had anything to do with me.

Rowan grimaces. "I probably shouldn't say this, but your parents sound like the most selfish people ever."

I laugh, though the sound is sad. "You're right. They are."

He rises to his feet, shoving his hands in his sweatpants' pockets. He looks awkward and uncomfortable, and I know I have everything to do with that. "Look..."

"I shouldn't have done what I did," I say for him, needing to get it off my chest. He frowns but I forge on. "I was trying to start a fight."

"You were?" He sounds surprised.

"Definitely. I was feeling vulnerable and unsure and I lashed out at you."

"But I made you feel that way. So that's on me." He clears his throat. "I'm sorry."

It feels like saying those two words took a lot out of him. I'm guessing Rowan Lancaster doesn't apologize for much.

"Are we arguing about who's at fault over last night? Because if we are, I have to take responsibility for encouraging you to come into my room."

He appears taken aback by what I said. "I was feeling vulnerable too. You got me to confess something I haven't admitted to anyone."

"Not even your best friend?"

Rowan shakes his head, his dark hair falling across his forehead. "Not sure if you've noticed yet, but I keep a lot of things to myself."

"I've noticed," I whisper, hating the flicker of hope that lights my chest. Maybe I could get him to share more with me.

His smile is faint, making that flicker in my chest grow. "I was thinking..."

"That sounds dangerous," I interrupt, teasing him.

"Yeah. It probably is. But maybe...we should each take on fifty percent of the burden from last night and call it even."

"That might be a good idea."

"Let's start over then." He pulls his hands out of his pockets and holds one out toward me. "Shake on it?"

I stare at his hand for a moment before lifting my gaze to his. "What exactly are we shaking on?"

"Resetting this...whatever it is we're doing this week."

"So you're basically admitting you don't know what we're doing either." There is something both reassuring and distressing in his admitting that.

"I don't. But I don't like that I upset you or hurt your feelings, Bells." His expression turns grave. "I'm sorry."

His second apology seems even more heartfelt. I can hear the sincerity in his voice. See it glowing in his eyes. He means it. And just like that, my heart cracks wide open, giving him all the room that he could ever need to slide right inside of it.

I take his offered hand and he yanks me toward him, slipping his arm around my shoulders and pressing his lips to my forehead, much like his dad did to his mom only minutes ago. I melt like the easy for Rowan Lancaster girl that I am.

"I'm an asshole," he murmurs against my temple.

"You are." I rest my hand against his chest, feeling his wildly beating heart beneath my palm. He's nervous. This boy is a constant surprise. "I'm sorry too."

"For stripping naked?"

I pull away slightly to stare into his eyes. "I don't know. Was that a bad thing?"

"It was an...unexpected thing." He's chuckling, and the sound warms my battered and bruised soul. "But it definitely wasn't a bad thing to witness."

"Let's just take this slow," I tell him, and his laughter dies. "We don't need to rush, do we? You said last night you didn't want a relationship."

"Is that what you want, Bells?"

"I...I don't know." I am a liar. I would say yes if he got on bended knee right now and asked me to marry him. I'm not even eighteen yet and I would run to the justice of the peace or whatever you call them and become his child bride. I am that enamored with this boy.

But I also don't know him like I thought I did. He believes he's peeling back my layers? I'm doing the same exact thing with him. There's so much more for me to discover about him, and then there's his family to consider too. I've not even been here for twenty-four hours and I'm already in love with all of them, especially his mother. She's so sweet. I feel bad that he ran to my defense and shut down her willingness to throw me a party. Yet there's also a part of me that loves that he did it because he could see I was uncomfortable.

It shows he pays attention to me, which doesn't happen very often. I'm mostly forgotten by everyone.

"I need to take a shower." I disentangle myself from his hold, immediately missing his warmth. A girl could get used to this sort of treatment, but that isn't all I want from Rowan. Earnest apologies and hugs and promises are nice but they don't mean anything if he can't follow through. And I know what it's like, dealing with someone like that. I've been promised lots of things throughout my life, only for those promises to almost always fall through.

Mainly from my parents.

Before I let Rowan back into my bed—I still can't believe he was in my bed—I want proof of his undying loyalty to me.

After all, I deserve the world.

TWENTY-ONE

ROWAN

I KEEP a respectable distance from Arabella because I think that's what she wants and also—I need it. I need to figure out what I'm doing with her. What we're doing with each other. My problem?

Every time she gets close, I can smell her. When our gazes meet, I'm reminded of the hazy glow I saw in her dark eyes last night when we kissed. And when I stare at her mouth for a fraction too long, I'm smacked with the urge to kiss her again.

And never stop.

It's dangerous, having her around. Why did I agree to my mother's suggestion again? I felt sorry for Bells. Imagining her stuck on campus bored out of her mind and with no one to talk to. I hated the idea of her alone. Despised it.

Now she's in my house, hanging out with my mom, laughing with my brother—and Beau has been a sullen little asshole since the moment we left campus so this feels major—and charming my dad. It's only Saturday night and she fits right in like she's been coming to my house for years during the holiday season. It's weird. It's also pretty great.

Terrifying. Absolutely, one hundred percent terrifying.

Dinner is in an hour and I'm in my room, hiding. From Bells, from my parents, from everyone because I feel awkward. I don't know how to act after last night, and while we had a good conversation earlier and she forgave me for pissing her off, I don't know where we stand. I asked for a reset and she agreed. We're taking it slow.

I can't forget the kiss or the sounds she made when my tongue first touched hers. The feeling of her soft body beneath mine. And then, when she got mad and stripped naked? That was a wild moment. One that is burned in my brain for all eternity. I want to see her naked again under better circumstances. Touch her everywhere with my hands and my mouth and my—

My phone rings, the distinct sound letting me know I'm getting a FaceTime call, and when I check to see who it is, my best friend's name flashes across the screen. I go ahead and answer it, leaning against my headboard as I wait for Callahan's face to appear. I hold my middle finger up to the camera as my greeting and when he finally appears, I see he's doing the same exact thing, revealing the giant grin on his face when he drops his hand.

"What's up, asshole?" he asks me with a laugh.

I stab my finger in the screen's direction one last time before I give it up. "Are you trying to rub it in that you're on vacation while I'm stuck here where it might snow tonight?"

He's sitting outside on a balcony and I can see swaying palm trees behind him and the sparkling blue ocean just beyond. Cal is wearing tropical print swim trunks and his skin is a faint red, his nose about three shades brighter. Someone forgot to apply enough sunscreen. "Snow? That sucks, dude."

"Tell me all about it. What's up?"

"Wanted to check in. See how things are going with your— guest." He lifts his brows in question, and all I can do is shake my head.

"Everything's fine." I clamp my mouth shut, not about to reveal all that happened last night. "We only got here yesterday."

"I realize that. Has she already won over your parents?"

How did he know? I keep my expression and my tone completely neutral. "They like her."

"I'm sure your mother *loves* her. I know how she is. This being the first time you've brought a girl home. Your mom is in heaven." Callahan's grin grows, if that's possible. "They're probably planning your wedding already."

"Shut up." I'm groaning, hating how accurate he is. "I don't plan on marrying her."

"Yet." Callahan laughs. "It's okay. You can admit it to me. You're into her."

My mind drifts. I *am* into her. It's hard to admit out loud but I am. "We're taking it slow."

"Who? You and Arabella? Seriously? I was just giving you shit." The shocked expression on my best friend's face is downright comical. "You're going to give this a try?"

"Yeah." I swallow hard. "You think it's a mistake?"

"No. Not at all. I say go for it."

I need to change the subject. All this talk of me and Arabella is making me sweat. "How's Mexico?"

"Beautiful. Hot. Lots of hot girls here too." He laughs. "Your sister seems like she's having a good time."

"I'm sure she is."

We make small talk and eventually Callahan ends the call because his dad lets him know they're going down to the pool. The one with the swim-up bar, Cal was sure to point out. Considering the legal drinking age in Mexico is eighteen, Callahan is having the time of his life getting drunk legally.

I decide to take a shower to look my best for dinner. For Arabella. The moment I step under the hot spray of water, my mind drifts, filled with thoughts of Bells naked. The perfect shape of her tits. Those hard little nipples. I didn't want to stare too long at her pussy but I have a faint, shadowy memory of it. It wasn't completely bare but it was framed by slender thighs. Her legs are long, and I can imagine her wrapping them around my hips when I slide inside her for the first time...

Opening my eyes, I glance down at my hard dick, curling my fingers around the base. I did this last night too. Jerking off to ease the tension that builds inside me whenever I'm around Arabella. Knowing what she looks like naked doesn't help my plight. Learning the taste of her lips doesn't either.

With a groan I lean against the cold tile wall, stroking my shaft. Losing myself in the sensation, imagining it's Arabella who's touching me. Encouraging me with softly spoken words and that mysterious smile on her face. She'd fall to her knees in front of me and part those lush lips, wrapping them around the head of my cock and pulling me deeper into her mouth. She'd suck and suck, her tongue dancing, her fingers gripping me tighter, a low moan sounding deep in her throat. She'd love every minute of this, her eyes sparkling with the knowledge that she's giving me so much pleasure.

Bells is a giver. I just know she is.

It only takes a few minutes accompanied by my vivid imagination before I'm coming in my hand. I bite my lower lip to restrain the groans that escape but the sound echoes against the tile walls and I wonder if anyone can hear me.

Fuck. I hope not.

TWENTY-TWO

ARABELLA

I'M in the middle of a clothing crisis when my phone rings. I check to see it's my mother and I ignore it, tearing through the clothes I hung up in my guest room closet, frantic to find just the right outfit. But nothing strikes me as appropriate. Not that this evening's meal is a formal affair. Rowan's mother reassured me I could show up in sweats and no one would bat an eyelash but just the idea of me doing that fills me with horror.

I love a good matching sweat outfit but to wear something like that for dinner with the Lancasters? Absolutely not.

My phone rings again, and exasperated, I answer it rudely, which is so out of character I don't even know what possessed me. "What?"

"There you are! Darling, I have wonderful, amazing news to share with you!"

So typical of my mother to ignore my rude tone, and for once, I'm grateful for it. "What is it?"

If she tells me she got last-minute plane tickets to Hong Kong for me, I'm going to flip out. Now that I'm at the Lancaster estate, that's the last place I want to go.

"Remember when I told you I had that friend who works for a certain prestigious jewelry atelier?"

"Mmm, hmm." I don't remember that at all but I'm going to pretend I do.

"Well, after many months of going back and forth, he's brought me an opportunity. For you." She pauses for only a second. "An internship with the jeweler. In Paris!"

I go completely still, my fingers curling around my phone so tight, it hurts. "What did you just say?"

"I know you used to enjoy making jewelry designs here and there, and when I became friendly with the creative director at the jewelry house, I started asking him about jobs there. It is a very tight-knit working space and they don't allow any old person to start working there," Mother explains.

"Okay." I draw the word out, gobsmacked. I adore that word. It's one Americans don't use often enough and they should. It's so apt for how I'm feeling in this very moment. "How do they even know I like to draw jewelry designs?"

"I showed him your designs, and he showed them to everyone else."

My heart goes into freefall. "Mother. Some of those designs were—"

"Amazing? I know, darling. I saw them. Your talent is spectacular, and I'm surprised you never pushed us to help you pursue it further."

Private, is the word I wanted to use. And old. But I remain quiet, remembering how I used to enjoy designing jewelry and she would encourage me. Little lockets and charms and pendants. Intricate bracelets dotted with precious stones in floral designs. It was a fun hobby but eventually I gave up because of my mother's obvious shock and faint disgust at my possible career choice.

"You want to work?" She had visibly shuddered, her shoulders shimmying as she shook her head in tandem. "That's so...beneath you."

Yes, that's what she said to me. Out loud. Talk about devastated. I was thirteen or fourteen and absolutely crushed by her response. I never brought it up to her again. As a matter of fact, I gave up designing jewelry and selling it to my new friends when I first started at Lancaster Prep because of what she said and how her words made me feel. Plus, it was just a phase. And now here she is, bringing it up to me like she's always been supportive, and actually doing something about it.

Deciding not to bring those memories up, I choose to be grateful instead because I'm a bigger person and I refuse to be petty in this moment. "What jewelry house are you referring to?"

When she says the name out loud, I suck in a surprised breath, nearly choking on it. Okay, that jewelry house is huge. Well-known and of the highest quality.

"Are you sure they want *me* to intern for them? I've never done this sort of thing before in my life."

"They're sure. You'll be an apprentice to one of the most prestigious designers there." I can hear the giddiness in her voice. "Aren't you excited? Isn't this amazing?"

"I'm...finding it hard to believe it's even true." I give up on searching through my clothes and collapse on a nearby chair, my brain going over our conversation. "I don't even know how you did this."

"I have my ways," she says, sounding mysterious. "Anything for you, darling."

My suspicions rise at her comment because it's a rare moment when she wants to do something for me. Everything my mother does is typically for herself. "When does this internship start?"

"January! Right after the new year. I thought it might be fun to spend the holidays in Paris. What do you think? We could stay at The Ritz and go shopping..."

Her words turn into a buzzing noise that I can't decipher, my thoughts overtaking everything else. January? I'm still in school. Christmas in Paris? That sounds like a dream and I would've jumped on the idea before.

Before this new side of Rowan. Before coming to his family's home and being so readily embraced by all of them.

"I still have school in January," I remind my mother, interrupting her. "I'm graduating in May."

"You have enough credits to graduate early. I've already checked," she reassures me.

"I do?" I mean, I sort of knew that but I didn't want to leave early because where would I go? I have no one to count on.

"Yes. Why stay at Lancaster Prep when you could be learning from one of the most prestigious jewelry designers in the world."

She has a point. "But I'll miss out on all of the senior things," I say, my voice small.

"What senior things?"

"Ditch day. Prom. Graduation." There are more special occasions throughout the rest of our senior year but I can't think of any others.

"Well." Her tone turns snotty, I can tell by just hearing her say that singular word. "If you want me to turn down this position for you because you don't want to miss out on senior ditch day, then I'll let them know."

"No." I clamp my lips shut, hating how I fell for her plan. She knew I'd protest. "I want to do it. I'll do it."

We're both quiet for a moment and I wonder if she's waiting for me to change my mind. But I won't. She's right. I need to take the opportunity and do this. I reach for my locket, the very one I designed for myself and had my mother's family jeweler design for me, worrying it with my fingers. Everything my mother is dumping on me is sending me into a mental spiral, but stroking the lightly etched front eases my anxiety.

"Excellent," Mother finally says. "Your father and I both think this is the perfect opportunity for you to further yourself."

"Instead of college?" I applied but only out of obligation to my guidance counselor. She told me I was smart and could have my pick of universities to attend, and I went along with her suggestions, applying to a variety of colleges, not caring about a single one of them.

"Darling, you don't want to go. You've been telling me that since you were ten."

"I have?" I don't remember ever saying that to her.

"Yes. Higher education isn't for you. You've always stressed that, and I think studying with a jeweler and learning their techniques is what you need."

"How long is this apprenticeship supposed to last?"

"As long as everything works out, it's for two years."

Two years. I'll be twenty when it's over. An entirely different person after living that long in Paris. Will I make friends? Have a boyfriend? A gorgeous Parisian man who whispers dirty French words in my ear while he slowly fucks me every night in my luxurious apartment my parents pay for?

I wrinkle my nose at the thought. God, that sounds awful.

"Does that deter you at all? The length of your apprenticeship?" Mother asks me.

"Not at all," I say, my voice calm. I sit up straighter. "That sounds perfect."

I ARRIVE in the formal dining room ten minutes early to find there's no one waiting and the table isn't set. Confused, I glance around, filled with the sudden and horrible feeling that maybe they're playing a trick on me. Maybe they left.

"We're eating in the kitchen tonight."

I whirl around to find Rowan standing there, dashing as ever despite the fact that he's wearing a faded pair of jeans and—oh my God—a gray hoodie. Sweats. To dinner.

Glancing down at myself, I take in the simple charcoal gray

sweater dress I chose to wear tonight, my legs bare and my feet clad in white Chanel sneakers. "I'm overdressed."

When I look at his face once more, it seems he's using every bit of restraint he can come up with not to crack a smile. "You're always overdressed, Bells."

I offer him a curtsy as my answer. "Where's the kitchen?"

"This way." He offers his arm to me like he's a true gentleman from the Regency and I take it, letting him lead me through the gorgeous house, neither of us saying a word. We haven't spent much time together today. Rowan hung out with his brother while I was either with his mom or wandering around the house by myself.

When we eventually end up in the kitchen, we find his family already seated around the round table.

"There you two are!" His mother rises to her feet, clasping her hands together. "I'll start serving right away."

"Sorry we were late." I settle into the closest open chair, right next to Beau. Rowan sits on the other side of me. "I was mistaken on where dinner was tonight."

"Sorry about that." Wren smiles at me. She keeps insisting I call her Wren instead of Mrs. Lancaster so I'm trying it out in my head. "We're going out tomorrow if that helps."

"I appreciate you letting me know." I duck my head, grabbing the cloth napkin folded in the center of my plate and drop it into my lap.

The conversation is quiet, everyone talking about their day and what they did. I don't add much to it, tempted to mention the phone call from my mother, but I don't want to look like I'm bragging. Plus, I'm not quite sure how I'm going to explain the situation to Rowan. Will he be supportive? Glad to be rid of me? Sad that I'm leaving? I don't know.

If I'm being real with myself, I don't want to know his reaction. What if it's not the one I want?

It's when their cook—a lovely woman named Marilee—takes away our salad plates that Rowan leans in toward me to murmur, "Are you all right?"

I pull away slightly to look into his eyes, noting the concern I see there. I put on a fake smile. "I'm fine. Why do you ask?"

"You're not very talkative." He pauses for only a moment. "And you've always got something to say."

"I'm just enjoying spending time with your family," I admit, which is partially true. I don't want to tell him I have a lot on my mind because then he'll ask what it is, and I don't want to explain myself. "Though I am a little tired."

"You should go to bed early then." The panic I see flare in his beautiful green eyes is almost comical. "And I'm not saying that because I want to sneak into your room later."

"What did you just say?"

His mother just overheard him say that. And I am. Horrified.

"I was kidding, Mom." I can practically feel the desperation radiating from Rowan as he tries to play it off.

"Are you sneaking into your guest's room in the middle of the night?" And now his father has pulled out the stern dad voice.

"Absolutely not," Rowan says with such conviction I could almost believe him. Almost.

The problem is, I know the truth.

Beau snickers, shutting up almost immediately when his father glares at him. I curl my hands into my lap, twisting the cloth napkin in my fingers and I put on a brave smile.

"Rowan didn't sneak into my room last night," I tell his parents, my voice calm. I am an excellent liar. I have been for years because I'm always having to mask my real feelings in front of certain people. Like my parents.

Like Rowan.

His parents' matching intensity is aimed right at me and I don't even squirm. I just keep my expression neutral, making sure I don't look at Rowan for fear the guilt will cross both of our faces.

"Make sure he doesn't," Crew Lancaster finally says, his deep voice giving off *I don't mess around* vibes. "There's a lock on your door, Arabella. Use it."

"Yes, sir," I murmur, ducking my head once more. I feel bad, like I did something awful, which I did. I lied to Rowan's parents, and I lie to my parents all the time, especially my mother. Not like she cares or notices. Nor would I ever get in trouble for doing it either. My mother is too oblivious to pay me any attention, even when I'm doing something bad.

With Rowan's parents, I feel like my lie would disappoint them if I ever revealed it. And they would punish me and Rowan for betraying their trust. I'd have to agree with them. I'm tempted to put my arms out at this very moment, fully expecting them to put handcuffs on my wrists and cart me off to juvenile hall.

If this happened later in the week, I'd deserve full blown jail and oh my God, I'm devastated. I rest my hand on my chest for a moment, trying to calm my racing heart when I feel it. Rowan's hand settling on my thigh and giving it a reassuring squeeze.

Okay. Maybe lying to his parents wasn't so bad after all.

TWENTY-THREE

ROWAN

I'M PRETTY sure something is wrong with Arabella, but she's not talking. And that's the problem. She's not her usual, nonstop talkative self and that's odd. She's always got something to say and has no problem saying it either.

What's her problem?

And it started before we had to lie to my parents, meaning that has nothing to do with her somber mood. It's not like I can ask her what's up at the dinner table. I'm sure whatever is bothering her, she's trying to keep private. Or maybe nothing is bothering her and it's a me problem.

Wait a minute. Maybe I am the problem and I'm the one who's bothering her.

Shit.

I'm in a terrible mood for the rest of dinner, despite the fact that Marilee made my favorite dessert—a giant slab of warm chocolate chip cookie with vanilla ice cream on top, melted to perfection. I take a few bites before I push my bowl away, not bothering to acknowledge the look Mom sends my way when she sees me do it.

"Not hungry?" Mom asks me in that soft voice that always takes me back to my childhood. When she'd ask if I was okay after a rough day and she could sense my unease. She's always had excellent mother's intuition and I don't want to trigger it tonight.

"Dinner was great. I ate too much." I pat my stomach for extra emphasis.

"Oh, Marilee, did you hear what Row said about your dinner?" Mom calls with a laugh.

"I did," Marilee says, beaming at me. Her favorite thing is feeding everyone, especially me. "Silly boy, not saving room for dessert."

I can feel my cheeks heat from her calling me a silly boy and I chance a glance in Arabella's direction, embarrassed. I love coming home but the problem with bringing someone who's never been here before—especially a female someone—is that the people closest to me can sometimes treat me like I'm still a little boy. Which sucks.

Bells is not even looking in my direction. She's too busy tapping away at her phone, texting someone. Who could it be?

I'm immediately filled with jealousy and that's some straight up bullshit. I have no right to be jealous of whoever she's talking to. She has a life outside of me. Hell, I've pushed her away more often than not and maybe she's done with me. Maybe she's being polite and merely tolerating my ass while she's stuck here for the rest of the week and—

"I hate to do this but I'm beat." Arabella rises to her feet and stretches her arms above her head, the hem of her sweater dress rising and showing off her bare thighs. Those thighs have been fantasy material for the last twenty-four hours, and seeing them in the flesh, close enough to touch, doesn't help matters. "I'm going to retire to my room for the evening."

"Aw, Arabella. I hope that you're feeling okay?" My mother frowns, her concern for Bells etched into her features. Mom already loves her but that's Mom's biggest problem. She falls fast and hard for anyone us kids bring around, eager to welcome them to the family and accept them as one of her own.

She has a big heart, and even Dad says it sometimes bites her in the ass.

"Oh, I'm feeling fine. I'm just full. And sleepy." Arabella even yawns for good measure, covering her mouth with her fist before she lets it drop. The sweet smile on her face would trick anyone. She looks perfectly fine but I know, I just fucking know, she's not. "I'll see you all in the morning."

After everyone, save for me, murmurs good night to her, Arabella exits the dining room, taking her delicious scent with her. I immediately miss her presence, but Dad doesn't give me long to think about her leaving. He waits approximately two minutes before he starts in on me.

"Rowan, we know you're eighteen years old and we understand what that's like. At least, I do more than anyone else at this table. But if you're actually sneaking into that sweet girl's room at night to do—I don't need any of the details—you need to stop."

I sink into my chair, wishing I'd left with Bells. Thank God he didn't launch into this speech with her still here.

"And with that, I'm out." Beau jumps to his feet and tosses his napkin in the center of his empty bowl. The kid ate every drop of his dessert and his dinner too. "Thanks, Mom. Thanks, Marilee."

Before either woman can say a word in response, my little brother is gone. The lucky fucker.

"I didn't sneak into her room," I insist, wondering if my lies are as convincing as Arabella's. She's great at it. "Like I said, I was just kidding around with her."

Dad stares at me, his gaze unwavering, and it takes all of the control I've got not to squirm. The man can be intimidating when he has to, and lucky for me, I haven't done too much to piss him off over the years. "She's a nice girl. Seems a little— fragile, if you ask me. Even a tad naïve? And I don't want to witness you taking advantage of her while you're both here this week."

"Take *advantage* of her?" I think of Bells basically daring me to sneak into her room. How she's already had sex with Bentley Saffron Jones—five times, I might add—and stripped naked in front of me last night because I made her angry. And he thinks *I* want to take advantage of her? "That's not what I'm doing."

"I hope not," Mom adds with a soft sigh. "She's the sweetest and your father is right. She does have this air of fragility around her."

I actually scoff. I can't help myself. "She's probably one of the toughest girls at our school. Nothing seems to ever get her down. She's always smiling, always friendly to everyone, even those who don't deserve her kindness. Bells told me she has shit parents who don't give a damn about her, which sucks. There are some girls who are always trying to intimidate her or make her feel bad, but I know they're really just jealous. And you should see some of the outfits she wears to school every day. She loves the attention. Does that sound like a fragile person to you?"

My parents go quiet, sharing a look before Mom speaks. "Have you ever considered that maybe she's seeking attention any way she can get it because she doesn't receive any from her terrible parents?"

Huh. There's a theory I never thought of before.

"Your mother has a point. Just—be careful with her, Row. You might believe she's strong, but is she really?" Dad's brows shoot up in question, and all I can do is shrug, trying to play it off but damn.

Damn.

The moment I can leave the kitchen, I'm out, racing through the house. Running up the stairs, sprinting down the corridor until I'm standing in front of Arabella's room, rapping my knuckles on the door in three short knocks. She doesn't respond, and being impatient, I yank my phone out of my pocket and send her a quick text.

Are you asleep?

With my luck, she is.

I wait, leaning against the wall, trying to scroll social media to occupy my mind but all I can think about is her. Fragile, devastated Arabella. Is that who she really is? Am I a blind asshole who's so wrapped up in my own lustful thoughts that I can't see her for who she actually is? If that's the case...

I'm a complete dick.

My phone buzzes with a text, clearing my brain fog.

Bells: **I'm taking a bath.**

I'm typing out a response when she sends another text.

Bells: **Did you want to talk to me?**

Me: **Yes.**

Bells: **Come in. The door is unlocked.**

I glance around the empty hall, breaking out in a sweat at the thought of getting caught slipping into her room. My dad would put my balls in a sling if he saw me doing this.

Bells: **I put too much bubble bath in the water and I'm drowning in it. You won't be able to see a thing if you're worried about that.**

Bells: **In case you're now disappointed knowing you can't see a thing, maybe we should talk later.**

Fuck that. I'm taking my opportunity now.

Testing the handle, the door opens with ease just as she promised, and I slip inside, shutting it carefully before I turn the lock. I move through the room, taking note of the clothes lying all over every available surface. A pile of shoes makes a little mountain at the foot of the bed and Arabella's scent lingers in the air, sweet as candy. She's been here for a little over twenty-four hours and the room is an absolute mess—*wrecked by Arabella* should be her tagline.

The adjoining bathroom door is ajar, and I can hear her singing along with a song that's playing. Sounds like Taylor Swift. I'm not a fan but my sister listened to her ad nauseum when we were younger and still does. I've picked up some of the lyrics by osmosis.

I pause in the doorway, my gaze finding Arabella sitting in the massive tub, her back to me. She wasn't lying about the bubbles. The tub is filled with them, even covering her shoulders. I can't see anything, just as she said.

What a fucking disappointment.

"I know you're lurking in the doorway, Rowan. Stop staring like a pervert and come talk to me," she calls.

Exhaling loud enough for her to hear my aggravation, I enter the bathroom and don't stop walking until I'm standing on the other side of the tub, turning to face her. Her dark hair is piled on top of her head in a messy bun, wavy tendrils curling around her damp face, which is all I can see thanks to the bubbles. I can see her neck too, that heart-shaped locket resting in the hollow of her throat. She never takes it off and I wonder why.

"You wanted to talk?" she asks, arching a delicate brow.

"I wanted to make sure you're okay." When she frowns, I forge on. "You said you were tired but you were lying."

She blinks at me. "How did you figure out I was lying? Do you think your parents realized it?"

I shake my head. "They don't know you like I do, Bells."

Her smile is slow. "Well, that's probably best—or is it? I haven't decided yet."

"Are you okay?" I ask the question again because I need to know. Did I hurt her feelings? Did my parents? Is she miserable here?

"I'm fine," is her glib answer. The tilt of her chin, the way she's watching me with that impassive expression on her beautiful face is telling me otherwise.

"You're still lying."

She lets the haughty expression fall and her arms slice through the wall of bubbles when she lifts them above her head, scattering said bubbles everywhere, most of them landing in her hair. "Stop trying to figure me out, Rowan. It's not polite, calling someone out straight to their face."

I settle in on the edge of the tub, leaning forward as I keep my gaze on hers. "You don't need to lie to me, Bells. Drop the pretense and tell me what's bothering you."

Her shoulders sag, the bubbles sinking in around her face, and when one floats in front of her, she blows it out of the way with pursed lips. "My mother called me."

"What did she call you?" I do my best to keep from smiling, trying to lighten the mood.

She rolls her eyes, her lips curling in the smallest smile. "She had some—news for me that I should be happy about, but I don't think I am."

The confusion in her voice fills me with panic. And I never panic. I didn't even panic when I got knocked on my ass and broke my ankle on the football field. I was pissed more than anything else. But my heart is racing and my mouth is dry. Why the hell do I feel like this news is going to be bad? "What kind of news?"

The music ends, Taylor finished singing about whatever asshole broke her heart this time around and the room is filled with silence.

Arabella studies me for a moment, quiet. Assessing. Like she might be afraid to reveal whatever her mom said to her. I keep my expression neutral, wanting her to see I'm open to what she's about to reveal but there's that tiny part of me that's clenched up tight. Worried as fuck.

"She got me an apprenticeship with a world-renowned jewelry house," she admits, her voice soft.

I let her words sink in. This sounds like a good thing and some of my worry eases. "That's—amazing."

"I suppose." She shrugs, her slender shoulders rising from the thick bubbles.

"Is that something you want to do?"

"When I was younger, it was everything I could've ever wanted. It's a well-known jeweler. My mother said she knows the creative director—how, I'm not sure—but she does buy a lot of jewelry from them so maybe that's why? It doesn't matter. Anyway, she asked him for a favor, and he offered me an internship to study with their team of designers."

Sounds like a major opportunity. "Will it be in New York?"

She slowly shakes her head. "In Paris. That's where their atelier is located."

My stomach sinks. Paris. That's far. "When would you start the internship?"

Arabella presses her lips together, her eyes somehow growing even bigger than normal as she watches me before she whispers, "January."

TWENTY-FOUR

ARABELLA

THE BATHROOM IS QUIET, save for the faint ringing in my ears as I wait for Rowan to say something. Anything. He doesn't respond at all. Just sits there on the tub's ledge, big and broody and unbearably handsome. The sudden image of him falling into the tub and settling right over me while he begs for me to never leave him again fills my brain, and breathlessly, I await his response.

"January?" He visibly swallows, the only telltale sign that he might be affected by my revelation. "You'd leave school early."

"I wouldn't be missing much." I lift one shoulder but I'm sure he can't see it thanks to all the bubbles it's buried under. "Just prom and graduation. Oh, and senior ditch day."

"Ditch day isn't that big of a deal."

"No, I suppose it's not." My voice is hollow, echoing in my head.

"I thought about leaving school early," he says, as nonchalant as ever. For once, I wish he was chalant. Full of big, overwhelming emotions that would leave me smugly confident about the way he feels about me. "I have enough credits to graduate early."

"Same."

He contemplates me, his dark hair falling across his forehead as it's wont to do. How would he react if I rose up on my knees and pushed the hair out of his eyes? Would his gaze drift downward, watching the bubbles slowly slide down my naked body? Would he touch me? After my reaction only twenty-four hours ago, he's probably terrified to lay a single finger on me, and I only have myself to blame.

"You can't pass up this opportunity if that's what you want to do," he finally says, his voice firm. "I didn't know you wanted to be a jewelry designer."

"It was always just a silly dream, especially when I was younger. Definitely not something I shared with anyone." It hasn't been my dream for years, that's why this offer feels so unexpected.

And odd. Terribly odd.

"I'm not just anyone, Bells." His deep voice sweeps over my skin, settling right between my thighs where I begin to throb. Not that anything's going to happen. Knowing us, I'll say something and ruin it. Or he will. We're both pretty shit at this... whatever it is we're doing.

"Right." I put on a blinding smile, hating myself for what I'm about to say. "You're an almighty Lancaster. Why wouldn't I confess my deepest, darkest secrets to you?"

He leans back slightly, taken aback by what I said, no doubt. "I wasn't meaning that. I was talking about us being..."

"Being what? *Friends?*" I let my smile fade the slightest bit. "I've never had friendly thoughts about you, Rowan."

His brows draw together in adorable confusion. I've got it so bad for this blind, dumb boy. "I don't believe that."

"No? What if I told you all of my thoughts involving you and me were absolutely, undoubtedly filthy?"

Sometimes, I wish I wasn't so impulsive. I just blurt out whatever's on my mind and damn the consequences.

Rowan blinks once, finally swiping the hair away from his face. "Is that why you're in the bath, Bells? Because I make you feel dirty?"

I burst out laughing, surprised by his question. Sort of turned on by it too. "Yes, Rowan. I'm a bad, dirty girl who needs to wash away all her sins."

He does the craziest thing, stretching his arm out, those long fingers dipping into the bubbles. He scoops out a rather large amount, his fingers dipping in the water, the edge of his sleeve getting wet. "How many times would I have to do that until all the bubbles were gone, hmm? Want to take a guess?"

"Are you trying to see me naked, Rowan Lancaster?"

"I already have, Arabella Huntley Thomas." He lifts a single brow. "What's your middle name?"

"What's yours?"

"I asked first." He scoops another handful of bubbles, pushing them out of the way, and I lift my knee, the water swirling around me. I can't believe I told him to come in here. But then again, I can. I have nothing to lose and everything to gain from this week with Rowan. It feels like so many things are on the line, especially now with my mother's unexpected call.

Maybe I could give myself freely to Rowan. Mind, body and soul. After all, we'd only have a short amount of time together before I'd leave for Paris if I do take this apprenticeship. He wouldn't be able to break my heart in six weeks, would he?

Impossible. That's not enough time to suffer from a broken heart. Look at how I've held it together around him the last few years. I'm a pro at dealing with constant rejection from Rowan. The majority of the time, he doesn't even realize he's rejecting me. Utterly clueless, as usual.

"Margaret," I finally answer in the barest whisper. "It was my grandmother's name."

"The royal one?"

I nod. "She was a marchioness."

"A what?"

"A marchioness. It's one level below a duchess, which is one level below a princess." A laugh escapes me. "I am a font of knowledge when it comes to useless royal facts."

"I'll have to remember that," he tells me with the gravest expression I think I've ever seen on his face.

"Like I said, it's useless. Besides, you know everything about American royalty, since your family is part of it." I level my gaze upon him once more. "Your middle name, Rowan? Are you going to share?"

"Reginald," Rowan admits, that familiar glower appearing on his face. "And don't ever repeat that."

I cover my mouth with my hand, hiding the gasp that escaped. "*Reginald?*"

The glower becomes more glower-y, if that's even a word. "I told you to never repeat it."

I drop my hand, making bubbles fly everywhere. "Rowan Reginald Lancaster?"

"It's my grandfather's name." His lips twist into a fierce grimace. "It's awful."

"I absolutely adore it," I say without hesitation.

"You're lying."

"I'm not." I shake my head. "I think it's cute."

"It is definitely not cute, Arabella Margaret Huntley Thomas." He actually chuckles. "That is a mouthful."

"Oh, you don't even know so you can't actually say that." I am smirking. He is smirking too.

"Did you just make a dirty joke?"

"More like an innuendo." I sit up straighter, my shoulders rising through the bubbles, though they still cling to my chest. My nipples are hard both from the cold air and his closeness, and I wonder what he might do if I cupped my breasts in an offering to him. Would he take me up on it or run screaming from the room?

I have a feeling he'd take me up on it. And if that doesn't make my core clench in anticipation, I don't know what else could.

"I got a lecture from my parents about you," he says, completely changing the subject.

"No." I rest my hand against my chest in mock horror, though I do feel bad. "What did they say?"

"That I shouldn't take advantage of you. My father brought up the sneaking into your room comment again." He leans back against the wall, his gaze dropping as he fiddles with his wet sleeve. "I wish they would've never heard that."

"It was a close call." I'm quiet for a moment, watching him. "Think they bought what I said?"

"Definitely. I didn't know you were such a good liar, Bells."

"I'm very talented in hiding my true feelings."

"Oh yeah?"

I nod and lean forward, still wondering if he could fit in the tub with me. It would be cramped but I think it's possible and would be so worth it. "I'm a mystery wrapped inside a riddle."

One side of his mouth lifts in a closed-mouth smile. "That's one way to describe you."

"Do you think it's accurate?"

"Definitely. Sometimes I can't figure you out."

"Good." I go on pure instinct and rise up on my knees like I envisioned only moments ago. The water slides down my exposed body, the bubbles clinging precariously to my chest. The bath water covers me from about the hips down but I suppose it doesn't matter since he saw everything last night. "My goal is to always leave you confused."

"Bells..." His voice drifts, his gaze raking along my body, lingering on the most important spots and making my skin tingle. "Those bubbles aren't going to keep you covered for long."

"Maybe I don't want them to." My voice is the barest whisper, my heart beating out of control in my throat. "Maybe you should touch me, Rowan."

His gaze lifts to mine, his hands remaining too far away from my body. "I thought you said we were moving too fast."

Knowing I could leave Lancaster Prep—Rowan—in January, now I feel like I'm not moving fast enough. "A girl is allowed to change her mind."

His gaze shifts downward again, and I can feel the bubbles sliding down my chest, exposing me. My own words leave me feeling exposed too. He's right, I did say we were moving too fast and we needed a reset, but my emotions are almost frantic with the need to know what it's like to be with this boy in any capacity possible. Whether it's more kissing or touching, I'll take whatever I can get. I would go on my knees for him, and I wouldn't do that for just anyone. I would also love to see him fall to his knees for me, but I can't imagine it. I'm the giver in this situation and he's the taker, and I'm okay with it.

I am.

"Are you fragile, Arabella?"

The softly worded question leaves me reeling and I fall back on my haunches, the water splashing all around me. I don't like that word. Fragile? It makes me feel weak. "No." I raise my voice. "I'm not."

"I didn't think so." He shakes his head once, and the next thing I know his hand is on my cheek, cradling the side of my face, and I lean into it, inhaling his delicious scent. The rough feeling of his fingers on my face as they slide along my skin, tracing a path I try my hardest to figure out. "You should get out of the tub. The water is getting cold."

"You don't want to join me?"

"I wouldn't fit."

"I bet you would if I sat on your lap," I suggest.

"You sit on my lap and God knows what might happen."

"Only good things," I say, my voice solemn.

"Things you'd want to happen?"

"Stop questioning everything and make a move, Rowan. I never figured you'd be so cautious." I paste on a smile to ease the sting of my words.

His hand drops from my face and for one breathless moment, I believed all was lost. I pushed him away with my impatience and he's leaving. But no. Instead, he reaches for my hand and rises to his feet, causing me to do the same. His grip tightens on mine when I wobble, the base of the tub slick, and he tilts his head to the side.

"You good?"

I nod and he lets go of my hand to reach for a towel hanging from the heated rack, shaking it out and holding it open for me. I gasp when he wraps the towel around my body and lifts me out of the tub, impressing me with his strength.

That's when I realize he isn't wearing his boot. I don't think he's been wearing it today at all, and I'm surprised his mother hasn't scolded him about it. Not that I want to think about his mom in this very moment but...

"You're not wearing your boot," I point out.

He grins, looking pleased with himself. "That's the first time you've noticed, huh. I haven't had it on all day. My parents haven't said a word about it."

"You're bad." I lightly slap at the front of his hoodie, marveling at the warm, solid strength of him beneath the soft cotton. Ugh, I'd love to strip him naked and kiss him all over his chest. Maybe lick his nipples—would he hate that? Or love it? Rain kisses all over the flat plane of his stomach before I shifted down lower. I've never really given a boy a blowjob before—I tried with you-know-who but he pushed me away and said he couldn't stand the idea of his penis being in my mouth, direct quote.

I shove all thoughts of him out of my brain too because I don't need to taint the night with those memories.

Once we're in the bedroom, Rowan sets me on my feet and I can't help but notice how careful he is with me. As if he does believe I'm fragile, and maybe that's not such a bad thing. The people closest to me in my life have zero regard for my feelings, save for the one who's standing in front of me.

My heart swells and I swallow hard, fighting off the over-whelming emotion that threatens to swarm. It doesn't help that he's drying me off with the thick, cozy towel that smells of lavender. I close my eyes when I feel his hands press against my chest. My stomach. Always keeping it respectful, my Rowan.

I can't help the smile that curves my lips at thinking of him as mine. Maybe he is. At least for a little while.

When he tucks the towel closer around my body, his head descends, his mouth brushing against my neck before he whispers, "Are you cold?"

I shake my head. "No."

"You're shivering." His lips move against my ear, causing me to break out in gooseflesh all over. "You've got goosebumps."

Even on my neck. My chest. Everywhere. I can feel them along with the tiny hairs on my body standing straight up. "It's your fault. You're being so nice. Taking care of me. No one—"

I stop talking, embarrassed. I shouldn't say it. He really will believe I'm fragile. A sad little girl in a big mean world.

"No one what?" he asks after a beat of silence. He slips his arms around my waist and hauls me to him, as close as I can get. Despite the towel around me, I feel naked and exposed and raw. I don't like it.

"No one ever really takes care of me," I finally admit, hating how scratchy my voice is. "I've always had to rely on myself."

Rowan goes still, and I wait, my heart in my throat, my head bent down so I can't look at him. Preparing myself for rejection. These are the things a girl should never admit to a boy she likes. I don't want to look too dependent or needy, though I swear I wouldn't be. I'm just being honest with him.

His hand touches my jaw, fingers slipping beneath my chin and with the gentlest pressure he encourages me to lift my head, our gazes meeting. I see nothing but tenderness in his eyes, something I've never noticed before and I've stared into those familiar green eyes a lot over the years. I part my lips, ready to say something when he speaks first.

"If you need me, Bells, you can count on me." His gaze takes on a fierce gleam that's difficult to look away from. "I promise."

TWENTY-FIVE

ARABELLA

IF HE KEEPS SAYING things like that, I'll never want to leave his side. Fuck Paris and my once-in-a-lifetime opportunity. This is a once-in-a-lifetime moment, being with Rowan.

"Are you ever going to kiss me again?" I ask, because sometimes a girl has to ask for what she wants.

His head dips and his mouth settles on mine, soft and sweet. A simple press of his lips, mine parting, eager for more, but he takes his time, kissing me over and over again. One of his large hands rests on my hip while the other is still tucked beneath my chin, keeping me in place, his thumb rubbing along my jaw. He touches his tongue to the corner of my mouth, streaking it across my lower lip and I dart my tongue out to touch his, earning a groan from him before he kisses me with more force.

Our tongues tangle and glide, teasingly soft and then with more pressure. He slips his arm around my waist, pulling me closer to him and I can feel his erection, hard against my belly. I wind my arms around his neck, diving my fingers into his soft hair and the movement causes my towel to fall to the floor in a heap. Leaving me completely naked.

We don't even pause in our kissing. No, it becomes even more intense between us, his hand cupping my face, his other hand sliding over one butt cheek. I moan into his mouth, wishing those magical fingers were stroking me between my legs but talk about moving fast.

Okay, what am I protesting? I want to move fast. I want all of it. I'm like a greedy little whore who's been shown what being with a boy you actually care about really feels like. And the greedy little whore buried deep inside me wants it all. Everything Rowan could possibly give me.

A squeal escapes me when I feel his hands slip under my ass and haul me up. I have no choice but to wrap my legs around his hips, our mouths still fused as he leads me over to the bed. He stumbles over the pile of shoes I left practically in the middle of the room, and I break the kiss first, my eyes cracking open to find he's already watching me.

"I could've killed us," he murmurs, his lips curved in a smirk.

"I'll direct you." I point. "The bed is right there."

He doesn't move.

"That's where you were taking me, right?" Deciding to incentivize the moment, I bury my face in his neck and start kissing and licking him there, his skin rough with stubble. Ugh, I love it. He's so manly, so big and strong as he hauls me around the bedroom. His hands are gripping my butt, his fingers close to where I want them the most and my God, I'm so wet, I can feel it. Am practically dripping, I'm so aroused.

"Rowan." I lift my face away from his neck and frown at him. "You're wasting time."

"I uh—I don't have any condoms." His cheeks turn the faintest red and oh, he's so cute. I wish I had my phone so I could take a photo and capture this moment forever. Instead, I'll have to store it in my memory bank and pull it out later when I'm feeling sad and alone in Paris, missing my Rowan.

"We can do plenty of things without condoms," I remind him, shifting in his arms and rubbing against him. Can he feel how wet I am? How hard my nipples are? I know he's reacting since I can feel his stiff dick beneath his jeans so yes. I'm affecting him.

He grins, and the sight of it takes my breath away. "You're right. Lots of things."

Without warning he deposits me on the bed and I almost scream when my body bounces on the mattress, I'm so surprised. My loose bun flops in front of my face and I push my hair out of my eyes just in time to catch him about to pull his hoodie off, but something stops him.

The giant wet spot on the front of his sweatshirt. Considering he dried me off most thoroughly, I know how that spot got there, and it isn't from water.

"Did you do this?" He points at the spot.

"No, you did. That's how hot you've made me." Oh, listen to me! Who am I right now?

Rowan makes an obvious statement. "You're wet."

Duh.

Lord, save me from my dirty thoughts, but he just yanked his sweatshirt off, revealing he was wearing nothing underneath it, and if I was wet before, I am positively drenched now because the man—not a boy, he is a man—has broad shoulders and developed pecs with the tiniest bit of dark hair in between them and a washboard stomach. Six-pack abs that I want to lick.

"Want to see?" I ask, my voice hoarse as I scramble across the bed so I can rest my elbows on the pillows behind me, my knees bent and feet firmly planted on the mattress. Slowly, like I've been practicing for this moment my entire life, I spread my legs, offering him a glimpse of my pussy.

His gaze is fixed on the very wet spot between my thighs, and without thought I drift my fingers down my front. Along the valley of my stomach and lower, past the little bit of pubic hair I have—I'm a girl who waxes but I don't like to be stripped completely bare—until I'm touching wet, hot flesh. I brush my index finger across my swollen clit and suck in a breath because oh my God, that felt good, and what makes it even better?

The hungry way Rowan is watching me. How his fingers flex into a fist before straightening out. His control is slipping, and I love it because I'm the one who makes him feel like that. I'm the one he wants.

I slide my fingers through all that sticky wetness before I hold my hand out toward him in an offering. "Want to taste?"

Rowan doesn't hesitate. Next thing I know, he's on me, his fingers curled around my wrist, holding my hand in place as he pulls my index finger into his mouth. He sucks it clean, his tongue swirling, his gaze never leaving mine and I've lost all ability to think, to speak, to function at the heated gleam I see in his eyes.

"Delicious," he murmurs before he licks all of my fingers, the flash of his tongue twisting up my insides and making me want to toss all worry aside and beg him to fuck me. We don't need condoms. He could pull out. Come all over my stomach and make a mess of me. I'd love every second of it.

But that's me being irresponsible.

He drops my hand and his mouth lands on mine in the greediest kiss I've ever experienced. It's messy and it's raw and we're completely out of control. Our teeth collide and it hurts but I don't even care. His tongue is everywhere and when he licks a hot path down my neck, moving so his big body is lying on top of me, his hips in between my spread legs, I just lie there and take it.

His hands wander as he shifts down my body, kissing a path down my center, between my breasts, along my stomach before coming back up, his mouth burning a path on the underside of one breast, then the other. I rest my hands on top of his head, tugging on his hair in a silent message and he takes the hint, his mouth finding my nipple, his tongue slowly circling around again and again, teasing me, making me twist beneath him. The cool air hits my wet flesh and I suck in a breath when I feel his fingers pinch and twist the other nipple, making it hurt.

Making it feel good.

He lavishes his attention on my breasts for what feels like forever. To the point that I can barely take it. Sucking my nipples into his mouth, then nibbling lightly on the tender flesh. He plays with me but won't let me play in return, and so I continue to remain still, reveling in the attention that he's feasting upon me. He's like a man who broke free from prison, tossing off the chains of his control and letting himself do whatever he wants, and I'm the willing participant, savoring every single second of his undivided attention.

When he slides his hand down until he's cupping me between my legs, I open my eyes to find he's already watching me with that intense green gaze. With careful precision he presses against me with a single finger until it's nestled between my folds. Testing me. Not really touching me but branding me all the same.

"Fuck," he mutters, his finger pressing deeper. "You're soaked."

It's almost embarrassing, how wet I am for him. But he seems pleased. He begins to stroke me, his movements a little jerky as if he's trying to find the right rhythm and when he flicks my clit by accident, I lift my hips, urging him to do it again. And he does.

Over and over and over again.

With Rowan, I'm not afraid to let him know what feels good. I was a fumbling fool with my previous sexual experience, and my partner was even worse, but with Rowan, I feel confident. Bold.

"Do that again," I whisper when he presses his thumb against my clit, and he does, flicking it. Rubbing it. "Just like that."

My clit is throbbing. Swollen. I'm desperate to come. I feel like I've been involved in some sort of foreplay with Rowan for years and finally, *finally* he's going to give me some relief.

He shifts downward, his mouth on my breast, lips enveloping my nipple and pulling it into his mouth. He tugs and sucks, his tongue swirling, his fingers busy between my thighs. The sound of my slippery flesh grows louder and louder as he strokes faster and faster, and I grip his head to my chest, arching my hips, moving with him, all worry about looking awkward flying out the window.

I just want to come. All over Rowan's fingers.

He increases his speed, tight little circles on my clit, and I'm crying out, thrashing my head back and forth on the pillow, my eyes tightly closed as I focus on the sensations that he's bringing out of me. What he's doing feels amazing. Overwhelming. I spread my legs as wide as I can, my thigh muscles aching, my feet braced on the bed as I smash my pussy against his hand, shifting up and down, desperate for more friction.

"Oh God, don't stop. Don'tstopdon'tstopdon'tstop." I am chanting, incoherent, riding his fingers like a shameless hussy and then it happens. I'm tipped right over the edge, straight into freefall, the orgasm sweeping through my body so fast, so hard, my mind goes blank.

Black.

I'm screaming his name and he slaps his hand over my mouth, silencing me. I'm still screaming, my voice muffled by his palm as I come all over his fingers just as I imagined. It's the most intense orgasm I've ever experienced in my life because while it's great that we can give ourselves so much pleasure, it definitely feels better when someone else is doing it to you.

Especially when that someone else is the crush of my life, Rowan Lancaster.

Once the trembling subsides and I'm quiet, Rowan finally removes his hand from my mouth. I crack open my eyes to find him watching me, slowly shaking his head.

"What?" I croak, clearing my throat, a shiver jolting through me, remnants from my delicious, fabulous, absolutely amazing orgasm.

"I should've known you were a screamer," he murmurs, and while it might sound like an insult, I know it's not. More like it's an example of Rowan being Rowan toward me, and I'm just being Arabella.

His Bells.

"I think I blacked out," I tell him, and he chuckles. Lifts his glistening fingers to his mouth and again, licks them clean.

Oh my God. It's so freaking hot when he does that. I clench my wet thighs together, can feel myself leaking everywhere, and I immediately want to feel those skilled fingers between my legs again.

Shifting into a sitting position, I throw myself at him and he catches me, his arms coming around my waist while I twist mine around his neck. We're face to face, his mouth smells like me and I lean in, licking at his lower lip and then the upper one with long, thorough strokes of my tongue. He groans, his hand coming up to catch the side of my head and keep me in place so he can kiss me but I shift away, smiling.

"I want your dick in my mouth, Rowan," I declare.

He chokes on his laughter, making me smile. "Jesus, Bells."

"I want it. I want you to come in my mouth. No! Wait, I want you to come on my face. My chest." I draw my fingers across my collarbone, letting them drift downward until I'm circling my nipple with just my index finger.

His laughter dies, his expression wondrous as he watches me. I'm sure he didn't expect me to say that, but that's my favorite thing to do. Shock him. "Are you sure..."

"Stop." It's my turn to clamp my hand over his mouth. "I am so sure. I've been fantasizing about it for months. Years, Row."

I drop my hand and his brows shoot straight up. "It's Row now, is it?"

"Yes, Row." I lean in and kiss him, my swollen lips resting on his before I pull away. "You've given me an orgasm so I'm calling you Row."

He's shaking his head. "You make zero sense, Bells."

"I think that's my best quality. That and I'm going to let you come down my throat." My smile is easy-breezy as I settle my hand over the front of his jeans, my fingers curling around the length of him. "Let's take these off."

TWENTY-SIX

ROWAN

I DON'T THINK I've ever heard that sultry voice come from Arabella before. The sound thick with pleasure and full of confidence. Her fingers are on the button fly of my jeans and she tugs them undone, every single one of them popping open with ease before she dives her hand inside, her nimble fingers curling around my dick and giving it a firm squeeze.

Swallowing hard, I inhale deeply, trying to gain some semblance of control, but damn that felt good. If she doesn't watch it, I might come in my goddamn boxer briefs, and that's the last thing I want.

This has been the fucking best night of my life and I'm still shocked it's happening with her. I had no idea Arabella would be like this, though I should've known. God, the moment she got close to coming she started screaming, and I was so freaked out my parents might hear us I went on instinct and placed my hand over her mouth, shutting her up. It was hot, seeing her like that. Desperate and straining, moaning against one hand while humping the other before she came all over it.

"Help me," she murmurs, and the next thing I know, I'm lifting my hips and she's pulling my jeans down along with my briefs. She's careful when she tugs them off my ankle and I appreciate her taking extra care with it because I forgot all about the fact that it's broken and still healing.

Huh. Maybe I'm the fragile one in this scenario.

"Lean back," she instructs me, and I do as she says, my head propped on the pillows so I can watch as she runs her hands over my chest, her fingers tripping over my rippling abs. "God, your body is unreal."

I've worked really hard to make this body unreal and I thought it all went to shit after my injury. But looks like I've still got it.

"And your dick is huge." Her eyes go wide when she takes it in. I try not to laugh but this is almost comical. In a sexy way but still comical. The girl doesn't hold back. "Like seriously, Row. How am I supposed to fit that in my mouth?"

"I'm sure you can figure it out." I tug on her hand and she falls into me, her mouth finding mine, our tongues tangling as she runs her fingers up and down my chest, making me shiver. I cup the back of her head, keeping her with me as I devour her mouth and damn, it would be so easy to just slip inside her. We're both naked and our bodies seem to fit like we're meant to be together but...

We don't have condoms. And there's that other little fact, the one I haven't admitted to her yet.

She hums when she finally pulls away from my still-seeking lips, her smile devilish as she shifts down the length of me, our gazes staying locked. She kisses my chest. Licks one nipple, then the other, making me groan. She kisses and licks her way across my abs and lower. Lower...

Until she's lying in between my spread legs, her fingers wrapping around the base of my shaft and giving it an experimental tug. I part my lips, trying to offer encouragement but no words come out. She's left me fucking speechless.

I've had a couple of blowjobs before, and every single one of them happened quickly. Lots of awkward fumbling around in the dark and me coming too fast because, shit, I was younger and horny and had no self-control. A gentle breeze could've coasted across my dick and I would've come everywhere.

It's not much better now, my self-control. Especially because the lights are on and I'm eating up a naked Arabella with my gaze. She's lying on her stomach and she's got her legs bent, her feet waving in the air as she plays around with my cock and I stare at her perfect heart-shaped ass. She's even more beautiful naked than she is clothed and swear to God, my heart expands at the realization.

That I'm the lucky bastard who gets to see her like this. Who made her come, who made her fucking scream.

"Your dick is perfect," she says, her sweet voice and odd compliment breaking through my thoughts. I glance down to find her watching me, a faint smile curling her swollen lips. "Seriously, Row. Is there anything about you that's not perfect?"

"My ankle," I choke out when she gives my dick a firm squeeze.

She actually giggles. "Come on. There has to be something else."

"My past inability to be nice to you," I admit.

Arabella goes still, her fingers still around my dick, her expression turning solemn. "You were never mean."

"Be real, Bells."

"I was a pest."

"That doesn't give me the excuse to be awful toward you."

"You were never awful..."

"Sort of," I interrupt.

"Well." She's smiling again, tugging on my cock, pulling it toward her mouth. Fuck. "You've made up for it. You're quite kind toward me now."

"I have to be. My dick is in your hands."

That lightens the mood completely and makes her laugh. The laugh dies the moment she touches her lips to the tip of my dick in the gentlest of kisses. She delivers one. Two. Three...and then dabs her tongue into the slit, swiping up the precum that had gathered there.

"Shit," I choke out, closing my eyes for only a second because I don't want to miss a thing. And Arabella doesn't disappoint.

She licks my dick like it's a popsicle she's savoring with long drags of her tongue, never fully taking me in her mouth and driving me out of my mind. Every muscle in my body strains, my stomach clenching, my balls drawing up. It doesn't matter that I jerked off in the shower earlier. I'm ready to blow all over her face right now and she hasn't even given me a proper BJ yet.

"Mmm," she murmurs just as she pulls me fully into her mouth, and all I can do is fall back against the pillows, closing my eyes.

One hundred percent focused on the gentle suction of her mouth. How her tongue glides around my cock. The firm grip of her fingers around my shaft as she squeezes and strokes. She's fucking good at this.

Excellent at it, really.

The slurping noises she makes when she releases me from her mouth are nearly my undoing. I reach for her, lifting my head and opening my eyes so I can watch as I push her hair away from her face. Her mouth is full of my dick, and when those big brown eyes meet mine, that's it.

"I'm gonna come," I warn her and Jesus, she deep-throats me, the head of my cock bumping the back of her throat before she pulls me all the way out.

Just in time for me to lose all control. With a groan, I'm coming, semen shooting everywhere. All over her chest. Her chin. Her neck. I'm like a fucking geyser, my entire body shuddering with the force of my orgasm, and when it's finally over, I collapse onto the mattress, my heart racing like I just ran across three football fields.

Goddamn.

I crane my neck when I feel the mattress shift, catching her bending toward the floor. She grabs the towel she discarded a while ago and wipes at her chest and neck, then her chin. I watch her, fascinated by every little thing she does, and when she drops the towel to crawl her way up so she's lying beside me, I curl my arm around her shoulders and haul her in closer. She nestles her head in that spot between my shoulder and neck, her hair tickling my skin, and I drop a kiss on her forehead like I can't help myself.

She drapes a slender arm across my chest, lodging her foot in between mine, always careful not to bump into my healing ankle. We are skin on skin, completely naked and spent.

"Did I do all right?" she finally asks after a few moments of silence. "The blowjob—was it good?"

"I don't know, you tell me." Is she for real right now? "Couldn't you tell by the fact that I came in like, two minutes?"

She giggles again and I savor the sound. "You did come pretty fast. I'm guessing it's been a while."

"Been a while since what?"

"Since you've come." She lifts up on one arm, staring at me. I stare right back. "How long has it been?"

"A couple of hours ago," I admit. When her eyes go wide, I explain myself. "I jerked off in the shower."

"Is that a common occurrence, Rowan?"

"We're back to Rowan, huh?" I brush the wild strands of hair away from her face, taking in her beauty. Without the glasses on, I can take note of her every little feature, and Arabella Hartley Thomas is fucking stunning. Or maybe that's my post-orgasmic haze talking. I'm not sure yet.

But yeah. She's gorgeous.

"Yes." She nods, serious. "Do you jerk off a lot?"

"Do you ever finger yourself in the shower?" I throw back at her.

"I prefer fingering myself in bed, if you must know." She lies back down, her head on my shoulder, her breath wafting across my skin making my dick stir. Though that might be happening because she just admitted to fingering herself. "And I can't remember the last time I did it."

"Really?"

A sigh escapes her. "Fine. I fingered myself last night after you left my bed. Happy now?"

"Arabella." I touch her face, slipping my fingers under her chin so she'll lift her head and meet my gaze. "I have never known someone like you. Ever."

She's smiling, looking so damn pleased with herself I realize I'll never forget this moment. This night. "I've been told before that I'm a unique individual."

"It's true." I lean in and kiss her. "If you need to hear praise, that was the best blowjob I've ever had in my life."

Bells tips her head to the side, kissing me, her tongue swiping at mine before she pulls away. "I went on total instinct. Truly, I had no idea what I was doing."

Is it wrong that I'm relieved she's not some blowjob pro? Because I am. "Your instincts were spot on."

"I also paid attention to you, Row. You have tells." Her hand wanders, brushing against my chest, my stomach, until she curls her fingers around my semi-hard dick. "Like what you did just now."

"What did I do?" Oh Jesus, she's stroking me. Bringing me back to life. I'm hard again. Already aching.

"You suck in a little breath when something feels good." She nips at my lower lip with her sharp teeth, making it sting at the same time she gives my cock a firm squeeze. "Maybe I should jerk you off this time and you can tell me how you like it."

"Only if you let me finger you while you tell me how you like it," I offer.

She grins.

"Deal."

TWENTY-SEVEN

ARABELLA

IT'S the day before Thanksgiving and I am in absolute heaven. The last four days have been unreal. Magical. Like I'm living in a fairy tale with Rowan Reginald Lancaster as my Prince Charming.

He went to the doctor Monday morning and came home boot-free and wearing the biggest smile I think I've ever seen. I'd like to think I'm partially responsible for that smile, though I understand ridding himself of the boot was a total relief for him. But still...

I can't forget the way he pulled me into a hall closet and kissed the crap out of me when no one was looking. Or how his brother caught us slipping out of the closet, a knowing smirk on Beau's face.

"Just friends," he said, smug with knowledge. "Uh huh."

Rowan didn't even care. There was no scowling or growling or the normal Rowan reactions. He just grabbed my hand and told everyone we were going for a walk. We've done that a lot over the last few days. Going on walks. But we never get far.

Instead, we find some secret alcove in the yard where we kiss and kiss until we're breathless and aching for each other. Our clothes disheveled and our hair messy and our mouths rubbed raw.

It's the nights that are my favorite. After the house has gone quiet and everyone's tucked away in their beds, Rowan sneaks into my room. Into my bed. His assured hands race all over me, stripping me bare, leaving me naked and wet and eager for more. Always wanting more. I thought I was a greedy whore before? I am greedier, ruthless and unapologetic with my wanting him. And he seems to love it. He doesn't judge me for running my mouth and saying silly things. Doesn't mind when I practically scream my head off when he makes me come. I've learned to cover my mouth, press a pillow to my face, whatever I need to do to keep my reactions quiet.

Ugh, I'm probably in love. I know that's what it is. He smiles at me and I feel like I'm going to burst into flames. He touches me and I want to throw myself at him. And while we haven't actually done it yet, we've done plenty of other things, and I'm still in shock that we've gotten this close. Me and Rowan. Row and Bells.

I like the way that sounds. I think he might too.

It's Wednesday afternoon and I'm in the kitchen with his mother and their cook, Marilee. We're working on the Thanksgiving menu and I'm currently peeling potatoes and it feels like such a traditional, pre-Thanksgiving dinner prep moment. I've never peeled potatoes in my life but Marilee kindly teaches me how to do it, and while I'm making a mess and peels are all over the sink, I'm having fun.

I am. Really.

"Arabella, I have a question for you," Wren declares at one point, and I nearly wound myself with the vegetable peeler when my hand slips on the potato. I let both drop into the sink and turn to find she's already watching me, her pretty green eyes full of caution mixed with hope.

Swallowing hard, I steel myself for what she might ask. Whenever a parent says this to me, it never ends well. And speaking of parents, I've been avoiding my mother, who's been calling daily. So completely unlike her but I know she wants a firm answer about the apprenticeship with the jeweler, and I'm not ready to give her one yet.

"What is it?" I ask, putting on my brightest smile. Like I'm a confident open book and not trembling with nerves.

"Your birthday is Friday and I know Rowan said you didn't want a party but...that was a few days ago and I wanted to check in with you and see if you're open to the possibility?" She pauses a beat before rushing onward. "It wouldn't be anything big. We could invite some of the family over. They always love an excuse for us to gather and celebrate. And while some of them are coming over tomorrow for the holiday, I'm sure they'll want to come over Friday too."

"They don't even know me," I whisper, shocked all over again that she would offer to do this for me.

"They'll get to know you and they'll love you like we do." She shifts away from the island where she was rolling out home-made pie crust—homemade by the very woman of the house, and I can't even imagine my mother doing something like this—her hands covered with flour.

The way Wren is looking at me, I think she might want to hug me, and I want her to hug me too, but we're a mess. I'm covered in potato juice, which I didn't even know was a thing, and she pauses right in front of me, her head tilted to the side. "But I understand if you don't want a party. Rowan has mentioned before that you're a private person—"

"I'm not," I interrupt. "I'm a blabbermouth who wants attention because quite honestly, my parents don't give it to me because they've never seemed to care. So yes, I'd love a party. A big, sparkly party with balloons and flowers and a massive cake that has sparklers instead of candles, though that might cause a house fire, I'm not sure. And we can play games and maybe eat pizza? I love pizza."

Wren Lancaster is beaming as she clutches her hands in front of her, her eyes sparkling like I imagine my cake might look Friday night—bright and fiery. "Oh, Arabella, you've made my day! Whatever you want for your party, we can put together. It'll be beautiful." She turns to look at Marilee, who's currently placing the crust Wren was just rolling out into a glass pie dish. "Marilee, I'm going to have to go make a few calls. I hope you don't mind."

"I've got this, Mrs. Lancaster. You should go with her, Arabella," Marilee tells me with a gentle smile. If I had a sweet and soft grandmother, this is who I'd want her to be like. Marilee is the best. No wonder the entire family loves her. "You need to go plan your party."

My potato duties forgotten, I hurriedly wash my hands, careful not to get any soap on the peeled potatoes in the strainer, before I leave the kitchen with Wren, excitement bubbling inside me as she leads me to her office. It's a gorgeous room with rose gold fixtures and a round marble table in the dead center of the room, a vase full of vibrant autumn-hued flowers the only burst of color in the otherwise muted room. There are art pieces hanging on the walls, massive pieces that are subtle in color and seem important. Like someone famous painted them all, though I have no idea who since I don't know much about art.

"Have a seat," Wren instructs, and I do as I'm told, settling into the cream-colored plush chair, watching as she sits across from me and cracks open the sleek Apple laptop, tapping away at the keys before she turns it to face me.

"What do you think of these flowers?" she asks as I gape at the photos on the screen.

"They're gorgeous," I say without hesitation.

"We'll order some balloons too. Fill them with helium and they can have ribbons hanging from them so they fill the ceiling in the family room. I think that will look beautiful." She turns the laptop back toward her and starts tapping again. "I used to hate my birthday."

My jaw drops. "Why?" I can't imagine this beautiful, happy woman hating anything, especially her birthday. It's a reason to celebrate and she seems to love any chance to have a party.

"My birthday just so happens to land on Christmas, and growing up, I hated that. I never felt like my day was special. It was a day for *everyone* to celebrate." Wren presses her lips together, silencing herself for a moment. "I sound selfish, but maybe I was. I am an only child, after all."

"I am too," I breathe, feeling like I have something in common with her. And while my birthday isn't on Christmas, I definitely know what it feels like to never feel seen on what's supposed to be a special day.

"Rowan mentioned that," his mother tells me, her voice soft. "We have some similarities."

We do, but I could never be half as beautiful or as elegant as the woman sitting in front of me. And she's so giving and thoughtful. Look at her wanting to throw me a party and she doesn't even know me. When I'm the hussy who's rolling around naked with her son in secret every night, right under her own roof.

My entire body goes hot at the realization. I am a bad person. I wonder if she can tell.

"He also mentioned that you don't spend much time with your parents," she adds, her voice gentle, like she's afraid I'm going to break if she speaks too harshly. Perhaps I will. I'm hanging on by a thread right now as it is, fighting the shame that wants to wash over me. "They travel a lot for work?"

I nod, swallowing past the lump in my throat. "My father works in finance. He's president of a bank in Hong Kong."

"Impressive," Wren murmurs, though I can tell she's not impressed at all. There's a gleam in her eyes that reminds me of Row when he's upset about something. "I don't want to speak out of turn but..."

"Please. Please speak out of turn," I urge, wanting to hear what she has to say.

"Well." She sits up straighter, brushing an imaginary hair away from her face. Trust me when I say her hair is perfection. "It sounds to me like your parents might—neglect you at times. Like now, for instance."

I don't even bother defending them. What's the point? "They're too busy to worry about me and my feelings."

Her expression shifts, full of sympathy but not—thank God—pity. "I know what it feels like, to have parents who were too wrapped up in their own lives to worry about their child. While

I have a solid relationship with my mother now, when I was your age, my parents were…not the best."

I don't speak, only send her a sympathetic look in return.

"I'm glad you agreed to come here for the week. It seems you're having a good time?"

The best time ever, is what I want to tell her. And not just because of Row either. I love the house and his parents and his brother and the housekeeper and their driver. I love their dog Oliver, a giant black lab who tries to knock me over with his sturdy body every time he sees me. I love my guest room and the giant bathtub and the sprawling backyard. Everything about this house has warm and cozy vibes despite its size and I never want to leave.

"I'm having a wonderful time. Thank you again for hosting me. I know it was last minute—"

"I always love having my children's friends come to stay with us," she says, interrupting me. "It's never an issue. We have more than enough room in this house. How are you and Row doing?"

I frown, not sure where she's going with this question.

"You two have seemed to grow closer." Her smile is small. She appears pleased with this turn of events and oh, how I can relate.

"We have." I sit up as straight as I can, squaring my shoulders and readjusting my glasses, which have clear frames. They are the ones I wear the most because they go with everything. "I think he might like me after all."

Wren laughs, and I can't help but laugh along with her. "Like you after all? I believe he's always liked you."

"No way. Not at all. I annoyed him. I might still, I'm not sure. I can be—a lot sometimes," I admit.

Her laughter dies and she gets a fierce look on her face, again reminding me of her oldest son. I kind of love it when he gets that look because it means he's fired up about something, and I do enjoy an impassioned Rowan. "You are not 'a lot,' as you say. Don't ever let anyone tell you that. You are just enough for many someones out there, including your friends and whoever you end up settling down with someday. If that's your choice. Maybe you never settle down. Maybe you want to wander around the world and live without restraints. Whatever you want, whatever you do, don't you ever feel like you're too much or a lot. I hate when people say that."

I blink back the tears that have sprung to my eyes, shocked by her outburst. How easily she defends me when my own mother used to chastise me for being over the top. All over the place. Unable to focus or sit still or calm down. I heard all of those phrases and more growing up, until I became a shell of myself whenever I was around them. Only when I'm at school do I act like my real self. Well, and here. I'm accepted by this family.

By Row.

The tears leak out of the corner of my eyes anyway, and I give in to my urges, leaping from my chair and going to Wren, who stands at the last second and envelops me in a big hug. I cling to her, pressing my face against her soft cashmere sweater, praying I don't get snot on it as I cry. She just holds me, running her hand over my hair and murmuring soothing words I can't really understand. I don't need to know what she's saying. Her comforting hug is more than enough.

I eventually pull away from her, a little embarrassed as I wipe the tears away from my face with shaky fingers. She hands me a tissue from the box that sits on the table and I take it, dabbing at my face and blowing my nose. I'm a mess but she's watching me. Quiet. Patient. Like a mother should be.

"I wish you were my mom," I admit, immediately wanting to take it back because then that means Rowan would be my brother and ew.

God, my thoughts are ridiculous sometimes.

"Oh, sweetheart." She pulls me back in for another hug, murmuring into my hair, "Maybe someday I will be."

TWENTY-EIGHT

ROWAN

IT'S THURSDAY. Thanksgiving. Our house is full of people. I don't know why my parents made the switch and decided to host the annual family dinner here instead of at Whit and Summer's house, but it is absolute chaos, and I'm dying to hide away in my room. Preferably with Arabella.

She's having way too much fun though so I could never ask her to do that. I watch as she sits with a few of my cousins in the family room, gabbing away with Iris, who is probably the only one who could outtalk her. They are going on and on about something, I can't even hear what, and they're both gesturing wildly, their arms in the air, their laughter filling the room, which makes me smile. The twins Paris and Pru watch them with envy in their eyes, probably wishing they could be as outspoken and wild as Iris and Arabella, though they're both already on the verge of being exactly like Iris from what I've observed over the years.

That's mildly terrifying.

"I miss your sister."

Turning at the sound of the familiar voice, I see Brooks Crosby standing there, clutching a drink in his hand with a grimace on his face. He's a big guy, taller and broader than me, and he can appear imposing to most. Once you get to know him though, you find out he's a giant teddy bear. He also happens to be Iris's boyfriend.

"You have a secret thing for Willow?" I ask him, raising my brows.

He scoffs, taking a giant gulp from his glass, his movements jittery. He seems extra nervous and I wonder what the hell his problem is. "More like I need Willow around for moral support. But she's too busy getting sunburned in Mexico."

Willow and Rhett FaceTimed us earlier, their red faces appearing on the screen made Mom give them a lecture about using sunscreen. The call didn't last long—who wants to be lectured on Thanksgiving? But I don't think my mom could help herself. She's always concerned about her children, especially when one of us is not around.

"More like you miss Rhett." They're best friends. Callahan and I have hung out a lot with Rhett and Brooks, and I get what he's saying—I miss the Bennett brothers too. It doesn't feel right, not having them here for the holiday.

"Right. Like you miss Callahan." Brooks takes another swig, then wipes at his sweaty brow. "It's fucking hot in here."

There are a lot of bodies in the house and the heater is blasting but it's not *that* hot. "You okay there, buddy?"

"Not really." Brooks rattles the ice in his glass before he drains it. "I'm stressed the hell out."

"Dealing with Iris on a daily basis is finally getting to you, huh?" I chuckle.

"Yeah, especially since she's moody and pregnant." Brooks immediately covers his mouth when I swing my head in his direction, the shock I'm feeling at his casual remark all over my face. "Ah, fuck. I wasn't supposed to say that out loud."

My jaw drops and I blink at him. What the actual... "Are you for real right now?"

He nods, clenching the glass tight in his meaty hand. "Her dad is going to murder me on the spot when he finds out."

"Iris is pregnant? Seriously? You guys are what...twenty?" I can't wrap my head around being a dad in two years. Hell no.

"Yeah, she's having my baby. And while I'm scared shitless, she's excited about it. Look at her." We both turn to watch Iris and Bells, who are now listening to whatever the twins are telling them, my gaze lingering on Iris for once instead of getting distracted by Arabella. "She's fucking glowing, man. I've never seen her look so beautiful."

She does look good. Her face is rounder, and she's got this big smile on it, like she's keeping a giant secret, which she is.

"It makes me wanna cry, knowing she's going to have my kid," he continues, his voice scratchy.

Brooks sounds like a man in love, and I give him a quick once-over, noting the googly-eyed expression on his face. Yeah, he looks like a man in love too. I'd be freaking the fuck out over bringing a baby into the world but all he's worried about is Whit Lancaster turning his wrath upon him when he finds out good ol' Brooksie impregnated his only daughter.

Which is a valid concern. I would never fuck with that guy. He's mean as shit and his son is the same. Grumpy assholes run far and deep in the Lancaster lineage.

I take a step closer to Brooks and lower my voice. "You haven't told her parents yet? Not even her mom?"

"No." Brooks shakes his head. "Haven't told mine either. And they're here. They're all here. Iris said tonight at dinner she's going to announce it to everyone, and I don't know if I'm ready for that."

Dinner tonight just got a lot more interesting, that's for damn sure.

"What are you cocksuckers whispering about?"

We both turn to find August there, his icy blue eyes raking over both of us, his upper lip curling in disgust. He's the oldest of the cousins, and when I was younger, I wanted to be him so fucking bad. I just wanted Augie to include me in everything he was doing, and he always treated me like shit. It's only been the past year or so that he actually acknowledges me in a semi-friendly manner instead of threatening to kick my ass, which is how he used to treat me.

Brooks sends me a look that says *please keep your lips zipped* before he turns to August, reaching to slap him on the back. August dodges away from him at the last second, sneering.

"Do not touch me. You're a fucking sweaty mess, Brooks. Are you drunk?"

Brooks drops his hand, defeated. "No, but I wish I was."

"Don't get another drink," I warn Brooks who was about to leave. "You should probably try and stay sober, don't you think?"

"Hell no." And with that, Brooks makes his escape.

August watches him go, then turns his attention to me. "What's his problem?"

No way am I telling August the news. He gets to find out with the rest of the family. "I have no idea. You know how he is."

"Always worried he's going to piss my father off? And me too?" August arches a brow.

"Exactly." I nod.

"How's the ankle?" August asks.

"Better. No boot." We both briefly glance down at my feet. "What's up with you?"

"I'm fucking sick of school. Bored out of my mind." He rolls his eyes. He's at one of the most elite private colleges in the country and is president of the fraternity there this year. You'd think he'd be on top of the world. "Pissed that I'll have to stay an extra semester and graduate next year."

"On the five-year plan?" I'm giving him shit and he doesn't like that.

"Wait until you get into college and find out how they rig the system and offer a class only during the fall semester. Meaning you can only take it once a year. Then you can talk to me about a five-year plan." August brushes his golden hair away from his brow, his irritation bubbling over as usual.

"I don't even know if I want to go to college," I admit. "I applied everywhere I might want to go, but we'll see."

I've never admitted that out loud. I've always been the dutiful son, doing as my parents say. The only time I rebelled was when

I joined the football team my freshman year. My mom was worried I'd injure myself and I promised I wouldn't. Then I go and do exactly that, proving her worry was warranted.

"What else are you going to do? Fuck around and travel the world while spending all of Daddy's money?"

"I came into the first part of my trust fund when I turned eighteen," I remind him. "Meaning it's my money."

"Right. Wait until you're twenty-one. Talk about having fuck you money." August actually grins.

"Fuck you money?" I've never heard that term before.

"Yeah. That's when you have so much wealth you can do whatever you want without consequences. Want to buy an NFL team? Fuck you, I can afford it. Want to buy a castle in Europe? Fuck you, I've got it covered." August tilts his head in my direction. "See where I'm going with this?"

"Definitely." I chuckle. So does August.

Damn, why does that feel like progress?

"Hey, guys! Whatcha talking about?"

I glance over my shoulder to find Arabella approaching us, a curious look on her face when she studies August, and I grab her hand, pulling her in so she's standing between us. He doesn't even acknowledge her. Just stands there with a bored expression on his face.

"Arabella Hartley Thomas, this is my cousin, August Lancaster," I say.

"Ah, I've heard of you," is how August greets her, tipping his head in her direction as acknowledgement. This is a moment for sure because it's rare August acknowledges anyone. "You came here with Rowan?"

She nods, her big gold hoop earrings swinging wildly. "His parents were kind enough to invite me to stay for the week. My parents live in Hong Kong and I couldn't see them during the holiday."

"Your dad is the big shot finance guy, right?"

"Yes, he is…" She glances over at me and I just stand there, paralyzed. I forgot I asked August to do a little investigating into Arabella's background. Shit. "And your father is the scariest Lancaster of them all, right?"

August full-blown laughs at Arabella's comment while she stands there like a serene princess. "I like her, Row. She's feisty."

He doesn't even know the half of it. I pull her in closer, staking my territory like the possessive ass I've become, and August notices because he notices everything, the fucker.

"Don't worry, cousin. I don't want to fuck your girl. I'll leave that all to you." Smirking, August offers a short bow to Arabella. "A pleasure meeting you. If you'll excuse me, I need a drink."

He leaves before we can say anything in response.

"He's a little…scary," Arabella says to me once my cousin is gone, shifting around so she's facing me, my hand falling away from her. She looks amazing, even though she's wearing the simplest of outfits: a soft black sweater and black wide-legged pants, that ever-present heart-shaped gold locket around her neck. Her hair is down and perfectly straight, those big gold hoops dangling from her ears, and her makeup is subtle, save for her mouth. Her lips are a deep, vivid red that gives her a sexy as fuck air, and she's wearing black frame glasses.

"He's a menace," I mutter, wishing I could kiss her but I'm not in the mood to make a spectacle in front of the entire family. I'll save it all up for later tonight.

We've been driving each other crazy the entire week—getting naked everywhere we can because it's like we can't keep our hands off each other. I've been trying to hold out, but it's proving more difficult as each day passes.

Here's my deal—I refuse to have actual sex with her until it's her birthday because, and I am a fucking sap for thinking this but I can't help it, I want the experience to be special. Memorable. For me and for her. But her patience is thin and so is mine. We've come close so many times, to the point that she begged for it last night. I refused and went down on her instead. I've never eaten pussy until Arabella, and she's so responsive, she makes me feel like a damn king every time I make her come.

The girl is excellent for my ego.

"Much like you're a menace?" When I scowl at her, she slaps at my chest. "Stop it. You enjoy being mean to everyone."

"Not as much as August does." I grab hold of her hand and intertwine our fingers, leaning in close to whisper in her ear, "Let's go find a closet and fuck around."

"Rowan," she scolds, which only makes me want her more. The scolding part. It's hot when she acts like I'm the bad one when she might be worse. "We're with your family."

"No one is paying attention."

She purses her lips together, trying to keep a straight face. "Someone might overhear us."

"Like I just said, no one cares. Trust me." I drop my voice a notch, whispering in her ear, "I bet I could have you coming on my face in less than five minutes."

Bells gets that look on her face, the one that tells me she's turned on. "Rowan."

"Arabella," I return, as serious as I can be.

She glances around, making sure nobody is close. "Make it four minutes and you've got a deal."

I grin. "Challenge accepted."

"I'll leave first." She steps away from me, her eyes shining with arousal. "Meet me in the first guest bathroom in the east wing."

"Give me two minutes." I slap her ass, making her gasp. "Go."

She scurries away and I watch her leave, smiling the entire time until I catch my brother shaking his head at me.

"Everyone knows you two are fucking," Beau whisper-yells.

His words don't even bother me. For the first time in my life, I welcome them. "I don't really fucking care," I tell him.

Just before I take off in search of Bells.

TWENTY-NINE

ARABELLA

MY NAKED BUTT is perched on the marble ledge of the gorgeous guest bathroom that resides in the east wing of the Lancaster household, my legs spread wide and Rowan's face buried between my thighs. His tongue laps at my clit, circling it. Sucking it between his lips. I've got one hand on the wall next to me and the other in Row's silky hair, holding him close, on the verge of coming.

Feels like I'm always on the verge of coming when I'm with him.

He's kneeling on the floor, his big hands pressed against the inside of my thighs, keeping me in place. My pants are discarded on the floor, a crumpled heap on top of my shoes and my glasses resting on top of them. My sweater is shoved halfway up my chest, my breasts exposed. I didn't wear underwear tonight. I've sort of given up on underwear this week because I prefer easy access, and Rowan always acts surprised when he finds out I'm not wearing a bra or panties.

I love giving this man surprises.

"Please don't stop," I gasp when he pauses and I glance down at him to find he's watching me. "What are you doing?"

"You're fucking beautiful," he declares, making my entire body flush with pleasure at his compliment. I can never get enough of them and he doesn't offer them up freely, so when he does say something like this, I know he means it. "Look at you."

"I can't," I croak, feeling silly. "The mirror is behind me."

He presses a wet, open-mouthed kiss on the inside of my thigh, tickling me. "I should take a picture."

"Absolutely freaking not." He chuckles and I tug on the ends of his hair, making him growl. "I mean it, Row. No photos. What if..."

Oh God, what if his *mother* found them? Or his *dad*? I would die.

D-I-E.

"Fine, no photos. Just watch me and burn this memory into your brain so it's there forever." He presses his face between my legs again, inhaling deeply. My stomach clenches when I feel his tongue slide over my clit. Search my folds. Tease my entry. My inner walls flex on nothing and I whimper, moaning when he slips a finger inside me. Then another. Fucking me steadily while he sucks my clit, driving me out of my mind.

We know how to make each other come fast and God, I love it. We've only been at it for approximately two minutes and I'm close. I love how he makes me feel filthy. Dirty—in the absolute best way. It seems he's just as into me as I am into him and triumph slips through me, knowing that I've finally got Rowan Lancaster where I've always wanted him.

He's mine. I know it.

My clit pulses rapidly in warning. I grab the back of his head and smash his face into my pussy, arching against him, rubbing shamelessly on his mouth and chin. I'm grinding, tipping my head down so I can watch, and when our gazes connect, I'm done for.

I fall completely apart, moaning low in my throat, trying my best to contain the noise I want to make. His eyes fall shut as he concentrates on my pussy, my poor overworked clit, and within seconds I'm pushing him away, unable to take it anymore.

Rowan leans back on his haunches while I try to control my breathing, my racing heart. He wipes at one corner of his mouth, then the other, sucking his thumb between his lips before he removes it and presses it upon my still throbbing clit.

"Oh. Shit." I bite the words out, banging my head against the mirror behind me when he slowly thrusts two fingers back inside my pussy, moving them in and out, bringing me to another orgasm that's somehow even more intense than the previous one. I nearly fall off the bathroom counter, and he grabs my knee, keeping me in place.

I'm shaking my head over and over, babbling like an idiot. "You have to stop, Row. I don't know if I can take it anymore."

He removes his fingers from inside my body and presses a gentle kiss on the inside of one damp thigh, then the other, before he rises to his feet. Bracing his hands on the counter, caging me in, he kisses me on the mouth, the salty taste of my pussy still lingering on his lips, and I kiss him back with as much enthusiasm as I can manage.

But I am spent. And it's all his fault.

"My poor sweet, Bells," he murmurs against my lips, and I swear, my heart stops, only to start back up again, beating triple time because of what he said.

I'm overwhelmed all over again, but not from the orgasms. No, it's emotion filling me up and threatening to pour out all over Rowan. He's not one to show how he's feeling, but in this moment, I feel cared for. Maybe even...

Loved?

No, I'm rushing things. Rushing, rushing, that's always my mode and I need to stop and savor what I've got. Rowan wrapped all around me with his mouth still on mine and our heated breaths mingling.

"We should go back out there," he finally says, and I nod, fighting my disappointment. Can't we stay in this bathroom forever?

He pulls away from me and grabs my sweater, straightening it out. He tugs it over my breasts until it's covering me to my waist, and I smile when he brushes the front of it while murmuring, "So soft."

When he catches me watching him with what I can only assume is a goofy look on my face, he tells me, "Not as soft as your skin though."

I am melting. Turning into pure liquid he'll have to gather up in a glass. I don't know how I'll ever put myself back together after this week. Everything has changed while we've been here but is it back to reality when we return to campus? Will I be his sweet Bells then? Or is it back to that girl who annoys him in class?

Snapping out of my dreamy state, I hurriedly finish getting dressed and smooth my hand over my hair while staring at my reflection in the mirror. My lipstick is a moot point, rubbed away within seconds of us slipping into this bathroom, thanks to Rowan kissing it all off. He digs around in the cabinet and finds a bottle of Listerine, both of us swishing it around in our mouths and spitting it into the sink while he turns the water on and rinses it away.

"Do I look presentable?" I turn to him after I wipe my face on the plush hand towel, slipping my glasses back on.

"Beautiful." He brushes strands of hair behind my ear, his gaze glowing with sincerity. "I miss the lipstick though."

"I left it upstairs in my room." I stand straighter. "Should I go get it?"

"If you want to." Rowan leans in and presses a soft kiss to my lips. "But hurry back. I think dinner is going to be served soon."

I exit the bathroom first, looking this way and that to make sure the coast is clear before I head for the staircase. I'm in my room seconds later, grabbing my phone to see if I have any notifications when it lights up in my hand as if sensing I was holding it.

It's my mother. I've avoided her long enough, and I have the perfect excuse to cut the call short—dinner is about to start.

"Mom, hi!" I greet her with all the enthusiasm I can muster as I grab the lipstick that I put on earlier and go into the connected bathroom.

"Darling! There you are! Happy Thanksgiving! And Happy Birthday!"

My heart soars at her remembering, but only a little bit. I had to remind her, after all. "Thank you. What time is it there?"

"Two in the morning. Your father and I just got back from our little trip with friends." She laughs. "We had the best time!"

"That's nice." I'm distracted, my head full of thoughts of Rowan and how much he likes the lipstick. I hit the speaker button on my phone screen and set the phone on the bathroom counter, uncapping the lipstick and carefully slicking it across my lips.

"Have you given the apprenticeship any more consideration? I need to give them an answer soon."

Nerves jangle in my stomach and make my hand shake. I set the lipstick on the counter and grab a tissue, wiping at the corner of my mouth. "How soon do they need an answer?"

"Yesterday," she says without hesitation.

"Perfect, considering it's still yesterday where I'm at." A nervous titter escapes me but she doesn't laugh in return.

"I'm serious, Arabella. We need to tell them right away. If you're not interested, there are plenty of other people who understand just how important this opportunity is and will gladly step in and fill the spot."

"Oh." I take a deep, shaky breath, trying to calm the full-blown panic that sweeps over me at her words. I grab my heart-shaped locket, rubbing my thumb over it like I do sometimes when I'm nervous. "Um..."

"If you're going to say no, please reconsider. This is the opportunity of a lifetime and I just know that you'll enjoy yourself once you're there. Isn't this what you've always dreamed of? Since you were a little girl? I remember you sitting at the dining room table with your jewelry kits strewn everywhere, concentrating so hard your tongue was sticking out while you lined up the different colored beads just so."

I blink at my reflection, startled she remembered. I always thought she gave me those kits so I'd leave her alone and she wouldn't have to deal with me. I was such an arts and crafts kid when I was younger, and Mother acted like that sort of thing was beneath her. And my father? He was never around so I don't recall him having any sort of reaction toward me beyond confusion.

"And all your sketchbooks you'd leave everywhere around the house when you were what? Eleven? Twelve? Full of designs, Arabella. Beautiful ones. You've got a special talent." Her voice lowers, and I swear it's even a little trembly. "Don't waste it, darling. Do something with it. My biggest regret is I didn't do anything with my talents when I was your age."

I'm stunned silent. My mother had secret hopes and dreams that had nothing to do with being married to a wealthy banker? I had no idea. "What was your talent?" I ask in a raspy voice.

"I enjoyed dabbling in a little writing here and there. Fantasy stories. They felt like fairy tales to me and I adored the world building. I might've even started writing a few, but I never finished a single one." Her words take on a rushed quality. "But that was before your father and he needs me. I don't have time to write fanciful stories that will probably go nowhere. I have other duties to perform."

I swallow hard, my vision blurring. Why am I crying? Because my mother gave up her dream for my father? A woman shouldn't have to give up anything for the love of her life. After all, we don't ask men to do that, so why should women?

Clearing my throat, I declare, "I'll do it. I'll take the apprenticeship."

She's silent for only a beat. "Darling, this is the best news! I'll let them know right away. They'll want you to come straight to Paris at the beginning of January, and I thought it might be nice to spend Christmas there? The three of us together? I know I mentioned it before, but we could stay at The Ritz. What do you think? We'll be right across the street from the atelier and we could all visit it together. Go on a little tour. Wouldn't that be amazing?"

"Yes." I sniff. "Amazing." I'm full-blown crying now. Not at the idea of taking the internship, but at the thought of leaving Rowan behind. Of not spending Christmas with him and his family. Being stuck in a glamorous hotel that isn't home and won't have a Christmas tree in the room, my parents most likely too busy to actually want to spend time with me.

I understand them—her—far better than she realizes. Yes, she's happy for me. This is the most thoughtful and nurturing I've seen her act toward me since I can remember. But she has her own motives too. Christmas in Paris sounds like a fantasy, something my mother literally just admitted that she likes. She might've gotten this opportunity for me, but it benefits her too.

Everything always does.

THIRTY
ROWAN

I KEEP GLANCING over at the arched doorway of the dining room, fully expecting to find Arabella rushing through it at any second, but she's still not back yet and we're all sitting down at the table while my mom and Marilee are in the kitchen, going over everything before the temporary staff they hired for the day bring all the dishes out.

"Where's your fuck buddy?" Beau leans in close to me and I jab him in the ribs with my elbow, making him grunt.

"Shut the fuck up," I snarl, anger flashing through me. "And don't call her that."

"Whoa. Sorry." Beau holds up his hands in defensive mode, turning his back on me and speaking to Brooks instead. That poor dude is so distracted I don't think he heard a word Beau said, and my little brother crosses his arms, pissed.

"I'm sitting somewhere else," Beau announces as he rises.

"Your mother put together a seating chart for the occasion," Dad says, his voice firm. "You're sitting there."

Beau drops back in his chair, his irritation obvious. "Still wish I could've seen Plymouth Rock."

"First of all, you were going to Cape Cod, and Plymouth Rock is nowhere near there. And trust me, I've seen it. It's not that big of a deal," I tell him but he only glares at me in response. And I don't think he gives a shit about a historic rock or where the Mayflower first landed. More like he wanted a shot at spending time with the girl who invited him to go.

Speaking of girls...my gaze goes to the empty doorway yet again, fighting the disappointment that tries to seep into my bones. Where is Arabella? She went upstairs to grab her lipstick what feels like hours ago.

I check my phone and see it's only been twenty minutes, but damn. Twenty minutes is plenty of time to grab a lipstick and come back downstairs. What is she doing? Is she okay? Is something wrong?

I push back my chair and stand, about to go in search of her when she magically appears, her eyes rimmed red and her expression solemn. She spots me and rushes over, sitting in the empty chair beside me and grabbing the folded napkin on her plate, shaking it out and placing it in her lap. "I'm sorry. I got a phone call."

I'm frowning so hard my forehead hurts. She won't really look at me and that's...weird. "Are you all right?"

She nods, her lips curled into a tight smile, her gaze flickering in my direction before she looks away. "I'm fine. Starving to death."

"Dinner is about to be served," I start just as Mom enters the dining room.

"It's ready," she announces, going to sit at the chair to the right of where Dad sits at the head of the table. "The dishes will be out momentarily."

Within seconds, servants fill the room, setting the dishes in between the flower arrangements and candle holders that line the center of the table. Mom went all out with this meal. There's even a cornucopia in the middle of the table, overflowing with flowers and various pieces of fruit. Once everything's brought out and our plates are full of food, Dad stands, holding a glass of wine.

"Before we eat, I'd like to say how grateful I am for everyone at this table. Not all of our family members could make it this year, but I appreciate all of you who are here for coming to our home and sharing this meal with us. Whit and Summer, thank you for letting us host this year. Wren has been wanting to put something together for Thanksgiving for a few years now, and from what I've seen so far, she's done a terrific job."

Mom beams as she tilts her head back, her gaze only for Dad.

"I'm thankful that everyone is happy and healthy. That we're spending this special day together. That we have new faces at the table, like Row's friend, Arabella."

She shifts in her seat when everyone turns their attention upon her, dipping her head, which is so unlike Arabella that I'm shocked. She's all about reveling in other people's attention. What the hell is wrong with her?

"To family," Dad concludes, lifting his glass into the air.

"To family," everyone else murmurs as they lift their glasses as well. My gaze cuts to Arabella and she looks like she could burst into tears at any moment. Leaning into her, I press my shoulder to hers, murmuring. "Bells. Something's wrong. I can tell."

Her smile is weak. "I'll tell you later. Let's enjoy dinner, hmm?"

Throughout the meal I'm attuned to every little thing Arabella does. She picks at her food, swirling it around with her fork like she's trying to make it appear she's eating. She's quiet and she is never quiet, always loving to chat about something. Anything. When Iris tries to engage her in conversation, Bells smiles and makes a quick comment, then drops her gaze.

I hate being kept in the dark. She's upset. And I'm dying to know what it is.

"We have an announcement," Iris says once everyone starts groaning about how they ate too much and the men grumble about needing to check the football scores. Her gaze goes to Brooks, and I glance over at him too. He's profusely sweating and his cheeks are red. I think he might be drunk. "Do you want to tell them Brooksie, or shall I?"

He inclines his head toward her. "You do the honors."

Her smile is coy, her eyes dancing with mischief because my cousin knows that she's about to drop a bomb. "Well...there will be another family member who'll be at the table next Thanksgiving. He or she will be arriving in approximately seven months, give or take."

The entire table goes silent. Brooks looks like he wants to slide under the table, and it figures my big-mouthed brother is the first one to break the tension.

"You knocked her up, Brooks? Holy shit!" Beau exclaims.

Everyone starts speaking at once and I can't make out who's saying what while Iris sits there and takes it all in, seemingly pleased with herself. The voices rise higher and higher, those who are speaking and trying to talk over the other until finally there's a bang on the table.

And that bang came from Whit Lancaster's fist.

"Enough!" Whit is glaring at poor Brooks, who's barely holding it together, and his face has turned green. If he pukes at the table, everybody is going to lose it. "Are you going to make an honest woman out of my daughter, Brooks?"

"Oh, Whit, stop it. We weren't married when August was born," his wife points out as she rises from her chair and goes to her daughter, pulling her to her feet and enveloping her in a hug. "My sweet girl. You're going to be a mother. Congratulations."

Iris clings to her mom, crying into her shoulder, and Whit goes to them as well, patting Iris's back awkwardly, like he's not sure what to do. Brooks stands, a little wobbly on his feet, but he manages to make his way over to Iris, who extracts herself from her mother's embrace to wrap her arms around Brooks. We're all watching them like it's a movie, the majority of us quiet, waiting for something to happen, for something to be said. And we're not disappointed.

Brooks drops to his knee in front of Iris, clutching her hand and staring up at her like she's his entire world. "Marry me, Iris. So we won't have a bastard child who's like your brother."

"I take offense to that," August mutters, shaking his head.

"Oh my God." Iris presses shaky fingers to her lips, nodding over and over again. "Yes, Brooks. Yes, I'll marry you."

He slips a giant diamond on her finger that he withdrew from his pocket and rises to his feet, delivering a deep kiss upon Iris's lips, who circles her arms around his neck and hauls him in closer. People start applauding, even the servers who've entered the room to clear the plates.

"This is so romantic," Arabella murmurs, tears shining in her eyes.

I rest my hand on her thigh, giving it a squeeze, and she turns to look at me, her gaze locking with mine. "You want to slip out of here?" I ask, my voice low.

She slowly shakes her head. "I wouldn't miss this moment for the world to sneak off and give you a hand job, Rowan. I appreciate you trying though."

I blow out a frustrated breath. "That's not what I wanted—"

"Later." She pats my thigh a couple of times before removing it. "I'm going to go congratulate the future bride and groom. And parents."

I watch her, baffled by her reactions. It feels like she's trying to avoid me, and I hate that. I also don't like how she thinks I wanted to get out of here only for her to give me a hand job or whatever. Right now, I'm not looking for sexual gratification. I'm concerned about her and want to make sure she's okay.

The realization hits. It's never only been about sex between us. I care about this girl. I think I always have, and this week my feelings for her have grown to the point that I can't think about anything else.

Only her.

I'm not pissed about the broken ankle or the opportunities missed with football. I'm not mad at the world or eager to get out of Lancaster Prep so I can get away from everyone. I'm actually happy to be here today, in the presence of my family, my cousins who we've all grown up together. It's a good day. It *was* a good day, until Arabella's mood had to throw everything off.

Throw me off.

I'm going to get to the bottom of this, whether she likes it or not. And I'm going to fix whatever it is that's bothering her too. I know I can.

I'd do anything for her.

THIRTY-ONE

ARABELLA

AFTER CHASING after Rowan Lancaster for what feels like the entirety of high school and finally catching him, I didn't think about how hard it would be to shake him—something I never thought I wanted. But Row has turned out to be far more determined than I thought—and completely unshakable.

Everywhere I go this evening, he's trailing behind me like a watchdog. And if he's not following me, he keeps his gaze on me wherever he stands, sits, whatever, tracking my every move. At school, he always seemed eager to get rid of me, and now he's become my shadow.

Any other day I'd find this endearing. I'd take it as a sign that he's into me and can't stand the thought of me ever leaving his sight. That's a lovely thing to consider, but in this moment, I'd rather he go away. I want to be alone with my thoughts and worries and feelings so I can overthink my recent, spontaneous decision and send myself into an anxiety spiral.

And I can't believe I just had that thought.

Earlier I tried to turn down dessert and you'd think I just gave Wren Lancaster the biggest insult of her life from the look on her face when I said no thank you. I immediately changed my answer to yes please because the last person I want to offend is Rowan's mother. She's so wonderful. Thoughtful and loving and sweet. I aspire to be like her one day, but I could never.

I think I have too much of my mother and father in me to ever be that perfect.

After dinner, we moved to the family room where the Thursday Night Football game is on but I've tuned it all out. I'm sitting in an overstuffed chair that looks like an antique and is probably worth thousands of dollars, balancing a plate of pumpkin pie on my lap, the whipped cream slowly melting thanks to the warmth of the room. I can't stand the idea of taking a single bite of it and I adore pumpkin pie. Pumpkin anything really. I am that basic bitch who's buying pumpkin spice lattes from Starbucks the second they're available, always ordering them hot despite the temperature outside. I love what I love and I refuse to feel judged about it.

My gaze goes to Rowan, who's blatantly watching me and doesn't bother looking away when I catch him. He's sitting on the couch flanked by his father and his uncle Grant, their gazes glued to the TV screen save for Row's. I smile at him because I don't know what else to do and his brows draw together with obvious concern. I can see the question in his eyes, and I don't want to answer it.

I don't know how.

Dropping my head, I grimace at the slice of pie on the plate and set it on the tiny table next to the chair. Marilee appears in front of me as if conjured by magic, dipping down to grab the plate, a frown on her face when she sees not a single bite has been taken from the slice of pie.

"Are you not feeling well?" Marilee asks me, concern filling her brown eyes. She's an amazing cook and I've eaten every last drop of the food she's prepared all week with the exception of today.

I want to weep at her question, the expression on her face. Everyone in this house cares. From the grumpy, arrogant men to the delightful women they married to the swarm of cousins who bombarded me with endless questions. Even Rowan's brother asked me if I had a problem when we were leaving the dining room earlier, his tone vaguely hostile.

He is currently mad at the world and not afraid to show it. All over a girl, according to Rowan. It figures.

"I'm just not very hungry," I tell Marilee. I pat my stomach. "I'm still full from dinner."

Her gaze narrows, and I wonder if she saw that I didn't eat my dinner either. But how could she know?

"Well, if you need anything, let me know," Marilee says, her voice full of doubt.

"Thank you," I say with a smile, grateful for her. Grateful for all of them. Grateful for the opportunity I've been given. The one that I'm taking despite all of the doubt currently swirling within me. Leaving Lancaster Prep early sounds like...

A terrible decision. I will miss everyone. Even Mrs. Guthrie, who probably won't miss me at all. But especially Rowan. What is he going to say when I tell him that I'm moving to Paris in January? That I'm spending the holiday season in another country and he'll most likely never see me again? Will he fall to his knees and beg me not to go?

I can't imagine it. That's not his style. Because he is a supportive person who was raised right by good parents, he will encourage me to go and chase my supposed dreams. But what if my dreams are now about him? And us?

Swallowing hard, I shake my head once, annoyed with my thoughts. I can't pin all of my hopes and dreams on a boy. I don't care if he makes me feel alive and kisses me like he never wants to stop. We're teenagers. According to the internet and anyone above the age of forty, we don't know what we want. We're going to change so much in the next few years we'll practically be unrecognizable to each other in the future. Once I've finished with my apprenticeship, who knows where it will take me. Certainly not back into Rowan's life. What's happening between us is a fleeting moment, just like I reminded myself it would be when my mother first told me about the position. I firmly believed six weeks wouldn't be enough time for me to fall completely in love with Rowan but I was wrong.

All it took was a few days. That's it. Meaning I am weak. A complete sucker for him. It's a terrible thing. A terrible, horrible thing and I'm a terrible, horrible person for being powerless to his lethal charm. He only has to look at me and I want to crumble at his feet.

My gaze finds him again and he's focused on his dad who's talking to him. Giving me the freedom to ogle him as much as I want. He's so gorgeous. The dark hair that's a tad too long and always falls across his forehead. Those beautiful green eyes and strong jaw. The sharp nose and lush mouth that brings me so much pleasure I shiver just thinking about it.

Maybe it's a good thing that I'm leaving. I need to learn how to stand on my own two feet and not find myself under the thumb of a powerful man who'll dictate what I do with my life. Not that Rowan would ever do that on purpose. But he's a Lancaster and they are one of the most powerful families in this country, if not the world. He will do something important with his life, and have huge influence. If I were to stay with him, would we eventually get married and I'd be the dutiful wife on his arm? The mother of future Lancasters who will go on to do important things like their father?

God, I am turning into my mother and if that doesn't make me want to fling myself off a bridge, I don't know what else will.

"Hey."

I glance over my shoulder to find August standing behind my chair, that permanent scowl on his face. It's funny but he reminds me of Rowan. Grumpy and dismissive when you first meet him, but I saw the potential in Rowan despite his growly ways and I can see it in August too. It's a front. They use their bad attitudes as a wall to protect them from God knows what. Having actual feelings?

Ugh, men. They are so silly.

"Hi," I say to August, keeping my voice soft. I don't dare ask him any questions because he'll probably respond with some snide comment and leave me as quickly as he approached.

"You're sitting all alone." He comes round the chair to stand directly in front of me, blocking me from Rowan's view. I'm sure he's doing this on purpose and I predict Row will make his way over here eventually. "What's wrong with you?"

His hostile tone almost makes me smile. It matches Beau's earlier, when he asked me if I had a problem. They all have decent mothers, so why are these boys freaked out by a woman who's feeling a little sad?

"If I told you, you'd laugh," is my answer.

That gets his attention. He tilts his head, contemplating me. His eyes are an intense, icy blue, and any other person who would be under this much scrutiny from him would probably wilt like a flower in the sun. But I have lots of practice dealing with Lancaster boys so I merely sit there, my hands curled in my lap, letting him look his fill.

"Tell me then," August finally says. "Let's see if I laugh or not."

Before I can open my mouth, he settles into the matching chair on the opposite side of the tiny table, leaning on the arm of the chair that's closest to me, giving me all of his attention. My gaze cuts to where Rowan sits and he's watching us. He doesn't look pleased. I probably only have a couple minutes tops before he interrupts us and drags me away like a jealous lover.

Once I start talking, it's like I can't stop. I spill my guts, telling August about my mother's call and the offer that came with it. How I used to love making jewelry and went through a stage where I sketched designs but have neglected it over the last few years. I don't admit to August that was my old obsession and my new obsession became...

Rowan.

That part is a little embarrassing so I keep it to myself.

"What jewelry brand is it?" August asks when I finish. "Cartier?"

I shake my head.

"Tiffany's?" He grimaces.

"No. And there's nothing wrong with Tiffany."

"If you say so." His voice is laced with doubt. "Who is it?"

When I offer up the name, he seems impressed. "My mother loves them."

"So does mine."

"Her wrists are usually dripping with their bracelets. She restrained herself today." August leans back in the chair, crossing his legs. Looking every inch the rich heir to a fortune that he is. "You'd be stupid to turn down the apprenticeship if that's what you really want to do with your life."

"I accepted it," I admit, knowing he would be real with me. He's too blunt to lie.

"Good." He nods once. "I don't think you'll regret it."

"I already do."

"Because of him?" The faint disgust in his voice is obvious. "Look, I think my cousin is a decent human. Sometimes he's annoying but that's only because he's younger than me and I've always felt that way about him."

"I think you were born annoyed with everyone," I tease, and his lips curl into the faintest smile, disappearing in a flash.

"My mother said I was an easy baby and full of joy. Then Iris came along and ruined everything," he admits.

"Aw, you had to share your parents' attention with someone else." I mock frown at him and his gaze narrows.

"Easy for you to say considering you're an only child," he drawls.

I frown. I've never told him that. He should know absolutely nothing about me. "And you know this how?"

His expression remains impassive. "Just an assumption."

"Uh huh."

An exasperated breath leaves him. "Fine. Your boyfriend had me investigate you."

My mouth pops open. "What?"

"Ask him about it." August rubs his jaw, his attention diverted. "You can ask him right now. Hello, Rowan."

"August," Rowan bites out.

My gaze goes to Row and I do a double take. His mouth is a straight line, his eyes blazing with anger, and a lesser person would fall apart if Rowan looked at them like he's staring at me. But I refuse to fold. Is he actually jealous of me talking to his cousin? Unbelievable.

"Can I talk to you, Arabella?" Rowan asks me, ignoring August completely.

With a chuckle, August rises to his feet. "I'll leave you two love-birds alone."

The moment he's gone, Rowan settles into the chair August just vacated. "What were you two talking about?"

"Nothing really. Making small talk." I shrug, trying to play it off, but then I remember what August said. "Well, he did reveal a little tidbit I didn't know about."

"Yeah? What's that?" His hostile tone is completely unwarranted.

"That you asked him to, and I quote, 'investigate me.'" I even add air quotes with my fingers, which I always thought was completely obnoxious.

But the expression on Rowan's face is worth me making the air quotes. "He told you that?"

"Is it true?"

He looks away, like he can't face me when he admits, "Yeah."

"Rowan." My voice is gentle but I still let the irritation shine through. He meets my gaze again and his miserable expression almost makes me go easy on him. Almost. "That's an invasion of my privacy."

"He didn't find out a lot. Not like he gave me your social security number or dug up those nudes you sent Bentley Saffron Jones."

I jump to my feet, hating the shame that washes over me thanks to his judgmental tone. "God, you're insufferable. And I never sent nude photos to Bentley. I've never sent nude photos to *anyone*."

Rowan stands, towering over me, and I tilt my head back, glaring. Giving as good as I get. "You need to stay away from August."

"Why? Are you jealous? Thinking I might lose interest in you, all because I'm having a casual conversation with him? Give me a break, Rowan. You must think I'm the shallowest person on the planet."

I leave him where he stands, exiting the family room as quickly as I can. No one says anything to me as I walk out and I'm grateful they're all preoccupied. My eyes are blurry as I make my way to the stairwell that leads to my room and I blink back the tears that want to escape, furious at my reaction. I can't let this boy make me cry just because he brings up stupid Bentley Saffron Jones. I regret ever telling him about my past, especially because he's never said a word about who he's been with.

His lack of honesty is frustrating. He's too secretive. Maybe because those secrets would shock me? I don't care who he's been with in the past or the number of girls he's had sex with. Who am I to judge?

"Arabella!"

I scurry up the steps when I hear his voice, desperate to get away from him. I need a little peace to clear my head and he's not giving me that.

Not at all.

"Stop, Bells! Come on!"

I increase my pace, breathing hard when I hit the top of the stairs, glancing over my shoulder to see he's gaining on me. I head for my bedroom door, crying out in frustration when I feel his fingers closing around my arm, stopping me. I turn on him, the tears flowing freely down my face, and the second he sees them, his entire demeanor shifts. Softens.

"I'm sorry." He lets go of my arm, framing my face with his big hands, his touch so gentle it makes the tears come faster. "I'm a jealous asshole. I hated seeing you talking to August, seeing you look like you were enjoying yourself. I'm a dick."

"You are," I say, my voice thick. "Just because I was talking to him doesn't mean I want to fuck him, Rowan."

His brows draw together. "I know, Bells. I know. I just—"

He quits speaking, leaning in to press his lips to my forehead, feather soft and making my belly flutter. "Forgive me. I should've never had August dig into your personal life. I was just—curious."

"All you had to do was ask. I'm an open book, remember?" I close my eyes when he brushes away the tears on my face with his thumbs. "I've told you everything whenever you have asked. Even the embarrassing stuff."

"You have," he agrees.

"While you've still kept your secrets." I open my eyes to find him frowning at me, confused as usual. "I have a question for you, and be honest."

"I will be."

"How many girls have you had sex with?"

THIRTY-TWO

ROWAN

I LET my hands fall away from her face at her question, my brain scrambling to come up with a lie. "Why does it matter?"

"Because I've been honest with you from the very start. I told you things I've never told anyone and you didn't judge me for it. Well, you sort of judge me for Bentley, but I think that's only because you're jealous, which isn't a good look for you, Rowan. There is nothing to be jealous of there. He's not worth your anger."

She's right. I'm jealous of any guy who's touched her before. I want her all to myself. I realized that when I watched her talk with August, who doesn't give anyone the time of day. But he talked to my Bells and I didn't like it.

Fuck that guy. He needs to stay away from her. I don't care what Arabella says. He's not harmless. He's a shark swimming in shallow waters looking for his next meal, and Bells is a tasty treat.

"How many girls, hmm? If the number is huge, that's okay." Her expression turns serious, her eyes still glassy from crying.

She's beautiful. She's all mine and I don't know why I'm so fucking stressed out over my answer but here I am, dodging it for as long as I can. "Every one of those girls has made you who you are today. Didn't Taylor Swift sing a song about that? What am I saying, she totally did. And I always thought it was unbelievable how she felt that way, but I can relate. I really can because those girls who loved you before made you into this version of yourself, and I like who you are, Row. I really do—"

"You're rambling, Bells." I drop a kiss to her lips, silencing her completely and she falls into me, her arms winding around my neck, her soft body pressed against my hard one. I love the shape of her, the way we fit perfectly together but she pulls away before I can deepen the kiss, extracting herself from my arms.

"Stop trying to distract me with your lips and just tell me." She steps closer again, resting her hands on my chest. "Please."

Tipping my head down, I press my forehead to hers, my heart hammering in my throat when I whisper, "Zero."

Her brows crinkle. She's silent for what feels like a million hours but is probably at the most fifteen seconds. "What?"

Of course, Bells would force me to repeat this. "My answer is zero."

She takes a step backward, her confusion obvious. "You've never been with...*anyone*?"

"Well, I have. I've messed around with a couple of girls. Nothing too serious." I think of the girl who broke my heart when I was a sophomore. Again, I refuse to think of her name—it doesn't deserve to take up space in my brain. But how she led me on only to get with someone else, fucking broke me a little.

Does that make me weak? Maybe, but I swore I would toughen up instead and never let another girl get under my skin like she did. Until now.

Until Arabella.

"I don't understand." She shakes her head.

"I haven't had sex with anyone else," I admit, my voice so damn low I can barely hear it. "I've never gone down on another girl either. Just you."

She blinks, her jaw working, like she wants to say something but can't come up with the words. Great. She's probably going to reject me. Fucking Bentley Saffron Jones has more experience than I do, and that guy looks like an asshole. I know this because I googled the prick and can't believe what a wimp he is. And my Bells had *sex* with that guy. Five fucking times.

I don't know if I'll ever fully get over it.

"Well." She clears her throat, squaring her shoulders. "You're really good at it, Rowan. Your instincts are on point."

It's my turn to not know what to say. How do I reply to that? Gee, thanks? Though I can't deny what she said is reassuring. I'm not a complete failure, though I already figured that out considering the way she comes every time I put my mouth on her.

"You've really never been with anyone else?" She rests her hands on my chest again, smoothing them up and down, and my body instantly reacts. Doesn't matter if we're arguing or I'm embarrassed or she's pissed, my dick jumps to life every time she puts her hands on me.

"Is it that big of a deal?"

"I suppose not." Her smile is small. "I'm your first."

"We haven't even done it yet." I touch the side of her head, threading my fingers through her soft hair.

"We will," she says with complete confidence. "You keep promising me that it's happening tomorrow. Like your dick is my birthday present."

I laugh. She says the most ridiculous things sometimes. "Maybe it is."

"That's not a bad present." Her laughter fades. "My only regret is that you weren't my first. I wish I would've saved myself instead of giving it away so easily."

"Your reasoning made sense. Don't have any regrets, Bells. You doing what you've done made you who you are right now." I tug on her, pulling her closer. Repeating the words she said to me. "And I like who you are."

"Oh, Rowan." She throws herself at me and I catch her, staggering a little from the unexpected force of her body, bumping into the wall. "I'm sorry I got mad at you."

"You haven't acted right all day," I point out, gathering her closer. Burying my face in her hair. "Are you feeling better?"

"No." Her answer is muffled against my chest and I slip my hand beneath her chin, forcing her to look at me.

"Tell me what's wrong," I demand.

She glances around the corridor, then takes my hand and leads me into her bedroom, shutting and locking the door behind us. "Sit." She points at the bed.

I do as she says, settling on the edge of the mattress, hating how uneasy I feel. This is probably nothing, though I'm sure I'm also in denial. It's not like her to act so down and out. She's cheerful all the time, even when she feels like her world is crumbling.

Arabella starts pacing in front of me, not speaking a damn word, and I finally can't take it anymore.

"Just say it," I demand, my voice sharp.

She comes to an abrupt stop directly in front of me, throwing her hands up in the air. "I'm taking that apprenticeship. In Paris."

I absorb her words, letting them soak in, fighting my automatic reaction to growl, "Hell no, you're not." That would be selfish of me, and while I can admit I'm a selfish person, I refuse to shit on her dreams. My father wouldn't do that to Mom, and I won't do that to Arabella.

That I'm even comparing my relationship with Bells to my parents is just...fucking mind-blowing.

"Okay." I say the word slowly.

"My mother convinced me that I can't pass up this opportunity."

"I agree. Your mother is right."

She appears taken aback by what I said, but forges on. "The position starts in January, so I won't return to school after winter break."

I can't imagine what Lancaster Prep will be like without Arabella there. She's in every single one of my classes. I wait for her out front every morning, eager to catch a glimpse of her, wanting to see what crazy outfit she's wearing. I'll miss that.

I'll miss her.

"My mother said she wants to spend Christmas in Paris." Her voice is barely above a whisper. "So right after finals, I'll be leaving for France, and I'll meet my parents there. We're going to stay at The Ritz through the holidays."

"That sounds nice," I say to fill up the silence in the room after her confession.

"No, it doesn't. It sounds dreadful. Christmas at a hotel? There will be no sparkling tree in our room. And we won't be with family or listening to Christmas carols. Do you love Christmas songs, Row? I do. I start listening to them early. I've been listening to them every day while we've been here, mostly when I'm taking a shower."

The last thing I want to listen to is a cheerful holiday song while I'm jacking off in the shower to thoughts of Arabella's beautiful naked body, so yeah, no shower Christmas carols for me.

"But I don't want to be the rotten only child who doesn't want to spend Christmas with her family when I'd much, much rather spend it with...you." She inhales sharply after her confession, the panicked look on her face telling me she can't believe she just said that.

Rising to my feet, I take her hands and clutch them in my own. "This is a great opportunity for you, Arabella. I'm glad you're doing it. I'll miss you at Christmas, but I understand that your parents want to spend the holiday with you before you leave them."

Leave them. That's funny. More like they're always leaving her.

"But I want to spend it with you," she whispers, her hands trembling in my grip. "You probably think I'm silly, but I've already envisioned it. Your family is so close and I—I love it here. I don't want to spend Christmas morning at a beautiful hotel. I mean, I'm sure it'll be gorgeously decorated everywhere we go, and we'll have a nice time, but that's not what Christmas is about. I want to be surrounded by family, even if they're not my own."

The tears start again and fuck me, I hate seeing them. I hate her parents for making her cry and forcing her to spend Christmas with them when it's obvious that's not what she wants.

It's not what I want either.

"I have to compromise for them every single time." She's crying for real now. "They forget all about me for the most part, but the moment my mother put in a good word for me and got me this apprenticeship? Now I'm supposed to be eternally grateful and eager to spend time with them in Paris. And I'll do it. I'm the dutiful daughter who always does what she's told, but I don't want to be there. Not when I can be with you."

I yank her into my arms and let her sob into my shoulder, running my hand over her hair, not saying a word because words won't comfort her right now. She's too upset and she's allowed to be. I don't know what it's like to have shitty parents because I'm fortunate—mine are the best. But they try their hardest because they didn't have great parents, and I guess I just lucked out to be born into a home full of love and a mom and dad who actually care about their kids and want the best for them.

"I'm sorry," I murmur against her hair, though my words feel useless. "We'll make the next few weeks the best we can."

She slowly pulls away so she can stare into my eyes, hers red-rimmed and her face flushed. "We will?"

I nod, wiping away her tears again, soaking them up with my fingers. "What have we got? Three weeks?"

"If that."

"And it's your birthday tomorrow."

Arabella nods. "I hate my birthday."

"You won't tomorrow. It's going to be the best birthday you've ever had. I guarantee it." I give her shoulders a little shake.

"You sound like a salesman." Her smile is tiny, and I take the small victory, even if she did just insult me. "But I'll trust you, Rowan."

"Good." I go still when she touches my face, her fingers drifting down my cheek. Tracing along my jaw.

"Thank you for trusting me," she murmurs, and I lean my cheek into her palm. "With your honest answer earlier."

It hits me that I do trust this girl. So damn much. I trust her with everything.

Including my heart.

THIRTY-THREE

ARABELLA

I WAKE UP SLOWLY, struggling to keep my eyes open at first. This bed is like sleeping on a cloud, as are the pillows, and I'm reluctant to leave it. Then I remember.

Sitting straight up, I push my hair out of my eyes and that's when I notice the single pink rose in a pink bud vase, sitting on my nightstand. There's an envelope sitting next to it and I grab it, opening the card to find a drawing of a fashionable dark-haired woman on the front of it, her long brown hair trailing behind her, her eyes covered in massive dark sunglasses.

The image reminds me of...me.

I crack open the card to find a simple Happy Birthday greeting, accompanied by a note.

I SAW this card when I went into town for last minute Thanksgiving supplies a few days ago and thought of you. You're a lovely young woman who makes our Rowan smile and that's a rare sight to see, so thank you. I hope you come to visit us again soon.

Xo,

Marilee

I CLUTCH the card to my chest, overwhelmed with emotion. Even their cook thought of me and snuck into my room to leave me a rose and a card. I cannot handle how sweet everyone in this house is.

I really can't.

There's a gentle knock on my door and I drop the card on the duvet cover, scrambling out of bed and snagging my robe that's on a nearby chair, hurriedly pulling it on as I go to answer the door. I fully expect to find Marilee standing there with a welcoming smile on her kind face but when I yank the door open, I'm surprised.

It's Wren, holding a tray in front of her. I spot the silver dome covering the plate, the cup of coffee and glass of orange juice, and another, smaller bud vase with a pale pink rose in it. I touch my chest, gasping. That she took time out of her day to bring me this? So thoughtful.

"Happy Birthday! Marilee made you breakfast, and I volunteered to bring it to you. I'm so glad you're awake." She gestures with the tray. "Can I come in?"

"Yes, of course." I step aside, holding the door open for her as she enters my bedroom. "You didn't have to bring me breakfast."

"But it's your birthday so let us all indulge you today. I have a feeling you're going to get utterly spoiled and it's going to be wonderful." She turns to look at me, standing right beside the bed. "Do you want to eat it in bed or at the desk?"

"In bed," I admit, running toward it and diving under the covers, my robe still covering me. I spread the covers over the top of me, making them nice and smooth before she settles the tray over my lap.

"Whew, it was heavy." Wren takes a step back, shaking out her hands. "Do you need any help?"

"No, I think I've got it." I lift the silver dome to find a plate filled with Marilee's perfectly scrambled eggs, two pieces of crisp bacon and two slices of whole wheat toast. "Aw, these are all my favorites. Thank you for bringing this to me."

"You're welcome." Wren clutches her hands in front of her, watching me. "Do you need anything else?"

I take in everything that's on the tray. Orange juice and a cup of coffee plus a few packets of sugar and creamer. The silverware and cloth napkin and even a couple of containers of strawberry jam cover the tray. "I think I've got everything I need."

"Good." She smiles, looking nervous, and I can't help but frown at her. "Rowan told me about your apprenticeship. It sounds wonderful, Arabella."

"Oh." When did he find time to tell her? It's barely eight o'clock and he fell asleep in my bed last night—both of us were too exhausted to mess around and that's fine. I enjoyed sleeping with Row, all snuggled up with him. He didn't seem to mind either. "Yes. I'm excited."

She watches me carefully. "You don't sound terribly excited."

. . .

"I AM." I put on my best, brightest smile. The one that is fake as hell. "I can't wait to go to Paris!"

"Have you been there before?"

"A few times."

"And you're spending Christmas at The Ritz."

I pause in scooping up a forkful of eggs. Boy, Rowan did tell her everything. "I am. With my parents."

"That sounds fun."

I meet her gaze. "Do you want me to be truthful?"

"Always."

"I prefer spending the holidays here. Your family is so...close. And kind. And fun. I really enjoyed yesterday." I tried to, at least. I was too preoccupied by what felt like my impulsive deci-sion. Leave it to my mother to put a damper on the holiday, and she's not even here. "Not that I'm a part of your family, but you make me feel that way. And I don't come from a big family. I've spent a lot of holidays by myself. Well, with servants. Or Lancaster Prep staff."

Wren settles right on the edge of my mattress, reaching out to rest her hand on top of my leg. "I hate hearing that. It breaks my heart, but I'm so glad that we've made you feel welcome. Rowan cares about you, Arabella. He just wants to see you happy."

Oh wow. This means he *really* talked about me with his mother and I...I don't know what to say. This moment feels important and I need to react properly.

"I care about him too," I admit.

Her smile is faint. "It's not easy making Rowan smile, especially after his accident, though he's always been a serious child. Since you've been here, it's rare to see Row not smiling. You're responsible for that."

I think of an angry Rowan yesterday when he got jealous over my conversation with August, and I'm glad she didn't see that. "He thinks I'm silly."

"I think he's in love with you." Wren slaps her hand over her mouth while I gape at her. She drops her hand and murmurs, "I probably shouldn't have said that."

My heart, my entire being, is glowing over what she said. "I think I'm in love with him too."

"I'm sure you don't want to talk about this with his mother, but if you do feel that way, tell him. Don't hold back, especially since you're leaving soon."

That's exactly why I wouldn't say anything. What's the point, if I'm going to Paris in a few weeks? Why would I admit that I'm in love with him when I can't be with him? It's best if I keep my feelings to myself and get over him as fast as I can. I'll be busy once I start my apprenticeship. I'll work hard every day to the point of exhaustion and then I won't think about him because I'll be too tired.

Right. Like I could forget him. I'm only fooling myself. Meaning I'm an absolute fool if I think I can "work hard" and erase him, and what we have shared, from my memories. Please.

"Okay, well, eat up! You have a big day planned." Wren jumps to her feet and rushes toward the door, turning to look at me one last time before she leaves. "Want me to tell Rowan you're awake?"

"If you'd like." I shrug, trying to play it off—play off my feelings for her son, which are big and overwhelming and enough to make me cry.

But I don't cry. I keep the smile fixed on my face until she shuts the door and once she's gone, I collapse against the stack of pillows behind me, jostling the tray on my lap. My appetite is gone and I feel terrible. Marilee fixed this breakfast for me as a special treat and I should enjoy it.

Determined, I sit back up and scoop up some eggs, shoving them in my mouth. Nibble on a slice of bacon. Add creamer to the coffee and take a sip. It's going to be a good day, even if I have to fake it.

ONCE I'VE TAKEN a shower and gotten ready for the day—Rowan never did come to my room, though he did send me a Happy Birthday text while I was in the shower—I make my way downstairs, bracing myself. I'm sure I'll be greeted by well wishes for my birthday and while it's nice, I'm not used to receiving acknowledgment from really...anyone. I've always preferred acting like it's just another normal day. That way I'm not disappointed.

But the moment I walk into the family room, I find Wren in the middle of the room, giving orders to Beau, who's standing on a ladder and moving the very balloons she said she would get for my party.

"Mom, this is dumb. The balloons look fine," Beau grumbles as he grabs hold of three streams and drags the balloons closer to where he is.

"Stop complaining and help your poor short mother out." Wren catches sight of me and beams. "There's the birthday girl! Tell Arabella Happy Birthday, Beau."

"Happy Birthday, Beau," he says, grinning.

I laugh. "Thank you."

Wren rolls her eyes, ignoring him. "I know it seems early, but we're setting up for your party. The guests should be showing up later this afternoon, around four or so? And we'll serve dinner—pizza, as per your request—and there's a DJ coming who'll set up in here and play music if anyone wants to dance."

"A DJ?" I'm shocked. I thought this was going to be a small, simple affair amongst the family.

"Well, we need music at a party, am I right? Though Whit was offended that I didn't ask him to help out. When the kids were younger, he was always the DJ at parties."

I can't even begin to imagine that. I didn't really speak to Whit Lancaster yesterday because he's thirty million times more intimidating than his son. And while that sounds like an exaggeration, it's really not.

"It's true," Beau pipes up, most likely because he saw the disbelief flit across my face. "He has great taste in music."

"See?" Wren's smile fades. "I'm thinking that maybe you should leave for a few hours? It's not that I want to get rid of you, but I don't want you to see everything we're doing for the party."

"Mom, she could help," Beau groans.

"The birthday girl does not have to help set up for her own party. That's a rule." Wren turns to face Beau, who's still standing on the ladder. She rests her hands on her hips. "Your father will be home soon. He texted me a few minutes ago that he finished his golf game."

Sheesh. How early did the man go play golf?

"And Marilee will help. Patrick said he would too."

"Isn't he the driver?" I ask.

"Patrick has been in our lives since we were teens. He and Crew are very close. He drives us wherever we need to go if we don't feel like doing it ourselves. He'll go pick up the children from school. He putters around the house and outside. He calls himself a jack of all trades." Wren laughs. "We tried to gently force him into retirement a few years ago, but he wouldn't hear of it. He's practically a part of the family."

"I call him Uncle Pat," Beau adds.

Wren shakes her head. "He does not."

The front door slams and we both turn to find Rowan entering the family room, his cheeks ruddy from the cold air outside, his hair windblown. He's wearing a thick black coat over a gray Lancaster Prep hoodie and a matching pair of sweatpants, and I've never seen him look better. It takes everything I've got within me not to hurl myself at him and beg him to run away with me.

Preferably not to Paris.

"Happy Birthday," he murmurs when his gaze lands on me, his perfect lips curved into a perfect smile. "Don't you look pretty today."

I swear I just heard the tiniest squeal come from his mother.

"Thank you." I am blushing. My face is hot and I'm shuffling my feet like I'm a bashful little girl. Such silly behavior because I am now officially an adult. "Where were you?"

"Had to run a quick errand." He jerks his thumb toward the foyer. "And I left the car out front. Thought maybe we could go for a drive?"

"That is a perfect idea. I want Arabella out of the house while we set up for her party." Wren gives me a gentle shove toward Rowan. "Go. Enjoy yourselves. Take her to lunch maybe."

"I never ate breakfast," Rowan admits.

"You're a growing boy, Rowan. You shouldn't skip a meal." I smile brightly at him. "Let's go get you fed."

We leave the house in a hurry, though I come to a stop on the steps when I see the car parked in the drive. "Is that your vehicle, Rowan?"

"Yeah." He stops to stand beside me, pride filling his voice. "That was my birthday present when I turned sixteen."

I glance over at him. "What is it?"

"A Ferrari—and it's fast as fuck." He lifts his brows. "Want to go for a spin?"

"I don't want to crash and possibly—die on my birthday," I tell him.

"I won't drive too fast." He holds his hand out toward me, his pinky extended. "Promise."

We hook pinkies and then he runs ahead of me, opening the passenger car door. "Get in, birthday girl."

I slide onto the smooth leather seat, sinking right in. He shuts the door and rounds the front of the car, giving me plenty of time to watch him, and when he catches me staring, he smiles. My breath catches in my throat at the sight of it. It feels so—intimate, the way he's looking at me right now. My heart flutters. My stomach flutters.

The spot between my legs flutters.

I'm still staring at him when he climbs into the driver's seat and starts the engine, which purrs like a kitten. A kitten that's really a tiger because I can practically feel the power in the rumbling sound. "You're looking at me funny."

"I've never seen you drive before."

"When I broke my ankle, my dad drove the car back here from campus because he didn't want me doing something stupid. Not that I could actually drive with that boot on my right foot," Rowan explains.

"You had this car on campus." I rest my hand against my chest. "I never knew."

What a missed opportunity. Not that Rowan was particularly interested in me before. It took a while for him to see just how perfect we are together.

"Well, yeah." He shrugs. "And I'll be driving it back there when we return to campus Sunday."

Ugh. School. Reality. I don't want to go back. I love it here. Everything is different at the Lancaster house, even Rowan himself. Once we're back on campus, people will be watching us. Most likely gossiping about us. Will the gossip and attention freak him out? What if he starts acting distant? I only have a few weeks left before I leave Lancaster Prep forever.

I push the thought out of my brain. I can't focus on that right now. Today is a good day. No negativity allowed.

"Are we going to keep sitting here or are you going to take me for a drive?" I'm goading him and he responds in typical boy fashion.

"Put your seat belt on, Bells." He grips the steering wheel and revs the engine, which roars like a lion. "And hold on."

He shifts the car into drive and hits the gas, the force of it all making my head knock back against the seat. I grip the handle on the passenger side door, my mouth hanging open as he whips the car around the circular drive, the tires squealing and the back end swaying.

"Rowan!" I'm yelling, my hair flying across my face when he lowers both windows, the cold air whipping into the interior of the car.

Tilting his head back, he laughs at me, his foot heavy on the gas, his hands firmly gripping the steering wheel. He peels out of the driveway onto the road and now we're going even faster.

"It's freezing!" I wrap my arms around myself.

"Aw, come on, Bells. Speeding down the road with the wind blasting across our faces on your eighteenth birthday—doesn't this feel like freedom?" He glances over at me, flashing that intimate smile at me once again before he returns his attention to the road.

"Stare straight ahead," I tell him, wagging my finger. "And don't go above the speed limit." He groans. "I mean it, Row! I'd like to arrive at our destination in one piece."

Rowan lets up on the gas, though I can see that he's still driving a little over the posted limit. He hits the button and both windows slide back up, the warmth from the heater filling the interior once again, and I relax against the seat.

"That's better," I murmur.

"You're no fun," he tells me, sounding like a pouty baby.

"Please." I settle my hand on his firm thigh and give it a squeeze. "I am the most fun you've ever had."

His chuckle is rich and warm and settles deep within me. "You're not wrong, Bells. You're not wrong."

THIRTY-FOUR

ARABELLA

ROWAN TAKES me to the closest town to their house, and it's the epitome of New England quaint. The trees have lost most of their leaves, thanks to the brisk weather, so the fall vibes have faded away which is fine since it's Black Friday and everything is all Christmas, all the time from now until December 25th.

The sidewalks are crowded with shoppers and it takes us a while to find a parking spot but finally we're outside, approaching the shops that line the street downtown.

"Where are we going?" I ask as I try to keep up with Rowan's long stride. Now that he's gotten rid of the boot, I have to practically run to match his pace.

"There's this coffee shop up ahead that has great breakfast sandwiches. And good coffee."

"Ooh, perfect. I would love to drink something festive." I rub my hands together, dropping them at my sides, and he does the craziest thing.

He grabs my hand, interlocking our fingers. And he keeps holding my hand as we make our way along the sidewalk. He even slows his steps so I don't have to make two for his every one and I am smiling. Grinning really, over this moment that feels so profound. Rowan Lancaster is holding my hand.

I repeat, Rowan Reginald Lancaster is holding my hand.

We enter the packed coffee shop and wait in line. I take everything in, loving how cute it is inside. There's a massive chalkboard hanging along the back wall with the menu and someone drew a massive wreath in the center of it, the ribbon entwined around the boughs saying, *Season's Greetings*. I cling to Rowan's arm and read the menu, tilting my head just enough that I'm sort of leaning it on his solid shoulder and I can feel him glancing down at me.

When I tilt my head back to smile up at him, he does another crazy thing.

He kisses me.

Right there in the middle of the crowded shop.

It's brief, nothing scandalous at all, but I feel that quick brush of his lips on mine all the way down to my toes. If I had a decent voice, I would be singing. Belting at the top of my lungs because I'm so, so happy.

"What are you going to get?" he asks me, knocking me out of my dream-like state.

"I want a gingerbread latte. Or maybe a peppermint white chocolate mocha." I lean into his shoulder again. "What are you going to get?"

"That breakfast sandwich I like, the one with bacon, and a vanilla latte. I don't like the real sweet drinks."

The coffee shop clears out a bit and by the time we're ordering at the counter, I can hear the Christmas music playing gently in the background. Frank Sinatra is crooning "Let it Snow! Let it Snow! Let it Snow!"

I feel like I'm in a movie. One of those sweet Hallmark Christmas movies or maybe a fun and sexy rom com on Netflix where the couple makes out a lot. Hallmark movies are sweet, but the couples rarely kiss until the movie is practically over.

I prefer a little more action in my holiday movies.

Once we've ordered, we find a tiny round table and settle in, our feet tangling together since we're so close to each other. Row sheds his coat, letting it hang on the back of his chair, and I rest my elbow on the table, propping my chin on my curled fist while I stare at him. He checks his phone before shoving it into the front pocket of his hoodie and when his gaze meets mine, his brows draw together.

"Are you staring at me, Bells?"

"I've been staring at you since you showed me your car, Row."

"I guess I won't give you shit for it since it's your birthday."

"Aw, thank you. That means a lot." I glance around the café before I return my attention to him. "I love it here."

"You haven't even tried it yet."

"I don't have to try the coffee to love it. It's so cute inside. I feel like I'm on a Christmas movie set."

"Do you hate having your birthday so close to Christmas?"

"I never really thought about it before." And that's because no one ever makes a big deal about my birthday, though I'm not going to say that out loud. I'm not in the mood to be a downer today.

"Hmm." He leans back against his chair, crossing his arms, his biceps all bulky and big. My Row is muscular and strong, and I love it. Anytime he's got his shirt off I want to lick him. And I have. Many times.

A wistful sigh leaves me. He arches his brow. I smirk.

"Should I ask you what you're thinking about?"

"Probably not. It's inappropriate."

He chuckles. "Now you have to tell me."

I slowly shake my head. "I'll tell you later."

"Tell me now."

"Rowan."

"Arabella."

I laugh and shake my head again. My cheeks are hot from embarrassment which doesn't happen much when I'm with Rowan. "I was admiring your...arms."

He glances down at them. "Yeah?"

"You have nice ones."

"Thank you."

"You have nice everything."

"You do too." His gaze rakes over me, setting my skin on fire.

"And once I started thinking about your nice arms, I thought of you shirtless and how I want to lick you every time you take your shirt off." I press my lips together, enjoying the heat I see flare in his gaze.

"We didn't really do much last night, huh."

"I wasn't in the mood." I shrug one shoulder and decide to be truthful. "It was an emotional day for me."

"How are you feeling today?"

"On top of the world, but a little worried about what your mother is planning." At his frown, I forge on. "What if she has us doing too many activities and we'll be tired at the end of the night?"

"I think you'll want to stay awake for the present I'm going to give you later tonight after the party is over." His suggestive tone is nearly my undoing. Forget tonight. Why not do it now instead?

"I might be exhausted from all the planned festivities." I'm lying. I'll never be too tired for him.

"Better keep drinking coffee all day then." They call his name at the counter and he stands, pausing right beside me, his intense gaze locking on mine. "I'm going to keep you up all night, Bells."

He leaves me a quivery mess to go grab our order, and I clutch my shaking hands together, resting them on top of the table. We're going to have sex tonight and I'm excited. Nervous. I was shit at it before with Bentley, but I blame my partner. And well, I blame myself. We were young and awkward and had no idea what we were doing.

It's not like that with Rowan. He makes me feel sexy. The way he looks at me, touches me, kisses me, it's wonderful. Mind-blowing. We are compatible sexually and it's never awkward or weird. Sometimes we're a little overenthusiastic and can get carried away, but it's always...fun.

Better than fun. It's hot. Despite his admitted inexperience, he knows what he's doing.

"Your face is red, Bells," he drawls, setting my to-go coffee cup in front of me. The barista drew the outline of a Christmas tree on the side of my cup, even adding a star on top. I smile at it before I take a sip.

"This is delicious." I take another sip of my gingerbread latte, setting it on the table in front of me while I watch Rowan unwrap his breakfast sandwich. "And you should never call a person out for blushing. It's not polite."

"I never claimed I was polite." He takes a big bite, and my stomach growls despite the fact that I ate breakfast not that long ago. And when he catches me staring at his sandwich, he holds it out toward me. "Want a bite?"

"I couldn't." I shake my head. "I already ate."

"And you're looking at this sandwich like how you used to look at me in class." He's grinning and I tear off a piece of the wrapper that was around his sandwich, balling it up and throwing it at him. It nails him right on the chin.

Ha. Take that, Rowan.

"You make me sound like a secret stalker," I accuse.

"You said it, not me. And there was nothing secret about your stalking." He takes another bite of his sandwich, humming as he chews. "This is fucking delicious."

My stomach growls again but the Christmas song "Happy Holiday" is playing so loudly Rowan can't hear it. I take a sip of my coffee, hoping it'll help subside my hunger.

The song ends and "Blue Christmas" comes on next.

"I love this song. It's so sad." I remain quiet, listening to it while Rowan eats his sandwich and I'm so preoccupied with the lyrics, swaying to the beat, I don't notice at first that Rowan has set the remainder of his sandwich on the wrapper and pushed it toward me.

"I don't like it when you say you're sad," he admits, gesturing at the sandwich with a flick of his chin. "You can have the rest."

"I couldn't. I don't want to take it away from you." I'm touched by his offer. "And I didn't say I was sad. I said the song was sad."

"Same diff for me," he admits. "Taste it, Bells. You won't regret it."

I do as he says, taking a big bite of the breakfast sandwich, and oh my God, he was right. It's delicious. I immediately take another bite, savoring the bacon and egg and cheese. The hint of potato. And is that hot sauce on it? "This is amazing," I say once I've swallowed.

"Right?" He takes a sip from his coffee. "You want to check out the shops?"

"I guess." I pause. "Is that what you want to do?"

"Mom said I needed to preoccupy you for the next few hours. We can come back to the house around two."

I check my phone. "That's three hours from now. What are we going to do until then?"

I don't want to shop. The only reason I'd want to wander around is so I could keep holding Rowan's hand and pretend we're really together. We haven't talked about the status of our relationship at all and I'm a little afraid to bring it up, especially now that I'm leaving.

"We could continue our drive," he suggests.

"That sounds better than shopping," I admit.

A lopsided smile appears on his face. "I'm shocked. Every girl I know wants to shop."

Don't get me wrong, I adore shopping. But wandering around for the next few hours and looking at cute trinkets in stores sounds like a waste of time. And we are running out of that.

"I'd rather be alone with you," I murmur.

His gaze takes on a warm glow and I'm breathless. "Whatever the birthday girl wants, the birthday girl gets."

THIRTY-FIVE

ROWAN

WE DRIVE AROUND AIMLESSLY AT FIRST until I come across a state park entrance, where I pull in. The parking lot is mostly empty, thanks to it being the day after Thanksgiving, and everyone is with family or out shopping—or whatever it is people do during the Thanksgiving weekend. Plus, it's fucking cold and clouds have been rolling in all morning, making the sky dark and ominous.

I drive along the path that winds through the park, pulling into a small lot that faces a lake, and when I shut off the engine, I turn to look at Arabella. She's wearing a soft smile and her gaze is kind of hazy.

Without hesitation I undo my seat belt and lean in, kissing her. Cupping the side of her face, gliding my fingers across her soft, smooth skin. She opens for me, our tongues meeting, and I shift in my seat, already impatient.

When it comes to Arabella, I'm always impatient.

She eventually undoes her seat belt, shifting forward so she can press her body against mine and I haul her into my arms, making her squeal. Within seconds she's on my lap, straddling me, our breaths coming fast as she leans in, pressing her forehead against mine.

"I've never made out with someone in a car before," she whispers, pressing her mouth against mine. "This is fun."

I shift beneath her, trying to get her off my hard dick but it's no use. She's everywhere, all over me, and do I really want her to move?

Hell no.

Resting my hands on her waist, I slip my fingers beneath the hem of her sweater, but she's got an oversized denim jacket on over it and it's getting in the way.

"You need to get rid of the jacket," I tell her.

She whips it off, tossing it into the back seat.

"Maybe you should get rid of your coat," she suggests.

I take it off, shoving it behind my seat.

"And your hoodie."

"But I don't have anything on under the hoodie." It's like she knew.

Arabella grins. "Perfect."

I slowly shrug out of the sweatshirt, never taking my gaze away from Arabella's, only when I whip the hoodie over my head. She tracks my every move, her lips parted, her eyes dilated. My girl is turned on.

I blink at her, startled by my thoughts. Calling her *my girl*.

But that's what she is. I can't stand the thought of anyone else even talking to her, let alone touching her. Kissing her.

She doesn't realize I'm having a total moment. She's too focused on my bare chest. I watch her as she takes off her glasses and carefully sets them on the dashboard before facing me once more. Without warning she leans in and brushes her mouth across my collarbone, delivering sweet, open-mouthed kisses on my skin.

Pressing my head into the seat, I close my eyes, savoring the feel of her damp lips on my chest. Her tongue. She said she liked licking me and she's proving that fact in this very moment. I cup the back of her head with both of my hands, sliding my fingers into the silky strands of her hair, and she tilts her head back, her gaze on mine.

"Should we do it right now?" she asks, breathless.

I frown. "Do what?"

"Have sex." She buries her face against my neck, her mouth moving when she speaks, making me shiver. "Tell me you have condoms."

I do. I had Pat buy me some a few days ago, and I owe that man big. But do I want to have sex with Arabella for the first time in a car?

"Not yet," I tell her.

She lifts away from my neck. "Why not?"

"I don't want to do it in the back seat. I'll be cramped up."

"We can do it right here." She reaches in between us, settling her hand right over my dick. It flexes beneath her touch. "It would be so hot, don't you think?"

Everything she does to me, with me, is hot as fuck. "Someone could catch us."

"That makes it even more exciting." She tries to look through the window, but it's covered in condensation. "No one is out there. We're safe."

Fuck, I sound like a girl in my own thoughts, but...

"I wanted tonight to be special. For your birthday."

And for myself. Arabella and I have done all kinds of things. We've done everything but have actual sex, but still...I want this first experience between us to happen tonight. After the party. In a bed. Where we can get naked and explore each other's bodies for hours. And if we want to have sex three times, then we can do it.

I don't want my first time with Arabella—my first time ever—to be a quick fuck in my car. We can do that later.

"You are so sweet," she murmurs, kissing me. "You act all grumpy and possessive but there's a romantic soul buried deep inside you."

I part my lips, ready to protest, but she kisses me before I can. And anyway...

I think she might be right. But I only have these romantic feelings for her.

"How about I give you a blowjob," she whispers against my lips. "You can push the seat back—I'd probably fit, don't you think?"

Bells glances over her shoulder, checking out the floorboard before she turns to face me again. "That way every time you drive this car, you'll remember the time I had my mouth full of your dick. Right here."

Jesus. I break out in a sweat at the mental image her words conjure up.

"But it's your birthday," I remind her, my voice weak. A man can only take so much, but turning down a blowjob?

"I want to." She smiles. "I think you've gone down on me enough times over the last few days that I owe you."

"I wasn't keeping count."

Her hand settles on the front of my sweats, fingers curling around my cock. "Maybe I was. Are you going to let me do this or do you want to wait until later?"

Is she making fun of me for what I said earlier? Fuck it, I don't care.

Reaching toward the side of the seat, I hit the button and push it so the seat slides all the way back. "I'm down."

She laughs, brushing the hair away from her face and looking like a total smoke show. Like the girl of all my secret sexual fantasies. "I knew you would be."

Once I've readjusted the steering wheel, she's kneeling in front of me, my sweats pulled down and my dick waving in front of her face. She grabs hold of the base and gives it a firm squeeze, sliding her tongue along her lips as she stares at it.

Fuck. All I wanna do is stuff my cock between her lips and choke her with it, but I need to play it cool.

"You seriously have the prettiest dick I've ever seen." She lets go of the base to trace her index finger along the flared head.

"The prettiest?" I am literally sweating, dying for her to suck me deep.

"It's perfect. Like, I could look up the word penis in the dictionary and there would be a photo of your dick accompanying the definition."

"You say the craziest shit," I murmur, shaking my head.

"Keeps life interesting, don't you think?" Her mischievous gaze locks with mine and I'm about to reply when she grabs hold of my cock and wraps her lips around just the head. Her cheeks hollow out as she sucks me deep, and I bump my head against the seat, closing my eyes.

But then I realize I can't watch her and that's my favorite thing to do so I open my eyes once more, my focus on her lips. How they slide up and down my shaft as she takes me as deep into her mouth as she can. She braces her hands on the inside of my thighs, her touch burning my skin. Burning me alive. It's so fucking hot in this car and she's so fucking hot, sucking me off like it's her favorite thing to do.

Maybe it is. With Arabella, I wouldn't doubt it. She's not afraid to ask for what she wants, and I like that about her. I like a lot of things about her.

I'm pretty sure I'm falling in love with her.

Reaching out, I brush her hair away from her face, holding it so I can see more clearly. She lifts her gaze to mine, that knowing look in her eye before she grips me tight with her fingers and bobs her head up and down, increasing her speed.

I'm already close. It takes only a few minutes for her to push me right over the edge every damn time and this moment in the car is no exception. Being all cramped up in my car while parked at a public park makes it even hotter. I lift my hips, needing her deeper, wanting her to suck harder, and as if she can read my mind, she does exactly that, her mouth like a fucking vacuum, her fingers squeezing around my shaft. She practically gags on my dick at one point and her eyes water, her gaze lifting to mine once more.

"I'm gonna come," I warn her but she never lifts away. She's a good girl who drinks every last drop. My stomach muscles constrict, my balls fucking tingle, and then it's happening. I'm coming with a shout, bracing my hand on the ceiling of the car, my cock throbbing as I unload in her mouth. She parts her lips at one point, letting me see the cum still in her mouth, and fuck me, I groan the loudest I think I've ever groaned.

"Now who's the screamer, hmm?" she says once I'm done and I'm sitting there like a boneless heap, unable to move. She braces her hands on my knees and somehow gets herself over the console and back into the passenger seat, wiping her mouth with the back of her hand. She reaches for the to-go coffee cup sitting in the cup holder and takes a sip. "Did you like it?"

I can only gape at her, unable to speak. Did I like it? I freaking loved it.

"It's not like you to be silent, Rowan. Did I just give you the best blowjob of your life or what?" She is grinning, pleased with herself.

Unable to resist, I reach for her, gripping the back of her head as I give her a long, tongue-filled kiss. We kiss and kiss until my cock acts like it wants more action and finally, reluctantly, I pull away from her delicious lips.

"We should go back to the house," I mumble, shoving my semi-hard dick back into my sweats before I dive behind the seat to grab my hoodie.

"But it's not two o'clock yet."

"I'll drive slow," I reassure her and when our gazes meet, I wonder if I look as dopey and as dreamy as she did back at the coffee shop. Because that's how I feel. I'm in a fucking haze with this girl.

And I don't mind. Not one bit.

THIRTY-SIX
ARABELLA

WE SNEAK back into the house around one thirty, going in through the door that's off the kitchen and running up the back staircase, me giggling the entire time while Rowan is constantly shushing me. I'm not afraid of getting caught. I don't think Wren would mind if we came back early, but Row is all twisted up over it and wants us to be quiet.

Whatever.

I'm still full of pride over that BJ I gave him. Talk about epic. Talk about feeling like a complete slut, though I always remind myself I'm only a slut for him. For my Rowan.

That's how I think of him lately. Mine. He's my favorite person in the entire world. I've had a crush on him for years and even wondered if it was love—not that I have any experience dealing with that emotion. But truly, I think it was more that I was in love with the *idea* of him. The persona he puts on at school. His extraordinary good looks and the way he moves. How I'd catch him looking at me the last few months—since we started our senior year—and saw interest in his gaze. Hunger. It wasn't just one-sided between us.

Obviously.

Now that we've become closer, I am without a doubt completely in love with him. This isn't a schoolgirl crush. This feels like the real deal. At least, I think it does. I don't have the best gauge when it comes to love.

"I need to get ready," I tell him once we're in the corridor where our bedrooms are. "Like take a shower, do my hair. Put on some makeup."

I want to look pretty—and I packed an outfit for a special occasion because I had a feeling that I'd need it. I am an overpacker and most of the time, it works to my advantage.

"Okay." He props his shoulder against the wall, watching me as I open my bedroom door. "Want to text me when you're done and we can head downstairs together?"

Smiling brightly, I blurt, "Sure!" Waving, I push the door open farther and practically run into the room, slamming it behind me and turning the lock.

I swear I hear him chuckle as he walks away.

All I can do is stand there for a moment and breathe. Collect my thoughts. Ponder over my earlier realization that I am in love with Rowan, which is exactly what I told myself I should *not* do. But as per usual, I went ahead and fell for him anyway.

How could I resist him? Not only is he wonderful and sweet and totally into me, but his family is wonderful too. And this house. They must sprinkle magic pixie dust in every room and even outside because it's exhilarating just spending time here.

As if I'm wrapped up in this delicious warm cocoon that I never want to leave. I wish these people were my family and that I belonged here for real. Not as a guest but as an actual member of their family.

A Lancaster.

But I'm not and I certainly can't entertain ludicrous thoughts like marrying Rowan. I am eighteen today and already contemplating marriage? Who am I?

A girl in love, whispers a tiny voice inside me.

More like a girl who's lost her common sense. I need to focus on the positives in my life, and while Rowan is one of them, there are many other good things happening to me.

Pushing away from the door, I make my way over to the closet and thumb through the clothes I brought with me, pulling out the dress I plan on wearing to my party. It might be a little over the top but that's my usual style wherever I go, meaning I'm staying on brand.

It's red and short, with straps that tie on my shoulders and a little flounce at the hem. It's pretty yet a little bit sexy, and I hope Rowan swallows his tongue when he sees me in it.

Well, not literally, but I am eager to see his reaction. And I'm not wearing anything underneath it either.

Happy Birthday to me.

I'm trying to do my hair in the bathroom, clad only in a plush terrycloth robe that was in the room when I got here when I hear a knock on my door.

Setting the hairdryer on the counter, I rush to the door, fully expecting it to be Rowan waiting for me but it's not.

It's Beau, wearing a grimace on his face as he peers around the massive flower bouquet that he's carrying.

"These came for you." He thrusts them toward me, and I have no other option but to take the heavy arrangement. "See ya."

"Wait!" He stops, turning to look at me. "Who sent these?"

"I don't know." He shrugs. His grumpy attitude is reminding me of his older brother and I can't help but find it endearing. "A delivery guy dropped them off and Mom said I had to bring them to you."

"Thank you." I smile at him, but he doesn't smile back. "Beau, I have a question."

His expression turns wary. "What is it?"

"Do you hate me?"

Eyes going wide, he furiously shakes his head. "No. No way. I barely know you, Arabella. How can I hate you?"

"Well, you're grumpy every time you're around me and you don't seem to like talking to me either." I clutch the flowers closer—they are gorgeous, mostly deep red roses and they remind me of my dress—and wait for his answer. I'm tired of dealing with grouchy Lancaster men. They need to be called out on their shit, even if they're only sixteen or however old Beau is.

"Sorry," he mutters, shuffling his feet and keeping his gaze downcast. Like he doesn't want to look at me. "I guess I'm still mad that I didn't get to do what I wanted for Thanksgiving break and my brother is allowed to have you over so you two can hook up anywhere you can in the house."

I peek out of the doorway, checking the corridor to make sure no one else is around before I wave my free hand at Beau. "Come inside, please."

His eyes wide, he follows me into my room, shutting the door behind him. I set the flower arrangement on the desk and turn to face him, resting my hands on my hips. Feeling stern and like I'm about to drop a big ol' lecture, which he deserves.

"Look, Beau. I know you think Rowan and I are together, but we're actually not. And while yes, I've had a crush on him and I'm grateful that we've become closer this week, Rowan's initial intention to invite me to your house—which is lovely, by the way —was as a friend. He felt sorry for me because I was supposed to stay on campus all week by myself."

Beau frowns. "By yourself? Where's your family?"

"My parents live in Hong Kong, and I have no brothers or sisters." I force a smile, hating how fragile I feel, making that confession. "Consider yourself lucky that you have parents who love you and your family that's so close. I wish I had what you have."

He blinks at me, quiet, and I'm sure I rendered him silent thanks to what I said. Well good. He's so wrapped up in his own problems, he deserves to see that other people have issues too.

"And I've seen the real Plymouth Rock," I add. "It's not that big of a deal."

He rolls his eyes. "Everyone loves telling me that. It had nothing to do with that stupid rock and everything to do with the girl."

"If she likes you as much as you seem to like her, she'll still be into you when we all go back to campus. And if she isn't? Then that's her loss. I happen to think you're a catch."

He stands up taller, puffing out his chest. "You do?"

"You're a Lancaster, Beau. Don't ever forget it." I make my way back to the door and hold it open. "Thank you for bringing the flowers, but I need to finish getting ready for my party. You're going, right?"

Beau slowly approaches the open door, stopping in front of me with the most earnest expression on his face, all traces of his anger gone. "I wouldn't miss it. Thanks for the pep talk, Arabella."

My smile is easy. "Anytime, Beau. See you in a bit."

Another door swings open, Beau glancing to his right, and I do the same. Rowan is standing outside his bedroom, a towel wrapped around his hips, his skin still damp, like he just sprinted out of the bathroom to find out who's in the hallway.

"What are you guys talking about?" His tone is casual though his body is tense and he's gripping the side of his towel like it's about to fall off at any second.

"Arabella got flowers for her birthday and Mom had me bring them up to her." Beau sends me a quick look before he says, "Bye."

He practically runs away, and I turn to face Rowan, amusement curling my lips. "You scared him."

"Good," Rowan grunts. "He should be used to it. I've scared him all his life."

"You're a mean brother."

"Not really." He shrugs, drawing my attention to his very naked chest. My gaze drops to the front of his towel and I think I can see the outline of his dick beneath it, but maybe that's my wild imagination playing tricks on me.

"You're also indecent." I wave a hand at him. "Put some clothes on."

His grin is strong enough to melt the panties straight off my body, if I were wearing any. "I thought you liked me this way best."

"Not at the moment." I rest my hands on my hips, much like I did in front of Beau not even a few minutes ago. "You're a distraction when I need to get ready."

"I can help you get ready." He puts the most innocent look I think I've ever seen on his face, but I know it's a ruse. "If you need me."

I always need him. My body is swaying like a flower outside seeking the sun. He is my sun and I am the flower that blooms only when he's shining his light—his smile, his attention— upon me.

"I appreciate the offer, but no thank you." I shake my head and make my way back into my room, peeking around the door to find he hasn't moved. "I'll text you when I'm ready, okay?"

"I'll be waiting," he murmurs, his gaze soaking me up, and I believe him.

Flashing a quick smile at him, I close the door, my gaze snagging on the flower arrangement. I make my way over to it, bending close to one of the roses and breathing in its rich, fragrant scent. Spotting a small envelope, I pluck it from the plastic stand and tear it open to find a card inside, the message typed out.

. . .

Happy Birthday, Bells. I hope it's the best day—you deserve it.

Xo,

Rowan

I CRUSH the card to my chest, closing my eyes. Of course, he sent me flowers. Of course, he hopes it's the best day and that I deserve it. He's trying to make me fall deeper in love with him and it's working. I can't resist him. I can't.

For the rest of my time here—and it is tragically limited—I am going to throw myself headfirst into everything. I am going to make this birthday the best day ever, and once we're back at Lancaster Prep, maybe then I'll try to create some distance between us. If I'm strong enough.

Though I'm probably not. I cannot resist him, and I think he feels the same way about me. We have become so completely intertwined with each other in such a rapid amount of time; I can't imagine me without him. It's going to hurt when I leave for Paris. So much.

I'm not sure I'll be able to survive it.

THIRTY-SEVEN

ROWAN

I PACE the length of my room while I wait for Arabella's text. She's taking forever but I should've known. I remember how long my sister used to take getting ready and Mom is the same way. It makes my impatience ratchet up to about a twelve versus a ten, which is where I usually hover.

Damn, I need to learn how to control my emotions, especially when it comes to Bells. Seeing her in her robe casually chatting with my brother in the hallway did something to me, and I know I'm being fucking ridiculous, but it bothered me. Made me jealous and we're talking about Beau. Arabella isn't interested in him. She's into me.

Acting like a possessive asshole isn't going to earn points with Arabella, though there might be a small part of her that likes it. I don't know. I'm curious about her conversation with my brother. I'd also love to know what she thought about the flowers I sent her. It was an impulsive move since I don't have an actual birthday gift for her tonight, and I hope she liked them.

I let out an aggravated breath, running a hand through my hair. I came to the conclusion while in the shower that I want Arabella to be my girlfriend. I care about her. Might even be in love with her, though I shouldn't tell her that. Not before she leaves for two years and I'll most likely never see her again.

Holy shit, my thoughts are dramatic, but I'm trying to be honest with myself. Out of sight, out of mind may be a cliché, but it's an accurate description. She'll become busy. I'll get busy. We'll drift apart and then it'll be over. Forgotten. Like we never existed together in the first place.

I rub at my chest, trying to ease the ache that forms there. The idea of not having Arabella in my life anymore...

It fucking hurts.

My phone buzzes and I check it, relieved to find it's from Arabella.

Bells: I'm ready! Will you be a gentleman and come pick me up at my door please?

Anything for her. I don't even bother responding to her text. I leave my room in record time and am knocking on her door, shoving my hands in my pockets while I wait for her to appear.

The door swings open and my jaw drops. She's fucking gorgeous in a vivid red dress that shows off her long legs and clings to her curves. There are bows on her shoulders, thanks to the straps that tie there, and all I can think about is undoing them later tonight, long after the party is over and we're in her room.

Swallowing hard, I croak, "Arabella."

It's all I can manage to say.

She grabs hold of her skirt and curtsies. "You look dashing tonight."

I sort of forgot what I was wearing, I'm too entranced with her. "Thanks. You're—beautiful."

Her cheeks turn the faintest pink, which is normally unheard of. Not much embarrasses her, but I feel like today I've been making her blush constantly. "Thank you. I'm so glad I brought this dress. I always like to pack a special occasion outfit because you never know."

Arabella pulls the door shut, smiling up at me. "Shall we?"

I offer her my arm, because she asked me to be a gentleman, and she curls hers around it.

Pulling her closer, I lead her along the hall when she murmurs, "Thank you for the flowers. They're beautiful."

"You're welcome." I let my gaze linger on her, appreciating the dress yet again. "Almost the same color as your dress."

"It's like you knew what color I would wear. Fate."

I've never believed in fate or destiny or any of that stuff. Horoscopes and signs and the stars aligned—it's all a bunch of shit. Though I can admit: Arabella is probably the one person who could convince me that sort of thing is true.

We head down the stairs and I slow my pace, accommodating for the very high heels she's wearing. They're black and make her legs look even longer than they are, and I can't help but let my gaze linger on them as we walk. I take her all in while she's quiet, her energy somewhat nervous, and I appreciate her beauty. Her long, wavy dark hair that trails down her back and the dress. All that skin on display, the front of it dipping low, giving me a view of her cleavage. Even the glasses she's wearing tonight are subtle. No flashy frames that draw people's attention. She looks nothing like the girl I go to school with and see in class every day.

No, Arabella looks like a woman. A beautiful, sophisticated woman, and I'm filled with the sudden urge to beg her to stay here. With me. Fuck Paris.

But I banish the thought because I can't be selfish. Not when it comes to this girl. She's accommodated for others—like her shitty parents—her entire life. She doesn't need me trying to tell her what to do. I refuse to be that guy. I'm greedy, but I'm not a selfish prick.

I'm not.

We come to a stop in the open doorway of the family room, which is living up to its description considering there's an absolute shit ton of my family clustered in there. I'm shocked by the turnout, and from the look on Bells's face, I'd say she is too.

"Happy Birthday, Arabella!" they all shout at once, as if they rehearsed it, and I step away from her so she can shine on her own, basking in their adoration.

I'm not lying when I say that either. Those that were with us yesterday for Thanksgiving told me they loved her and thought she was a great match for me—plenty of the women said this, especially my aunt Charlotte, who is a not-so-secret romantic.

"She looks at you like she's in love with you," Charlotte had told me yesterday, and my gaze somehow finds her now, where she's standing next to my uncle Perry, both of them beaming. She raises a brow, as if she's quietly telling me something, and I get it. I do.

Arabella does look at me like she's in love with me and the look is reciprocated. Feels like all of her birthday guests are looking at her the same way, and they don't even really know her that well yet.

"Oh my gosh, you guys! I can't believe you did all of this for me!" Arabella is absorbed by them as they circle around her, giving me the chance to check out the decorations and everything my mom put together for this party. There are what looks like hundreds of balloons hanging from the ceiling and fresh flower arrangements are set on every available surface. There are servers standing at the ready with silver trays covered with appetizers, and I watch as my mother nods at one of them, launching them all into action as they start circulating through the room. There's a makeshift bar set up in one corner and a DJ on the opposite side, who's currently playing gentle background music as everyone mingles and wishes Arabella a happy birthday.

"Your mother went all out."

I glance to my left to find my dad standing next to me, a proud look on his face. "She really did."

"She likes Arabella." His gaze turns sharp when he levels it on me. "Don't fuck this up."

If I was drinking something, I'd most certainly choke on it at his warning. "What makes you say I'm going to fuck it up?"

"You're a male Lancaster. We don't always make the best decisions." Dad gestures toward Whit, who's standing at the bar with his wife. "Just ask him."

We've heard the story of Whit chasing after Summer when she was in Paris—ironic—since we were little kids, though I'm sure the version we know is a more cleaned-up version of the truth.

"And the men who aren't Lancasters? They never hesitate to go after who they want. Like Spencer." Dad nods in his direction. He's with his son Christopher, though I have no idea where Sylvie is. "And Weston. He's the biggest sap out of all of us."

"Right, and you're not?" I turn to face him, the disbelief obvious in my voice. "Come on, Dad. You spent a million bucks on Mom when you guys were my age."

"She loved that painting." His tone is wistful and before he can start talking about the infamous *A Million Kisses in Your Lifetime*, I keep talking.

"And you loved her."

"You caught me." He throws his arms up, though he doesn't look mad. "I would've done anything for her. I still feel that way."

My gaze hones in on Bells, who's laughing with Iris and Brooks, August approaching them and pulling her in for a hug. I narrow my eyes, ready to cause fucking chaos when I see him put his hands on her, but it's a brief hug and she disentangles herself quickly.

Beside me, Dad starts chuckling. "If you're trying to deny how you feel about her, don't bother. I can see it written all over your face. Pretty sure you were considering murdering August just now."

A rough exhale leaves me. "I need to stop being so possessive."

"There's no point." Dad slaps me on the shoulder. "It's what we do in this family."

"What are you two talking about?" Mom asks, her cheeks flushed, no doubt from the glass of champagne she just emptied. The party is barely getting started and Mom's already lit.

"Nothing, Birdy." Dad pulls her in for a hug and a too long kiss. "Just giving junior here some advice."

"Junior?" I swipe a champagne flute off the tray of one of the servers who walks by. "Seriously?"

"Do you think Arabella likes the party?" Mom's worried tone almost makes me smile.

"She loves it. Look at her. I don't think she's ever had this kind of party before that's all about her." I appreciate my mom doing so much for her.

Mom scowls. "And isn't that awful? Her parents sound like a nightmare."

"According to Grant, they are," Dad adds. We both send him questioning looks and he explains himself. "We were talking about her parents last night. He mentioned that first night you guys came home that he sold them an apartment in Manhattan. He says the father is a pretentious asshole and his wife is a first-class snob. Considering Grant could, and I quote, 'eat them for fucking dinner,' he thought they were, and I quote again, 'horribly obnoxious people.'"

Mom and I share a look, anger coursing through my blood. I hate Arabella's parents and I've never even met them.

"When I was her age, my parents were kind of awful," Mom admits.

"Even Grandma?" I love my grandma. She's always overindulged all of us and used to come and stay with us during the summer for weeks at a time. Or we'd go to her house. She doesn't travel as much as she used to but we still see her often, especially during Christmas. She likes to spend Thanksgiving going on a cruise with her friends. It's been an annual tradition for her the last few years.

"When my parents were still married, they were—awful." Mom winces. "Wrapped up in their own problems all the time. My father showered me with attention but now I look back and think he did that to make my mother angry."

I hate hearing that. My grandfather died when I was little, so I don't have many memories of him.

"I relate to Arabella more than I like to admit. I could've been her, or she could've been me." Mom's smile is small. "But she's got a lot more strength than I ever did."

"I don't know about that, babe." Dad wraps her up in his arms, kissing her yet again, like he can't help himself. Mom pats him on the chest, smiling up at him. "You have always been one of the strongest women I've known."

I drain my glass in one massive swallow, setting it on a nearby table.

"I'm going to leave you two alone," I inform them before I take off, not in the mood to get caught up in their conversation. I've heard the majority of their stories before and I'm more in the mood to make my own stories tonight.

With Arabella.

She spots me as I approach her, her expression shifting, a big smile stretching across her pretty face. I smile back, letting all of the emotions I feel toward her shine in my eyes, and she goes still, clutching a champagne flute that's still full of golden, bubbly liquid, her big brown eyes tracking my every step as I make my way toward her.

I'll never forget this moment. The way she's watching me, surrounded by my family, that red dress and those black heels. The lipstick she's wearing is the same shade as the dress, and I imagine kissing it off her. Right in front of everyone.

Once I'm standing before her, I haul her into my arms and do exactly that, kissing her soundly to the hoots and hollers of everybody in the room. There's even a smattering of applause, someone whistles loudly, and when we break apart, I reach out, brushing the corner of her mouth, smudging her lipstick.

"Couldn't resist," I murmur, and she laughs, wrapping her arms around my neck...

Just before she kisses me again.

THIRTY-EIGHT

ARABELLA

ROWAN WAS CORRECT. This has been the best night of my life. The best birthday I've ever experienced. There was plenty of champagne and delicious appetizers, and the adults turned a blind eye to us drinking since we weren't going anywhere tonight. The pizza was delicious, coming from an Italian place nearby, and the cake was heart-shaped and frosted white, *Happy Birthday Arabella* spelled out in pink frosting across the top of it. Everyone sang to me and I just stood there in the glow of the candles on top of the cake, wanting to cry at how sweet they were being.

Especially Rowan.

Once the cake was served, I opened presents and so many of them brought me something. Gift cards and nail polish and body lotions, typical girly stuff. The twins Paris and Pru made me a stack of friendship bracelets and I've had them on ever since, proud to wear them. Wren and Crew gave me a hot pink cashmere sweater that is so bright, I could probably stop traffic when I wear it, but it's also so me. I clutched it to my chest and blubbered my thank you, almost crying yet again.

I've been on the verge of tears all night. My own parents don't treat me this well on my birthday. I haven't heard from them all day, not that I'm surprised. Mother did wish me a happy birthday yesterday, but I think she had ulterior motives. Specifically trying to get the answer out of me about the apprenticeship.

After the gifts were opened, the DJ started playing music and everyone is currently dancing in the middle of the makeshift dance floor. Even Rowan, who doesn't have the best rhythm, but he's cute for trying. He's been in good spirits all evening. Haven't spotted a single scowl on his handsome face, not once.

He's dressed to perfection too, in black pants and a pale gray button-down that he left open at the throat. I want to press my mouth right at that spot and inhale his spicy scent but I restrain myself. It's bad enough how we kissed in front of everyone, but I'm guessing it wasn't that much of a surprise. The only groan I heard came from Beau but I think it was all in good fun.

Poor little frustrated boy. He'll get his chance with a girl someday.

The music stops, and a slow song comes on. All the parents are out on the floor, swaying to the music and I wait, breathless as Row wraps me up in his strong arms.

He doesn't disappoint, sweeping me into his embrace and holding me close. I twine my arms around his neck, the two of us shuffling to the beat, and I rest my cheek against his hard chest, taking note of his rapidly beating heart.

"Are you having fun?" His low murmur rumbles in his chest and I lift away to stare into his eyes.

"It's the best birthday I've ever had," I admit. There are no lies detected in that statement. I don't know how anyone could ever top this day.

"Good." He leans in, kissing my forehead. "Everyone went all out for you."

"They didn't have to," I protest but he shakes his head once.

"Pretty sure they all wanted to." He smiles, his eyes glowing. "My family likes you."

"I like them." I love them. I wish they were mine, but alas...

They're not.

"The cake was delicious," I blurt, unsure what to say next because that heated gleam in Row's gaze is starting to make me feel squirmy.

In the very best way.

"It was good." He sounds amused.

"And the pizza," I tack on.

"That's my favorite place."

"I think I ate four pieces." Should I have admitted that? Probably not. Oh well.

"I ate five, I think." He's grinning. So am I. But my grin fades when he dips his head and whispers in my ear, "When can we get out of here?"

I tilt my head down, shivering from his mouth brushing against my earlobe. "I can't leave my party early."

"Says who?"

"Says me." I lift my head to look at him. "That would be rude."

"And Arabella Hartley Thomas is never, ever rude," he teases.

"You're right. I'm not." I sound a little snotty and I remind myself of my mom which is just...no. Not good.

His expression shifts, turning dreadfully serious. "I want to be alone with you. I've been looking forward to this moment all day."

I can't tear my gaze away from his. He's so sincere. So sweet. The sweetest I've ever seen him act toward me. I think back to a week ago, when we drove here. How excited I was. How I knew my entire life was going to change and I was right in so many ways.

Even some unexpected ones.

"I've been looking forward to it too." I press my lips together and glance about the room, noting how there are less people in it. Some have already left. The room is not nearly as crowded as when the party first started, and it's close to eleven thirty. "How long does your mother have the DJ hired for tonight?"

"That's a good question. I'll ask her after this song."

We shuffle around the dance floor, his hands sliding down, almost covering my butt and I send him a stern look. "You're really going to grope me in front of your parents?"

"I don't think they're paying us any attention." He slides his hand over my right butt cheek, giving it a firm squeeze and making me yelp. "I can't help myself. I've been dying to touch you all night."

"You *have* been touching me all night."

"Not in the way I want to."

The promise in his voice is making me a quivery mess. My knees are knocking and everything. "You're bad."

"You like it."

He's right. I do.

The song ends and I excuse myself to use the bathroom while Row goes in search of his mother. By the time I'm finished and am washing my hands in the very bathroom where Rowan had me sprawled out naked and his mouth buried between my thighs, my phone buzzes on the counter.

It's my mother calling.

"Darling, where are you? Aren't you on campus?" This is how my mother greets me.

"No, I went home with a friend to spend the holiday with their family. Remember?"

See how I carefully choose my words so she can't detect the gender of my friend? I'm not dumb.

"Who exactly are you with?"

A sigh escapes me and I decide to be truthful. "Rowan Lancaster."

"Rowan *Lancaster*? Are you serious? Are the two of you dating?"

"No." I have no idea how to describe what I'm doing with Rowan to my mother. Fucking around? She would never approve. Or maybe she would. I don't know. "We're friends."

"Well, that's the kind of friend any girl would want to have. A Lancaster." She sounds in absolute awe over the revelation. "They're a powerful family."

"They're a nice family. They had a party for me and everything."

"That's right. It's still your birthday!"

"For approximately thirty minutes, yes." I stare at my reflection in the mirror, pleased that my makeup is still good. My lipstick is mostly faded but that's okay. My cheeks are flushed, thanks to the alcohol we've consumed, though I've stopped drinking. I noticed Rowan has too. I think we want to be sober for what's about to happen.

My stomach flutters with nerves at the thought, which is silly. We've done a lot of things together. I've seen him naked. He's seen me naked. What's the big deal?

"I just made it." She laughs but I remain quiet. My disappointment in her, in my father too, hits me hard.

All I ever wanted was for my parents to show me some love. Shower me with affection. At the very least, acknowledge my existence. But they can't be bothered with it, with me, and that...

God, it hurts.

The Lancasters are virtual strangers and look how easily they accepted me. Showering me with attention and love and gifts. Making my birthday the absolute best ever, despite only meeting me a few days ago. It's unfair, how terrible my parents are.

"Well, Happy Birthday, Arabella. I hope you've had a nice day," she says, filling up the silence because it's obvious I'm not in the mood to speak.

"Thank you." My voice is clipped. Formal. And she can hear it.

"You do understand that we're busy," she says, an irritated sigh escaping her and anger seeps into my skin. "We've had this conversation before."

"Right." Ad nauseum, if I'm being real with myself. I don't know how many times I've heard the, *we want what's best for you, and that comes with your father working terribly hard to give you whatever you need.*

They've never really given me what I need. Maybe I didn't want the best. Maybe I just wanted them. In my life. Supporting me.

"I wish you could understand. Not everything is about you."

That's a good one. "It's never really about me, is it?"

She goes silent and I suppose I should feel triumphant, but I don't. It hurts more that my reality is this: I have parents who don't give a shit about me and then they try and make me feel bad when I complain—well, that's how my mother treats me. I rarely speak to my father. We don't spend much time together, and never one-on-one. Does he even remember my name? What I look like?

"I have a question." I clear my throat, the idea striking me, and I brace myself, scared of her answer.

"What is it?" Mother asks warily.

"Did you get me that apprenticeship because you remembered how much I loved sketching and making jewelry? Or did you do that because you wanted more of an in with the jeweler?"

She actually bursts out laughing, like what I'm asking is hilarious to her. All while I stand in the bathroom with my back to the mirror because I don't want to see the furious expression on my face.

"I don't need an 'in' with the jeweler, darling. I am one of their best customers. You wouldn't believe how much money I've spent there over the years. I can get whatever I want from them. Whatever. I. Want. And that apprenticeship? It's a rare thing. They don't offer it to just anyone, and once you get there, you'll have to prove yourself. But if you don't want to do it, then say so. I'll let them know you don't have what it takes."

With those last words, she ends the call.

Leaving me reeling.

THIRTY-NINE

ROWAN

AFTER SEARCHING FOR HER, I find Arabella in the foyer, a dazed expression on her pretty face as she hugs my family members before they leave. Every time the door swings open, a blast of freezing cold air rushes in, and I see the goosebumps dotting her exposed flesh.

Going to her, I slip my arm around her shoulders and she startles, her head jerking up, gaze meeting mine. "Oh. Hey."

"Hey." She seems completely out of it, her eyes dull, her skin pale. "Are you all right?"

"No. No, I'm not." Shaking her head, her face crumples and her eyes are glassy with unshed tears.

My heart freezing, I steer her around and we head for the stairwell. "Let's get out of here."

"But I didn't thank everyone for coming." She digs her heels in, not budging, and I drop my arm from her shoulders, snagging up her hand instead.

"You've already thanked everyone enough. Come on, Bells. Let's get you into bed." All thoughts of having sex with this girl go out the window, and I'm okay with it. Too worried by the zombie-like look on her face. How she's talking like a robot. What happened? Why is she upset? Because it's obvious. Tears are streaming down her face and little hiccups leave her, like she's trying to hold back from full-blown sobbing.

Shit. Shit, shit, shit.

We walk up the stairs in silence, her icy hand curled around mine. I lead her down the hall and she stumbles over her feet, like she's not watching where she's going, and I wrap my arm around her waist, steadying her.

"Come on," I murmur, stopping in front of her closed bedroom door. "Let's get you inside."

She goes willingly when I open the door, my arm dropping from her waist. I shut the door and find her standing in the middle of the room, her shoulders shaking.

I go to her and pull her into my arms, letting her sob into my shirt while I run my fingers through her hair. I don't say any useless words. I don't think anything would comfort her in this moment and she'll explain when she's ready. There's the tiniest flicker inside me that worries it's something I did, but what could it be?

This isn't about me. I can feel it.

"I-I'm s-sorry." She pulls away slightly, and I do what I always do when she cries—brush her tears away with a gentle sweep of my thumb, absorbing them into my skin. If I could take away all her pain, to make her stop crying, I would.

"Why are you apologizing?"

"I-I'm ruining the night." She takes a deep breath, holds it for a second and then lets it out slowly. Shakily. "I don't know why I'm so upset."

"What happened?" I tilt my head, peering at her. Trying to look into her eyes. "If you don't want to talk about it, I understand."

"No." Arabella slowly shakes her head, sniffling. "I-I need to talk about it. My mother called me."

"She did? When?"

"When I went to the bathroom. I was washing my hands and she was calling. I thought about my birthday but I had to remind her of it. She forgets about me all the time, and I was just—I was so mad at her, Rowan. Mad at the both of them. They don't care about me. They never have, and in that particular moment while I listened to her talk, all I could do was compare her and my father to your family. How accepting they are of me. How they showered me with attention and gifts and...and love. My parents don't love me, or if they do, they don't know how to show it." More tears flow and I crush her to me, holding her as close as I can. Trying to absorb all of that pain emanating from her.

I hate this. I hate her parents too. They make her feel like garbage, on what should be a happy day too.

"What exactly did she say to you?" I ask, my voice cautious. I don't want to pry, but I assume her mother must've said something awful.

Arabella lifts her head again, her gaze filled with anger. "She implied that I'm ungrateful and self-absorbed, and maybe I shouldn't take that apprenticeship. I asked her if she really did it for me or to give her an in with the jeweler, which was dumb on my part. She needs no in. Her money is what gets her whatever she wants—well, my father's money."

"And she didn't like that."

"Absolutely not." She shakes her head. "She implied I don't have what it takes because I questioned her, and that's unfair. But everything she does is unfair, so at least she stayed consistent."

"I guess you can always count on her then." I smile, trying to ease her sadness.

"Right?" A sigh leaves her and she slowly shakes her head, running her hand down my chest. My skin burns beneath the thin fabric of my shirt just from her touch. "I usually don't let her upset me like this, but she was extra rude. Even hung up on me."

"I'm sorry." I curve my fingers around her chin, smoothing my thumb along her jaw. "I hate that she hurt you."

"I'll be okay," Arabella whispers.

I'm hit with the sudden urge to tell her not to go to Paris. To stay here with me. Finish out our senior year together. I don't want her to leave. What the hell am I going to do when she's gone? It'll be weird not seeing her in every single class, every single day. I'll miss her. She's become a part of me. If Arabella leaves, she's going to take my fucking heart with her. And there's no if about it. She is leaving for another damn country and I can't do anything about it. Asking her to stay is the most selfish thing I could ever do. I have to let her go.

Even if I don't want to.

Another shuddery sigh leaves her, and I can tell she's still rattled. "I'm so tired."

Her lids are heavy and she sways into me like she can hardly stand.

"Come on, let's get you undressed." Pulling away, I take her hand and lead her over to the bed, turning her so that I'm standing behind her. I unzip the back of her dress, my gaze eating up all that bare flesh I'm exposing, but I tell my dirty thoughts to calm the fuck down.

We're not doing what I'd hoped we'd be doing tonight, and that's okay. This girl needs me to comfort her, not fuck her into oblivion.

"Are you trying to strip me, Rowan?" A glimmer of normal Bells shines in that one question and I smile, pushing the straps of her dress aside, watching them fall off her shoulders.

"I know you're sleepy," I tell her, wanting her to get that I'm not trying anything.

The dress falls in a heap at her feet, revealing that she wore nothing underneath it, and my eyes widen slightly, taking her in. Her body is beautiful, even from behind. Her perfect heart-shaped ass and those long, sexy legs.

I curl my hands into fists, fighting the need to touch her. She turns her head, watching me from over her shoulder and she smiles.

"I'm not made of glass," she murmurs. "You can touch me."

I settle my hands on the dip of her waist immediately, curling my fingers into her soft, warm skin. She's not cold anymore, but her flesh is covered with goosebumps anyway. Most likely from me. "I hate that she made you so fucking sad."

"Forget her." Arabella turns to face me, and my gaze drops to her chest because it always does. "Eyes up here, Lancaster."

Her amused tone makes me smile and I meet her gaze, pulling her into me, my mouth finding hers in a gentle kiss. Despite what she said, I'm still treating her like she's fragile by restraining myself. Keeping the kiss simple, my tongue swiping at her lips. She parts them immediately and I slide my tongue against hers, savoring her taste. Reveling in the way she molds her body to mine, her fingers going to the front of my shirt and undoing the buttons.

"I need you," she murmurs against my lips, and my heart trips over itself at the urgency in her voice. "Help me forget, Rowan."

I unleash on her as if I have no control, which I don't when it comes to her. My hands are everywhere, wandering all over her naked body as I steer us closer to the bed. Next thing I know she's falling backward and I'm following after her, careful to brace my weight so I don't crush her. Not that she seems to mind. She wraps her legs around my hips, grinding her naked pussy on my dick, making me throb.

Making me ache.

I didn't think we'd do this. Not after spotting her looking devastated not even fifteen minutes ago in the foyer. God, seeing her like that. Broken and vulnerable and in shock, all I wanted to do was hold her close and protect her. I still feel that way. Seeing her hurt, hurts me. And I've never felt that way before about anyone, save my mom, and that's a different kind of emotion.

What I feel for Arabella is all-consuming. Overpowering. Even a little confusing.

It's love. That's what it has to be, and I've heard the speech time and again over the years from my father. From any Lancaster really. Once you find that one person, it's over. They are it. Yours forever.

That's Arabella. She's it. My forever. But how can I tell her that when she's going to leave in a matter of weeks? I refuse to hold her back. I am more than willing to sacrifice my feelings for her.

Even if it ends up leaving me with a broken heart.

FORTY

ARABELLA

ALL ANGRY, frustrated thoughts involving my parents—specifically my mother—flee from my brain the moment Rowan puts his hands on my naked body. He became the only thing I could focus on. The only one I wanted. I'm lying crushed beneath him on the bed as he kisses me along my neck, nibbling and licking me there, and I have my hands in his soft hair, wishing I would've taken his shirt off before we fell onto the bed.

I'm desperate to feel his skin on mine.

Impatient, I shove at the shirt, pushing it off his shoulders, and he lifts away from me, hurriedly taking it off and tossing it on the floor before he resumes kissing my neck. I race my hands all over his back, his shoulders. Along his sides. Slip my fingers beneath the waistband of his pants, wishing those were gone too.

I want him as naked as I am.

No one makes me feel as good, as whole, as Rowan does. He was so sweet earlier, trying his hardest to comfort me and it worked.

He was all I needed. Everything I wanted. And when he unzipped my dress, I could feel his restraint. His uncertainty. He settled his big, warm hands on my hips, and I knew.

This is what I wanted to help me take my mind off my troubles.

"You have condoms, right?" I'm just making sure because oh my God, I can't wait anymore. If he says no, I am willing to be reckless and let him inside me without one. He can pull out. I just had my period the week before so I should be good. Right?

He lifts his head from my neck, his hand settling on my right breast. "Yeah."

A shiver streaks down my spine at the rough sound of his voice. And when he lowers his head, his lips brushing against my distended nipple, I cry out, curling my fingers into his hair. Holding him close.

I wish I didn't ever have to let him go.

Rowan rains kisses all over my body, his hands everywhere. Curving around my breasts, along my waist, my hips. Fingers brushing between my thighs, testing me. I'm soaked, I can hear his fingers sliding up and down, circling my clit. One thick finger presses inside me. I close my eyes, holding my breath, my stomach constricting, skin tightening in anticipation of him moving within me.

"Fuck, you're already so wet, Bells," he murmurs when he lifts away from me, his fingers still working their magic between my thighs.

I decide I can't lie. "I want you."

When I open my eyes, I find him watching me, his hair mussed, his lids heavy, his lips parted. He's handsome. Gorgeous. And all mine.

Mine.

Mine.

Mine.

"I want you too," he murmurs, shifting back up over me, our gazes locking. He dips his head, his hungry mouth settling on mine, and I open up to him, reaching between us and fumbling with the front of his pants. Once I've got the button undone, I tug on the zipper, diving my hand inside and brushing my fingers against the front of his boxer briefs. His erection.

He's hard. Hot. I'm impatient, shoving at his pants, his boxers. He pulls away and takes care of them for me, stripping off the rest of his clothes until he's gloriously naked. The moment he lies down on top of me, trapping me beneath him, I run my hands up and down his smooth back, his firm ass.

Rowan has a beautiful body. Far more defined than mine. I don't exercise much, unless you consider constantly changing clothes to get your outfit just right a sport.

Prior to the accident, he was an elite athlete who worked out constantly. I know he has regrets about his broken ankle. Would he have pursued football in college? He still could if he wanted to. Would he go to a big university while I'm stuck in Paris?

Pushing all of those thoughts out of my head, I focus on him. I lift my head, pressing my mouth against the center of his chest, his heart thundering beneath my lips, and I smile, knowing that I do that to him.

A week ago, I could've never imagined we'd get to this point, but here we are.

Here we are.

"Your skin is so soft." His tone is reverent as he strokes his fingers across my stomach before sliding his hand up to cup my breast. "I never want to stop touching you."

"Don't stop. Please." I sound like I'm begging but I don't care. "Just—keep doing what you're doing."

His smile is slow and sure and the sight of it makes my pussy throb. "There's my girl."

My entire body flushes at him calling me his girl. He is really trying to destroy me, isn't he. With a few choice words and his hands and mouth, I'm a wreck. A wreck for him.

He kisses me before I can say anything else, stealing my words, my thoughts. I give into his greedy kiss, even greedier than him, our tongues tangling and teeth clashing and hands roaming. I've got his cock firmly in my grip, sliding up and down, rubbing my thumb across the head, smearing the precum everywhere.

"Jesus," he grunts, thrusting into my hand. "I don't know if I'm going to last much longer."

"Get the condoms," I demand, impatient. I'm tired of waiting.

I need him inside me.

He crawls off me and goes to grab his pants from the floor, pulling out a single condom that he must've been carrying in his pocket. He stands at the foot of the bed, tearing the wrapper open and pulling the condom out before he settles the ring over the tip of his dick, slowly rolling it on.

I watch with obvious interest, pressing my thighs together to stave off the ache. He lifts his head, his dark green gaze meeting mine, and I see nothing but pure heat there. All that want and need that matches the emotions swirling within me.

Unable to stop myself, I sit up, propped against the pillows as I spread my legs wide, offering myself to him.

His gaze turns even darker. "Touch yourself, Bells."

I do as he demands without question, settling my fingers between my thighs, rubbing tiny circles upon my clit. It tingles. Throbs. I moan, my gaze still locked on his, my fingers busy. His gaze drops, watching my quick fingers, and then he's back on the bed with me, pushing my hand aside so he can touch me instead.

"Are you close?" His voice is gravelly, making me flush hot, and I nod, a whimper leaving me when he slips a finger inside me and thrusts, his thumb pressing on my clit. He knows exactly what to do—all of the sneaking around for the last few days has taught him well. Within seconds I'm coming, the orgasm slamming into me. I cry out, pressing my lips together the moment I hear myself, not wanting anyone else to hear us either.

He removes his hand from between my legs, readjusting himself, and next thing I know, he's right there, his erection brushing against my still pulsing clit, and I suck in a sharp breath, realizing the moment is happening.

Finally.

"Oh fuck." He slips inside me, just the head, and pauses there, his arms straining, his eyes falling closed. I watch him, fascinated by his reaction. His restraint is impressive, though I can tell his arms are shaking slightly. "You feel so fucking good."

"You do too," I whisper, wrapping my arms around him. He pushes deeper, filling me more and more, until he's completely inside me and he pauses, hanging his head.

I squirm beneath him, trying to get comfortable. It stings a little —it's been a while since I've had sex and I'm sorry to even think about him, but Bentley wasn't nearly as thick as Rowan is—and I take a deep, shuddery breath, clenching my inner walls around him to test it out.

His loud groan could probably wake up the entire household.

"Shh." I rest my hand lightly over his mouth, shutting him up. "They'll be banging down my door in seconds if you keep that up."

Rowan's eyes go almost comically wide and I drop my hand, smiling. He leans in, his mouth on mine and the kiss turns wild as he starts to move. Pulling almost all the way out before he pushes back in, the slow drag of his cock causing little tendrils of pleasure to spread throughout my body. Our bodies start to move together, rocking, our hips thrusting in consummate rhythm. I arch against him, sending him deeper, tightening around him and he presses his face into my neck with a groan.

"You keep that up, I'm going to come," he threatens, his voice dark. "And I don't want to. Not yet."

I cling to him, letting him fuck me, reveling in the sensation. In the knowledge of him being with me like this. The two of us together. It feels right. Perfect. And I'm going to ruin it all by leaving him.

Closing my eyes, I fight against it, focusing instead on the pleasure. The thrill of being in his arms, connected to him. As close as two people can be.

Rowan increases his pace, his hips moving, and I let him. I'm not close to orgasm yet but I'd rather he become lost in me and lose control completely. I'm okay with it. Beyond okay.

"I'm." He thrusts. "Going to." Another flex of his hips, sending him deeper. "Come."

I nod my encouragement, hooking my legs around his hips, sending him further. He's buried deep, hitting a part of my body I don't think I've ever felt before, and the next thing I know, he's coming, a long, shuddery groan leaving him when he thrusts one last time, holding his hips against me as he orgasms.

Cracking open my eyes, I watch him, fascinated. His muscles strain, the tendons in his neck thick, his body covered in a light sheen of sweat. Without warning he collapses on top of me, always careful of his weight and that he doesn't crush me, and I wrap my arms around him, drifting my nails up and down his back, making him shiver.

"Holy. Shit." He kisses my neck. "That was..."

"All right?" Amusement laces my voice.

He lifts away from me, his gaze serious. "Amazing. Like, what the fuck were we waiting for?"

"I don't know. We could've been doing this days ago. You know I was game." I smile, trying to keep it light and staying focused on him. If I let my thoughts wander, I'll start to get sad and that's the last thing I want.

"I've wasted time." His expression, his voice are both gravely serious. "Guess I know what we're doing tomorrow."

I slap his shoulder, making him grin. "We can't, Rowan. We need to spend time with your parents before we—go back."

Those two words hang in the air, foreboding. Go back to Lancaster Prep. Go back to real life. Go back to the limited time we have together.

He pulls out of me and gets out of bed, going to the bathroom to dispose of the condom, I assume. I hear the toilet flush and water run in the sink and then he's back, sliding into the bed. Pulling me into his arms. I rest my head against his chest, the steady rhythm of his heart filling me with contentment.

"You didn't come, did you?"

I tilt my head back, meeting his gaze. "No. I mean, I did right before—"

He flips me so I'm lying on my back once more, his torso settling between my legs, his gaze full of mischief. "Want to rectify that?"

"Umm..." My voice drifts when he slides down my body, leaving a trail of kisses on my skin, his mouth brushing one hip bone, then the other. "Okay."

And then he proceeds to do just that.

FORTY-ONE

ARABELLA

IT'S Sunday afternoon and we're in Rowan's Ferrari, headed back to Lancaster Prep. Beau is in the back seat with his headphones on and his focus on his phone and nothing else. I'm in the passenger seat, and I keep sneaking looks at Rowan, both loving and hating how attractive I find him when he drives.

What am I even thinking? Everything he does, I find attractive. The crush I had on Rowan has bloomed into something bigger after spending the last ten days with him. I'm consumed. He's all I think about, and the best thing?

I'm pretty sure he feels the same way I do.

That's also a rather depressing realization, because I'm leaving. My mother texted me yesterday with all of the information about our upcoming Paris trip. She sent me a link to the first-class ticket she booked for me. I'm flying by myself to Paris and meeting them at the hotel. There will be someone there to escort me from the concourse and help me through customs, gathering my luggage before I'm driven to the hotel. She's taken care of everything, and I suppose I should've thanked her but I barely responded at all.

I'm still mad at her. She's most likely still irritated with me as well, and that's fine. I'm okay with it. I thought it was interesting that I fly out the evening of the last day of school, Friday the Thirteenth. Fitting, no?

I hate it. Feels like I'm going to my impending doom.

"Tired?" Rowan asks me, his deep voice breaking through my depressing thoughts.

"Oh." I smile then shake my head. "No. Just thinking."

He doesn't ask what about and I'm glad. I don't want to tell him.

Instead, he reaches out, settling his hand on my knee and giving it a squeeze. Yesterday was a good day. We went to that cafe and picked up breakfast sandwiches and coffee before we went to the same park where we messed around in his car. This time, we sat outside at a picnic table, sharing a bench, the two of us bundled up since it was freezing cold, even though it was sunny. We talked, always keeping things light. I took the breaded ends of my sandwich and threw them at the ducks that waddled up to our table, and they fought over those pieces in a frenzy of quacking and feathers flying, making us both laugh.

There was something about Rowan yesterday—the last few days, really—that was so at ease. No more scowling. No more grumpy remarks or grumbling. He's smiling more. He's paying close attention to me at all times and he's just...

He's sweet.

I knew he had it in him.

"I don't want to go back to school," I admit, my voice so low he might not have heard me, but he did. I can tell by the way his hand tenses on my knee and he gives me another squeeze.

"Why not?"

"Real life sucks." I turn in my seat so I can study him, leaning my cheek against the headrest. "Can't we just stay here forever?"

His smile is wistful. "We only have a few more months and then school is done forever."

"I only have a few more weeks, and then I'm gone," I remind him.

"Right." He removes his hand from my knee, settling it on the steering wheel. "I forgot."

I don't know how he could, considering it's been on the forefront of my mind since I found out. Maybe it's not that big of a deal that I'm leaving. Maybe he won't miss me. Maybe he's—maybe he's glad that I'll be gone.

No. He would never feel that way. He cares about me too much. I know he does. I saw it in the way he treated me Friday night. And even yesterday. After our experience at the park, we went back to his house and hung out with his mom and dad, watching a movie. It was fun. Then we all went out to dinner, Rowan's aunt Charlotte and uncle Perry and their children joining us. Once we came back to the house, we both said we were tired and went to bed early.

All lies. Row snuck into my room and we did it all night. It was amazing. I lost track of how many orgasms he gave me—three? Four? Whatever the number was, I was left in a heap of boneless exhaustion by the time we were done, and I fell into a deep, dreamless sleep. When I woke up hours later, he was gone.

Like he'd never even been there.

Traffic is terrible on the way back to campus, as if everyone is headed back home, and we finally arrive almost an hour later than it should've taken us. The sun has already set and it's mostly dark, the lights that line the walkways on campus are on. The moment Rowan shuts off the engine, Beau is out of the car, taking his duffel bag with him.

"See you guys tomorrow," he calls before he dashes off.

Rowan and I slowly get out of the car, both of us going to the trunk. I watch as he pops it open and pulls each of my bags out of its depth. I can't believe he fit them all in there, but he worked a miracle.

"Thank you," I tell him once he's done. I don't know how I'm going to manage all three of the suitcases back to my room, but I'll figure something out. "I've got this."

"Arabella." His voice is tinged with irritation, like he can't believe I said that. "I'm walking you back to your room."

"Oh." Why am I assuming everything's going to go back to the way it was, when everything between us has changed? I'm being ridiculous, but at least I'm being consistent. "Okay. I appreciate that."

He slams the trunk lid so hard I jump. And when I glance over at him, I see that scowl. The one I'm so familiar with but somehow, it feels different. "What's wrong with you?"

"I—nothing is wrong with me." I wring my hands together,

fighting the nerves that are swarming me. "This is weird, you know?"

"What's weird?" He approaches me slowly, as if he's afraid I'm going to dash off at the last second, and I wait for him, breathless, my eyes falling shut when he touches my cheek, rubbing his palm against my skin.

"The one thing that felt familiar to me now that we're back on campus is the scowl you aimed in my direction." I lean my face into his hand, closing my eyes for the briefest moment. "I'm not used to kind Rowan while being here."

"Bells." I crack open my eyes to meet his gaze once more. "You need to get used to kind Rowan, as you call me."

"Really?" I curl my fingers around his wrist, hanging on to him. "So this wasn't all a dream?"

He slowly shakes his head, his lips curling in amusement. "It definitely wasn't a dream. The last week actually happened."

"Thank God," I breathe, making him chuckle.

"Tomorrow, when we're all back in class, everyone is going to know that you're mine." His tone is fierce and he pulls me in closer, dropping a possessive kiss to my lips.

"We have a lot of projects to work on together," I remind him. "American Government and psychology."

"Ah yeah. I told my mom about that and she laughed. That's how she first got together with my dad. Skov paired them up for a psychology project. Before that, she believed he hated her."

"No way. Who could hate your mom?" I'm smiling. I love that we experienced something similar to his parents, though we're together now. We didn't need a psychology project to make it happen. "That's so funny."

"That's what my mom said." His expression turns serious. "Look, we have to make the most of the time we have left together, don't you think?"

I nod, my heart lodging in my throat. "We only have a few weeks."

"I know. Two to be exact, right?"

"Yes. My mom booked my ticket. I'm leaving on the thirteenth."

"You're not staying over the weekend?" His brows draw together and he looks sad, something I rarely see.

"No. My mom said something about how she wanted to spend as much time as possible in Paris. It's her favorite city."

"Okay. Well." He says nothing else, dropping his hand from my face and leaving me where I stand, grabbing the handles of two of my suitcases. "Can you get that one?"

"Yes." I go to the carry-on suitcase he didn't grab and extend the handle, pulling it behind me as I start walking. Row keeps up with my brisk pace and I realize everything is different. Rowan no longer has the boot on his foot so he can walk at a normal speed. I'm sure he still needs to take it easy, but I'd guess he can go back to working out. Maybe concentrate on football for his future? It's something we've never discussed.

Maybe I don't have the right to discuss it with him because I won't be around anymore. I won't see what happens to him, but I'm still curious. So curious that by the time we're at my dorm suite and he's bringing my suitcases into my room, I have to ask.

"Do you still want to play football?"

He goes still for a moment before turning to face me. "I would love to, but I don't think my ankle can handle it. That fucker broke it in two places."

"I remember," I murmur. It was a heart-stopping moment, one I'd rather forget.

"I talked about it with my coach, and he warned against me trying for college. I had some interest before the accident, even a couple of offers, but I haven't heard anything since that playoff game." A ragged exhale escapes and he thrusts his fingers in his hair, pushing it away from his face. "I don't think it's going to happen."

"I'm so sorry." I feel awkward. I don't know what to do. I'm tempted to offer him comfort, but from his body language I don't think he wants it.

"It's okay." He shrugs. "We don't always get what we want, right?"

"Right," I whisper.

I've never related to something more than what he just said. I'm not getting what I want, and neither is he. Our timing is all wrong.

And it sucks.

FORTY-TWO

ROWAN

TIME IS GOING by too damn fast.

I try to savor every moment I can with Arabella but we hit the ground running the moment we were back in class. We're bombarded with assignments and projects and tests. We have the group assignments in two classes and while we're able to chat and flirt and I can sneak in a touch here and there, it's not enough.

It's never enough where she's concerned.

Arabella's school workload has become more intense thanks to her leaving early. She has enough credits to graduate, but there's still some work to be done, and my Bells is tired. She's also nervous. Scared.

I still don't want her to go, but I remain quiet. Encouraging her instead, always trying to lift her up. Sometimes I'm trying so damn hard I feel like I'm talking to one of my teammates before we go out onto the field, about to face a formidable opponent.

After being in school for a few days, I went to talk to my coach, asking him what my future options were. And while they weren't terrible, they weren't necessarily what I wanted to hear either. Coach warned me the colleges that offered are still interested, but they want to make sure my ankle is good to go and right now...

It's not.

Not sure what I was thinking—I don't have a future as a football player. Definitely not professionally. I'm no Callahan Bennett who comes from a long line of ex-NFL superstars. He's a wide receiver and has tons of offers, all of the big D1 universities dying to snap him up thanks to his family's legacy. And then there's the fact that he's a great football player. He's so modest about it too, like it's no big deal.

I'm with him right now in the training room after school. It's Thursday. The weekend is almost here and the minutes keep ticking right on by. Counting down to the moment she'll leave me.

I can barely stand the thought.

We're both running on treadmills, and I catch Callahan shaking his head, smiling to himself. I yank out my AirPod.

"What's so funny?" I ask.

"I don't know. My thoughts were wandering and I got stuck on the idea of you and Arabella actually together. I go away to Mexico for a week and come back to you all lovey-dovey toward each other," Cal explains, chuckling.

"Lovey-dovey?" I take offense to that.

"You two are all over each other at lunch."

In my dreams. Bells won't let me get too crazy with PDA. Claims she's not that kind of girl in public. In private though?

Watch out.

"Define 'all over each other.'" I slow my pace, wincing when I feel a twinge in my ankle.

"Holding hands. Sitting close. Lost in your own little world. I never thought I'd see the day that Rowan Lancaster fell in love. With Arabella too. I mean, I could've predicted that shit, but then again, I didn't think it would happen."

I come to a complete stop, staring at my tan friend. The guy looks like he went on a tropical vacation and I'm envious. Not that I would change what happened to me while I was on Thanksgiving break. "You think I'm in love with her?"

Cal comes to a stop as well. "Well, aren't you? You're totally into her. You talk about her all the time."

"I do not."

"You do."

"You're the one who brought her up."

"Because you two are practically shoving your relationship in my face. I'm not complaining. I think it's great," he adds, no doubt noticing the snarl on my face at the shoving in his face remark. "You've been so closed off the last couple of years. You know how many girls would talk to me, asking how I could help them get access to you? The list was endless."

"Did Arabella ever talk to you about me?" I feel like an idiot for asking, but I have to know.

"That's what's so funny. She never did. Not really. I mean, we would talk at parties, and sometimes we would talk about you, but she never asked if I could help her out. It's like she worked her magic on you and eventually figured you out. I like her with you. She makes you less serious."

"She's leaving."

Callahan frowns. "What do you mean?"

"She's graduating early. Leaving after we take our finals. Moving to Paris to work for a famous jeweler. She'll be an apprentice to designers and study there for like...two years." I absently rub at my chest, trying to ease the always present ache there. Saying it out loud makes it all too real and I fucking hate it.

"She won't come back after winter break?" When I shake my head no, Cal whistles low. "That blows, man. You're going to miss her."

"Yeah. That's why I can't tell her I love her." I clamp my lips shut, startled I said it out loud. But damn it, it's true. I'm in love with her. I can't stand the thought of her not being in my life. Why'd I have to go and fall in love with her now? I should've done it months ago. Years ago.

We've wasted so much time.

More like I have. She's been chasing after me for over two years and like a dumbass, I blew her off. Didn't think she was my type. Instead, she's turned into my only type. The only girl I want.

"Why can't you tell her?"

"And make her feel like shit when she leaves? I won't do it." I shake my head. "It's a mistake."

"Maybe she wants to know where she stands with you. It'll make her feel more secure, knowing that the two of you are in love."

"Since when did you become a relationship expert?" I taunt.

"I'm not, but I have an older sister. And a dad who's always big on talking about his feelings." Cal shrugs. "You should tell her, bro. She'll love it."

"What if she isn't in love with me?"

Callahan bursts out laughing. "Are you fucking for real right now? That girl adores you. She's been crushing on you since sophomore year. Everyone knows she's in love with you."

I think about what Cal said when we're done with our workout and I'm taking a quick shower. When I hurriedly get dressed before I go in search of her. She told me she'd be in the library working on an English essay, and I find her quickly, deep in the stacks in the back of the building, sitting alone at a table and tapping her foot to the beat of whatever she's listening to on her headphones.

Stopping behind a tall shelf loaded with books, I spy on her for a bit like a creepy stalker. Her outfits aren't as wild since we've come back, though she's still putting in a little effort. Today she has on that bright pink sweater my parents gave her for her birthday, wearing it over her white button-down, and the glasses with the bright pink frames. Guthrie barely gave her a second glance when Arabella glided into first period. Even complimented her on the sweater, and I swear Bells was disappointed.

She likes causing a bit of a scandal. Our being together has done exactly that. The rumors started the moment we arrived on campus Monday hand in hand. I wanted to show everyone that she belonged to me. After that first day back, I was satisfied with the point I made.

They all know.

"Rowan, you're freaking me out."

My gaze jerks to her face but she's not even looking at me, though her lips are curled in the faintest smile. Stepping away from the bookshelf, I go to the table and sit across from her, watching as she hits a button on her phone screen and takes off her headphones, setting them down.

"How did you know I was there?"

"I saw you. Well, I smelled you first. You have a very distinct scent." She has that dreamy look on her face that she gets sometimes, mostly when she's looking at me.

"You *smelled* me? Is that a good thing?" I took a shower right after we worked out. No way do I stink.

"It's a great thing. You smell delicious." She reaches out and grabs my hand, picking it up and bringing it to her nose. She gives my wrist a sniff. "It's your cologne."

I did spray some on after my shower, right before I put on clothes.

"You like it?"

"I absolutely love it." She smiles and drops my hand, and I become entranced with her beauty like I always do and say the first thing that comes to my mind. That's been heavy on my mind since my conversation with Callahan. Even before that.

"I love you." The words come out of me as if I have no control over myself.

Her smile fades and her brows come together in confusion. "What did you just say?"

"I said..." Aw fuck. Did I do this all wrong? I should've told her this in a more romantic setting. When we're alone in my room and she's naked in my bed. Not in the back of the school library where it smells like old books and dust. But she loves books. She likes to read. Maybe she does find this moment romantic. "That I love you."

She's blinking rapidly, like she might have something in her eye, but I realize that her eyes are filled with tears and if that doesn't make me feel like shit...

"No one ever really says that to me," she whispers, then swallows hard. "That they love me."

I rest my clenched hands on my thighs, wishing I could punch something. I hate hearing that. Her parents are so fucking shitty.

Bells blinks again. "I'm not used to hearing it."

"Well, get used to it." I sound lame. I feel lame. I should've kept my mouth shut. Stupid Callahan. His advice was for shit.

I hear the scrape of her chair being pushed back and she stands. Rounds the table until she's in front of me. Next thing I know she's trying to sit in my lap and I let her, scooting my chair back to accommodate her. She straddles me, her skirt flaring, and I can feel the thin cotton of her panties. Her heat pressing against my junk.

She winds her arms around my neck, her gaze level on mine when she whispers, "I love you too, Rowan."

The relief I feel at hearing those words is followed swiftly by complete and total elation. Bracing my hands on the table just behind her, I cage her in, trapping her, though I know she's going nowhere. There's nowhere she'd rather be than right here in my arms.

I feel the same way.

Leaning in, I kiss her, keeping it chaste. No tongue. We're in the library for Christ's sake, but she won't have it. She parts her lips for me, her tongue darting out, and then it's on. The kiss turns wild and I wrap my arms around her slender waist, my hands pressing into the cashmere-soft sweater. She's got her hands buried in my hair and she's pressing her chest to mine. Grinding her sweet little pussy against my already hard cock.

"Think anyone will come back here?" she asks, her mouth still on mine.

"With our luck, I'm positive someone will come back here." I devour her mouth to keep her from encouraging me to take this further, enjoying the moment. Imprinting it on my memory for later, when she's gone.

That thought sobers me completely and I end the kiss, rearing back from her still-seeking lips. "We need to stop."

She frowns, a little pout forming. "You're no fun."

"You're seriously calling me no fun right now?" I rise up on my feet, taking her with me because she doesn't weigh that much. She squeals, her arms tightening around my neck as she wraps her legs around my waist, and I send her a stern look. "You're loud."

"You're strong," she returns, shifting in my arms. "What are you doing?"

"You'll see." I carry her deeper into the building, leaving behind our stuff at the table. Until we're at the very back of the library and I find one of those study rooms that no one uses, giving the handle a quick twist with my fingers before kicking open the door.

"I've never been in this room before," she starts but I seal my mouth over hers, shutting her up, pinning her against the door. She returns my kiss with matching enthusiasm, moaning low in her throat. The sound so damn sexy, I press against her, letting her feel what she does to me.

She turns me inside out. Makes me want things I can't have. Like her.

Forever.

FORTY-THREE

ARABELLA

THE WORDS RUN through my mind on repeat.

I love you.

I can't believe Rowan said it—that he said it first. I never thought it would happen like this. I don't think he did either, from the shocked expression on his face after he said those three little words.

I love you.

There's a hint of desperation in the way he's touching me. Kissing me. My energy matches his, my moves just as frantic. I tug on the hem of his gray Lancaster Prep hoodie, shoving my hands under the fabric to encounter smooth, warm skin. If I could reach, I'd slip my hand down the front of his joggers, but the way I'm positioned has me limited and I groan in frustration.

He breaks the kiss, staring down at me with those heated eyes, his breaths coming fast. I stare back at him, unable to speak, not sure what I could even say. Sorry I'm leaving soon? I regret that we don't have much time left together? I love you so much it's going to physically hurt me to not see you again?

Rowan licks his lips and parts them, like he's going to say something, but I don't want to hear it. Instead, I hook my hand around the back of his neck and pull him down until his mouth is back on mine. All is right in the world when he's kissing me.

I wish he would never stop.

His hands slip beneath my sweater and I can feel his frustration when he encounters my uniform shirt. I went with layers today because it's cold outside. A winter storm is coming tonight, and we should wake up tomorrow to a fresh layer of snow. Those are always my favorite days at school for some reason. That first snow is magical. Until it turns dirty brown and is slushy or worse—when it freezes into a solid wall of ice.

When he pulls away from my lips and presses his mouth to my neck, I murmur, "I want you inside me."

I have no problem asking for what I want, especially with Rowan. He likes it. I know he does. I can tell from the agonizing groan that leaves him, how his hands grip my butt, fingers sliding beneath my panties to touch my flesh. I am wet and aching for him, and it's risky, doing this in the library. But we're locked away in a tiny room that no one ever uses, and the library will be open for hours, still. No one will find us.

I hope.

Within seconds, he's got my sweater shoved up under my chin, his fingers undoing the buttons of my shirt hurriedly before he tears it open and his hands settle over my breasts. Cupping them. Kneading them, his thumbs brushing against my nipples. I press my lips together to keep from crying out, not wanting to attract any attention but he knows just how to touch me to make me melt.

"Please tell me you have a condom," I murmur.

"In my wallet." He shifts closer. "Grab it for me."

I do as he asks, pulling the wallet out of his back pocket. It's made of black leather and is slim, and I crack it open, yanking out the single condom that's tucked inside. I slide his wallet back into his pocket and hold the condom up between two fingers to show him.

"Help me put it on." When I frown, he goes on. "I don't want to let go of you."

Aw. I adore him so much.

Probably too much.

We fumble around. I shove his joggers and boxers down halfway to his thighs, helping him roll on the condom. He shoves my panties aside, exposing me, and when he slides deep inside, I bang my head against the door, overcome with sensation. The perfect glide of his cock as he pulls almost all the way out before pushing back in. His hungry mouth back on mine, his tongue matching the same rhythm as he fucks me.

All finesse is lost in seconds when he lets his emotions take over. He fucks me hard against the door, my butt banging against it with his every thrust. All I can do is revel in it, just take it, the pleasure growing inside me, spreading everywhere, settling in between my thighs. My clit pulses and I squeeze my eyes shut, holding on to him for dear life as he slams into me over and over. Until I'm crying out. Falling apart. Orgasmic tremors take over my body, and I come so hard, it's like I can't breathe. Can't think. It goes on and on and at one point, I hear him shout, the shudders taking over his body. He's coming too. And then it's over.

Gradually, I become aware of my surroundings. Rowan still inside me. The sound of his harsh breathing in my ear, his mouth right there. My butt aches, still pressed against the old, slightly rough door, and my legs are wound so tightly around his waist, I wonder if we'll ever be able to break apart.

But we have to. No matter how much I would love to stay locked with Row forever, I can't.

He kisses my cheek before pulling out of me, then sets me on my feet. I step away from him and search the room with my gaze, spotting a box of tissues sitting on a shelf that runs the entirety of one wall. I go to it and snatch a tissue out of the box, handing it to him and he takes care of the condom, wrapping it up and tossing it in the trash.

Once we're both put back together, it becomes almost awkward. And it's never awkward between us. Not anymore. We're always in tune, as if we know what the other needs and now, there's this weird...space between us. Despite us declaring our "I love yous," it doesn't feel right.

I don't know what to say so I blurt out the first thing that comes to me.

"I have a paper I need to finish."

He sends me a look I can't decipher, brushing the hair out of his eyes. "I'll let you get back to it then."

Within seconds, he's gone, leaving me alone. He didn't kiss me or tell me he loved me, and I would've really liked to hear him say that again. Though the fact that he does love me brings me happiness—and an equal amount of pain. Maybe he feels the same way. What we're doing is going to end badly.

Especially for me.

I'm BACK in my dorm room and at my desk trying to finish that damn English essay when there's a knock on my door. I rush to answer it, fully expecting to find Rowan standing there. But instead, it's my friends, Hadley and Simone.

"You've been ignoring us," is how Hadley greets me, Simone nodding in agreement. "We just wanted to tell you that."

I blink at them, shocked at the slightly hostile tone in her voice. "I'm sorry. Ever since I came back to campus I've been—"

"Busy messing around with Row? Yeah, we noticed." Hadley shoves her way past me, entering my room with Simone trailing behind her. I shut the door and turn to face them, my gaze locking on the gift bag Simone is carrying. Hmm.

Hadley gets right to the point. "We miss you. We get that you're with your dream man and probably having really great sex or whatever, but you used to hang out with us all the time and we miss having you around."

Simone holds up the gift bag. "We got you a birthday present."

"You guys." I rest my hand on my chest, touched by the gesture. "You didn't have to do that."

"Well, we're your friends. Of course, we want to give you a gift for your birthday." Simone shakes the bag. "Take it."

I do as she asks and peek inside the bag to find it's full of an abundance of tissue paper. Shoving it aside, I pull out a box. "What is this?"

"Open it and find out," Hadley encourages.

I set the bag and tissue paper on my desk and crack open the box to find a pair of earrings. They're in the shape of a starfish, with tiny crystals dotting them in a variety of shades of blue. "They're beautiful."

"I found them in the Bahamas and texted Simone a photo. She agreed they looked like something you would wear," Hadley explains.

"I adore them. Really." I glance up to find my friends watching me. "Thank you."

"You're welcome," Simone says with a faint smile.

"How was the Bahamas?" I ask Hadley before I turn to Simone. "And what did your parents think of your boyfriend?" The realization smacks into me. "We have a lot to catch up on."

"If you weren't hanging all over Rowan every minute of the day, you'd already know by now." The snide tone in Hadley's voice is obvious. Even Simone sends her a questioning look. "I'm sorry. I sound like a bitch, but it's just so unlike you, Arabella. You've always been there for us. Through thick and thin. It feels weird not having you around. We—"

"We miss talking to you," Simone finishes for her, offering me a gentle smile. "I get wanting to spend time with your new boyfriend, but please don't forget about us."

"I never thought you would," Hadley adds. "Maybe that's why I'm...so mad about it."

My heart crumples and I go to them, wrapping them both up in a group hug, clinging to them. They cling back, squeezing me tightly, and honestly, I've never felt so loved. This isn't like what I experience with Rowan, though. My friendships with these girls go back a few years. I've known Hadley the longest and while I valued their friendship, I never actually believed either of them thought of me in the same way.

I'm used to being ignored. Forgotten. And instead of reaching out to my friends when I returned from break and telling them all of my good news, I ignored them completely, when I should know better.

"I'm the worst friend ever," I confess with a sniff when I pull away from them.

Simone shakes her head. "No, you're more like the best friend ever. That's why we missed you so much."

"It's true," Hadley agrees. "We were hoping you'd want to hang out tonight."

I think of the paper that I still need to finish. I've become too distracted by my hot encounter with Row in the library and I can't focus. It's due tomorrow at midnight so I still have a little time.

"I'd love to," I tell them, glancing down at the box that's still clutched in my hand. "I love my gift. Thank you again."

"Did you have a good birthday?" Simone asks.

"The best one I've ever had," I say without hesitation.

"Thanks to Rowan?" Simone's smile is sly.

"Definitely. But also, his entire family is...so sweet."

"Unlike Rowan?" Hadley asks.

I immediately feel defensive. "He is sweet, once you get to know him."

They both make the *oooh* sound and I start laughing, my defensive feelings evaporating. I have to remember that he was grumpy toward everyone and had been for a while. Hadley even warned me about him, which is amusing to me now. Imagine if I'd taken her advice? Talk about a missed opportunity.

"Stop. You guys are embarrassing me." I can feel my cheeks go warm.

"You need to fill us in. I feel like I know nothing," Simone says, going to my bed and collapsing on top of it.

"There is a lot I have to tell you." I think of me leaving for Paris. "And some of it you're not going to believe."

Simone pats the mattress, Hadley joining her. "Okay, it's time. Spill your guts, please."

I join them, stretching my body out and settling my head on a pillow. "What do you want to hear about first?"

They both practically scream my boyfriend's name and I launch into my story, spilling my guts, just as Simone requested. And by the time I'm finished, I know by the grave looks on their faces that they feel sorry for me. Which I suppose is expected.

I feel sorry for myself too.

FORTY-FOUR
ARABELLA

NO MATTER how fiercely I might cling to them, the days sweep right past me, and I try my best to spend time with everyone who wants me around. Does this mean I bring my friends and Row's friends together more often? Yes. Now, the girls and I sit with the boys at lunch. Even during breakfast. After school. We hang out constantly whenever we can find some free time, and while I love it and I'm going to miss everyone when I leave, it's Rowan who I want to be with the most.

My stoic boyfriend. The one who keeps his chin up and his emotions locked tight. That one moment of complete honesty when he told me he loved me and then proceeded to fuck me straight into oblivion feels like a fluke. He hasn't said he loves me ever since, and I don't know if that's because of self-preservation or if he regrets saying it. Maybe he didn't mean it.

But I see the way he looks at me when he thinks I'm not paying attention. He's lovesick. I recognize the symptoms because I'm lovesick too. Over him.

Have I told him I love him since that moment in the library? No. I'm playing the same game he is and it's dumb. We're being dumb. It's like I can't help myself though.

We're still having sex. Any chance we can get, we're doing it. It gets better every time it happens too because of course it does. I'm going to become so addicted to him, so helplessly in love with him, that it'll be a massive struggle for me to leave.

Which I'm about to do in less than a week.

It's Saturday night and we're all in Rowan's suite. He invited all of his friends and a few extra people to turn it into a real party and there is plenty of alcohol flowing. Music is playing on a tiny speaker that Callahan brought with him, the bass thumping extra hard and there are even snacks, provided by me.

I am all about snacks. So are my friends. What's a party without food?

"You do realize this is a going away party for you, right, Arabella?" Hadley is clutching one of those skinny cans of High Noon, swigging from it every few seconds and swaying on her feet. Is this her third can already? Her fourth?

I'm monitoring my alcohol intake because I want to remain relatively sober in the hopes that I'll have a little heart-to-heart conversation with Rowan later. After everyone has left, which isn't happening anytime soon. It's not even ten o'clock and the place is packed with people, and according to Hadley, they're all here celebrating...me?

"I had no idea," I tell her because I didn't.

Hadley rolls her eyes. She's extra sassy when she drinks, which is saying a lot. "*Duh*. This is all about you." She waves her can around, her gaze searching the room. "This suite is massive."

"He's a Lancaster. They have privileges." I shrug, not bothered by it in the least. Though if you'd asked me a month ago about the size of his dorm suite, I would've complained out of jealousy. I need the closet space.

Well. I guess I don't need it anymore.

"Right. Like getting away with having a party in his room and no one from admin saying a word." Hadley grins and lifts her can in a salute before taking a sip. "You picked a good one."

I absorb her words, knowing they're true. I did pick a good one. And he picked me too, making all of my dreams come true. My mother getting this opportunity for me is another dream coming true.

So why am I dreading going to Paris? The closer we get to the day I fly out, the more uncomfortable I become. And nervous. I'm so nervous. There's a big part of me that doesn't want to leave. Knowing I won't see Rowan every day makes my heart break a little. To the point that it feels like I'm on death row and I'm counting down the days until my execution.

That is incredibly dramatic of me to think, but typical. I am the most dramatic person I know.

Letting my worry take over, I work the locket on my necklace back and forth, rubbing my finger against the etched heart. I keep messing with it lately and I've noticed the clasp isn't in the best condition.

"Hey." Rowan appears at my side, his mouth pressing against my cheek in a brief kiss, and I can smell the alcohol emanating from him. "You having fun?"

"I was telling her how you planned this party just for her," Hadley says to Rowan.

"Yeah?" He turns his attention to me. "You didn't figure that out yet?"

I shrug, feeling silly. "I thought it was just another Saturday night at Row's dorm room."

He shakes his head. "I don't have parties."

"Like never," Hadley adds.

"Right. I never want anyone in here getting drunk and making a mess," he further explains.

"Because he has OCD." Hadley smiles, swinging back and forth, reminding me of a little kid. It's obvious she is feeling the liquor coursing through her veins.

Rowan glares at her, his irritation also obvious. "I don't have OCD."

"Could've fooled me," she murmurs, holding the can in front of her lips before she drains the last of it. "I need another one."

She's gone before I can tell her I'd take one too.

"Your friend is drunk." He sounds vaguely amused, which is a relief. I don't want him mad at Hadley. She almost always speaks her mind, which is why I think we're friends. We have similar traits.

"She's having fun." I stare at his handsome face, tracking his features. I feel like there is always something new I notice when I look at him. For instance, why haven't I ever noticed how thick his eyelashes are? I'm envious. I don't get that kind of thickness unless I apply about ten coats of mascara and look at him, blinking those eyelashes at me. His eyes are too pretty. They are my downfall.

Everything about him is my downfall.

His expression shifts into serious mode. "Are you having fun?"

I nod, wishing he would say the words I want to hear. One more time, that's all I ask. I don't feel like I savored them enough the first time he said them. Probably because I was in so much shock when he did. "I'm having a great time."

"You're not drinking."

"I'm not a big drinker."

"I'm not either. Got that drilled into my head when I was playing football. Alcohol just adds unnecessary calories."

"Makes sense," I murmur, hating how stilted our conversations have felt the last couple of days. We are circling around each other like we don't know what to do and that is just the dumbest thing ever.

"Yeah. Tonight, I'm cutting loose." He glances at the red Solo cup he's currently clutching. "Callahan even got a keg."

"I saw." It's outside on the tiny patio that Rowan has off his room. A patio—it's like he's living the high life here on campus. No one has a patio.

"You want a beer?" He lifts his cup toward me.

"No." I shake my head. "I'd rather know why you're being so weird toward me lately."

He appears startled by my blunt question but I can't take it anymore. We're just wasting time at this point and I have no idea what he's doing. Subconsciously trying to push me away? Wishing he would've never admitted that he loved me? Has he changed his mind and now he can't wait to get rid of me? Was this party just a ruse to appease me and make me think he's still into me when he's so not?

See how my insecurities run rampant? Inside I'm a twisted mess but my outward appearance, I'm serene. Calm and controlled. Acting like this in front of Rowan, as if nothing bothers me, makes me feel...

Fake.

"I'm not being weird toward you." His voice is calm, his expression void of any emotion and I'm impressed.

I'm also a little mad.

"You so are." I rest my hands on my hips. "If you don't want to be with me anymore, just say it."

Rowan frowns. "What the hell are you talking about?"

"You tell me you love me a couple of days ago and now you're acting like you're...running scared. Running away from *me*. Like, all the time. It's been awkward between us ever since you said it when you fucked me in the library. I don't get it, Rowan. Why did you say that if you didn't mean it? Do you feel sorry for me because no one else loves me?" I am yelling, not that anyone notices thanks to the loud music playing.

He blinks, startled by my outburst. "We shouldn't be having this conversation right now."

"Then when are we going to have it? I'm only here for approximately six more days. *Six*." I hold up my hands to show him exactly how many that is with my fingers. "And then I'm gone. In another country and we won't get to see each other much. Though from the way you're acting, I think you might be glad to get rid of me."

I storm off before he can say another word, overcome with emotion. Anger. Feeling stupid too. I should've never said that. Again, all of my insecurities have been building up inside me, bit by bit, and this is the result. Me exploding all over him and acting like a damn fool.

I shove my way through the crowds of people in his dorm suite. It's tightly packed with unfamiliar faces and I don't even care if I'm rude. By the time I'm at the front door, I'm sweating and puffing and my head hurts. My eyes do too thanks to me fighting back tears.

I hate it here. I hate this stupid party. I'm not having a good time. I'd rather be alone with Rowan but clearly, he doesn't want to be alone with me, so I'm out.

Opening the door, I exit his suite and run down the hall, realizing the moment I walk outside that I left my coat behind. Well, he can keep it. I have plenty of coats and I don't need that one.

It's freezing outside, though the snow we got a few nights ago has mostly melted away. The sidewalks are slick and they'll probably ice up overnight, and I watch my step at first, eventually giving up and breaking out into a run. I just want to be in my room alone. That way I can cry my eyes out in peace.

I glance over my shoulder right as I approach my dorm building to find that no one is behind me, and the disappointment is so strong, I swear I nearly collapse. I fully expected him to chase after me. Grab hold of my arm and pull me in close, like he's done before. Reassure me in that warm, deep voice of his that I'm wrong. That he loves me and wishes I could stay with him forever.

But absolutely nothing like that happens. I wasn't followed by Rowan or anyone, for that matter. I'm alone in front of my dorm building and the realization is difficult to face. That I was right all along. No one loves me. I'm completely unlovable.

Sniffing, I push my way inside through the double doors and practically run down the hallway toward my room on the first floor. I have a suite as well, though it's not nearly as big as Rowan's, but I love it just the same. When I walk inside, I see the stack of boxes in the corner of my room, already filled up with most of my belongings. I only have the necessities out to get me through the rest of the week, and I don't even know where any of this stuff is going. Some will be making the journey to Paris with me, but I can't take all of these things. I'll be staying in a two-room flat that's close to the jeweler's atelier and there are no actual closets in the place. It's like my worst nightmare is coming true. No real closet space? Heaven forbid.

A slight hysterical laugh sounds and it takes me a second to realize it's me. I'm the one who laughed like that. Who's crying as well. Who can't believe the boy who supposedly loves her treated her like he did. I'm starting to think I wish he would've never told me he loved me in the first place. Now that I know what it feels like, to be loved by Rowan Lancaster, even for a brief moment?

It's terrible. Addicting. Something I'll always crave and probably never receive again.

I fall apart once I'm in my dorm room, throwing myself on the bed and crying my eyes out into the pillow, my sobs muffled. Like a sadist I keep checking my phone, fully expecting a text from Rowan.

But one never comes.

FORTY-FIVE

ROWAN

I AM AN ASSHOLE.

I'm chasing after Arabella through the swarms of people filling my dorm suite but I'm stopped by slender, cold fingers touching my arm. I look down to find it's her drunk friend Hadley who stopped me.

"You shouldn't lead her on," is what she yells at me.

I frown. "What the fuck are you talking about?"

"You've made her upset." She inclines her head in the direction Arabella just ran past. She's probably all the way to the door by now. "And you're only digging a deeper hole for yourself. For her. Lavishing all of your attention on her. Throwing this big party for her. She didn't even know it was a going away party. Why didn't you tell her?"

Because I know how Bells reacts to a lot of attention when it comes from other people—not well. She's a contradiction. Dressing outrageously so everyone notices her, yet when she finds out someone wants to do something for her out of the kindness of their heart, like throw a get together in her honor, she freaks out. Almost like she believes she doesn't deserve it, which I think is the root of the problem.

"I really don't need your advice on how I should treat Arabella," I tell Hadley, my tone snide because I'm pissed. I jerk my arm away from her hand. "Besides, you're drunk."

"What, like it's a fatal flaw? The problem is when I drink, I get realllll truthful." Hadley's eyes narrow and she sways on her feet. "She's leaving soon. Like in a matter of days."

No shit is what I want to say. "I know."

"Why are you making it harder for her to go? This is the job of a lifetime for her. When we first met, it was all she would talk about. All she would do."

"What do you mean?"

"Make jewelry! She had all of these kits and tools. Beads and stones, and gold and silver chains. A fat sketchbook that she filled with drawings. She was obsessed. Until she met you." Hadley actually sneers. "Once we started going here and she saw you, her obsession shifted. To you. She forgot all about making jewelry."

"You act like it's my fault her interests changed." And she has to be exaggerating. No way did Bells just stop making jewelry and switch her entire focus on me. I don't even remember much about her from our freshman year. It was our sophomore year when I first started noticing her.

"Because it is, Row. Like, what the fuck? Your ego is so huge that you can't even take responsibility for ruining her? That's exactly what you did, you know. She wasn't interested in any other guy, though so many of them were into her. All she could focus on was you. Perfect Rowan Lancaster and his perfect hair and perfect face and perfect smile, playing perfect football and getting perfect grades. Your only flaw was your rude ass, but she never seemed to mind. I was glad you got your ankle broken because it proved to me that you were actually human." Hadley shakes her head, her lip curled in disgust.

Damn, that's harsh. She's glad I broke my ankle? Who says that to a person? "What the hell did I do to you to make you hate me so much?"

"I don't hate you. I hate what you did to my friend. Wrapped her around your little finger and you weren't even aware of it! Now you're acting like you're into her and she's over the moon. She is madly in love with you and if you told her to, she'd probably say no to that apprenticeship and stay here with you. You need to cut her loose. Let her get away from you once and for all." She's swaying again, making me nervous, and I swear her face turns pale.

"Are you okay?" I may be pissed at Hadley for saying all of this shit, but maybe she really is just being a good friend. Could she be right? Am I holding Arabella back? Would she stay here if I asked her to?

I can't even entertain the thought.

"I'm fucking great," Hadley announces.

Right before she pukes on my shoes.

It's chaos after that. Girls are squealing and guys are shouting, getting out of the way of Hadley the barf machine. The smell rises, making other people nearby nearly throw up themselves, and someone pushes open the sliding glass door, letting a blast of freezing cold air inside, which helps alleviate the smell somewhat.

Thank God.

I head for the slider, walking carefully, my feet squishing, which is fucking disgusting. The moment I'm outside, I'm kicking off my shoes and shedding my socks. Tearing off my jeans, which are covered in vomit splatter, until I'm standing just outside in only my sweater and a pair of boxer briefs, shivering.

"What happened to you?" Callahan asks. He's been monitoring the keg all night and he's bundled up like he's ready for a snowstorm.

"Hadley threw up on my feet." Cal looks ready to bust up laughing but I point at him. "It's not fucking funny. Can you go check on her? And then get everyone else out of here? This party is over."

Callahan's expression turns serious. "Sure man. I'll take care of everything. You need some fresh clothes?"

"I need to jump in the shower."

"Follow after me and you can hide out in your bedroom." Cal frowns. "Where's Arabella?"

"She left already." My tone is clipped, my head still spinning from everything Hadley threw at me.

"Got it." Callahan nods. He's smart enough not to ask me any more questions. "Let me get rid of everybody. You go take a shower."

I clap him on the shoulder, giving it a firm shake before he goes inside, me right behind him. I veer off toward my bedroom while Callahan goes in search of Hadley. Once I've locked my bedroom door, I'm in the bathroom, getting rid of the rest of my clothes and checking my phone real quick to see if Arabella has texted or called me.

She has not.

Dumping my phone on the counter, I turn on the shower and wait for the water to heat up, stripping off my boxers before I step under the extra hot spray. Closing my eyes, I soak my head, wishing I could get rid of the nasty thoughts running through my brain.

I should be pissed at Hadley for calling me out so thoroughly, but I'm not. She said some harsh truths. Things I didn't even know. She made me feel like I'm only using Arabella, and fuck.

Is that true?

Exhausted, I press my hands against the tile wall, standing directly under the water and letting it pour over me. I close my eyes and think of Bells. How she lashed out at me when I played dumb over her "being weird" comment. I have been acting weird—because I don't know what to do or how to feel. It's wrecking me, knowing that she's leaving. Slowly tearing me apart inside, but I have to be the strong one. I don't want her to know how I really feel. I'm not about to put a damper on her going away to Paris and working a dream job, especially after everything Hadley told me.

Still can't believe she threw up all over my feet. God, that was disgusting.

Once I've taken a quick shower, I'm toweling off, checking my phone yet again. No word from Arabella but I do receive a text from Callahan accompanied by a photo.

Cal: **They're all gone. Got rid of everyone. Simone walked Hadley back to her room. She's okay. Just embarrassed.**

The photo is of my empty dorm suite. It's a wreck and I see remnants of vomit in the middle of the room but it's on a rug I can get professionally cleaned, and if I have to, I'll roll it up and store it outside until I call someone out to clean it up. No way am I letting that rug stay in my room, especially if it still stinks.

I consider texting Arabella to see if she's all right, but she's probably still mad at me. Might be best to wait until the morning.

I throw on some clothes and head out into the living area, grimacing when I see the mess left behind. I tackle the rug first, shoving furniture out of the way so I can roll it up. The stench is awful, and I hold my breath, hauling the rug outside and leaning it against the wall and under the overhang in case it rains or snows.

Damn that sucked. This entire night did if I'm being real with myself. I pissed off the girl I love, and I got my ass handed to me by her drunk best friend. Feels like I'm messing everything up, and I sort of am. Only because I can't be real with myself.

More like because I can't be real with her. Arabella.

I'm too energized to call it for the night. Instead, I decide to clean up around the place, throwing everything away that was left behind. I'm almost done when I spot something gleaming just under the small table that sits right by my door. Bending down, I scoop it up, discovering that it's a necklace. The one that Arabella wears all the time. It must've fallen off. Does she realize it?

Cracking open the locket, I stare at the tiny empty picture frames inside, remembering how she told me she hasn't found the right person to put inside it yet. Fuck, that makes me sad.

I grip the necklace in my hand and drop it into the top drawer of my dresser. That's the safest place for it and no way do I want to lose it. That locket means too much to her.

By the time I'm collapsing into bed, it's well past midnight. I grab my phone to check notifications but still nothing from Bells. I decide to send her a text.

Me: **Hey, Hadley cornered me and wouldn't stop talking, and she threw up everywhere. I had to take care of her and the mess. I'm sorry if I pissed you off. We should talk in the morning.**

After I send it, I wait for a reply.

But I never get one.

FORTY-SIX

ARABELLA

IT TOOK ALL of my mostly depleted energy to force myself out of bed at a decent hour. I put on a black crewneck and matching sweatpants, threw my hair up into the sloppiest bun ever seen, and made it to the dining hall just in time to get breakfast, since they stop serving at ten thirty.

Got in under the wire since I walked in at approximately ten twenty-five.

I order a skinny vanilla latte and a bagel with extra cream cheese, eager to drown myself in dairy products. Once I've grabbed my breakfast, I spy Simone and Hadley occupying a table, Simone rubbing Hadley's back. Her face looks positively green.

Forgetting all of my Rowan-related troubles—I hate how we ended things last night and I really don't know how to respond to the text he sent me when I was already asleep—I head over to the table and settle in across from them.

"Hads, are you okay?" I keep my voice gentle because from

outward appearance, she looks like she's suffering through an epic hangover.

"I drank way too much. I still don't feel right," she answers, sounding miserable.

"Ugh, that's the worst." I take a sip from my latte, grateful I didn't really drink much at all last night. "You were definitely feeling yourself."

Simone sends me a stern look while Hadley groans and buries her head in her arms. "Don't remind me."

"She got so drunk, she threw up on Rowan," Simone whispers.

I nearly spill my latte at her revelation. He mentioned her throwing up, but not on him. "What? When exactly did she do this?"

"Right after you left. I was telling him off and then...I just barfed on his shoes." Hadley lifts her head, her misery written all over her face.

"Telling him off?" Worry fills me. "About what?"

"About you. I told him I was tired of him leading you on."

"Hadley—"

"And then I told him that he can't ruin your dreams. You used to love designing jewelry. You were obsessed with it. Until you became obsessed with him." Hadley shakes her head. "He changed you, Arabella. You can't let yourself get wrapped up in a boy so much that they distract you from your future."

"I'm not letting him distract me from my future." Ooh, I don't like that she did this. I can only imagine what she might've said to Rowan. And how dumb does she think I am? "I'm leaving for Paris in five days, remember."

"But you don't want to go," Hadley points out. Simone remains quiet, which is her normal stance.

"It's not that I don't want to go. I just know I'm going to miss it here—and I'll miss Rowan."

"Right. Because it's all about Rowan. Rowan this and Rowan that." Hadley makes a face. "I told him you were obsessed with him and that he should let you go."

"Hadley," Simone murmurs, shaking her head, while I gape at my friend.

"You actually said that to him?" I am incredulous. I'm also angry.

Why did she do that? She needs to stay out of my relationship.

"You know how I am when I drink. My mouth gets big and I probably say too much." Hadley winces. "I was only telling him that stuff to protect you. He needed to know."

It's my turn to bury my face in my hands. My appetite is gone. I don't even want the latte anymore. I can't believe she told him that. "You were definitely too harsh."

"I don't care! He deserved to hear it. It's not healthy, how wrapped up you are in him. I'm only watching out for you," Hadley cries.

"He told me he loved me, Hads. Rowan *loves* me. Our relationship is definitely not one-sided." She meant well. She always means well, but this time, she took things a little too far.

Distressed, I reach for my locket, but I grasp at nothing. It's not there. I wrap my fingers around the base of my neck, fully expecting to feel the chain move beneath them but it's gone.

"Oh no," I whisper. "My necklace."

"I noticed you weren't wearing it," Simone says. "And you've always got it on."

"It must've fallen off." Frantic, I jump to my feet, looking under the table but it's not there. "I wonder where I lost it."

"You should retrace your steps." Simone stands. "Do you need help?"

"Yes. Yes, I do." I grip the back of the chair I just vacated, running over my every step in my mind. "I came straight here from my room so I guess we should start from there."

"I'll help too." Hadley makes her way over to me and wraps me up in a hug, resting her head on my shoulder. All I can do is pat her back awkwardly, still kind of mad with her but also kind of not? I don't know how to feel. "I'm sorry, Arabella. I should've never opened my big mouth."

I say nothing. I'm not about to lie and say it's okay, or it's all right because it's not. She had no business saying what she did to Rowan. She says she did it because she was watching out for me, but it feels more like she made everything worse.

The three of us retrace my steps through the dining hall and then outside, on the lookout for my locket, but we don't spot it. We enter the dorm building, make our way to my room and find nothing. Once I'm in my room, I take apart my bed, figuring I lost it when I was sleeping, but after I tear off the blankets and sheets, I come up empty.

"It's not in here." Simone emerges from my tiny bathroom, coming to a stop when she sees my face and no doubt the tears shining in my eyes. "Aw, we'll find it, Arabella. I know we will."

"I made that locket. I drew it and my mom took it to a jeweler and had it created for me." I let the tears fall, then wipe them off my cheeks, frustrated with myself. Why didn't I notice it was gone sooner? "I haven't taken it off in all the time I've owned it. It's my favorite thing in the whole world."

"Did you have pictures in it so someone might know it belongs to you? Though pretty much everyone knows you wear that necklace," Hadley says.

"The locket was...empty." Just like my life. Barren of love for my entire existence until these last few weeks. And lucky me, right when I find love and can put a photo in the locket, of Rowan, I lose it.

This feels like foreshadowing. Like I'm about to lose everything that matters to me. Am I afraid of change? Am I terrified of losing Rowan?

Yes, and yes.

Why did I agree to this apprenticeship again?

"How about at the party?" Hadley asks. "Do you think you could've lost it there?"

I remember thinking about the loose clasp at one point last night. "Maybe."

"You should ask Rowan if he found it," Simone suggests.

"Maybe I should." I sink my teeth into my lower lip, hating how unsure I feel at the thought of texting him. "I'll go to his room."

"Shouldn't you text him first?" Hadley asks.

"No." I shake my head, determination filling me. "I'm going over there. Right now. But you guys don't have to go with me."

"Thank God." Hadley sighs loudly. "I'm so embarrassed about throwing up on his feet. I don't think I can face him yet."

I can't imagine how grossed out Rowan was about her vomiting on him. I'm sure he never wants to talk about it again.

"You've got this," Simone says, reaching out to squeeze my hand. She can probably see how nervous I am, while Hadley is still thinking about what happened last night. "And you might luck out. He probably found your necklace."

"I hope so." I squeeze her hand back, grateful for her. Grateful for both of my friends. Despite the fact that Hadley could've driven Rowan away.

But he's made of stronger stuff than that.

I hope.

I KNOCK on Rowan's door and he answers almost immediately, jerking the door open with a thunderous look on his handsome face. The moment he sees it's me, his expression softens and he opens the door wider. "Hey."

"Hey." I wave like the awkward soul that I am. "How are you?"

"Not good."

I didn't expect him to be so honest. "Me neither."

"You want to come in?"

"Sure." I enter his room, noticing right away that the rug is gone and the entire place is devoid of any party evidence. "Did you have help getting this all cleaned up?"

"Cal helped a little, but I did most of it." He reaches behind, rubbing at the back of his neck, his T-shirt rising and offering me a glimpse of his flat stomach. My traitorous body tingles at seeing that sliver of skin and I tell myself to calm down.

"Wow, *the* Rowan Lancaster cleaning up after a party?" I'm teasing.

"I had to. Your friend threw up all over my feet." He makes a face. "And the rug. I had to toss it outside."

"Right." I wince in sympathy. "She told me about that."

"You saw Hadley?"

"Yeah, in the dining hall. She feels terrible about throwing up on you."

"Does she feel bad for accusing me of holding you back and ruining your life?" Row's brows shoot up.

"She didn't tell you that you ruined my life...did she?" She better not have.

"Not quite in those words, but she made me feel like shit. I didn't know...any of that stuff she said to me last night."

I duck my head, embarrassed. "You had to have known I had a massive crush on you."

"Well, yeah. You made that pretty obvious."

I lift my head at his slightly amused tone. "What made you give in, then? Because you had no other prospects? Thought you should take advantage of the one girl who consistently offered herself to you?"

"No. It was never like that, Bells. I had—a crush on you too," he admits.

Unable to help it, I burst out laughing while he just stands there, gripping the back of his neck with both hands now, seemingly lost. Uncomfortable. I don't know how to describe it. "You're kidding."

He slowly shakes his head, dropping his hands at his sides. "Nope."

"You had a crush on me."

"Yeah." Rowan starts to approach me while I remain stock-still. It's as if I'm frozen in place. "Like I told you before, we wasted a lot of time. And I'm sorry if I upset you last night. That is the last thing I wanted to do. I've been in this weird place ever since you told me you were leaving."

"Me too," I admit softly. "And I leave in five days."

"I know."

"We have finals all this week."

He scowls. "Don't remind me."

"We have to do well on them if we want to get into college," I remind him.

"I assumed you weren't going to college since you got this apprenticeship."

"What if it doesn't work out? What if I hate it there?"

Rowan takes another step closer, and I can almost reach out and touch him. "You won't hate it. It's going to work out, Bells. I can feel it."

I blink at him.

"If that's what you want," he adds, taking that final step, standing right in front of me. "I've been weird toward you because I don't know how to act."

"That's silly. It's just me."

"Just you. It's never 'just you,' Bells. You've become everything to me. I'm consumed with you. You're all I think about and you're leaving me." The pain I see on his face hurts me too. "I never want to make you feel bad for doing that. You have to do what's best for you, and I support whatever your choice is but I have to be real with you—losing you? It hurts."

I throw myself at him, pressing my face against his chest, sighing with relief when I feel his strong arms close around me. We cling to each other, silent until I tilt my head back at the same time that he looks down at me.

"It hurts me too. That's why we need to make the most of these last few days together, don't you think? I know we have finals and we should probably study for them, and I have to pack up my entire life before I go to Paris. But I want to spend these last days with you, Rowan." I send him a pleading look, needing him to be on the same page as me. "Every minute I can steal away with you, I want it. I need it."

He lets go of me and for a moment, I'm scared he's going to push me away. But then his hands land on my face and he cups my cheeks, his fingers streaking across my skin, feather soft, while he stares into my eyes. "I love you, Bells."

I forget all my stress, all my worries at hearing him say those words. "I love you too."

"I'm in this with you. For as long as I can have you." He drops a kiss on my forehead and I lean into it, exhaling softly. "Stay with me today."

"Yes," I whisper. "Yes."

There's no place I'd rather be.

FORTY-SEVEN

ARABELLA

THE WEEK FLIES by in a whirlwind of turning in final projects, studying for tests, dividing up my things and boxing the items that I'm sending to my parents' apartment in Manhattan—their suggestion—and I finish packing my belongings that I'm taking with me to Paris. My mother has been in constant contact with me, which is unheard of. Telling me the flat she's found for me to live in isn't too far from the atelier, within walking distance. She's texted me my work schedule and some of the names of the people I'll be working with.

Maurice is her point of contact at the jeweler. He's one of the creative directors and has worked there for years. She speaks of him often and fondly, and I can only hope that I'll like him too. More importantly—I hope that he'll like me.

If I'm not preparing to leave or studying for finals, I'm with Rowan. We spend every free moment together and I'm so grateful for this time with him. I just want to feel connected to him. Revel in his love and affection for as long as possible, before it's taken away from me. Though I suppose I only have myself to blame for all of it. I'm the one who's leaving. If I wanted to stay,

I could. But it's too late now. I'm committed. I must go through with this. I refuse to live my life with what ifs looming over my head. *What if I'd never gone to Paris?* What then?

For once, my mother did something for me. I have to take the opportunity she gave me. She may not tell me she loves me often, if ever, but this is a sign of her love for her child. I know it is.

By the time it's Friday morning, my last scheduled final is for first period. Statistics. Mrs. Guthrie's class. I haven't seen her this week and I put all of my effort into my outfit just for her. The second I enter the classroom, I spot her sitting behind her desk, her gaze on the door, on me. Like she was waiting for my appearance.

I hope I didn't disappoint.

"Arabella! There you are!" She starts to laugh, shaking her head. "Oh...my."

I stand there proud in front of the rows of desks, doing a little curtsy, holding out the ends of my uniform skirt as I dip down. I'm wearing my white button-down but I left the last few buttons undone so I could knot the ends together just above my navel, showing off my belly. I've got a cropped gray cardigan on over it, and sheer white knee socks, along with my new favorite Dior loafers on my feet. My hair is done in two braids and I've got my standard black-framed glasses on. It's not too outrageous of an outfit, but I'm hoping she can guess who I'm emulating.

"This reminds me of something," Mrs. Guthrie says, tapping her index finger against her pursed lips as she studies me. "I've seen this look before."

"Go on," I encourage, nodding.

She stands there for a second, her gaze narrowing before she snaps her fingers, pointing at me. "Britney Spears from her 'Hit me Baby One More Time' video."

"You're right!" I'm laughing. So is she.

"Oh, Arabella." Her laughter dies and she's shaking her head. "I'm going to miss you."

My heart hurts at the sincerity I hear in her voice. "I'm going to miss you too." I hesitate. "Are you going to write me up?"

"No! Of course not." Her voice softens. "It's your last day here. Why would I get you in trouble? There's no point."

Her response leaves me feeling a little defeated. I sort of wanted to strut into the headmaster's office and get a lecture. It's been a long time and I wanted to finish attending Lancaster Prep on a high note, but I suppose Mrs. Guthrie is right. Why write me up when I'm leaving?

And seriously, only I would think it would be fun getting written up and sent to the headmaster's office. Something is wrong with me. I think it's that constant need to seek attention —even if it's bad—that I have in me. Yes, I'm aware of it. Yes, I rarely acknowledge it, but I know it's there. Maybe I don't feel that way as much anymore because I have Rowan giving me all the attention I need.

"Are you excited to be going to Paris?" Mrs. Guthrie asks, pulling me from my thoughts.

"Yes. Definitely." I nod, going for enthusiasm. "I can't wait. It's going to be such a wonderful experience, I know it."

"I remember when you used to sell your jewelry in the dining hall during lunch. I bought a bracelet from you."

"You did?" I frown, trying to remember. That was so long ago. Beginning of my freshman year, when I was looking for friends any way I could. Selling jewelry was one way to bring people to me as a conversation starter. It's how I became friends with Simone. Hadley helped me sometimes, always talking up my jewelry designs to anyone who would listen.

I'm going to miss my friends.

"Definitely. Everyone on staff was impressed with your work, but then you sort of...stopped." Mrs. Guthrie holds her arm out and pulls up her sleeve, showing off the delicate gold chain bracelet around her wrist. "I'm wearing it in honor of your last day."

I go to her and check out the bracelet, vaguely recognizing it. There are blue stones on it in various shades, and the way I set them gives it an ombre effect. It's pretty. I can see why she was drawn to it. Mrs. Guthrie likes to wear blue.

"Thank you for supporting me back then," I tell her.

"You're easy to support—we've all adored having you in class, Arabella. Even if you test my patience with your outlandish outfits." Her smile is kind. "Are you ready for the final?"

I stand up straight, snapping my heels together and giving her a salute. "As ready as I can be."

We both laugh and suddenly, the hairs on the back of my neck rise. Glancing over my shoulder, I watch as Rowan slips into the room, a smile appearing on his face when he catches me staring.

My heart aches, full of love for him. And longing. So much longing. I'm already mourning the loss of him and it hasn't even happened yet, but it's happening soon. He's taking me to the airport right after we finish school, and I know I'm going to break down and sob like a giant baby when I have to leave him. I don't want to do it.

But I will. I have to.

Even if leaving him will shatter my heart into a million pieces.

THE DRIVE to the airport is long and mostly silent, me nervously clinging to his hand when I can, which is for most of the ride there. He doesn't say much because I think he knows that words are useless. We've already discussed this moment many times. He knows my feelings. I know his. We don't want this to be over, but there's a tiny part of me that recognizes it already is. The moment I'm gone, our future is uncertain. Or more like, our future is over.

There's no point.

But for now, I'm clinging to him like he's my lifeline, and he's indulging me. I appreciate his kindness. His love for me. I never believed this moment would be possible, but here I am, in Rowan Lancaster's car, somewhat secure that this boy—this man —loves me.

Until he won't anymore. And that's not his fault. I won't be here. I gain his love only to leave him. This isn't his fault.

It's all mine.

We arrive at the airport and we're at the point where he has the option to park his car and walk me in or drop me off at the departure section. "You sure you don't want me to go with you into the airport?"

"No." I am shaking my head on repeat. I will fall apart if he does that. Bad enough that I have to leave him at his car in front of all the harried travelers desperate to get inside as fast as possible. I'm flying first class and have TSA Precheck. The lines are usually a breeze for me and we're here early enough. I almost wish we were late. That would give me more time with him. "I can do this."

His gaze softens. "I never said you couldn't do this. I just thought you might want me there."

"I appreciate you." I pat his firm thigh, thinking of last night. We had sex and I cried afterward, which is pitiful, but I couldn't help myself. It was the last time. Everything just feels so damn final and I hate it.

Hate it.

He eventually pulls the car to the curb and cuts the engine before he gets out. I follow after him, grabbing my carry-on from the back seat of his car while he grabs my suitcases from the trunk. How he fit them in there, I'm still not sure, but I'm not going to question him. I just stand there on the edge of the curb, my travel backpack slung over my shoulder and the carry-on at my feet.

"Have a porter help you." He nods toward the airline employees standing behind the counter outside who are checking in people's luggage. "You can't carry all of this."

"I can manage." I nod, pressing my lips together so I don't say something stupid. Like, *take me back to Lancaster Prep now, please.*

I can't do that. I need to be strong.

"I have something for you." He pulls a small box out of his jacket pocket, handing it to me.

"You didn't need to get me a gift." I take the box from him, frowning when I see the words written on top of the box in his familiar script.

Keep me in your heart.

"Open it," he says, his voice gruff.

I lift the lid to see there's a dark blue velvet jewelry box inside. And when I pop it open, it's my heart locket nestled within.

"Oh my God," I whisper, lifting my gaze to his. "I meant to ask you if you ever found this a week ago and I just...I forgot."

I was too distracted by him that I forgot about my necklace completely. When he had it all along, like it was meant to be.

"I was surprised you never brought it up. I found it that night of the party." He flicks his chin at me. "Open the locket."

With trembling fingers, I crack it open to find tiny photos of the two of us in each frame. One is from my birthday party at his parents' house that someone must've taken of us and another one is a selfie we just took a few nights ago, when we were lying on his bed together, our heads close, our smiles genuine. Though he's not looking at the camera.

He's looking at me.

And all the love that's shining in his eyes makes the tears fall from my eyes, one after the other.

"Oh, Rowan." I am crying. Hard. "I love it."

"Fuck, Bells." He crushes me to his chest, his mouth on my temple. "Don't cry, baby. It'll be all right."

I sob into the front of his shirt. "I just—I don't want to leave you."

"You have to." He pulls away slightly, cupping my face. "Wear the locket and don't forget me, okay? I know you're going to be busy, but we can FaceTime and catch up every night."

"You'll be busy too. We'll be on different time zones. I don't know—" I press my lips together, unable to finish my sentence.

I don't know if this is going to work.

That's what I wanted to say, but I don't. Why put doubt into this moment? It's already there, lingering around us like a cloud, but to say it out loud makes it real. And that's something I can't face right now.

"Let me put it on you." He takes the box from me and pulls the necklace out. I can tell it's a new chain, gold and shimmery in the sunlight because of course the weather is wonderful today. Like a reminder that I'm about to go to gloomy, rainy Paris. The weather is for shit there currently and has been for the last week. "Turn around."

I offer my back to him and he drapes the necklace around me, clasping it together. I touch the locket, rub my fingers across the etched front, my heart feeling like it's going to burst. Whirling around, I face him, throwing my arms around his neck and holding on to him with all my might. "I love it. I love you. Thank you."

"Don't ever take it off," he says fiercely.

"I won't. I promise."

"I love you, Bells. So fucking much." He pulls away from me slightly and kisses me right there in front of everyone. A long, intense, tongue-filled kiss that makes it even more difficult for me to break away. But I do.

I have to.

"Don't cry," he demands but it's too late. "Come on. I'll help you with your luggage."

He's about to take the heaviest suitcase for me but a man wearing an airport police uniform approaches him. "Sir, you can't leave your car at the curb. You have to move it."

"She needs help with her luggage," Row protests, but the officer shakes his head.

"Those are the rules. And I can help her." The officer takes my luggage from Rowan while I stand there, helpless. "Ready, miss?"

I look at Rowan, seeing the sadness filling his green eyes, and I fling myself at him one last time, hugging him tight, rising up on my tiptoes so I can whisper in his ear. "I love you. I'll miss you."

"Text me," he says, his arms wrapped tightly around my waist. "Let me know your flight took off on time."

"I will." I keep my gaze trained on his face, desperate to memorize every single feature. Every little flaw and characteristic that makes him look like that. He is perfect. And he was mine. But now, I'm afraid...

He isn't mine anymore.

"And text me when you land in Paris." He runs a hand along the side of my head, fingers streaking through my hair. "I need to know you're safe."

"Okay. I'll keep you updated. Promise."

One last kiss, our lips lingering and finally I pull away. It's the hardest thing I've ever done.

"Bye, Bells." His voice is a harsh whisper and I swear his eyes are glassy with unshed tears. For me.

Seeing that makes me want to bawl like a baby, but a newfound thread of strength curls through me, and I stand taller, straightening my shoulders.

"Bye, Rowan." It hurts to speak. Hurts more to keep looking at him and I turn away, smiling at the officer who's been waiting patiently for me. As if he knew how rough this goodbye was for us.

I tell myself not to look back. It'll only break my heart even more but like the sadist that I am, I finally glance over my shoulder to find Rowan standing there, leaning against his car, watching me go. He lifts his hand up in a silent wave and I do the same, quickly turning forward, telling myself I need to focus on my future.

Without Rowan.

FORTY-EIGHT

ARABELLA

THE FLIGHT IS UNEVENTFUL. We take off on time and the trip is smooth. I try to fall asleep but it's not easy. My thoughts are too chaotic, too full of a sad Rowan watching me leave. We texted for the last hour of me waiting in the airline lounge, after he arrived back at Lancaster Prep. He is supposed to leave for his parents' house early Saturday morning, and he told me that the campus was quiet. Downright ominous. No one was really there, save for him and Beau, and he was contemplating leaving that night after all.

I told him he should and he agreed. And then I lost all connection with him while I flew to another country to start my new life. Without him. Without any of my friends. Dependent on my parents.

Talk about taking a risk.

Once the plane touches ground, I send him a text letting him know that I landed, and he responds, saying he's at home, already in bed.

I'm jealous. His house is my favorite place to go.

I'm grateful my mother arranged for an escort to take care of me at the airport when I arrive in Paris, because I feel helpless. Even a little scared. The man greets me within seconds of my leaving the plane and he helps me through customs, picking up my luggage and escorting me outside to the driver that's waiting to take me to the hotel.

It's a long drive, made worse by traffic. The car is a sleek, newer model Mercedes and the driver is silent, listening to the radio, which plays nothing but songs sung in French. I stare outside the window, watching the city rush past me, the sky gloomy and dark. The streets are wet and everyone is bundled up, and I'm thankful I wore my favorite coat that feels like being embraced by a real-life teddy bear. It's cozy and warm and a little bit of a comfort, though not nearly enough.

By the time we arrive at the hotel, I'm exhausted and ready to collapse into bed. I don't care if my mother told me I should try to stay up and get through the day to adjust to the time. I didn't get much rest on the plane and all I can think about is falling into a deep, dreamless sleep for hours.

I texted my mother to let her know I was on my way, and she greets me inside the hotel lobby, gliding across the marble floor and sweeping me into her arms while I just stand there and take it.

"Darling, it's so good to see you! It's been too long. Let me look at you." She pulls away from me, her hands still on my arms as her gaze sweeps over me. "You look tired."

"Gee thanks. Nice seeing you too." I look around the opulent lobby, my gaze snagging on the stairwell with the intricate iron railing. "Please tell me that leads up to our room."

"What?" She turns to examine what I'm staring at. "No, darling. Our elevator is over here."

I let her take my hand and lead me to this other mysterious elevator while she's telling the bellman in French where to take my luggage. I don't say anything. I'm too tired, like she said. Mentally spent and in desperate need of sleep.

We ride up in the narrow elevator with the bench seat and I settle on top of it, leaning against the wall and closing my eyes. Mother is talking nonstop about our beautiful suite and how I have my own room, and by the time we're exiting the elevator and she's dragging me down the hall, I'm ready to beg her to please stop talking.

Maybe that's where I get it from.

The room is ridiculously extravagant because of course it is, and I come to a stop to look at the sketches that are framed in gold that hang on the wall.

"Karl Lagerfeld drew those," Mom informs me, referring to the former designer of Chanel who died a few years ago. "They're of Coco Chanel."

"Wow." I love them. I love fashion but it's like I can't focus right now. I'm literally swaying on my feet, reminding myself of Hadley last weekend when she got drunk.

"This is the Coco Chanel suite. You saw the sign on the door, no?" Mother's delicate brows shoot up, her expression almost... condescending?

"I didn't notice." I try to smile. "I'm so tired, Mother. I'd like to sleep for a bit."

"You shouldn't, my darling. Try and stay up for a while, don't you think? Maybe you should take a nice shower."

"That will only make me sleepier." I glance around the neutral-toned living area. "Where's Father?"

"He's still in Hong Kong. Working." The brittle smile on her face is surprising. She doesn't seem pleased. "He hopes to be here in the next few days."

"The next few days?" I'm frowning so hard my forehead hurts. "Why are we here so early then? Christmas isn't for another two weeks!"

"More like ten days, but who's counting? And doesn't it sound like fun, going Christmas shopping here? We can wander around the Rue Cambon or perhaps the Avenue Montaigne? The Dior store is to die for there, and I notice you're wearing your loafers. Perhaps we could pick you up some new shoes. A bag or some clothes." Mother beams, her hands clasped in front of her, and I try to smile in return but it feels too forced. Too fake.

I let it drop.

"Please just let me sleep for a bit and then we can go shopping?" I fight the yawn that wants to come but give in at the last second, hoping she'll take it as a hint. "A few hours are all I ask for."

"All right, darling." She guides me to the bedroom that will be mine for the next two weeks. "Get some rest. I won't let you sleep for too long though. You need to get adjusted to the clock here."

"I have plenty of time for that. Good night." I practically shut the door in her face, breathing a sigh of relief once she's out of sight.

I'm disappointed that my father isn't here, but I'm also not surprised. This is how he operates. Consumed with work, always putting it above his family no matter what. I've maybe had two conversations with the man in the past four years, no joke. I'm not even sure he'd recognize me on the street if I walked past him. For that matter, I'm not sure if I'd recognize him, it's been that long since I've spent time in his presence.

Banishing all thoughts of my father out of my mind, I take a quick shower and then dry myself off with the thick, peach-colored towels The Ritz is known for. I wrap myself in a hotel robe and run a brush through my hair before I exit the bathroom.

I come to a stop when I hear the low tones of my mother's voice. Without thought, I whip open my bedroom door to find my mother pacing around the living area, her phone pressed to her ear.

"...I can't get away right now. No, she just arrived, but she's sleeping." She pauses and I can hear a man's voice. My father's? I can't tell. "What if she wakes up and discovers I'm not here?"

More talking from the other person on the phone while my mother goes to the window that overlooks the Vendome, pushing back the curtains and staring outside. I can practically feel the nervous energy emanating from her and I retreat, carefully closing the door so she doesn't hear me.

Who is she talking to? I don't think it's my father.

I don't know who it is.

When I crack my eyes open, the room is dark, the drapes pulled tightly closed, not allowing even a sliver of light in. I sit up in bed, shoving my hair out of my face, looking around. Completely disoriented.

Real life dawns slowly. I'm in Paris. At The Ritz.

Reaching toward the nightstand, I grab my phone and tap the screen to check the time. It's past five o'clock, closer to five thirty.

I slide out of bed and peek through the curtains to see it's dark outside and the street lamps are on. The sun has already set. I slept the entire day away and my mother let me.

Odd.

I flop back into bed and check my phone, smiling when I see how many texts I have from Row.

Rowan: **I bet you're sleeping.**

Rowan: **I miss you.**

Rowan: **Text me when you wake up. My mom says hi.**

Rowan: **She misses you. Everyone does.**

This text is accompanied by a photo of his beautiful mom in the kitchen, waving at the camera, a frowning Beau right behind her.

I miss her. I miss all of them. I'm in an unfamiliar place with my mother who feels like a stranger and I'd rather be with Rowan's family. When I was there, I felt like I was home and I barely knew them.

Well, it doesn't feel like that anymore. I know them. I know Rowan especially. And I miss him terribly.

Me: **I'm awake. I slept all day. I can't believe my mother let me.**

Rowan: **Why wouldn't she let you? I'm sure you're exhausted. You didn't sleep on the plane?**

Me: **I couldn't sleep. I was thinking too much.**

Rowan: **About what?**

Me: **You.**

My eyes fill with tears and I wipe them away, frustrated. I can't keep this up. All the crying isn't good for me.

Rowan: **I love you.**

Seeing those three words just makes me cry more.

Me: **I love you too.**

My phone rings in my hands and I gasp, dropping it onto the duvet. It's my mother and I pick my phone back up, answering her call.

"You're awake!" is how she greets me. I can hear the murmurs of conversation in the background, the clinking of glasses. Music. "You should come down here and have drinks with us."

"Where are you?"

"At Bar Hemingway, in the hotel. It's marvelous here. And you can drink legally since you're eighteen now." Her voice warms. "Come down, darling. You'll love it. We'll save you a seat."

"Who are you with—" She ends the call before I can finish my sentence.

What is going on?

I receive another text from Rowan as I'm crawling out of bed.

Rowan: **Are you going out to dinner tonight?**

Me: **My mother is currently in the Hemingway Bar and basically demanded I go down and join her.**

Rowan: **Is your father with her?**

Me: **No. He's still in Hong Kong. He's a workaholic and won't be here for another few days. I'm sure he'll drop dead at his desk someday.**

I'm rifling through my suitcase and trying to come up with an outfit when he texts me back.

Rowan: **You should take this opportunity to talk to your mom. Try to catch up with her. Make amends. Whatever it is you think you need to do.**

I stare at what he just sent me, realizing that he's right. It would probably help if we had a heart-to-heart. Not that I need to clear the air with her or anything, but I would love to get to know the woman who gave birth to me.

Me: **That's a good idea. I think I'll try and do that.**

Rowan: **Text me later and let me know how everything goes.**

Me: **I will.**

I send him a string of red heart emojis and he sends me a bunch of kissy face emojis in return.

Smiling, for the first time in days, I feel confident. Maybe everything is going to work out after all.

FORTY-NINE

ARABELLA

I ENTER Bar Hemingway twenty minutes later, wearing a simple black dress with an equally simple black cardigan over it, both pieces trimmed with white. I've brought out designer everything. Chanel dress and sweater. Chanel bag. Prada pointy-toe flats. I am ready for Paris. Ready for my mother.

I see the back of her dark blonde head, her hair twisted into an elegant chignon, a string of gleaming pearls around her neck. She's talking animatedly, her hands waving in the air, the light glinting off the giant diamond wedding ring on her finger. I hear the gentle tinkle of her laugh, a man's chuckle accompanied with it, and that's when I realize she's sitting with a stranger in a bar on a Saturday night, the two of them cozied up together, his gaze for her and no one else.

And that man is most certainly not my father.

Uneasy, I make my way to their table, coming to a stop in front of it. The man notices me first, nudging my mother's arm and indicating my presence with a tilt of his head, and my mother's face brightens when she sees me. She leaps to her feet, pulling me in for a hug.

"You made it," she murmurs against my cheek before pulling away. "You look lovely. Chanel?"

I nod, not surprised at all that she'd notice. "You bought it for me last Christmas."

"Hmm. Well then, it's out of season." She sniffs and I realize my error. I can never get it right with her. "We'll need to find you some new outfits to wear when we go shopping. I do adore the shoes, though."

They're a soft, buttery shade of yellow and the top of each shoe is decorated with matching yellow leather flowers. I was going for a pop of unexpected color and it looks like I earned her approval there.

"And the black classic flap," Mother continues, referring to my bag. "You can't go wrong with it. Don't ever get rid of that bag, darling. The prices just keep going up every season. Have you heard about the latest increase?"

"I won't get rid of it." My smile is brittle. I could not care less about the Chanel price increase. "And no, I hadn't heard." My gaze shifts to the handsome older man who's remained seated, watching us with an amused expression on his face. "Who's your friend?"

"Ah, this, my darling, is my friend Maurice. The gentleman who helped you get your apprenticeship. He's their creative director," Mother says proudly.

Maurice rises to his feet in one smooth motion, stepping away from the round table to stand in front of me. "A pleasure to meet you, Arabella."

He takes my hand and presses a brief, dry kiss to the back of it, and I can't help but wonder if this is how he greets all of his coworkers.

Is that what I am? A coworker? Or am I a student there? And is this man my boss somehow? I don't think so, but I'm not sure. If I'm being real with myself, I don't care for the way my mother was sitting so closely to him. It was almost too intimate. If my father saw her like that, I'm sure he wouldn't approve.

"Nice meeting you too," I murmur, snatching my hand away from him a little too quickly.

"Let's sit down," Mother says, and we do, crowded around the tiny table, my mother shifting closer to Maurice as if she's sat with him like that a thousand times.

I watch them carefully as they speak to each other in rapid-fire French, too fast for me to keep up. I can snatch a few words out of the air but for the most part, I have no idea what they're saying.

And I'm dying to know.

A server approaches our table and Mother orders a bottle of champagne.

"We have much to celebrate," she says once the server drops off a silver cup of the biggest olives I've ever seen, accompanied by a glass jar of toothpicks. "I'm so proud of you, Arabella! This is going to be a once-in-a-lifetime experience for you."

"Thank you." I turn to Maurice. "And thank you for offering me the job. I'm excited to start."

"You're welcome." He inclines his dark head toward me. He's got a swarthy complexion, his dark hair curling at the ends and swept away from his face, a hint of gray at the temples. His brown eyes are extra dark and he has a nice smile. Extremely white teeth. "You'll be assisting some of the most renowned jewelry designers in the business, Arabella. I hope you can appreciate the opportunity you've been given at such a young age."

My smile stays frozen on my face. I hate how he said that. As if I don't understand the importance of this position I'm about to start. That I'm possibly too young to take anything seriously.

"I'm very appreciative," I tell him. "This has been a dream of mine for years."

Such a lie. This hasn't been my dream for years. I'm only saying this for my mother's sake.

"You should've seen her sketchbooks, Mo. They were filled with the most adorable designs! Very creative. And she made all sorts of little jewelry trinkets when she was in middle school. Why, she even sold some to her classmates her freshman year in high school. Isn't that cute?"

Mother laughs. So does Maurice. All I can do is sit there, hating how silly she makes me sound. How she diminishes what I've done with the tone of her voice.

"The cutest," Maurice says, his gaze shifting to me. His eyes roam over my face, my entire upper half, and I withstand the shiver that wants to overtake me. That felt a little...

Creepy.

"The necklace she has on? She designed it herself. I had it created at my favorite jeweler." Mother waves at my heart locket.

Maurice doesn't even bother to look. "I thought I was your favorite jeweler." He rests his hand against his chest, seemingly offended.

"You are, darling. Never worry about that. I'm referring to the place I used to go to when Arabella was younger. How long ago was that?" Mother asks me.

"Five years ago? Six?" I answer through clenched teeth, disappointed that my plans for this evening are essentially ruined thanks to Maurice's presence. There will be no catching up between my mother and me. Seems like she's too interested in him anyway, to pay any attention to me.

The champagne arrives and the server pours each of us a glass, Mother raising hers in a toast once he's gone. We clink glasses and I take a sip, the crisp, cold alcohol sharp on my tongue. I remain quiet while Mother and Maurice talk, occasionally sipping on my champagne. I tune them out completely because it's obvious they don't care what I have to say or what I might think about...anything, and I suddenly miss Rowan so badly I could almost cry.

His parents wouldn't treat me this way. None of his adult family members would. They'd include me in their conversations and show genuine interest in what I had to say. They made me feel welcome. On the other hand, here's my mother, ignoring me like I don't even exist.

It hurts. Worse, it makes me angry. Why did I take this apprenticeship again?

"Darling, we need to leave soon. Our reservation is at eight and traffic might be terrible." I thought Mother was speaking to me, but she called *Maurice* darling, her gaze sultry.

Hmm.

Mother signs for the bill and then we're outside, being escorted into a taxi. We're all crammed into the back seat, Mother seated in the middle, her and Maurice talking in low tones while I stare out the window, admiring the Christmas lights. We drive through a neighborhood of similar looking buildings and I look through people's windows, trying to see inside. I spot a few Christmas trees. I even see what appears to be a party going on in one house, the living space crowded with loads of people dressed in their holiday best, everyone seemingly clutching a glass and smiling.

I don't even know that many people to invite to a holiday party. When I was younger, my mother was always hosting some sort of event for my father's work colleagues. I wonder if she still does that. If they have big parties and have tons of people over and serve delicious little appetizers. They were always formal affairs, where I would have to dress up, and I'd never feel comfortable. Not like how I felt at the party the Lancasters threw for me. It was such an intimate, special moment where I felt well and truly loved.

We arrive at our destination approximately thirty minutes later and take an elevator to enter the restaurant. It's modern and elegant and someplace my mother would absolutely adore. We're seated by the windows with a perfect view of the sparkling Eiffel Tower in front of us, and I assume I'm supposed to be impressed so I do the proper amount of oohing and aahing over the view before I bury my head in the menu and try to figure out something to eat.

"This is one of the hottest restaurants in Paris right now," Mother tells me. "Took me ages to get a reservation."

"It's beautiful."

"The view is unparalleled. You'll have to take photos and share with your friends," she suggests, and I nod dutifully.

The only person I would want to show this view to is Rowan, and I haven't even told my mother that we're actually together yet. Which feels like a travesty, though I doubt she'd care. Or would she? She recognizes the Lancaster name, and that impressed her when I mentioned him before, which is so shallow.

But that's my mother. Impressed by expensive things and important names, and if I told her I was dating a Lancaster, she'd probably love it.

Instead, I keep my mouth shut and order a Coke from the server, earning a disappointed look from Mother once the server walks away.

"A Coke, Arabella? Seriously?" Mother shakes her head. "I thought you'd be eager to order a drink now that you're eighteen and it's legal here."

"I need something to keep me awake," I say, though really, I just want a Coke. What's so wrong with that?

"It's not very..." She lowers her voice. "Sophisticated."

I want to roll my eyes but I restrain myself. I'd hoped I wouldn't receive so much judgment from her, but I should've known better. This is typical behavior for my mother and I hate that I'm disappointed.

Isn't the definition of crazy doing the same thing every time yet expecting different results? This is on me, not her. She is who she is, and I know this. Why do I keep hoping she'll change?

She won't. She never will.

I get through dinner by concentrating on the view and not on the table conversation. After we finish eating, I take some photos of the Eiffel Tower while my mother and Maurice go wait for a taxi. It was my mother's suggestion and I thought nothing of it.

Until I start heading for the taxi stand and I spot them standing close together. I come to a stop, feeling like a spy as I watch Maurice bend his head in my mother's direction. She tilts her head back, a faint smile curling her lips right before his mouth touches hers in a passionate kiss.

I can't move. It's like I can't even breathe. They kiss and kiss, and I'm almost embarrassed to witness their passionate display but I refuse to look away. No one else around them gives them a second glance and I feel like a prude.

And then I don't because this is my mother, and this man is most definitely not my father, and why in the world did Maurice offer me this apprenticeship again? Certainly not based on my talent. Not that I think I have much. I haven't picked up a sketchbook in years. Hadley wasn't too far off with her assessment. I was obsessed with jewelry until I became obsessed with boys. Specifically, Rowan.

In other words, I acted like a normal teen. Who wasn't making jewelry in middle school? All of my friends were. It was fun. I still like being crafty but to design creations for a world-renowned jeweler in the heart of Paris?

That has never been my dream.

They finally end the kiss and Maurice gets into a car, my mother waving at him until he shuts the door. The moment the car pulls

away from the curb, I'm walking toward her, my steps determined, my anger bubbling inside me.

"There you are! Isn't the Eiffel Tower beautiful at night?"
Mother smiles and I take in her features. The flushed cheeks
and the sparkling eyes and the slightly swollen lips. She looks
like a woman who was just kissed. A woman who is in love—
with a man who isn't my father.

"Beautiful," I agree through tight lips, not wanting to unleash on
her in front of all of these people on the street on a Saturday
night.

"Let's get a taxi and head back to the hotel," she suggests.

We sit in the back of the cab in stone-cold silence, Mother oblivious to my anger. I'm on the phone, texting Rowan incessantly,
telling him everything.

Me: **I hate it here. My mother is her usual self and
completely self-absorbed. The weather is terrible
and so cold. My father isn't here because he puts
work before family every single time and my
mother is having an affair with the man who got
me the apprenticeship.**

Rowan types and types, that little gray bubble staying on the
screen for what feels like hours until finally, his response comes
through.

Row: **I was going to give you an inspirational speech
about keeping a positive attitude because it can't
be that bad. You're in Paris. But are you for real
about your mom?**

Me: **I am. I caught them kissing outside when they
didn't know I was watching. He came with us to**

dinner. They talked to each other the entire night and completely ignored me. She doesn't care about me. She did this for herself so she'd have an excuse to come to Paris and see HIM. This was never about me and always about her.

Row: **Can you talk?**

Me: **Not right now. But I'll call you soon.**

Row: **Okay.**

The moment we arrive at the hotel, I'm out of the car like a shot, murmuring a thank you to the man who opened the car door for me. I'm practically running to the elevator, my flat shoes slapping against the marble floor and echoing in the spacious lobby.

I'm waiting at the elevator when my mother approaches, slightly out of breath. "You were so fast."

"I want to get back to the room." I can't even look at her, I'm so disgusted.

"Tired?"

Of you, is what I want to say, but I don't. "Yes."

My tone is clipped and she notices. "Are you all right? Your dinner not agree with you?"

That's one way to put it.

"I don't want to talk about it." I march into the elevator the moment the doors slide open, Mother following me in.

"We're not going to start that little game," she says once the doors close and the elevator starts its ascent. "I refuse to have you act like a pouty baby. Do you know how hard I worked to get you that apprenticeship? How difficult it was? The prestige this position carries is unparalleled, and you'd rather flounce around like an ungrateful brat. Do you realize you barely spoke a word to Maurice during dinner? That man is going to be your superior and you wouldn't even look his way."

The doors open and I'm out of the elevator, practically sprinting to our hotel room door. Pissed at myself once I get there because I don't have a key. I wait impatiently, Mother sauntering her way down the hall, stalling because it irritates me, and I ball my hands into fists, wishing I was anywhere but here.

Why did I think this would work out? How was I so blind?

"Your father would be so disappointed in you," she mutters when she's finally in front of the door, unlocking it with a wave of her key card. "He wanted this for you more than anything else in the world."

What a crock. I bet he doesn't even care.

"More like he'd be extremely disappointed in you," I retort, pushing my way into the room.

She trails after me, snagging my hand and forcing me to turn and face her. "What in the world are you talking about?"

"Does Father know?"

I see the flicker of alarm in her eyes but otherwise, her expression remains calm. "Know what?"

"That you're fucking Maurice?"

FIFTY

ARABELLA

THE CRACK of her palm across my cheek is loud in the hushed silence of the room, the move so unexpected, all I can do is stand there in stunned silence, clutching the cheek my mother just slapped, my skin hot and throbbing from the force of her hand.

"You—hit me," I whisper.

"You are a vulgar and rude young lady." She tilts her head up, staring down her nose at me. "How dare you speak to me that way?"

"I'm speaking the truth!"

"You know nothing."

"I saw you. When you sent me away to take photos of the Eiffel Tower. He kissed you! And it wasn't the way two friends kiss when they're saying goodbye either. There were—tongues involved."

A full body shiver moves through me because gross.

She gasps, resting her hand against her chest. "You can't speak to me like this."

"What? Speak the truth? Do you have a problem with that?" I can feel the tears forming in the corner of my eyes and I wish I wouldn't cry over everything but I do. I cry when I'm sad or happy and also when I'm angry. "Does Father know about your affair with Maurice? How long have the two of you been together anyway?"

My mother crumples right in front of me. Falling to the couch and covering her face with her hands, her slender shoulders gently shaking. I worry for a moment that I upset her too much but then I remember that she hit me, and I let my anger fuel my reaction. I don't feel bad for her.

She did this to herself.

"Of course, your father doesn't know. How can I tell him? I don't even know if he'd care if he found out. He's so wrapped up in his work. It consumes him and leaves me with...nothing."

Crossing my arms, I stand in front of her, needing more details. "Go on."

"I met Maurice earlier this year. When I came to Paris for Fashion Week. He charmed me completely and the next thing I knew, we were at a bar and he bought me a drink. And then another—and then another one after that. He let me talk all night and he listened. I'd never felt so seen. The next day I went to the store where he works and he personally showed me all of the pieces they had. I foolishly spent over one hundred thousand euros on a pile of jewelry I didn't even particularly want. Not that your father cared. He said I deserved it—which I do, for putting up with him. Maurice stayed in constant contact with me and our conversations became more...intimate. The next thing I knew, I was looking for any excuse to come to Paris."

Closing my eyes, I take a deep, fortifying breath before I open them and speak. "Like finding your daughter an apprenticeship at his place of business? That would certainly give you all the excuses for coming here."

She drops her hands from her face, glaring at me. Her cheeks are dry and her eyes are clear so the crying moment was clearly a false production. "I did that for *you*, Arabella. You really did enjoy making jewelry—"

"When I was thirteen!" I practically screech, throwing my hands up in the air. "I didn't care much about it once I got into high school. It was just a hobby, Mother. A stage I went through —lots of girls my age went through that sort of thing. I never wanted it to be my life's work."

Mother stares at me, her lips working, and I can tell she's trying to come up with the right thing to say but failing miserably. "You loved it," is all she can manage.

"Maybe in another life I did, but this isn't me. This isn't what I want." I look around the gorgeous suite, but all I can see is how boring everything looks. Sterile. This isn't a lived-in space. It's perfectly put together and chic but I don't like it. It's cold, just like anywhere my parents choose to live.

I don't want this life anymore. I never really did.

She remains quiet, her head bent, her phone sitting next to her on the couch lighting up with a notification. She picks it up and types a response, and something tells me that text is from Maurice.

"Why don't you just tell Father you don't want to be with him anymore? Then you can be with Maurice," I suggest, which only makes her laugh.

"You silly, foolish child. You make it sound so simple."

"Isn't it?"

"No." She shakes her head. "It most certainly is not. To leave your father would be to leave the status that comes with being married to him. The status and the immense wealth."

"Wouldn't he take care of you?"

"He would, but it wouldn't be the same." She shakes her head. "You wouldn't understand."

"I'm not a child."

"And yet, you are." She rises to her feet, standing directly in front of me. "I'm sorry that I slapped you. What I did—is unforgiveable."

She's right. I don't know if I can ever forgive her for what she did.

"But when you said that to me, using such—ugly words. I was shocked." She shakes her head. "Perhaps that's all you see Maurice and me as, but we are more than that. He is in love with me, and I'm in love with him."

I wrinkle my nose. I hate hearing that. Even though I'm not close to him, this is all incredibly unfair to my father.

"But again, you wouldn't understand what I'm trying to tell you. When a person is so in love with another, they are desperate to see them. In any way they can."

If she only knew about Rowan, she'd know I definitely understand. "I don't want to do this apprenticeship." She parts her
lips to speak but I keep on talking. "I'm not going to be the
excuse for you to keep coming to Paris. That's the only reason
you set this up. You didn't do it for me. You did it for yourself."

"That's not true," she whispers but I shake my head, cutting her
off again.

"What's worse is, you don't even see it." I take a deep breath,
exhaling slowly. "I'm booking the next flight out of here."

"Where will you go? It's winter break! Spend part of it here
with me. I'll take you shopping." Her smile is small. "Somehow
convince you that you might want to stay here after all."

"No." I shake my head. "I agreed to this because deep down, all
I ever wanted was to earn your approval. At the very least, gain
your attention. You've been oblivious to everything I've done for
years. I finally saw this chance as a way to make you proud of
me. To make you want to spend time with me and see me. Your
daughter. Your only child."

The tears fall from my eyes and she tries to wrap her arms
around me but I dodge out of her way. "You don't care about
me. You never really have."

"That's unfair, Arabella. I do care. So very much."

Her words mean nothing. Her actions are everything.

"It's sad, how you think this is your way of showing me love.
When really, you're so focused on what you can gain out of
what you've supposedly done for me." I stand up taller, feeling
stronger than I think I ever have before. "I'm going home as soon
as possible. You can tell Maurice I turned down his apprentice-

ship. I'm not going to be the excuse you're looking for to continually sneak around with this man."

Mother's face turns about twenty shades of red, she's so angry. "You little fool. What do you think you're ever going to amount to? I give you an opportunity others would kill for and you'd rather be lazy and spend your father's money."

"You should understand. That's exactly what you do." My voice is eerily calm, as is my demeanor. I refuse to let her hurt me. I've given her that power for the last eighteen years. I'm done.

Another gasp escapes her, and I see the way her hand rises up and she catches herself. What, like she was going to try and slap me again? "Little bitch. I should lock you away in this room and not let you out for a couple of days. Tell everyone you're sick. It's what you deserve."

"You try that and I'll call my father right now and tell him everything." I hold my hand up, showing her my phone that's clutched between my fingers. "That would ruin your little plan, wouldn't it?"

"Go ahead. Call him. You're not brave enough to tell him." She flicks her chin at me.

"Want to bet?" I speed dial my father's number and hold my phone to my ear, waiting for it to connect. Mother marches right up to me, snatching the phone out of my hand and hitting the red button to end the call. "Hey!"

"You're not leaving, and your father isn't going to bail you out, either. You need to stay, Arabella. This is a good opportunity for you." She reluctantly gives me my phone and I pocket it before she can take it again.

"More like a good opportunity for *you*." I stress the last word, though it's not like she's going to see how selfish she's being. She never does.

Mother smiles, her eyes sparkling and all I can do is stare. I'm baffled by how easily she turns it on, like a light switch. "Come on. If you don't take the apprenticeship, then at least stay here with me for a few days. It could be fun! Don't you want to shop? Paris is beautiful during the holiday season."

"We don't need to pretend we have this wonderful, close relationship, Mother. There's no point. I don't want to go shopping at Dior and Chanel. It means nothing to me—you can't buy my love no matter how hard you try. None of this means anything to you either. Just let me go home."

"To Lancaster Prep?" She raises her brows. "No one will be there waiting for you."

Ouch. It's as if she knows how miserable I was, spending holidays on campus when no one was really around, but she flat out doesn't care.

"No. To my—friend's house." I stand up taller. "My boyfriend's house."

"What? You have a boyfriend?"

I nod, for the first time since she slapped me, feeling good again. Feeling positive. "Yes. I do. I told you about him."

The skeptical look on her face tells me she thinks I'm full of it. "Oh really? What's his name?"

"Rowan Lancaster."

She scoffs. "A Lancaster, darling? I'm sure he's just using you."

Her automatic assumption hurts, but I refuse to show it. "You don't even know him."

"For all I know, you don't either. And you're not going anywhere. You're staying right here." Her smile is triumphant. "With me."

FIFTY-ONE

ROWAN

I'M PACING the kitchen to the annoyingly cheerful Christmas music my mother has playing in the background while she makes cookies, and Willow is helping her. She arrived this morning from college, and they're having the best time bonding over holiday cookie recipes while I feel like I'm slowly dying inside, waiting for Arabella to text me.

"What's wrong with you?" Willow asks, her tone vaguely hostile as any older sister's voice can be.

"He's waiting for his girlfriend to call him," Mom answers for me.

"You have a girlfriend?" Willow sounds surprised.

My gaze shifts to Mom. "You didn't tell her?"

"I figured that's your personal life. It should be up to you to let her know you have someone you care about."

"Who is she?" Willow asks.

"Arabella Hartley Thomas." I start pacing again because just saying her name out loud is enough to send me into a spiral.

"Wait a minute. Isn't that the girl who used to drive you crazy?" Willow frowns.

"One and the same." I nod.

"Now she drives him crazy in another way," Mom says, sounding amused. Willow laughs. "She's a lovely girl. I think you'd adore her."

"I probably would. You should invite her over."

"Can't. She's in Paris."

"Oh." They share a look but I ignore them. "Hopefully I meet her sometime soon."

My phone buzzes and I check it to see a notification from Arabella.

Bells: **Can you talk?**

"I'll be right back," I tell them as I sprint out of the kitchen and up to my bedroom. Only once the door is locked do I call her.

"Are you okay?" is how I greet her when she answers.

The shaky exhale I hear is enough to tell me that no. She's not. "I want to come home."

"Then come home."

"I have nowhere to go." She sniffs and fuck, she's crying.

"Yeah, you do. Come here."

"My mother is basically holding my bag hostage so I can't get a flight out of here. She has my wallet."

"Book the flight on your phone. You have your account numbers saved in there, don't you?"

"I don't know. I mean, I have apps but I-I never book a flight for myself. She always does it for me." Arabella is full-blown crying now. "I just want to leave. I told her I don't want that apprenticeship. I only did it to make her proud of me but she really set that up so she could have an excuse to see her secret lover whenever she wanted. She—she used me."

"Aw, Bells." I settle on the edge of my bed, hanging my head as I listen to her sob. "I can come and get you."

"How?"

"We have a private plane. The family does."

She actually starts to laugh and though it sounds sad, at least she's not crying anymore. "Of course, you do. I should've known."

"I can make a call and fly out by tonight—at the latest tomorrow morning." I put her on speaker and open the text thread between me and my dad, sending him a quick message. "Tell me and I'll make it happen, Bells."

"You would do that for me?" She sounds so full of doubt and I fucking hate that. Her parents are the worst.

"I would do anything for you, Arabella. Just say the word and I'll be there."

She's quiet for a moment, most likely absorbing my words, and finally she speaks. "Come get me, Rowan. I need you."

"Done. I'll keep you posted." I pause, reading my dad's response to my question. "I can leave tonight."

"Okay. Please do. I'm at The Ritz."

"That's a nice hotel."

"In the Coco Chanel suite, being held prisoner. Doesn't sound so nice, does it?" A shaky laugh leaves her. "I can't believe I'm making jokes."

"Better than crying. Dry your eyes, baby. I'm on my way." I rise to my feet, contemplate packing a bag but fuck it. "I'll let you know when we fly out and my estimated time of arrival."

"Okay." She pauses. "Row?"

"Yeah?"

"I love you."

"Love you too."

I end the call and decide to gather a few things after all, shoving extra clothes in my backpack before I sling it over my arm and head down the stairs. I make my way to the kitchen where the Christmas songs are now playing at full blast and my sister and mom are singing along, Mom rolling out dough on the counter while Willow is taking a sheet of cookies out of the oven. The moment Mom spots me, she turns down the volume on her phone, causing Willow to turn around and watch me as well.

"Where are you going?" Mom asks.

I grip the strap of my backpack. "I'm flying to Paris to get my girl."

FIFTY-TWO

ARABELLA

I FEEL like the Princess and the Pea. Isn't that the story where the girl was held captive in a tower? Or maybe that was Rapunzel. Yes, it was Rapunzel, and she could only escape by letting her hair down and the prince crawled up to save her, using her long hair like a rope. Or something like that.

I think I'm getting my fairy tales confused.

Whatever. How about this: I feel like a princess locked away from her prince but instead of an imposing castle in the middle of nowhere, I'm in the Coco Chanel suite at The Ritz, locked in my room and my mother won't let me out. Like that's going to convince me to stay and do this apprenticeship.

My mother has clearly lost it. She refuses to listen to me, and I didn't bother arguing with her once I heard from Rowan when he was at the airport. His plane was set to leave at five o'clock his time, which would have him arriving around six thirty in the morning here. Dreadfully early, but I don't care. I just want to see him. I need him to get me out of here and take me home. Back to his parents' house.

Where I feel like I belong.

He called me when he got to the plane, full of reassurances, telling me he loved me. I held it together and didn't cry, too happy that he was coming to my rescue like only a true prince would. Once we got off the phone, I fell asleep, only to wake up with a gasp, sitting straight up in bed.

It's six thirty-three.

I check my phone but I haven't heard from him yet. I am almost out of battery—Mother won't let me have my charger, which is silly, but she's acting ridiculous so I suppose I shouldn't be surprised. I'm limping my phone along by shutting all of my apps off and keeping it on low power mode but even doing all of that, my battery only has nineteen percent left.

I need him to get here soon.

Sliding out of bed, I go to the window and pull the curtains back, staring out at the Vendome square in front of me. It's mostly empty, all of the shops closed and not many people outside. In fact, there are only the employees of the hotel out front, helping someone get into a car. My gaze drops to the door handles in front of me and I realize this is a small balcony.

Duh.

I test the handle and it opens with ease. I step out onto the balcony and breathe in the cold air, shivering when the gentle breeze hits me. At the very least, I can talk to Rowan outside like this if he can't get a hold of me. Which I doubt it'll get that bad but hey.

I need options.

Going back into my bedroom, I carefully shut the doors, trying to stay quiet. I check my phone yet again and this time I do have a text message from Rowan.

Row: **Just landed. Give me some time and once I'm on the road and headed to the hotel, I'll text you. Be ready to go.**

Oh my God. I am giddy with relief. And flushed with love. No one has ever dropped whatever they were doing to run to my rescue. Not even my parents.

This boy...he really does love me.

Me: **I'm ready to leave whenever you get here. Just... hurry.**

Row: **I'm trying. Made sure to arrange for a car to take me there before we took off. Depends on traffic but I'm about forty minutes away.**

Me: **I'll be waiting for you. Thank you.**

Row: **Anything for you, Bells. I hope you know that.**

I do. I know it now. I have more faith in him than anyone else in my life.

I take the quickest shower because I don't want to miss his call. I change into the comfiest clothes I brought—a cream-colored matching sweat set—and dry my hair. I don't bother putting on makeup, I don't waste my time looking for a special pair of glasses to wear to make my outfit pop. I am myself. No pretense, no need to try and get someone's attention. I already have it.

Once I've packed my suitcase, I go out onto the balcony and wait for his arrival. The morning sky is still dark, but the area we're staying in is slowly coming to life. There is more traffic on the street, and people appearing on the sidewalks. I spy the retail store for the jeweler I was supposed to work for across the street, and I'm filled with sadness.

Then, I remember this opportunity was never about me. My mother planned on using me to see her lover as much as possible.

All of the regret is gone, just like that.

I remain on the balcony for so long, I watch the sky grow lighter as the sun rises. It feels good out in the fresh air, knowing I'm leaving soon. That I'm not stuck here. I have options.

And this makes me think of my mother, who might feel like she's run out of options. She's in a loveless marriage but won't leave because she's scared to be alone, even though I assume she'd still have Maurice. But she's afraid to lose the status being married to my father brings her. She'll sacrifice all happiness for that status, and I can't help but think that's a horrible way to live her life.

I refuse to be like her. Someday when I have children, I'm going to lavish them with so much love, they'll be sick of me. And I won't even care because my children will always be secure in the knowledge that I love them. They will matter to me, and I will celebrate them every chance I can get.

But I can't worry about that. I don't want kids for a long time still. I'm barely eighteen. Me and Rowan as parents now?

No, thank you.

There's a knock on my door and I turn, watching as the door swings open and there stands my mother. I step to the side, blocked by the curtains, but able to watch as she enters the room. She looks around, her expression one of utter disbelief that she can't find me. She goes into the bathroom and rummages around, then darts back into the bedroom, her gaze wild.

"Arabella!" She is screeching. I don't think I've ever heard her sound so panicked. "Where are you?"

"Looking for me?" I emerge from my hiding spot, coming in from the balcony. I turn and carefully shut the doors before I face her once more.

She's seething. Her face is flushed red and her gaze is full of fire. "What were you going to do? Jump from the balcony?"

"I'm not that stupid." I push past her and go to my suitcase, zipping it closed. "I'm leaving."

"Good luck. I have your wallet with your ID in it."

"And I have my passport in my backpack." I point at where it sits by my suitcase. "You can keep my bag and my wallet. I don't need it."

"How do you think you're getting out of here if I won't let you out?" She arches a brow, crossing her arms.

"Do you think by forcing me to remain in Paris that you're somehow convincing me to stay? Hate to break it to you, but you're wrong. I won't be your excuse to spend time with your secret lover." I stare at her like she's lost it, which she has. She can't keep me trapped in here forever. "I'm an adult. If you continue to keep me in this room, I'm calling the police and telling them you're holding me captive."

Mother laughs. "I dare you to do just that. You're my child and still under my care. I can keep you in this room for as long as I like."

"You're really going to dare me again, hmm?" I go to the phone that's on the desk and pick it up. "You want to risk people finding out that I filed a police report against you for attempted kidnapping? What would Father think about that?"

I've got her. I see the worry on her face. The way her skin pales slightly at my threat. "You wouldn't."

"I would. You dared me to, and I'm never one to back down."

A ragged sigh leaves her and she shakes her head. "Go ahead then. Leave. Good luck on finding any financial support with your parents not helping you."

"I came into my own money the second I turned eighteen," I remind her. The woman neglects me so badly she doesn't even remember I collected on my first trust fund. "I have plenty of money to get by. I don't need much."

She laughs, and the sound is...unkind.

"Keep telling yourself that. You're a spoiled little brat. I feel sorry for the man who you'll end up with someday."

As if on cue, there's a knock on our suite door and Mother leaves me where I stand to go answer it. After I've grabbed my back-pack and suitcases, I try my best to push them out of the room, lingering in the living area when I hear the man I love's familiar voice speaking to my mother.

"Where's Arabella?" He sounds furious.

"Who are you—wait a minute, you can't just push your way into my suite, young man. Who do you think you are?" Mother is positively indignant.

"Your daughter's boyfriend," he practically growls, suddenly appearing in the room. His expression, his entire demeanor shifts when he sees me, and the moment we lock gazes, I run to him, straight into his open arms. He holds me close, his hand cupping the back of my head, his mouth on my temple.

We cling to each other for a moment until I finally pull away to stare into his handsome face. It feels like an eternity since I last saw him, even though it's only been a couple of days, and I've never felt such total relief at being reunited with someone.

The most important person in my life.

"This is your boyfriend, Arabella? This rude boar of a young man who has barged into our suite? Has no one taught you any manners?"

"I've learned plenty, ma'am. My mother taught me well."

Mother snorts. "Who is your mother?"

"Wren Lancaster."

All the color drains from her face, and she squeaks, "Your mother is Wren Lancaster?" She sends me a questioning look. "You were telling me the truth?"

"Of course, I was. Why would I lie?" I roll my eyes.

Rowan's expression is like granite as he glares at my mother. "I've come to take Arabella home."

"Home? Where, pray tell, is she going?"

"My house, where she's more than welcome. And where you are most definitely not." He turns to look at me, his gaze softening. "You ready, Bells?"

I nod. "I need help with my suitcases."

"I've got it." He takes two of them and I take the others, the backpack slung across my back. Mother hands me my Chanel bag—reluctantly—but she doesn't offer to hug me. Doesn't say she loves me, but when does she ever?

"You'll regret this," Mother says as we're exiting the suite. "This might be the silliest thing you've ever done, Arabella."

I pause, glancing over my shoulder at her. She looks so very small in her pale ivory silk robe, the belt cinched around her too slender waist. She's a shell of herself and with no makeup on and no designer clothing, she's like a shadow. There are such dark hollows under her eyes that I wonder if she gets any sleep. She looks exhausted. "I don't regret leaving at all. This apprenticeship, this entire trip to Paris, was never about me and all about you. I don't know how you can live with yourself with the way you've neglected me all of these years. I think in the end, you'll be the one full of regret."

She blinks at me, no doubt shocked by my words.

"Goodbye, Mother." I turn away, letting the door slam shut behind me. And when I glance back a few seconds later, on the off chance she has one last thing to say to me, I'm not surprised, nor am I disappointed to see she's not there.

After all, that's what I expected.

FIFTY-THREE

ROWAN

I STARE at the girl I love who is currently sitting across from me on the Lancaster family private plane, eagerly taking the glass of champagne from the flight attendant who's tending to our needs on this trip back to New York. We were given new staff on this return flight, and I'm not sure how this all works, but I'm just grateful to be on the plane and about to take off with Arabella.

The moment the flight attendant leaves us alone, Arabella takes a big sip, sighing once she swallows. "Delicious. And it tastes extra good because I'm on a plane and about to go home."

We didn't really talk much about it on the drive back to the airport, but I need to make sure she's doing this for the right reasons. She gave me bits and pieces about what happened between her and her mother, and while I think Arabella has every right to want to get out of here, I want to make sure she's not doing this only for me.

I don't want to be responsible for her leaving this chance to do something that she's always dreamed of. I refuse to be the sole reason.

"Bells." I take a swig of my own champagne, a little baffled that we're drinking it before ten in the morning, but when in Paris, I guess. "We need to talk."

Her lips form into a pout. "Seriously, Rowan? I just had one of the most traumatic experiences of my life and you want to have a serious talk?"

I nod, needing to get this out of the way. "I want to make sure you're doing this for all the right reasons."

"Doing what?" She appears baffled.

"Leaving Paris. Leaving the job opportunity that they gave you." I hold up my hand when she's about to speak. "I want to make sure this isn't all about—me."

I sound like an egotistical ass, but I have to know.

"Well, of course, part of this has to do with you. The moment my plane took off, I missed you. I never wanted to leave you. I was a complete mess, but I tried to make the best of it. I wanted this to work, for me and for my parents. The moment I saw my mother though, everything felt off. My father couldn't even make it here, and now I wonder if he was ever scheduled to come to Paris this early. I don't think so. I believe my mother lied to me. She lies about a lot of things, I'm discovering."

"Make sure you put your seat belts on, please," the flight attendant says, reappearing in front of us like magic. "The captain let me know that we're about to take off."

We both put on our seat belts, Arabella polishing off the rest of her champagne quickly.

"Your mother was involved with the man who hired you?" I ask, needing to get back to it.

Arabella nods. "Yes. But she won't leave my father, and it's all so—dumb. And pathetic really. She has nothing else. No one else but Maurice, and how honest are that man's intentions? He might be using my mother for her money as well. It's a big, twisted mess, and I refuse to let my mother use me as her excuse to come to Paris to see her lover, because that's what this was all about. It had nothing to do with me. I can't even remember the last time I sketched a jewelry design, let alone even thought about making jewelry until she told me about this."

"You don't want to design jewelry?" I raise my brows.

She slowly shakes her head. "It was fun while it lasted, and I got this beautiful locket out of the experience, but no. I don't want to be a jewelry designer. I only took the apprenticeship because for some dumb reason, I wanted to earn my parents' approval."

"You're not dumb for wanting their approval," I tell her, my heart aching for her. I'm lucky that my parents are so involved in my life, even though I sometimes hate it. But never for long. I'd rather have attentive parents like mine than Arabella's.

"Are you sure? Because I feel dumb for wanting something I don't think I'll ever get." She shrugs.

I watch as she smooths her thumb across the front of the locket. "I'm glad you didn't lose that."

"And I'm glad you found it." Her smile is small, and I'm filled with overwhelming love for her, having her sitting across from me like this.

Undoing my seat belt, I switch sides and sit right next to her, leaning in to drop a kiss on her lips. "I love you, Bells. More than anything in this world."

Her eyes are glowing, full of happiness and so much love, I can literally feel it emanating from her. "I love you too. I'm so glad to be going home with you."

I grab hold of her hand and interlock our fingers. "Are you going back to school after winter break?"

"Duh, of course I am. What else am I going to do?" She leans into me, resting her head on my shoulder. "Though I suppose I could do whatever I want since they let me graduate early."

"Don't get any weird ideas." I bring our clutched hands up to my mouth and drop a kiss on her knuckles. The plane starts to move and I catch Arabella watching me. "Finish the school year with me."

"I will," she whispers. "I don't ever want to leave your side again."

"You don't have to."

"Your parents are okay with me being there over Christmas?"

"I think you could move in forever and my parents would be fine with it. They adore you."

"I adore them." She kisses me this time, her lips lingering, and I can't wait to get her alone. I can't believe she's coming back with me. We were apart for what, maybe three days? Two? Felt like a lifetime. And now I've got her back. I'm so fucking lucky.

"My sister is home. You'll get to meet Willow."

"I can't wait." Her face falls and she chews on her lower lip. "I hope she likes me."

"She'll love you. And you get to spend Christmas with us."

"That'll be amazing. We'll have to go shopping. I want to buy everyone a present. All of your family."

"That's...a lot of people, Bells."

"I don't care. I want to do it. They've all been so kind to me, so accepting. I've never had that before. They make me feel like I'm a part of something. A part of your family," she admits, her voice quivering.

I touch her cheek with my free hand, threading my fingers in her soft hair as we stare into each other's eyes. "You're a part of something, Bells. A part of me. You're buried so deep in my heart I don't know how you're ever going to get out."

"I don't want to," she whispers. "Keep me in your heart. Always."

"Always," I repeat, brushing her lips with mine. "I love you, Arabella."

"I love you too, Rowan." She smiles when I kiss her again. "You need to keep this PG-rated, sir. We can't get frisky on the flight."

"I'm not the one who said anything about getting frisky. And who uses that word anyway?"

"Me. I do." She kisses me again. "And you didn't say it. I did. Because I've been thinking about it. I've missed you. A lot."

"I missed you too." We kiss again, and when the flight attendant walks by, we spring apart, both of us breathing a little heavier.

"We should join the mile high club," Arabella suggests because of course she does.

"I don't know. The bathroom is kind of cramped." I don't bother bringing up there's an actual bedroom on this plane. I think she likes the idea of us doing it in the bathroom.

"You're always bringing that up," she points out.

"Because I'm tall."

"True." She sighs. "I'm not scared, Row. Besides, I'm flexible."

Fuck. She is pretty flexible.

"Maybe," I hedge.

"Maybe? We have a long flight ahead of us. We'll need to fill the time with all sorts of—things." Her tone is pure mischief. The flight attendant is about to walk past us yet again when Bells stops her. "Can I get a blanket, please?"

"Of course." Within seconds the flight attendant is handing Arabella a blanket, and she shakes it out once she's gone, draping it over the two of us.

"There. Now I can give you a hand job and no one will know." She settles her hand right over my dick, which twitches in agreement with her statement.

"Bells...." I'm not about to turn that offer down, no matter how risky it might be. Besides, I think my girl likes it when things are a little risky.

"Please stop trying to act all prim and proper, Rowan Reginald Lancaster. I know you missed me."

I cup her cheek, staring into her dark brown eyes. Carefully, I pull her glasses off and fold them up, handing them to her before I lean in and kiss her. "I missed you so fucking much, Bells. You are my entire world."

She wraps her fingers around my wrist, clinging to me. "Do you think we're too young to feel that way, Row?"

"I don't care if we are or not." I kiss her again. I don't ever want to stop. "It's how I feel. You're the most important person in my life. I love you. I would do anything for you."

"Like hop on your family's private plane and fly to Paris to rescue me?" she asks.

"Yeah. Exactly like that. Anything to keep you safe and make you happy," I tell her, meaning every word I say.

"You make me happy, Rowan. You taught me how to love."

"You always had that in you, baby. You just didn't know it until you met me." I am grinning. Feeling cocky because everything for once is going one hundred percent right.

"Oh, you." She lightly slaps my chest. "I missed my arrogant Rowan."

"You like it when I'm a cocky asshole?" I raise my brows.

"I love everything about you." She kisses me once. Twice. Three times. "Don't ever stop loving me."

"Like I could," I whisper.

Impossible. She's embedded in my heart, just like I told her.

Forever.

EPILOGUE

Arabella

CHRISTMAS *Eve*

"This has been the most magical Christmas season I've ever experienced," I declare to the entire room, not that anyone is listening to me. With my parents, this sort of reaction would upset me because they never, ever pay attention to anything I say, but right now? In this moment? I don't mind.

The room is full of people and they're all rowdy. Laughing and yelling and having a great time. I've never seen anything like it. All of the holidays I've experienced were refined and dignified. Being with this family, one of the most dignified and refined families in the country, they are anything but during the holiday season.

I am loving every second of it.

"Cookies?" Willow appears before us, holding out a giant platter of a variety of cookies for us to choose from. I'm sitting on a loveseat wedged between Callahan and Rowan, squished in the middle because both of them take up a lot of space.

The boys grunt their response and between the two of them, they clear almost half the platter while I take a singular frosted cookie in the shape of a bell.

"Thank you," I say like the polite person I am while the boys shove their mouths full of cookies, murmuring their approval. I roll my eyes at Willow who rolls her eyes in return before moving on.

I nibble on my cookie, watching the chaos unfold. It's like living in a holiday movie—maybe because everything is so spirited that it feels surreal. The dads are all wearing hideous Christmas-themed sweaters their wives got for them, and they're all good sports about it, save for Arch Lancaster, who keeps complaining about the fact that his sweater is pink. With three fluffy white kittens on the front of it, wearing Santa hats.

I suppose if I were a man, I'd be complaining too.

Presents were passed out already—it's their annual celebration for the entire family to open presents and spend the day together. This year, Crew and Wren are hosting because for some unknown reason, Wren wanted to hold the big holiday events this year. I think it's because she enjoys the ruckus having the family over causes. It's pure chaos, and I don't think I've ever seen her smile slip. She's enjoying every second of it, and so am I.

I'm thinking Wren was right. Maybe we are similar.

My mother sent me a text wishing me a happy Christmas this morning and I responded in kind. I'm still angry with her, but it's not like me to be so blatantly unkind, but that's also me being fake. I guess I learned from the best, didn't I?

After what happened in Paris, I'm worried something is wrong with my mother. I know my parents' relationship isn't in the best place, but it's not up to me to fix it.

They need to figure that out on their own.

I hate how she tried to trick me only for her benefit. It's disappointing when you realize your parents don't really care about you, even though I've known this for years. I suppose I can't help but feel like it's true when one of my parents acts like they're trying to change. Eventually, I probably won't believe in them but for now, I still have that tiny flicker of hope burning deep inside me. Truly?

I hope I never lose it. Being bitter is probably easier, but I am an eternal optimist.

"Hey. Your cookie is a bell. Like you." I glance up to find Rowan smiling at me. He is extra handsome tonight, but I think he's extra handsome every night. "Bells. Get it?"

"Yes, Rowan." I take a big bite out of my cookie and then offer him the rest, which he takes. "Here's a piece of me, just for you."

"I eat Bells on the regular," he says with a wolfish grin.

"And with that, I'm the fuck out of here." Callahan leaps to his feet and takes off, heading over to where his brother is standing with their parents. The Bennetts are celebrating the holiday with the Lancasters this year, which makes the house even more crowded and hmm.

Maybe that's why Wren wanted to have the party at her house. To include her most-likely future in-laws.

"Poor Cal," Rowan says once his friend is gone, leaning back into the couch and taking me along with him. He slings his arm around my shoulders and pulls me in close so I'm practically lying on top of him. "We just grossed him out."

"I think you enjoy grossing him out." I gaze up at him, lovesick as usual. My feelings for Row grow more and more each day, to the point that sometimes I feel like I might explode.

"Busted." He chuckles then kisses my forehead. "We should go up to my room."

"And miss out on everything? Not yet." I try to pull away from him when he comes at me with his lips but there's no use. He's got me firmly planted by his side, his arm still around me. He kisses me right on the mouth in front of everyone and I revel in the sweet taste of his lips. The warmth of his body seeping into mine. All is right in my world and I don't think I've ever felt this content.

There is suddenly a tinkling noise, like silverware hitting glass, and the room goes silent. It's Rhett who's trying to get everyone's attention, with Willow by his side, and they both appear nervous, standing in front of the massive marble fireplace, which currently has a fire going inside it.

"We have an announcement to make," Rhett says, his voice slightly shaky. Oh my, he *is* nervous. He is one of the most confident people I've ever met, save for his dad, Eli. "We've been keeping this secret for a while but—"

"You're pregnant!" Iris yells, rubbing her belly. It's not that big yet but I know she's just thrilled to be having a baby. "Please make it true so our babies can grow up together."

"Sorry, Iris. I'm definitely not pregnant." Willow holds out her hand, a giant diamond on her finger that wasn't there earlier when she was passing out cookies. "But we are engaged!"

The room erupts in a chorus of "congratulations!" with Wren and Crew running over to them and embracing their daughter. Rhett shakes Crew's hand before Crew pulls him into a hug and then Ava and Eli are joining them. Iris starts taking photos of everyone, and all I can do is sit there and smile, dreaming of the day it'll be my turn to make this announcement with Rowan.

Am I jumping ahead of myself? Yes, most definitely. But do I think Rowan and I are in it for the long haul?

Absolutely.

"My dad predicted this," Row says, watching them.

"He did?"

"Yeah. Or maybe it was my mom? I remember when they told me and I thought it sounded crazy." He shakes his head. "It wasn't that long ago either. Before Thanksgiving? All I could think was they were too young to get engaged. Tied down. Sounded like a death sentence."

"And now?" I whisper, my heart racing in anticipation of his answer.

"Now I can see it. With you." He kisses the tip of my nose. "But not for a while yet. We really are too young."

"I agree." I smile at him, misty-eyed. So many emotional moments happening today. My romantic heart can barely take it. "We should go congratulate the future bride and groom."

"Okay."

"And then we should go to your room." My smile grows wider. "Don't you think?"

"Best idea you've had all day, Bells." He releases his hold on me and stands, offering his hand. "Let's go."

WE'RE in his room about an hour later, after all the congratulating and picture taking. I'm tired and I can tell Rowan is too, but we're never too exhausted to do you-know-what, which means my entire body is tingling in anticipation.

But like the girl I am who enjoys drawing things out on occasion, I go to his bedroom window and check outside. "Look! It's snowing!"

Rowan looms behind me—I can see him in the reflection of the glass—and he leans in close, squinting his eyes as he peers into the darkness. "I can barely see it."

"Trust me. It's snowing." He wraps his arms around my middle and I rest my hands on top of his, leaning against his chest. "The perfect end to a perfect day."

"We haven't even got to the most perfect part of all yet." He brushes my hair away and presses his mouth to my neck. "You smell fucking delicious."

"New perfume Iris got me." She said it would drive Rowan out of his mind, and while I thought that was a strange comment to make about her cousin, I suppose she was right.

"I love it. Don't ever stop wearing it." His lips are hot on my skin and I shiver when he shifts his hands beneath the hem of my sweater, touching bare flesh. "I should fuck you right here."

"Rowan." I stretch his name out, like I don't approve of his suggestion, which is the biggest lie I've ever told. He could fuck me wherever he wants to and I wouldn't mind. I used to be the one who made the more daring suggestions but lately, he's been pushing my boundaries—and his own—more and more. It's fun.

Maybe a little dangerous. But that's what makes it so thrilling.

"Stop. You fucking love it." Next thing I know, his hands are on my breasts, cupping and kneading my flesh, his growl of approval when he discovers I'm not wearing a bra making my pussy throb. You'd think he'd know by now that I'm not a big fan of underwear when I'm with him, but he acts surprised every single time.

"Keep your gaze on the window, Bells," he demands before he whips my sweater off, leaving me naked from the waist up. I can see myself. See him. His big hands cover my breasts once more, fingers toying with my nipples, and I lock my knees so my legs don't buckle.

He slides his hands down my stomach, resting his chin on my shoulder and watching our reflection as he undoes the button of my pants, shoving them down so they're bunched around my knees. "No panties."

"I never wear panties when I'm with you. Unless I'm on my period."

Which was last week and God, I was horny. I gave him at least three blowjobs in a two- day span and he got me off by letting me rub against his knee and thigh. I'd heard orgasms help with cramps and that turned out to be true. On the third night of my period, he begged me to have sex and I finally let him, worried there would be a blood bath, but he said it wouldn't bother him.

Ugh, he's perfect for me. And I think I'm perfect for him.

"I love it." He cups my pussy, holding me there, and when he murmurs, "Spread your legs," I almost fall apart right there thanks to the deep timbre of his voice.

I do as he says because he tells me on occasion that I'm a good girl and good girls do what they're told. And then he's stroking me, the wet sounds filling the room and making me moan. I lean my head back against his shoulder, melting into him as he plays with me, his fingers pushing inside while he presses his thumb against my clit. Over and over again, faster and faster. Taking me higher and higher and just when I'm about to come, my breath catching and my entire body going still, he stops.

Leaving me frustrated. Breathing hard and ready to curse him out.

But he's not wasting any time, hurriedly undoing his jeans and shoving them down his legs, toeing off his shoes and then stepping out of the jeans, kicking them away. I realize he's not wearing any underwear either, and I glance over my shoulder to examine his glorious cock. It really is the prettiest one I've ever seen, not that I've seen many.

Well, that's a lie. I've seen plenty online, but I've seen only two in person, and one doesn't count because it was always dark when I was fumbling around with Bentley and he never really wanted me to see it. Save for the time I tried to give him a blowjob but we were outside, and again, it was too dark for me to see much. And why am I thinking of Bentley again?

"Stay facing forward," Rowan demands gruffly, and all thoughts of BSJ leave my mind as anticipation tingles throughout my body.

I remain in place, my entire body shaky, and he helps me take off my pants, his hands brushing against my inner thighs, making me squeal.

"Brace your hands on the window." I slap my palms against the windowsill and spread my legs, anticipating the command before he gives it, and I hear his murmur of approval. "Good girl."

I love it when he calls me that. I love it when he speaks, period. I am so one hundred percent focused on him, I could probably come just by his command. We should try that someday...

I hear the crinkle of a condom wrapper and I close my eyes. Hang my head. Waiting. Within seconds he's got his hand on my hip. "Bend forward," he whispers, and I do so without hesitation, crying out when he fills me up with one sure thrust.

"Open your eyes," he tells me, as both of us still, me getting used to him being inside me like this. We haven't tried a position like this before and I want to do it again. Immediately.

My eyes open and I see him behind me, his naked chest. He must've taken off his sweater when I wasn't paying attention and now, he's as naked as me. His gaze locks with mine and slowly, he starts to move. In and out, keeping a steady pace. The pressure already starts to build inside me, growing with his every thrust, and I curl my fingers into the wooden sill, hanging on for dear life.

His pace increases. Faster. And faster. Our skin slaps together, the sound echoing in his cavernous bedroom, and oh God, I'm going to come. My legs are shaking. Tingling, like I'm losing sensation in them and I arch my back, causing him to go even deeper, which has both of us groaning.

And then I'm coming, my inner walls flexing around his shaft, squeezing as my clit pulses over and over. I can't breathe and for a second there I can't see either, and just when I think I might die from the pleasure of it all, I come to, aware that he's coming now, his hips slamming one last time against my ass before he holds himself there, his groan loud.

The worrisome type of loud.

When he's finished, he leans over me, kissing a hot path down my spine, his hands on my hips turning, spinning me around to face him once he's slid out of me. I wrap my arms around his neck and kiss him with everything I've got. It's a mash of teeth and tongues and lips and I tell him I love him once. Twice. Maybe even three times. I don't know.

I lose count.

He picks me up and carries me to the bed, depositing me there, and then he goes to the bathroom, where he gets rid of the condom. He's sliding into bed seconds later, wrapping me up so I'm surrounded by nothing but sweat-covered skin and I can feel his cock. He's hard again already. All for me.

"I fucking love you, Bells," is what he murmurs against my neck, kissing me there, making me giggle because it tickles. His fingers poke into my sides, making me laugh louder, and then he's kissing me again. Rolling me over so he's on top of me, his face hanging in mine. "We need to replace the photos in here."

His fingers brush against my locket. My neck.

"Why?" I'm confused. I love the photos that are in my locket.

"I don't want to forget this night." He stretches across me, reaching for his phone and the next thing I know he's got his head pressed close to mine, the camera aimed right at us. "Smile, baby."

"I am naked, Rowan," I remind him, trying to sound stern, but he just shakes his head, laughing.

"I won't get your tits in the pic. Come on, Arabella. Do it for me."

He knows just what to say to get me. I would do anything for him.

So I pose for the photo, smiling. We're cheek to cheek and body to body, and I realize once he's taken the photo, that I will never, ever forget this night either. Especially now that we've documented it. Merry Christmas to me.

Merry Christmas to us.

ACKNOWLEDGEMENTS

This book was born from bad reviews.

Let me explain myself: sometimes, writers (me) will scroll through Goodreads reviews. The good and the bad. Sometimes, we even get tagged in bad reviews on social media, and guys, that is truly just...not necessary. If we want to seek out bad reviews, we'll go looking for them. Like I said above, ha ha.

Anyway, I read a lot of reviews from various Lancaster Prep books that criticized my FMCs. How they are all starting to feel the same. Meek and quiet and virginal. So I decided to create a completely different FMC for my Rowan Lancaster. I wanted her to be bold, a little outrageous and NOT a virgin. I took the bad reviews as a challenge and in the end, I think I created one of my all time favorite female characters ever.

Miss Arabella Hartley Thomas.

And now, I am SO protective of her. She has my heart, just like she has Rowan's and while I write this acknowledgement on July 21, 2024, I must admit I love her the most out of any of my Lancaster cast, and I love so many of them! All she wants is to be seen and loved, and she never feels like anyone cares. Until she practically forces her way into Row's life, and then all the rest of the Lancasters fall in love with her too, just like Rowan. Even August. Oh August...he's next, peeps. And I cannot wait to write his book. *Cackles*

So I must acknowledge all of the people who left me shitty reviews and criticized my FMCs. I see you and THANK YOU for calling me out. You challenged me and in the end, I feel like I created someone pretty great. And even if you don't agree, that's okay. I'm hoping the readers who love Lancaster Prep will also love my Bells. Because I think she's pretty special.

p.s. - If you enjoyed **KEEP ME IN YOUR HEART**, it would mean everything to me if you left a review on the retailer site you bought it from, or on Goodreads. Thank you so much!